A CHORD OF SILVER MOONS

SONGS OF ARYAM

BOOK ONE

TYLISHA WASHINGTON

Book Cover by Helena Santana

ISBN 979-8-9899640-2-4 (paperback)

ISBN 979-8-9899640-3-1 (ebook)

1st edition 2024

For my sister and first fan, Sade,
and for my 6th-grade teacher, Mrs. Pace,
who once called me "Future Author."

The Gate at Eroden's Pass
Zorel's Caves
Gedra
Sea
Tower of Stones

The Burning Temples

Zehir

The Scorched Wood

Amaro Bay

l Island

APITAL CITY

Immortal Soul Forest

Marad

Scales

Irez

CHAPTER ONE

One kiss won't kill me.

Ranee claims that other guardians have fallen prey to the Omission for less, wiped out by the oath humming in their blood in the same beat that they dissonate from their Pulse. Moons forbid I pine after a handsome boy with even a fleeting thought. Ranee says the oath prohibits even the slightest infraction, that it will snuff out a guardian in the space of a sixteenth note. One measure, a guardian's heart sings a fervent ballad of devotion. The next, it rests.

But Ranee is my monitor. It's her sacred duty to say bloodcurdling things like that. Things to scare me straight and keep me from having too much fun.

Eyes closed, we sit on woven mats beside the sea, the morning sun hot on our heads. A stray bead of sweat breaks from my frizzy hairline straight down the ridge of my nose, dangling on the tip. I am not supposed to wipe it away. Instead, I should acknowledge the way it tickles and release it from my awareness. Acknowledge and release the tiny pebble poking through my mat, too, and the faint thirst tickling my throat.

Easier said than done.

I wriggle my nose, and when that fails to dislodge the droplet, I crack one eye open and peek at Ranee.

My monitor sits serenely on her mat, unbothered by the giant ant scurrying across her calf or the warm breeze toying with a strand of her dark, wavy hair. I wipe the droplet away with a quick swipe and drop my hand back onto my knee, palm skyward, closing my eyes and counting out three breaths before I'm caught.

"Ahem," Ranee chastises. I don't have to open my eyes to know she's raising her brow in disapproval.

"Sorry," I blurt out, straightening my back. I get my breaths back in rhythm and try to quiet my thoughts, letting the sea's gentle roar wash over my senses.

We've been doing this first thing every morning since before I can remember. Wake up before the break of day. Greet the sun at the water's edge. Sit. Eyes closed. Palms up. Breathe and search.

Even on a day like today, when there's so much to do to prepare for tonight, we search, ignoring the fruitlessness of sixteen score. Ranee still has hope that I'll discover my oju, I guess, even if I am four score past the average age most guardians find theirs.

"Steady your breath," my monitor instructs. "Imagine the glen."

There's no need for her to describe it in detail, the way she used to do when I was younger. In my mind, I have stood at the heart of this valley a thousand times before. Green, rugged mountains stretch toward an azure sky in my mind's eye. Crisp, clear air flows around me, scented with fresh earth and pine from the forest beyond the hills and a faint hint of salt from the distant sea.

Water surges over a distant cliff, roaring softly in the

distance. Everything looks the way it always has, no new threads to follow.

Another bead of sweat trickles down the side of my face. I lick my lips and find them too dry. That won't do. I need them soft. Maybe the berry balm Ranee made last week will help. I sink my teeth into my lower lip and tease it the way my friend Katina told me I should if I want to draw someone's attention to my mouth.

"Ahem."

Moons. I got distracted again.

I open my eyes to find Ranee watching me, a knowing look on her face, and a smile. She shakes her head. "Why do I get the feeling you're thinking about something *other* than finding your oju?"

"Can you blame me?" I crawl onto her mat, and we sit side by side. "Dragon's Fall starts today."

She lets out a sharp laugh. "As if I could forget. It's not like you haven't been marking the days leading up to it on our bedroom wall or anything."

I nudge my shoulder against hers, earning another laugh. "Are you sure you don't want to go?" I ask. We rarely go to town, and we've *never* gone during the monthlong celebration of humanity's triumph over the dragons near a thousand score ago. "I know guardians are supposed to be devout, but there's no such rule stating that Monitors can't have some fun from time to time."

Ranee rests her hands on her knees and lets out a long breath. "I have a different idea of fun. Besides, I had my share of Dragon's Falls before you were born."

"When you lived on Capital Island?" I ask. It's hard for me to imagine Ranee's life before she became my monitor. All I know is that she trained at the palace and that, despite leaving behind her homeland, she somehow loved it there.

"Before" is all Ranee murmurs, before reversing to our first subject. "Did you really have no luck this morning?" she asks.

I shake my head before resting it on her shoulder. No luck any morning.

She studies me. "You seriously didn't notice anything new?"

The waterfall crosses my mind. Maybe its roar was a little louder today than it was yesterday. Or maybe I just imagined that it was louder. Either way, it's not worth getting Ranee's hopes up. I shake my head. "Everything was like it always is. Are you really that surprised?"

Ranee stares at me a second longer, then relents with a sigh. She turns and surveys the beach. It's just the two of us. Very few people from the village would dare the hike through the shadowy forest surrounding us to get here. "We can train here today."

I interlock my fingers with hers and squeeze. "Or . . . "

She gives me a sideways glance. "Or what?"

"You could show me that dance again."

She hums thoughtfully. "Dances carry stories," she muses, "and a capable guardian should be able to decode them, I suppose." She drops my hand. "Alright. I'll show you. Close your eyes."

I do.

"Listen for the heartbeat of the past," she instructs. "The drums speak in layers. That low thrum you hear is the anchor, steady and deep, like the roots of a tree older than a hundred score. The sharper, higher beats are the footsteps of your ancestors prancing along cobblestone paths. The music moves in waves, both grounded and free."

I open my eyes to find her smiling at me.

"Do you hear it?" she asks.

I nod, and I do. I hear and feel the music coursing through me, a song that makes me feel rooted and loose all at once.

Ranee extends her arms like wings. At the drums' direction, she leans forward slightly at the waist and then back again, her hands bobbing at the wrist in concert. Following her lead, I raise a hand in front of my face and twirl. We carve patterns in the air, dipping and twisting and spinning. I sigh and relish the breeze on my skin.

"What story does this dance tell?" I ask as Ranee slows, curving toward the ground in a graceful bow.

My monitor straightens up. "It tells a small part of mine," she admits. "I'm still working on it. What do you think?"

I seize her hands and squeeze, bouncing on the balls of my toes. "I think it's beautiful," I gush. "It makes me feel like I'm flying." There are so many questions I want to ask her about it, about her past in general, but a sudden gust of wind stirs the treetops, sending down a shower of leaves.

Ranee's eyes narrow as she scans our surroundings. She squeezes my hands before letting go. "Let's go home," she says, striding for the path that weaves through the forest, leading back to our tiny cottage nestled among the trees.

I lock arms with her as we fall into step. "Thank you," I murmur.

She knows what for.

A FEW MEASURES LATER, we stand before the full-length mirror in our shared bedroom. A cool breeze flutters through the window, carrying irresistible notes that lure my hips into their rhythm. The festivities in town began shortly after Ranee and I returned home this morning. I danced my way through today's chores and training as sporadic bursts of music drifted to us from Irez.

Ranee swats my side, her golden-brown fingers leaving my skin smarting a little. "Hold still, Aryam," she chides before snapping my wings into place. The wings arch above my head, cascading downward in a soft rush of purple and blue nightfall feathers. The evening colors complement my handsewn, seashell-covered bodysuit perfectly.

I bounce on the balls of my feet and grin at my reflection, twisting and turning in the mirror as I study myself from each angle. "This is perfect."

Behind me, Ranee smirks. "Oh? Not too childish?" she quips, mimicking how I sounded when I begged for a different costume a few weeks ago. I wanted a fiery two-piece that conjured sunlight and dragon fire, something that would make me look irresistible to a certain crimson-eyed boy I met over the summer. The modest one-piece she's made me instead evokes twilight and sea breeze—a subtler kind of romantic.

I stick my tongue out at Ranee, and she laughs, shaking her head. "I've been too lenient with you," she says. "I should be keeping you home tonight. We have training in the morning, after all."

"We have training every morning," I point out.

"Though, lately, you've often managed to avoid it," she retorts. Even though her tone is playful, it carries an undercurrent of suspicion, but she doesn't outright pry. Not today.

After a beat, Ranee says, "I have something for you."

She squeezes behind me, careful not to fall over the footboard of my bed, and pulls open the bottom drawer of the wooden wardrobe crammed between the bedroom door and window. The item she retrieves is wrapped in white linen, embroidered with the showy pink flowers she says adorned her childhood home. I hold my breath tight as she peels the cloth away, revealing a silver tiara clip lined with auger shells. My eyes dart to the tear-shaped crystal resting at its center.

"Your costume wouldn't be complete without this," she says, extending the clip toward me.

I cradle it gently in the palm of my hand. "How did you . . . " The words catch in my throat as I gape at the sapphire crystal. It's not just a fragile piece of sea glass plucked from the offerings of the morning tide. This crystal is worth something. "Where did you even find the coin?" I stammer.

There's not much coin to go around our island to begin with, and since neither of us has time for employment, we're poorer than most. Being a guardian doesn't pay so well.

Ranee smirks, mischief shimmering in her eyes. She won't tell me. "A special gift for a special girl" is all she says before easing the clip out of my hands and sliding it into my hair. It fits perfectly between the two puffs atop the bubble braids she segmented my hair into earlier this morning, each neatly descending in black puffs to my shoulders. My heart flutters at the sight of the girl staring back at me through the looking glass. She looks positively regal, like an Aziza princess plucked from a children's tale.

Ranee runs a thumb along my hairline, smoothing an errant baby hair, then leans into my ear. "You look beautiful, Ary," she croons before pinching the skin above my elbow. "Don't let it go to your head."

I laugh and bat her hand away. "You're too late," I say. My head's already full of knowing that when he sees me tonight, Kyrel Durago won't be able to take his eyes off me. For a moment, I let myself picture him with that smoldering gaze and those charming freckles of his. I see his tall, lean figure etched out in the light of our white moon as he takes my hand in his and . . .

"Do you remember your oath?"

Ranee's gentle voice shreds through my fantasy. Our eyes

meet through the glass. She watches me with an otherworldly stillness, concern glistening in her eyes.

She hates to ask that question, always has, but she must. As my monitor, it's her duty to ensure that I stay in rhythm. The oath is clear.

Never fall in love.

Never care for anyone at all, aside from the princess I'm bound by blood to serve.

I must train and wait. Train for battle. Wait until I'm called to her side. *If* I'm ever called to her side. Never mind that no guardian has been summoned to the capital in almost a thousand score.

A *thousand score*.

My smile slowly returns as I remember how long the empire of Beldemar has been at peace, how long humans have been free of dragon rule and terror, and how unlikely it is that anything I do matters at all. I won't fall in love. I won't do anything reckless.

Just one kiss.

That's all I want tonight. It doesn't have to mean anything.

"*Ary*," Ranee warns. Even when she's scolding me, her voice is soft. Warm. Like a hug. Sometimes, I suspect that she sympathizes with my plight. Alas. "Promise me you'll remember."

I put on my best smile. "I'll remember," I vow.

She purses her lips to one side, unconvinced. I can see her debating whether letting me go into town tonight is worth the risk of encouraging my recklessness. "If you think there might be too much temptation . . . "

"You promised I could go," I interrupt, knowing better than to let her finish that line of thought. "This score is special." I've sat every Dragon's Fall out for fifteen score, forbidden to venture into town during the entire month of its celebration, but this score has to be different.

Ranee freezes and eventually releases a long sigh. "It is special," she acknowledges, and her gaze turns inward, drifting off to some faraway, secret corner of her mind. It's the same place where she's hiding the answer to how she found enough coin to buy my crystal. "How nice it is that King Felix honors us this score by sending a gift to our humble little village for the Dragon's Fall Carnival," she murmurs.

"He sent the gift to *all* the rural villages in Marad to honor Princess Marleyn on her sixteenth birthday," I remind her. *Our* sixteenth birthday, as well as that of the other three guardians who were bound to her at birth. They live somewhere on Beldemar's other three islands. "I doubt he was really thinking of two glorified servants."

Ranee shrinks back, her pained gaze flinching away from mine as I realize how spiteful I sound. How dissonant. I want to take the words back, but I can't. Whenever I think about her, about the princess, all I can think is how happy I am that I'm far away from her, that the empire is at peace and the burden of duty may fall on the next generation of guardians and not mine.

Somehow, Ranee knows I think this way.

My attitude is a poor reflection of her moral guidance, of the scores she's poured into molding and preparing me, of the sacrifices she's made. She's trained me to be better.

"I . . . I'm sorry," I choke.

She shakes her head. "You should hurry if you're going to get to Irez before dark," she suggests. "Do you want me to walk you through the forest?"

And even though I do, I shake my head and put on my best smile again. Besides, if I show up with my monitor in tow, my friends will never let me hear the end of it. "No, thank you. I'll be fine."

. . .

I'M NOT FINE.

The eerie stillness of the Immortal Soul Forest always turns my stomach. Aside from an occasional shudder of wind here and a flicker of light there, my hurried breaths and shuffling feet are the only signs of life. Even animals do not dwell in this wood, for the colossal trees that tower overhead in austere silence are dead living things, as old as the island itself.

They had souls once. Ranee says they communicated in treesong, their stories stretching far and wide across the island in a symphony of whispers. Now hollow silence reigns.

I hurry along, trying not to be spooked by silhouettes or to scan the trees for traces of shadow thieves and other ancient tricksters that the logical part of my brain tells me no longer exist in this realm.

Long ago, Prince Donomar defeated the dragon king and banished all those horrid creatures to the Shadows, I remind myself. That's what Dragon's Fall is all about, after all, a celebration of humanity's triumph over all things akbarrin. Prince Donomar ensured that the creatures could not return by placing a seal on the akbarrin realm.

But knowing what I know can't stop me from feeling what I feel, and what I feel, currently, is a shaking in my limbs and an uncanny sense that something is out there watching me.

It takes twenty beats longer than usual to reach the forest's edge, twenty beats of chills skittering over my skin and of tears threatening to ruin my makeup. I shuffle along as fast as I can, my wings growing heavier with each step and bearing down on my shoulders. It's just like Ranee to sneak in that extra bit of strength training on what should be the best night of my life.

With a sigh of relief, I shake off my nerves as the forest finally falls behind me.

The brightly colored block houses that crowd Irez's tropical hills are a welcome sight to my blurry eyes, as are the streets swarming with currents of brown and yellow bodies of every shade, all dressed in costumes as resourceful and colorful as mine. The divine aroma of sweet breads, dumplings, and curried meats curls beneath my nostrils, hooking me like a fish and reeling me in. My mouth waters at the thought of indulging in the delicacies offered by the street vendors, many of whom have traveled from as far as Capital Island to share their goods.

And then a lump forms in my throat.

I forgot to ask Ranee for coin.

Tears threaten to fall anew but stop when I hear my name.

"Ary! Over here."

My friends wait for me near the edge of town, outside the stone washhouse where Kyrel makes five coin a week cleaning clothes for the villagers who can afford the service. Securing that job for him took effort. The same features that I find attractive about him make others uneasy, and it didn't help that he came to Irez mysteriously—orphaned and alone. But Darien's father owns the shop, and Katina's aunt is a patron there. Once I convinced my friends that he was good, they helped with the rest.

Standing on the curb outside the building, a lanky, tan-skinned boy with dark, bushy hair and frizzy sideburns that look like two caterpillars inching down the sides of his face waves a frantic arm in the air.

"Over here!" Darien calls again. A tall headdress made of straw grass and feathers bobs on his head as he waves, one side of the headband sliding down over his eye. The rest of his costume is a sea stone–studded loincloth, leaving his pale, yellow stomach and untanned upper thighs on full display.

Despite my despair over forgotten coin, I can't help but

giggle. "What are you wearing?" I ask, stepping over the line where the dirt road becomes cobblestone.

"He thinks that ridiculous costume will get him noticed by the storyguard." Katina sits by his feet, paring her fingernails with a sanding stick, her face a deliberate mask of disinterest. The ruby-red paint on her fingernails, most likely a gift her mother sent her from the capital, matches her costume—a two-piece rich in reds, oranges, and rust, much like the one I begged Ranee for. Her brown eyes roll toward me, aloof at first, then filled with something closer to delight as she takes me in.

"Okay, pigtails," she exclaims, snapping her fingers to punctuate each syllable.

I tug self-consciously at one of my braids and wonder if that was a compliment. Katina's own hair is braided into an elegant coiffure, rising into a puffy afro bun at the top of her head. She raises her two well-oiled hands and waits for Darien and me to pull her to her feet. We clasp our hands around hers, and I'm too conscious of how rough my own must feel. Where I start my days with sprints and exercises, Katina starts hers with servant-drawn baths and massages.

"I can't believe Ranee let you out," Darien says.

"It took you long enough to get here," Katina pitches in, dusting her thighs free of tiny specks of dirt and gravel from the ground. When she finishes, she prods at the crystal dangling from my tiara. "This is nice," she comments, but there's a question embedded in her tone. She narrows her eyes. "It almost looks real." Suspicion clouds her face as she studies it a tick longer, then shrugs. "Probably not, though," she says, before sauntering off for her wings, resting on a wooden crate near the washhouse door.

"I like your pigtails, Ary," Darien says. "You look just like Dragon Princess Nalini—I mean, in her human form, of course."

I flash him a grateful smile. "Thanks. And you look like . . ." I pause to study his outfit. "An ancient griot?" I guess.

Darien's answering smile assures me that I've said the right thing. He glances at Katina before lowering his voice and asking, "Do *you* think the storyguard will notice?"

I grin. "Of course they will." I don't tell him that it would be difficult for anyone not to notice him in that absurd costume, not when being accepted into the ranks of the storyguard and traveling Beldemar is his biggest dream. Even if the odds are stacked against him as a washman's son.

He isn't the only one with a fool's heart.

"Darien, help me with my wings!"

Darien playfully rolls his eyes before answering our friend's summons. He tries to hide it, but I notice him snatching looks at me as he helps Katina.

"Have you been crying, pigtails?" A new voice sends a staticky shimmer down my spine. Kyrel steps out of the shadow of the washhouse's entryway, warm sunlight cascading over his freckled honey-brown skin and igniting the copper-red twists atop his head. My breath catches in my throat, head swimming as it always does at the sight of him. I feel weightless, like I could float to the moon.

Only one word anchors me to the ground. *Pigtails.* So, he heard that?

I drop his gaze, finding it suddenly hard to look at him.

Kyrel strolls forward and touches his finger to my chin, tilting my gaze upward to meet his. "Don't tell me you're still afraid of the forest."

I brush his hand away. "No," I mumble defensively. "I just . . . " I can see Darien and Katina listening in. They're going to mock me mercilessly for this. "I forgot coin for food, okay?"

Kyrel smiles slyly, glancing toward the forest. "Alright," he says, shrugging. "If you're not afraid, just run home and grab some coin. We'll wait."

"No!" Katina and I protest simultaneously.

"We're late enough as it is," Katina says. She throws a pointed look in my direction. "If you wanted to eat, you shouldn't have been so forgetful." She shrugs and turns her nose up. "I guess now you'll just have to go without."

A whine escapes my lips, but my friends laugh. "She's only teasing, pigtails," Kyrel reassures me with a wink. "I have enough for the two of us." He squints curiously at my forehead, at the crystal resting there, before starting into the village with Darien at his side.

Katina takes up my side as I follow. She elbows me in the ribs. "He forgets how much you eat," she remarks.

I elbow her back, protesting with a laugh. "Kati, that's *so* unfair."

Her laugh dwarfs mine. "Tonight's the night, then, eh?" she asks. "Finally going to make your move?" She lowers her voice and leans in conspiratorially. "What does your *monitor* have to say about that?"

"Keep your voice down," I hiss. "What if someone hears you?"

It was a mistake, a mistake to tell her the truth about what Ranee and I truly are, monitor and guardian, not a young widow looking after the orphaned child of a dear friend, as most people think. But Katina is the only person nosey enough to inquire, and I kind of like having a friend to share my secrets with, even if I shouldn't.

Katina wouldn't tell anyone.

CHAPTER TWO

The king's gift to our humble village awaits us at the village square—an enormous Dragon King puppet and the fifty members of the royal storyguard it takes to maneuver it. A stream of masquers, people dressed like all manner of akbarrin, flow toward it. My friends and I merge with the stream of make-believe pixies, Aziza Fae, and trolls. I bump into a tall man playing a convincing bonsam. He snarls at me, baring sharp fangs.

I scream, eliciting a burst of laughter from the masquer. He swipes at me with wooden claws before surging ahead in the stream. A hand slides into mine, interlocking fingers, and Katina pulls me toward her. "Girl, you're so embarrassing sometimes," she says. She lowers her voice. "I thought you were supposed to be training to fight these things."

My eyes jet toward the others. "Not too loud," I remind her. But neither of the boys is paying attention to us. Darien is too busy flexing nonexistent muscles at a pair of giggling girls who certainly aren't laughing for the reason he thinks they are, and Kyrel saunters coolly ahead of us, hands resting in his pockets. I squeeze Katina's hand. "These costumes are a lot scarier than the pictures in Ranee's story scrolls, okay?"

Although I've had my share of nightmares about those, too.

Katina laughs. "For all of Beldemar's sake, I hope we never have to rely on *you* to face the akbarrin," she says, her jest cutting deeper than she could possibly intend.

I let out a sheepish chuckle. "Yeah. I hope so, too."

Kyrel glances at us over his shoulder, and Katina mercifully lets the conversation go, shifting her attention to a bejeweled pair of sandals worn by a pretty woman masquing as an Aziza Fae. "Ooh," she squeals. "I want those."

But I stare at Kyrel and wonder if he overheard us just now. As if he can sense my eyes boring into the back of his head, he turns and looks at me. The flashing white smile he gives me seems to sparkle in the sunlight.

No. He couldn't have heard.

I smile back. I bite my lower lip, just like I practiced this morning. His eyes widen slightly just before he turns and faces front. Katina giggles, squeezing my hand. *Smooth,* her eyes seem to say.

The Dragon King puppet wriggles and writhes, its body crammed in a zigzag that fills the village square. Its red and orange plumes shimmer in the sunlight as it pulses to the syncopated rhythm the drummers' palms pound out along the square's periphery. It shakes its massive head from side to side, three large horns poking through a stringy white mane. From the tributary streets feeding into the square and the balconies surrounding it, masquers and others just along for the thrill jeer and heckle at the beast, assaulting it with balls of confetti and powdered paint.

I flinch as a canon fires more confetti over our heads. The round-faced woman beside me snarls at the dragon king, bright orange paint dripping down her face like ruined kohl. All around me, people roar with feral delight, hurling curses and insults at the paper dragon king.

I take a step back. "This isn't . . . " I look at Katina as she cackles as rotten fruit strikes the dragon king. "It's . . . "

"Not what you expected?" My wings back into Kyrel's chest. He steadies me with his hands, bending slightly so his mouth is next to my ear.

I look around at all the faces twisted with cruelty. "Not really," I admit.

I know the dragon king despised us all.

I know he wanted us dead. But . . .

"This is just kind of . . . "

"Barbaric, right?" Kyrel hums.

That he's here, touching my shoulders and finishing my sentences, is almost enough to quell the unease growing inside me. Katina's right. There's no way *I* could ever face the akbarrin.

One, no oju.

Two, I don't want to. And now seeing the gleeful vitriol that surrounds me makes me want to even less.

Three . . . I note the warmth of Kyrel's palms against my shoulders.

"C'mon. It's starting," Katina cries.

Another canon fires confetti. Scraps of orange, red, and maroon paper rain down on our heads. The Dragon King uncoils and charges up an open road, the only one not blocked by masquers. Men and women wearing costumes made of bark and wigs of long grass and twigs dash after him on stilts, the eyes of their wooden masks painted red—herders, wicked, feral creatures the Dragon King once sent out to round up his enemies. They'd blend in with the trees so that by the time anyone saw them, it was already too late.

Now they drive us up to the cliffs, parading us through the

city for onlookers to admire. Overhead, apartment residents shower us with more confetti and paint powder, cheering us on. Normal, cheerful people watching a parade. I grin and wave at a little girl clamoring about my hair from her balcony. She tugs eagerly on her mother's arm.

This is what I was looking forward to. A festive celebration. Not whatever that was back in the town square.

The giddiness fades once we're outside of Irez, trekking along narrow switchbacks under the glaring sun. My feet are bricks scraping along the rocky ground. The wings dig into my shoulders, making my back ache almost as bad as when Ranee makes me jog with a pack basket full of apples strapped to it. But the food baby sitting rock heavy in my stomach is the worst of it. I may have indulged myself in one too many desserts.

"If you hadn't eaten so much aifu, you wouldn't be complaining," Katina unhelpfully points out.

"*If you hadn't eaten so much aifu, you wouldn't be complaining,*" I mimic.

"I'll carry your wings for you, Ary," Darien offers.

But Kyrel steps between us. "Cheer up," he says. "We're almost there."

Beads of sweat sprout along my hairline as we finally reach the meeting cliff. The Dragon King slithers onto the stage while the masquers swarm the water stations, where volunteers dole out water infused with sweet cucumbers and purple-and-white pansies. Katina and I shed our wings and, with hundreds of others, cram onto the wooden benches that arc before the bandshell while Kyrel and Darien fetch our drinks.

"Wow," Katina breathes at my side.

I'm too busy staring after Kyrel, watching how he easily maneuvers through the crowd, coming toward us with two cups of water in his hands. Darien clumsily follows, splashing water on his feet, but Kyrel doesn't lose a drop. "Wow what?" I murmur.

Katina sighs. "I always forget how beautiful it is up here."

Kyrel catches me staring and curves his lips into a half smile. He doesn't do that for everyone. Smile, that is. "Yeah. Beautiful," I agree.

Katina laughs. "I'm talking about *this*." I follow her hand as it swoops in a wide arc, indicating the colorful village below, the majestic forest, and the sea glittering in the distance. She drops her hand in her lap. "Of course, it's not near as beautiful as the capital, but it's cute."

"Are you ever going back to the capital?" I ask. "To live with your mom?" Katina's been here since we were little. Sometimes, I'm surprised she even remembers the capital.

She huffs. "Obviously."

A hush settles over the crowd as the show begins. Kyrel squeezes into the spot next to me and hands me my water, our fingers grazing. I gasp, jerking my eyes forward.

On stage, the royal storyguard reenacts the final events that led to Beldemar's freedom from dragon rule. The four human kings and queens of Beldemar's largest islands appear: Bre'onna of Jara, Kalisha of Marad, Lamont of Gedra, and Treveon of Zehir. The monarchs lose at first, divided by human quarrels. Then Prince Donomar rises and unites them and becomes the human high king.

That's when the tides turn.

I clasp my hands over my heart as the actress who plays Princess Nalini graces the stage—Princess Nalini, the dragon princess who fell so in love with the human prince that she betrayed her father and sided with the humans in the war. The dragon princess who saved all our lives and forfeited her own.

When she and Prince Donomar stand over the Dragon King's corpse, I drop one of my hands to my side and inch my fingers toward Kyrel's, only to find . . . nothing. I whip my head toward where he'd been sitting. He isn't there.

The crowd erupts into dance as the show ends and the bands start playing. Katina grabs my hand and pulls me out into the open. She starts dancing first, moving her hands and hips so fast to the beat. All around me, people dance like leaves caught in a wild wind. Anyone could see that the dance Ranee taught me doesn't fit in here.

It's too slow, too formal.

Like something you would see in a ballroom.

I cover my mouth to suppress my laughter as another dancer stumbles between us. This dance is out of my league. I cup my hands around my mouth and yell to Katina over the drums, "I can't do this!"

She's dancing with a boy, their hips swaying side to side in unison. Without looking at me, she points toward a copse of trees. "He went that way."

I force my way through the crowd and emerge with a gasp, like I'm coming up from water. Kyrel leans against a tree near the cliff's edge, his body a silhouette against the backdrop of a bright moon, his hair glowing redder.

My heart thrums in my chest. He's chosen the perfect spot. This is definitely where I kiss him.

Kyrel turns as I approach, his crimson eyes brooding. They soften with surprise. "Ary?" Ary, not pigtails. That's a good start.

"You're missing the party," I say. I'd imagined us having at least one dance together before we snuck away to a place like this.

He shrugs. "Yeah. Dragon's Fall is not really my thing," he confesses. It explains why he hasn't dressed up, why he's wearing his signature black fitted caftan and pants, embroidered with neat golden swirls. It's the same suit he wore last summer when he first came to this village.

I try not to think about how I've gushed about this carnival nonstop for weeks. "So, why'd you come?" I ask.

Kyrel chuckles. It's always a surprising thing when he does something like that, surprising and intoxicating. "Isn't it obvious?" he asks. He's crossed the space between us to lift my chin with a gentle finger. Our gazes hold each other. "Because you'd be here." His gaze flickers up to my tiara, then back to my eyes.

Dizzying blood rushes to my head. "Beautiful," he murmurs. I stare at his lips as they frame the word as if I need to see its shape to believe my ears.

I lean forward. I don't worry about breaking oaths or committing treason because what's happening will only last for one night and no one will ever know about it. I tilt my chin upward, press onto my toes, and pucker my lips slightly. I close my eyes, graceful and alluring, just like I've practiced, and brace mentally for the impact of his lips against mine.

Except, it never comes. I pitch forward, stumbling into thin air. Kyrel's darted toward the opening that led me to him, his ear tilted toward the party. "Do you hear that?" he asks.

I groan, wondering how he could have possibly moved so fast.

He holds up a finger. "Shh," he commands.

I stalk toward him, a shrinking feeling in my chest. But then I hear it, too, a commotion rising above the sounds of celebration. The whinnying of horses and the rumbling of wheels. The music halts. A man's voice cuts through the ensuing silence. "Aryam Sinanan!"

My eyes widen as Kyrel turns toward me with questioning eyes.

"No," I stammer, stumbling back a step.

My name being yelled that way, in that voice, can only mean one thing. But this can't be happening. I stare wide-eyed at Kyrel, drinking in his handsome face and reliving the last half day. Too short. I look at his lips. We need more time.

Kyrel's shoulders tense. "What's going on?" he demands, but I shake my head.

Run. I want to run.

But Ranee would be heartbroken, and the oath would destroy me.

Numbly, my feet carry me back to the party. The crowd parts before me, peeling back like curtains to reveal a travel coach drawn by two enormous blue-black steeds. Two soldiers sit on the box seat, their captain standing on the coach step so that he might see over the crowd. I see Katina and Darien standing just in front of him, Katina's wide eyes trying to connect with mine, but I can't meet her gaze.

Somehow, the captain knows who I am when he sees me. The tall, rugged, yellow-haired man hops down to the ground and pulls open the coach door. Ranee sits inside with a meager bag of our belongings. Our eyes meet, hers filled with tears. "I'm sorry, Moonsong," she whispers.

Hearing the pet name she's used for me since I was a baby snaps me out of my trance, and the reality that I will never see Irez or any of my friends again comes crashing down, but I don't look back at them, not even as they start calling my name nor as hot tears stream down my cheeks. Instead, I hide my face in my hands and sob as the coach carries us away.

CHAPTER THREE

"You could have at least waited until I kissed him!" The words spill out amid a torrent of bitter tears as the coach carries me away from the only home I've ever known. I think of the people I'll never see again. Darien. Katina. Kyrel. I'll even miss Mr. Sama, Darien's ill-tempered father, who often complains that Katina and I are bad influences on his lazy son.

Sitting on the bench across from us, the captain folds his arms across his chest. His eyes narrow, his lips curling into a sly smile as he says, "You do know romances are forbidden for members of your rank?"

"Of course she knows," Ranee cuts in before I can respond. Her soft voice is sharper than I've ever heard it. She sets a trembling hand on my knee, and I realize the sharpness of her voice is meant to conceal the shaking in her hands. "She remembers her oath," she says. She turns to me, eyes wide. "Don't you, Ary?"

I stare at her fingertips curled around my kneecap and feel the weight of her alarm digging in. A warning. A plea to say the right thing.

"Yes." My own voice rings flat and hollow inside my head. The tears dry up. "I only meant to have a little fun tonight, nothing more than that." I add, belatedly, "Sir." How either of them could think the oath would allow anything more is beyond me. It would turn my heart to ice before letting it fall in love. It would tighten its leash and blind my eyes toward anyone besides the princess.

That's how it's supposed to work.

Ranee loosens her grip on my knee. A soft exhale parts her lips. She meets the captain's gaze with unflinching steel in her own. A flicker of amusement dances across his eyes before he relents with a shrug. Ranee slides her hand beside mine on the bench, our pinkie fingers touching, but that's the closest she allows herself to come to holding my hand. "Why is she being summoned?" she asks.

The captain's face blanches, that smug look vanishing. He clears his throat. "King Felix is dead," he announces.

Ranee's gasp is so sharp, I flinch, and her next word so soft, I have to strain to hear it above the sound of my own heart pounding in my ears. "How?"

Dead. The king of Beldemar is dead. The man who sent that beautiful puppet to Irez, who loved his daughter so much he wanted even the farthest, poorest village to celebrate her sixteenth score in style. How could someone like that be dead?

"He was assassinated."

Ranee leans forward. "Assassinated how?" she presses, her voice so tight, it sounds like it might shatter. I wonder if she knew the king personally. She must have since the palace served as her training ground. That's the only explanation I can fathom for my monitor's rare slip in composure.

The captain strokes his throat as if doing so makes it easier to swallow the lump that seems to be lodged there, easier to relay his horrible news. "We have reason to believe akbarrin were involved."

"Akbarrin?" I blurt out. That tightness in my chest clutches harder as images from scores of bedside tales fill my head, images of monsters and immortal tricksters and other creatures that can wield the world's akbarra, its energy, to wreak havoc on its inhabitants. I shake my head. "The akbarrin have been banished," I remind him. "They're trapped in the Shadows. They have been for near a thousand score."

They must be, because if they aren't and they're going after members of the royal family, it's my job to fight them. I can't even walk through the Immortal Soul Forest alone without succumbing to tears. I could hardly stand a parade where people just *pretended* to be akbarrin.

"Are you afraid, guardian?" the captain asks.

"No," I stammer. Yes. Definitely yes.

Ranee's finger brushes against mine, anchoring me in her steady calm. "I've prepared her well for this," she says. "The princess will be safe."

He stares at me with narrow, assessing eyes. Then, wordlessly, he raps a knuckle against the small window between our cabin and the box seat. The carriage rolls to a halt, and the broad-shouldered captain squeezes through the narrow door to relieve himself in the forest.

"Ranee." I'm clasping her hand, willing my tears back from falling. The cabin feels too small. It can't possibly hold enough air for the two of us. I want to turn back time, set the stagecoach's wheels in reverse, take us home to where none of this has ever happened.

It's because I tried to kiss him, isn't it? Maybe this is the universe's way of trying to punish me.

She strokes the side of my face before easing my tiara from

my hair. She plucks the crystal from the center and tosses the clip onto the floor. "I've given you what childhood I could, Ary," she says, pulling a silver chain from her pocket. "Most Monitors would even say I've spoiled you." She smiles softly and pulls something else from her other pocket—a small, tear-shaped silver cage that opens like a clam. She tucks the crystal inside before closing it and threading the silver chain through the clasps. Then she loops the chain around my neck. "I don't regret a single tick of the life we built together, from the day I carried you to Irez on my back."

She held nineteen score when she became my monitor, the youngest in her cohort, and the sharpest.

The crystal falls between my breasts, resting against my sternum. I tuck my chin into my chest and watch as a tear rolls down my cheek and splashes onto the sapphire stone.

Ranee lifts my gaze to meet hers. "But we must put duty before self," she commands, "now more than ever."

I force myself to nod, even though my heart screams that none of this is fair. But it wasn't fair for Ranee, either. She could have chosen a life instead of coming here. She could have had a husband and a family and a home.

Instead, she chose me.

And she's complained far less in sixteen score than I have in this one night. Ranee gave up everything to train and raise me. I nod again.

"Good." Ranee leans forward to kiss my forehead, and I savor her scent, one of forest and sea, one of home. She tugs a hooded poncho over my head and pulls the hem as I thread my arms through the sleeves. I use them to wipe away the last of my tears. I start to pull the crystal from beneath the cloth, but Ranee stops me, resting her hand over my own. "From now on, keep it hidden," she instructs.

I tilt my head. "Why?"

Rather than answer, Ranee squeezes my hand fondly before pulling away as the captain climbs back into the cabin.

I'll ask her later, then. I turn toward the captain as the coach starts forward again and ask, "What happened to the king's guardians?"

Ranee braces herself beside me, and even the captain looks uncomfortable. He clears his throat. "The oath claimed their lives," he answers, "when they failed to protect their king."

I cling to Ranee's hand and fight back the terror that claws at my throat.

A SLEEPLESS NIGHT creeps by despite the coach's swift pace as it cuts through the forest. "What kind of horses *are* these?" I asked Ranee earlier when the coach first accelerated and the world outside became a blur. The horses move faster than any I've ever seen.

"They're omiayo," the smug captain had pitched in, "creatures of wind and sea." In other words, akbarrin. I should have felt vindicated after all these score of suspecting that some managed to slip through the barriers between our world and theirs, scores of being teased by my friends. Instead, I felt squeamish.

Hours later, the nausea remains.

We've exchanged the gloomy, silent Immortal Soul Forest for its greener, noisier neighbor. The *chiri chiri chiri* of a thousand poisonous tree frogs drowns out the wheels crunching against the rocky road, joined by baritone croaks of bull lizards and the exuberant whinnies of the omiayo. With my heart pounding in my ears, I strain to hear what other manner of beast might be prowling these woods.

What manner of akbarrin besides the omiayo.

I sit at the edge of my seat, which is how I find myself flying across the cabin into the captain's arms when the coach jolts. I quickly disentangle myself only to fall into him again as the coach sinks into one wheel. My head smacks against his firm chest. I struggle to get free. "What was that?"

Ranee hooks her arms beneath my armpits and hauls me back onto our bench as the captain scrambles for the door and thrusts it open. "Dex? Joan?" he calls out to his second and third, the two people in the driver's seat.

"Just snagged a wheel!" a gruff voice calls back. "You'd better see this, Captain Aric!"

A wall of silence slams down upon us. "What happened to the frogs?" I whisper. Even the dauntless bull lizards have stopped croaking.

Not a good sign.

And the omiayo . . . their unbridled whinnies vanish on the wind.

Ranee moves slowly, cautiously setting me aside. Her eyes dart toward the window, then to the captain, steady and calculating. "After you, Captain Aric." She says his name like she's known him her whole life. That's Ranee. Always ready to take charge when needed.

The captain nods firmly and slides a hand to the hilt of the blade strapped at his side. "Be ready for anything," he commands before pushing the door open. It creaks on its hinges.

Ranee leans forward, preparing to go after him. I catch her by the wrist. "Ranee, you know I can't fight them without . . . "

Her eyes hold mine, and she drops her voice low and firm. "Aryam, do as I've trained you," she instructs, "and you will be fine."

That tightness in my chest loosens, fluttering away as I force my heart to calm. "Right," I confirm. I crawl out of the cabin after her.

The faulty wheel sits at an angle, ripped from the axle. The two soldiers, Dex and Joan, fiddle with it. The horses, as I suspected, are nowhere to be seen. The tall man, Dex, squats and tries with all his might to raise the coach while the powerfully built woman, Joan, pushes against the wheel.

"Step aside." There's so much authority in Ranee's voice that the soldiers obey without question. Even the captain bows to that authority, sidestepping so that she can pass him, but his hand doesn't leave the hilt. One glance at the wheel tells me all I need to know about why he's so on edge.

No ditch. No exposed root. No protruding rock. Not a single logical reason for the wheel to have broken off the way it has. Instead, a woody vine, green and thick and *wrong*, snakes through the wheel's spokes, strangling the hub.

"Where did that come from?" I ask. None of the trees around us have vines.

A branch snaps behind us. Something rustles in the bush. We whirl around instantly, Dex and Joan flanking me and Ranee, the captain standing before us. Ranee wraps her fingers around my wrist, her grip tight.

Another snap of a twig, a whistling sound as something shoots through the air, then the startled gurgles bubbling out of throats. I glance to each side. Dex and Joan raise their hands to their necks, tugging at the vines wrapped around them. The rest happens so quickly. The vines go taut, the soldiers' eyes bulge in terror, and then they fly headfirst into the bush.

Captain Aric draws his weapon, an ordinary sword with a wide blade. Sturdy, but perhaps not enough to defeat whatever creature lurks behind the bush. "Roaring seas," he swears. "Get behind me." I'm quick to do as he says.

Screaming. I expect to hear screaming from Dex and Joan, but I don't. The akbarrin granted them swift deaths, then. My imagination runs rampant as I try to predict what sort of creature could so easily overcome such capable-looking soldiers —Dex with the height of a bonsam and Joan with her muscular arms.

Leaves crunch underfoot. The bushes rustle again. A whimper escapes my lips, but I reel it in at a peremptory glance from Ranee. The captain flexes his fingers and adjusts his grip on the hilt. "I'll hold it off," he says. "Get ready to run." Beats ago, I didn't like this man. Now I think I could hug him.

The creature emerges from the bush.

I see its eyes first. They glow bright yellow, hovering six feet above the ground. The body appears afterward, the ancient face a wooden mask with foliage for brow and beard, and a bare chest and arms that look as though they've been chiseled by the demigod of carpentry himself. All resemblance to mankind stops at his waist, his lower half furry and hooved.

"Father Wood." We all breathe the name of the legendary guardian of the forests in unison. More than an akbarrin, he's a demigod. But even those were banished after the war. The vengeful fire burning in the forest guardian's eyes tells me exactly what he thinks of that banishment.

"The dock is not far from here," Captain Aric informs us in a low voice. "There'll be a boat waiting to take you to the capital. Go." He raises his sword above his head and roars as he charges forward. Father Wood answers the roar with a battle cry of his own and thrusts his arm toward Captain Aric. His arm splinters into vines. The captain reacts with surprising quickness, slicing through the vines as they come.

But Father Wood just shoots more. Anyone with eyes can see that he'll soon overwhelm his opponent.

I struggle to tear my gaze away from them. As much as my instincts tell me to run, I can't fathom leaving behind a person who would sacrifice himself for me, even if he's just doing so to allow me to go sacrifice myself for someone else.

Ranee seizes my wrist and pulls me away. Before I can see what happens next, we're running down the narrow, overgrown road, thick, humid air shoving down our lungs as we draw nearer to the sea. My sense catches up with me. I remember the stories Ranee told me in my youth. "Father Wood is a protector," I pant, between heavy breaths. "Not a monster or a murderer."

Ranee nudges me forward. "I suppose being locked in the Shadows for nearly ten hundred score has made him a little onery." Her voice is so smooth compared to mine, her breath so easy. She pulls up to my side and smirks a little. "I bet now you wish you *actually* went for all those runs I sent you on, rather than sneaking off to play with your friends."

"*Ranee*," I protest. What a terrible time for a joke, but it takes the edge off just a little. I let out a petulant huff, realizing that was her aim. "I didn't think you knew about that." But I shouldn't be surprised. Ranee has an uncanny talent for knowing all the things I get up to, even when I think I've done a superb job of covering my tracks.

I'll never know how she does it.

We find the port dark and quiet, except for the sound of water lapping gently against the lone wooden dock that stretches out into the sea, lit by a single lantern flickering at the end and the moon sitting low on the horizon. I stumble to a stop and gape at the boat awaiting us, a sleek wooden vessel without a sail or oar in sight.

"That isn't what I had in mind when Captain Aric said 'boat,'" I grumble. "Where's the crew? How are we supposed to sail it?" I thought there would be a real ship with a crew to man it. A crew with weapons. Maybe even some with the ability to call oju.

Because, regardless of what Ranee said before, that's what we need right now.

Oju.

Only the legendary spirit weapon of the guardians will aid us against an opponent like Father Wood.

Ranee puts two fingers in her mouth and throws a loud summoning whistle into the night. Wild whinnies answer from the sea. The omiayo.

"Oh," I murmur, gazing at my monitor. "How did you know to—"

"Later," she cuts me off. "We need to keep moving." She races to the dock and darts out onto it first, the wood groaning under her feet.

I test the first plank with a hesitant push of my foot against the wood. It holds. The trees rumble behind us. A man screams. Captain Aric. I take a breath and yell out to Ranee. "Wait!"

She turns back, her eyes full of question, but she finds the answer in my own.

"We can't just leave him."

Ranee answers sternly. "Ary, the captain made his choice. He knows how important it is that we get you to the capital."

To the princess awaiting my aid. But the oath hasn't boiled my blood yet, so she must be fine. Safe. Unlike the man who took on an akbarrin demigod to buy me time. I open my mouth to explain this to Ranee, but then I see it. Rising behind her. A woman with skin of obsidian and hair of coils as black as the nighttime sea. She emerges from the water, the black scales of her serpentine lower half flickering in the moonlight.

Of course. Father Wood does have a wife after all—Mama River, guardian of all things water and protectress of mothers and daughters. But her eyes are all wrong. They lack love and warmth and burn with malice.

"Ranee, look out!" I cry.

She turns and ducks just in time, narrowly evading the scaled tale that swoops over her head. She scrambles off the dock, turning her back to the sand. Mama River's tail slams down against the wood, crashing through it. The dock splinters and breaks, and the demigoddess vanishes beneath the surface.

"What do we do now?" I huff, peering over Ranee's shoulder at the black, quiet water. The boat bobs at the end of what remains of the dock. Ranee reaches around her back for the staff that sits in two pieces above her hips. In a fluid motion, she unsheathes it and unites the two pieces with a crisp click.

"We do what we must," she asserts, her voice husky and winded. Something feral glints in her eye, something I've never seen in her before. Without looking away from the water, she nudges me with an elbow. "Outside my right thigh."

I slip my hand along the outside of her thigh and find a small dagger holstered beneath the flap of her tunic. Carefully, I slide it out. My breath catches at the sight of the gleaming silver. She can't possibly mean it. "Ranee," I hiss, "we cannot fight the mother of the sea."

She flexes her fingers and adjusts her grip on the staff. "She has chosen her side," she replies. "Whatever you do, don't turn your back on her."

"As the legends say," I acknowledge, but I frown. She isn't listening to me. I must get through to her. "This isn't right." None of this is right. Father Wood and Mama River are—*were* good.

Ranee sweeps a foot across the sand and sets her stance. "For the princess," she murmurs. "And for Beldemar." She glances at me. "They are one and the same, Ary. Remember your duty to both."

Mama River emerges from the sea, water trickling down her firm, majestic body. Cold sweeps through my blood, settling in my gut and my fingers, but my training sets in, too. I match my monitor's stance, and the two of us fan out, the soft, black sands shifting beneath the balls of our feet.

Mama River slithers ashore, those glowing eyes darting between us and settling on me, on the stone at my chest. Surprise registers on her face, her eyes widening slightly. She sneers at Ranee and then dashes for me, reaching for my throat. The dagger trembles in my hand. I can't bring myself to raise it, even in my own defense. I take a step back, letting the dagger fall to the sand.

I lower my chin to my chest in a show of deference. Mama River slows. A good sign. Maybe I can appeal to the goodness that must still reside in her heart. Maybe I can put an end to whatever is going on here.

But I don't get a word out.

Ranee strikes, leaping into the air and swinging her wooden staff down toward the akbarrin demigoddess's head. Mama River blocks the blow with her forearm and snarls, the sound vicious and inhuman. "You will regret that, insolent daughter," she hisses.

And then they are a haze of motion, Ranee a flurry of swift blows and mathematic precision, and Mama River an angry blur of fanged attacks and lunges.

"Stop!" I plead. I step toward them, but something catches my ankle, wraps around it, and tugs it back. My body pitches forward. My feet fly from under me. I land on my stomach, face level with the sea, just as Mama River tackles Ranee into the water and plunges her under. The sea rages as they continue their struggle below its surface.

I twist and see a vine wrapped around my ankle. My gaze follows the vine back to the forest, to Father Wood as he emerges with three wild boars squealing frantically in his wake.

"Aryam!" My attention snaps back to the water, where Ranee has fought her way to the surface. She raises her staff as Mama River's tail coils around her and snaps it back into two halves. She slams the sharper half down with brute force and punctures the scaly skin. Mama River's terrible shrill pummels my ears as Ranee slumps forward in her grasp, exhausted.

She's put up an impossible effort, but she won't last much longer. I reach for her. "Ranee!"

My body slides back as Father Wood reels me toward him. I flip onto my back and manage to sit, grabbing my discarded dagger in the process. I lean forward and saw at the vine. It snaps. I roll onto my hands and knees, crawling for my monitor as Mama River submerges with her again.

This time, the water swallows them quietly. Ranee isn't fighting back.

Another vine catches my waist. Two more seize my arms. Father Wood raises me into the air. I struggle against the vines, twisting and pulling to no avail. Father Wood turns my body to face his. The water behind me is still and silent. "Let me go," I plead. A vine tightens on my wrist, forcing my hand open. The dagger falls to the sand.

In the end, I won't even make it to Princess Marleyn's side.

And all because I never saw this day coming.

Because I didn't train hard enough.

Drawing in a sharp breath, I try to fling my consciousness into the glen in a final, desperate attempt to find my oju, but the crushing force of Father Wood's vines makes it impossible to find calm. Tears stream down my cheeks as my eyes meet his. His ancient face is stern and solemn, his eyes filled with . . . sorrow, then sharp focus as they settle on the crystal at my chest.

Father Wood raises a hand toward it, and just as his fingers brush against the cool stone, a bright flare tears through his chest—a blade engulfed in fire. I snap free of his hold as Father Wood bursts into flames, then disintegrates into ash that flutters away on the sea breeze. The boars at his feet squeal in terror.

I fall to my knees, the ash of the forest guardian blowing into my face.

A girl with a massive mane of golden curls stands in his place, wielding a flaming sword. She salutes me with a triumphant smile. “Guardian Maya at your service,” she announces with a dramatic bow.

And then the burning sword in her hand vanishes because it wasn’t a physical sword at all. It was her oju.

CHAPTER FOUR

The boars spiral into a frenzy, their frantic grunts escalating into a crescendo of ear-shattering squeals. They wriggle and writhe, and their plump bodies undulate with each shriek. They look like they're in terrible pain. I fall back onto my elbows and scramble to get away as they shuffle toward me, then press my hands against my ears to block out the horrid noise. The boars topple over, and the sickening crunch of cracking bones overtakes their squeals. I watch as their bodies twist, break, and stretch. Fur falls away from skin. Snouts shrink into noses. The creatures morph into something less porcine and something more . . .

Human.

Bile churns in my gut.

A few beats later, the three once-pigs huddle in fetal position, half-naked and fully *human*. The first to recover raises himself onto all fours, retching before forcing himself to stand. A thin, slimy layer of black hair coats his pale chest. He tugs at the ancient scrap of cloth fastened around his waist. Captain Aric. Dex and Joan whimper behind him, covered in the same strange fur and wearing similar scraps.

Captain Aric tries to dust off the sand that clings to his skin, grunting his displeasure. It's no use. The sand is everywhere. The captain abandons the effort. "That," he says, seemingly fighting off a wave of nausea, "was utterly terrifying." He frowns down at himself, then frowns further as he notices me, still propped on my elbows. I don't miss the grim relief in his eyes. He scans the beach. "Where's . . . "

I'm scrambling to my feet before he can say her name. Between Guardian Maya's appearance and the boars' transformation, I got distracted. I rush for the now-tranquil water, finding no sign of my monitor or Mama River anywhere. I wade in chest deep. The cold water steals the air from my lungs. Her name tears from throat. "Ranee!"

But yelling for her conjures nothing, not even the faintest splash.

I dive in, the freezing water hurling my body further into shock, forcing me to gasp for breath. It goes down my windpipes like icy fire. But I stay under, even as the saltwater stings my eyes, even though it's too dark to see anything despite the sun's soft glow on the horizon.

Dawn.

Arms hook under my own and heave me to the surface. Captain Aric pulls me against his chest. "Whoa, kid. There's no one here." His tone is so different than it was earlier, absent of condescension. Instead, I hear pity.

Dawn.

I can't let this happen. I can't let the sun rise without her here by my side.

I've already lost everything.

I can't lose her, too.

I shake my head and fight to free myself from Captain Aric's grasp, fire still burning in my lungs. "She's still here," I insist. "She needs help." My last glimpse of her, enervated in the demigoddess's clutches, flashes before my eyes. I drop my weight in his arms, desperate to get underwater again. "We have to help her."

But he drags me toward the ruined dock. When we get close enough, Dex reaches down and hoists me up. When I lunge for the edge again, he and Joan restrain me. I try to wrestle myself free, but they're too strong. The captain pulls himself up onto the dock and grabs me firmly by the shoulders. "Pull yourself together, guardian," he commands.

The words hit hard. Numbness falls over my body, and I slacken in the soldiers' arms. I stare at the dark water as a devastating emptiness swells inside my chest.

Guardian.

"What kind of guardian doesn't fight?" I whisper, hoarse.

Ranee gave me a dagger, and I dropped it.

"You couldn't endanger yourself," Captain Aric reasons. His fingers press into my shoulders like he's trying to squeeze some sense into me. "Not when you need to get to Princess Marleyn. I am sure Monitor Ranee understood that."

My gaze flickers up to his. I blink, trying to process the horror behind the truth. "Did I . . . " I retch, unable to voice the question. Did I drop the dagger because of my oath to the princess? Did being chained to her stop me from trying to save Ranee? I double over, clutching my stomach.

Oh, Moons. What's going to happen to her?

Legends say Mama River drives her victims to the seabed, sometimes to their deaths, sometimes to their torment. Her vicious words clatter through my head.

You will regret that, insolent daughter.

I retch again, spilling the contents of my stomach onto the captain's bare feet. Joan's arms tighten around me, keeping me from collapsing into my own sick.

"Are the four of you headed to the capital, too?" A bubbly voice fills the silence.

I freeze as I remember Guardian Maya.

The girl with the flame sword oju.

My head lifts to find her standing at the edge of the dock, a graceful smile on her face. She's just a girl, maybe the same age as me. But she isn't from Marad. Maradis favor blues and purples, like the scales of their ancient patron dragon. Maya wears orange with red accents. Those are the colors of Zehir, the sibling kingdom that shares our island.

No one answers her question. Captain Aric calmly steps out of my vomit puddle as Dex hands him the dagger I left on shore. "Who are you?"

Maya's smile doesn't fade. She bares her pale wrist to us and brushes a thumb over the exposed skin. A faint symbol glows there: two moons, one three-quarters of the way eclipsed by the other. It's the same symbol that would appear on my wrist if I performed the same motion.

Captain Aric loosens his grip on the dagger. "One of Princess Marleyn's guardians, then," he observes, relief in his voice. "Now we have two of you." His attention shifts to his feet, his lip curling with disgust. The captain plops down at the edge of the dock and plunges his feet into the water. "We need to head to the capital," he says over his shoulder.

Joan eases her hold on my arm. "Captain, should we really head out to sea?" she asks. "You know, with"—she casts me a pitying glance—"you-know-*who* in the water?"

"Don't worry," Guardian Maya reassures her. "If the akbarrin gets close, I'll just call my oju again." That bright smile returns, then fades as she tilts her head and studies me. "Why didn't you call yours?"

The heat of their curious gazes warms my skin. I avert my gaze to the glittering sea and think of all the mornings I should have spent taking my time in the glen more seriously. All the mornings I spent plotting exploits with my friends and fantasizing about a boy instead.

"I don't have one," I confess.

If I did, I could have saved the only person who has ever truly known me.

WE PILE INTO THE BOAT. Captain Aric summons the omiayo and fastens their straps to the fitted rings on the boat's bow. Then he takes the boatman's seat and holds their reins. Dex and Joan push us off from the dock, and Captain Aric commands the omiayo to go. The water horses unleash vivacious whinnies and charge out to sea. A ripple of waves fans out in our wake.

No one says anything when I curl up on the deck floor, pressing my back against the concave wall and pulling my knees into my chest. It isn't until we surge past the barrier of the breakwater that Joan starts chattering, maybe to take her mind off of the choppy sea.

"Doesn't make sense," she says from the bench where she huddles against Dex. "I thought all guardians have oju—fire oju from Zehir." She nods toward Maya. "Plant oju from Jara. Animal from Gedra." She gestures toward each of the islands in the distance, somewhere beyond Capital Island. The soldier levels a pointed look toward me. "And pure akbarra from Marad."

I flinch. As if I need reminding. Not only should I have an oju—I should have the most powerful oju of all the guardians in my quartet, just as the Guardian of Marad has always held the strongest oju. I should be their leader.

Instead, when it mattered most, I dropped the dagger.

I curl further into myself, squeezing my legs just a little

tighter. I have no answer, no words to defend myself. No words. A tear rolls down my cheek and splashes onto my forearm. I turn my head to hide the ones still brimming in my eyes.

Joan backs off.

Sometime later, Maya slides from her seat into the space before me, perching on her knees. She assesses me for a beat before stating, "You were really close to her." Her gentle voice overflows with wonder. "It's . . . "—she pauses, searching for the right word—"*rare* for a guardian and her monitor to be so close."

Her observation makes me curious enough to lift my head and face her. I glance beyond her at the shrinking shoreline. "Where's your monitor?" I ask, only now realizing that she arrived at the clandestine port without one.

She straightens. "We were separated," she replies, somewhat carefully. Her dark brown eyes reveal no trace of sadness, but I notice the slight pause before that final word. *Separated.* There's more there, a story maybe, but she doesn't offer it, and I don't ask.

A good guardian minds her secrets.

Maya continues. "I suspect Monitor Ahiel has returned to Gadara." I try to conjure an image of Zehir's capital, a charred city famous for its ales and spirits, but my imagination comes up short.

Maya doesn't seem sad about leaving Monitor Ahiel behind, but I detect something else. Disapproval, maybe. She quickly hides it behind an inviting smile, and I get the feeling that she's the type who would never openly criticize another.

"Tell me about her," she entreats. "Your monitor."

When I hesitate, she insists.

"Go on. Maybe it will help you feel better."

As if losing my monitor, the only person who has known me since my birth, is only a minor inconvenience. But then I remember. It *should* be. A monitor's duty is to devote herself to the upbringing and training of her guardian. The guardian's duty is to focus solely on serving her Pulse.

Ranee did her job.

It's my turn to do mine.

Her final advice plays in my memory: *We must put duty before self.*

I straighten my back, just a little. She would want me to try to put this behind me. She would demand that I let it go. Above everything, she would urge me to keep searching.

Maybe if I do that—maybe if I find my oju and secure the princess—maybe my monitor will be less disapproving when I show up to rescue her.

Because no matter what she says, no matter what the oath demands, I won't abandon her. I squeeze my eyes shut and brace myself for the omission to smite me—but nothing happens. I pop one eye open to find a bemused look on Maya's kind face. She gives me an encouraging smile, and I remember her request.

"Right," I murmur. I sift through the sparse details Ranee's given me about her family and life before she became my monitor. It isn't much.

"She's Jaran," I share. "She's never admitted it, but I think she comes from a wealthy family." My monitor's small tells give her away, like how she always manages to smell like rain and flowers despite our strenuous activities and lack of coin, and how she prepares finer meals than any eatery in town.

And there's the dance she taught me, too elegant and traditional for common gatherings and festivals.

I tell Maya this and other things. I tell her about how Ranee likes art, cooking, and storytelling, about the things she taught me. With each fact I share, the tightness in my chest and throat loosens a little. It doesn't quite quell the grief, but it keeps me from feeling like breaking.

That will have to be enough until I can find her.

"She does sound much better than Ahiel," Maya comments when I've finished, but again, her tone doesn't invite questioning. She smiles brightly. "I guess I can understand how leaving someone like that behind might be difficult, but you don't have to feel so alone. We're chorus sisters now. We have each other."

Chorus sisters.

Inexorably linked by the song of our hearts.

I smile back at her the best I can. I just hope she still feels this way once she realizes how terribly unprepared I am.

CHAPTER FIVE

A measure or two after zenith, Capital Island emerges on the horizon, a black giant slumbering in the hazy distance. I sit just behind the bow, watching as Captain Aric drives the omiayo toward the island. Horses made of wind and water in our realm all this time. Days ago, it would have been a joke that Katina whispered to make my skin crawl. Today, it's real. All real.

Captain Aric's waistcloth catches a gust of wind, flapping upward. I quickly turn away, grateful that there's little left in my stomach to throw up. We left most of our provisions in the carriage and have long since devoured the meager supply of flame seeds Maya carried with her. Little grows in Zehir after the fire that devastated their half of the island a thousand score ago, but the spicy flame seeds are a resilient breed.

Much like Maya.

My chorus sister ascends the steps from the main deck and, stifling a giggle at the captain's expense, hurries to sit beside me. She pushes her mass of gold curls over her shoulder before neatly folding her hands into her lap. "It won't be long now," she says, her excitement palpable through the bright gleam in her eyes.

I can't blame her for being happy. I've lost everything that's ever mattered to me in the span of a night, but Maya's gained the world in the same time frame. For hundreds of score, guardians have trained and died in isolation, never meeting their pulses or their chorus brothers and sisters, feeding every fiber of their being into a prophecy they would never see fulfilled. Most never have what Ranee dared to give me. A childhood and a home. I, too, would be happy to see an end to that sort of loneliness.

That's why I go along with it, squeezing Maya's hand in turn when she squeezes mine.

"I hear the palace's Library of Light has some of the oldest texts in the empire," she says. "Maybe you'll find something there to help unlock your oju."

"Maybe," I agree, although it isn't just my oju that I want information on. It's the oath. There must be a way of saving Ranee without breaking it, without sentencing myself to omission before I can even try.

Another measure ticks by, and the blurry beast on the horizon begins to reveal its true colors. A canopy of green ornaments its hills, stretching high and wide across the island. Closer to the sea, a cluster of colorful rooftops sparkles in the sun. As the land rises higher toward the mountain, the distance between the rooftops grows. Trees and buildings alike vanish into the thick ring of fog at the very top.

Our ship crests a small wave into the calmer waters surrounding the island, so clear I can see the sand several feet below the surface and the rainbow of fish darting through seaweed and coral. Captain Aric and his crew guide the small ship into the harbor that sprawls at the base of the island. It's a proper port with every sort of ship flowing in all directions.

A half measure later, we're docking at the outer edge of the pier, away from all the great cargo ships. We're met by a party of soldiers whose mouths are agape at the sight of their scantily clad captain and his second and third.

Maya disembarks first, closing the gap between ship and dock in a graceful leap. After landing, she sweeps her hair over her shoulder, then turns and extends a hand for me. I wait for the gangplank to settle before I venture off the ship, clasping her hand to avoid slipping into the water.

"Thank you," I say, as she pulls me ashore. As soon as my feet find solid ground, I pull my hand back from hers and tuck it into the folds of my poncho.

Captain Aric and the others clamber across the gangplank behind me. One of the new soldiers waiting on the dock clears his throat. "Uh, Captain? Your clothes?" he inquires, respectfully averting his eyes.

Captain Aric's face glows impossibly redder, already ruddy with exertion from crossing the sea. "Don't just stand there," he barks. "Find us replacements." Maya giggles as the soldier scurries away, and the captain shoots her a sharp look in return. She stops, but her smile doesn't fade. It's only when his stern brown eyes turn to me that I realize I'm holding in a laugh, too, despite everything. I slide a hand over my mouth to conceal my smile.

A few beats later, the soldier returns with the requested clothing and, panting, doles it out between Captain Aric and the others. "Dex, Joan, you're dismissed," Captain Aric grumbles after snatching his clothes, a colorful ensemble that appears to have come from a vendor's booth. "Go get yourselves cleaned up." He tugs on a bright pair of trousers and a garish tunic before striding toward the bustling city. Maya and I exchange amused glances before taking our cue to follow.

More people than I ever imagined could be in one place at

one time mill about the cobbled streets of Beldemar's capital, people of every shade of brown and yellow—just like in Marad—but people of paler hues, too, like Maya and Captain Aric. They wear a myriad of traditional colors and fabrics from all corners of the empire. I see every shade of green from Jara, brown and tan from Gedra, orange and red from Zehir, and all the blues and purples of Marad.

Laughter and singing fill the streets, along with the most savory aromas from street vendors and pop-up eateries at every other corner. Kitesmen dash through the streets, pulling paper dragons behind them on gentle breezes, weaving between streamers and paper lanterns. There's not one sign of a people mourning their slain king.

I quicken my step to reach Captain Aric's side. "They're still celebrating," I point out. "Shouldn't they be—"

"They don't know," he grunts tersely, before I can finish that question.

Surprise stills my feet. "They don't know?" I repeat. The words sound far away, even though they're coming from my own mouth. I scramble to make sense of them, wondering if I've heard him correctly. How can they not know?

"That kind of makes our job easier," Maya reasons, taking up his other side. "Don't you think?"

"I . . . guess you're right," I concede.

She has a point. It would be easier to get to the princess, easier to protect her if no one knew, if Beldemar wasn't in complete pandemonium following the unprecedented assassination of one of its noblest kings.

"But . . . " I trail off. It still feels so wrong for a man who loved his daughter so well that he honored her across kingdoms to die unnoticed. "When will someone tell them?" I demand.

Instead of answering, Captain Aric veers right, steering me by the elbow toward a wooden booth crammed between two other vendors. An old woman stands behind the counter, wearing the traditional green garb of Jara and doling out heaping ladles of corn soup to a long line of customers. She flashes a toothless smile when she spots the captain and waves him to the front of the line, folds of skin cascading over her cheeks in a way that makes it hard not to gape at her.

"Captain," she greets Captain Aric as we approach. She's already filling a bowl for him. "It's been a while since I've seen you at my booth." There's something ancient and grating about her voice that makes my spine tingle, but Captain Aric issues a courteous nod to the old woman and accepts the bowl.

All thoughts of the eerie old woman vanish as Captain Aric passes the corn soup to me. I take in a glorious whiff, sorting the scents with my nose: coconut, plantains, garlic, pepper, thyme, and so many more, mixed to sweet and spicy perfection. It's a Jaran novelty Ranee has prepared for me only a handful of times, times she claimed I deserved a treat for working so hard. But I knew two things were true. I wasn't working *that* hard, and she made the fancy dishes around the same time each score.

The old woman's gummy smile widens as she watches me guzzle the first several spoonsful. I remember to thank her after a few more gulps. Then Maya and I carry our soup, along with two thick slices of bread each, over to a wooden table near the road. Aric follows with a bowl of his own. We eat in silence, and for once, I'm happy not to be teased about the fact that I go back for seconds . . . and second seconds. Best of all, the old woman doesn't charge me coin for any of it.

"Anything for a friend of the captain's." She grins, handing me my third bowl. But this time, she's slower to release the bowl. That sagging skin above her right eye pulls up a little farther as she squints at my chest. I glance down to see the crystal peeking out from the triangle cut in my poncho. "That's a pretty stone you have there, girl," she remarks. "Where did you get it?"

I tuck the crystal back under my collar and try to suppress a flood of images from the past several measures: Ranee settling the stone on my tiara, eyes beaming with pride. Her ripping it off again and fixing it to the chain. Father Wood's gnarled hand reaching for it before a blade of fire pierces his chest.

I swallow. "It's nothing special," I murmur gently but firmly, tugging the bowl free. I bow respectfully to the elder. "Thank you for your kindness." I ignore Captain Aric's and Maya's curious glances as I slide back into my seat. The third bowl goes down slower than the first two, but neither says anything until I'm finished.

Once we're all good and full, Captain Aric slaps his knees, signaling the end of the meal, then hails a small carriage to carry us up the mountain toward the palace that sits above the fog. I sense eyes on me and look back at the vendor's booth, but the old woman has vanished from her post, her line of customers dispersed.

WITH THE ACHE I feel in my legs and back, I welcome the carriage as a small drop of mercy in a stream of merciless events. Inside the cabin, Maya flits from side to side, marveling at all the sights. "This place is nothing like Zehir," she says. "I'm sure you know."

I do. "My friend Darien is a bit of a scrollhead," I reply. "He told me all about how King Elrey made his last stand there." And burned the land so badly that even hundreds of score later, it hasn't greened again.

Maya tilts her head to one side, fixing me with a quizzical stare.

"What?" I ask, worrying my fingers over the fray of my sleeves.

A placid smile graces her face. "I'm happy you were able to make friends somehow," she says. "It's strange news but not unpleasant."

All the same, my carelessness makes me cringe. Moons, I need to try harder to fit in. She already thinks me strange for loving my guardian. "What about you?" I ask. "Was there really no one?"

"Friends?" she clarifies. She shakes her head. "People were wary of me, especially once I started wielding fire. Besides, Monitor Ahiel was stern with anyone he thought distracting. Once, I think he even broke a poor guy's nose for asking me to dance. Ahiel always insisted on going to dances. He'd say that understanding noble culture was an important part of my training, but I think he just liked the wine."

Her hand flies to her mouth. "Oh. I don't think I should have said that."

Monitor Ahiel sounds like a charm, but I'll spare Maya's feelings and tuck this morsel of information away for another time. Besides, something else stands out to me about what she's shared.

"People knew who you were?" I ask. "What you were meant to do?" For once, I don't feel like the odd one. Secrecy is a guardian's mantle, after all. In my case, it was near freedom.

She looks surprised. "Why wouldn't they?" she asks. "The guardian rank is the most honored in all the land. I was practically a celebrity. Weren't you?"

I shake my head, doubt creeping in. "Ranee always said fame would be a distraction and that safety and honor went hand in hand with anonymity." I've always taken her word for it, never questioned her. I wonder if I should have. Why would she insist on secrecy if it wasn't law?

"I suppose every monitor has his or her way of rearing his or her guardian," Maya says after a moment.

"I guess," I muse. Even if her reasons weren't clear, I'm grateful Ranee raised me the way she did. I don't think I could handle people being afraid of me. What if Darien, Katina, and Kyrel couldn't speak to me? That would be too lonely. My eyes meet with Captain Aric's, and I find he's been staring.

He clears his throat. "From what I've heard about it, every monitor has their own opinion on the matter," he enlightens us. "Some prefer humble seclusion. Others fancy the prestige that comes with one of the most coveted positions in society."

I think of Monitor Ahiel's penchant for glamorous parties and nod. It helps to know that Ranee's preference for isolation was maybe more about her than me. Besides, she's the one who rarely ever went into town. She never forbade me from going.

The cluster of buildings thins out as the carriage climbs higher and higher up the mountain. Capital Forest's spindly fingers, hairy with moss, creep between bamboo houses until there are no more houses to be seen. Just dense rainforest. Maya releases a heavy, satisfied breath. "This place just smells so . . . alive," she says.

Captain Aric scoffs at that. "One way of putting it," he remarks, tugging at his collar. Feeling the beads of sweat percolating along my hairline, I'm more inclined to side with him. But at least it's cooler here, this high up the mountain, and growing cooler still as we ascend into a damp mist. At last, we've reached the fog. It rolls around us, an impenetrable blanket of white, and pushes against the senses.

Maya's hand slides over mine, anchoring me against the rush of adrenaline flooding my body. I feel something in the fog, something age-old and sinister prodding at the barrier of my mind. I gasp. "Do either of you feel that?" I whisper.

Captain Aric sits forward. "Feel what?"

I peer out at the blinding fog. "I think something's out there."

Captain Aric groans, slumping back into his seat. "Relax, guardian," he grumbles.

A shadow passes in my peripheral vision, just beyond the wall fog. I flinch, turning toward the other side of the carriage. "There!" I redirect them, but they turn too achingly slow. The shadow is gone.

Captain Aric frowns and fixes me with a disapproving stare before relenting with a sigh. "You've been through a lot in a very short time," he says. "It's enough to make anyone jumpy."

Maya squeezes my hand, gentle and firm.

So, they both think I'm crazy.

"I really did feel something," I murmur, freeing my hand from hers, but I know better than to try to make them believe me. Instead, I peer out into the rolling fog and search for monsters. Maybe one will jump out and try to eat us. Then they'll believe me.

A faint chill cools my breastbone, drawing my gaze down to the crystal pressed against my skin. The *glowing* crystal pressed against my skin. I throw my hand over it and wrap my fingers around it, squeezing tight enough for my fingernails to press little crescent moons in my palm.

When I open my fist, one finger at a time, the crystal appears to be normal.

Maybe the captain and my chorus sister are right.

Maybe I'm imagining things.

I let out my breath as we emerge from the fog.

The summit of Capital Island is flatter and more expansive than I ever imagined it could be. Green fields stretch on either side of the carriage, sparsely adorned with gnarled, crooked little trees with bright green canopies. The trees look capable of scuttling off, their pale trunks splintering into foot-like branches at the base, all twisting and curving.

I'm sure whoever planted them there meant for them to be beautiful and not so ghastly.

"Are you okay?" Maya asks, watching me with warm, attentive eyes.

"Don't tell me you're afraid of the trees, too," Captain Aric taunts.

I stick my tongue out at him. "I think you were nicer as a pig," I mumble, eliciting a sharp laugh from Maya. She quickly covers it up.

The captain blanches, then clears his throat and straightens up. "Guardians," he says, his lips pursed tightly as he stares at me, "welcome to the palace of Beldemar."

CHAPTER SIX

A motley collection of arches, domes, and towers looms before us, somehow blending the artistry of all four kingdoms. My jaw drops at the sight of a palace that balances the severity of Gedra's arid sands with the verdant beauty of Jara's dense jungles and the freeness of Marad's breezy seaside hills with the obsidian purity of Zehir's scorched lands.

"I nearly forgot," Maya marvels as we pass under a black pointed arch. "The four kings and queens once dwelled here beneath the same roof."

"That was under dragon rule almost a thousand score ago," Captain Aric points out, a note of caution in his voice. "Through those monarchs, the dragons divided us against ourselves and ruled us more easily because of it. There is only one royal bloodline now—the Sinanan bloodline."

A reminder that discussing that part of our history treads dangerously close to both dissonance and treason. For once, it's Maya's face that burns red. "Of course, Captain," she agrees. "There's only one royal family. I just meant . . . the palace is so beautifully diverse. I feel like I'm somewhere new and somewhere old all at once."

"I agree," I blurt out in her defense before Captain Aric can chastise her further. Maya smiles gratefully and sits back in her seat.

I allow myself a fleeting thought of the four ancient queens and kings of the empire. They were traitors, all of them. After Donomar united them to defeat King Elrey, they turned on him and brought him down. With his dying breath, he cursed them, ensuring that they would never betray Beldemar again. Their descendants would be scattered and nameless, a chosen few born with a faint trace of arkbarra in their blood and bound at birth in service to Donomar Sinanan's children.

Even my surname belongs to the princess.

I don't expect for there to be any ceremony about our arrival, especially so late in the day, but Maya and I find two attendants awaiting us at the gatehouse. The elder of the two inclines her head slightly as Maya and I climb out of the carriage, while the younger one curtsies. They could be grandmother and granddaughter, both with the same high cheekbones, rich ochre skin, and shimmering dark eyes.

"At last, you're here," the older woman speaks. "I am Chamberlain Kemi. My family has managed the royal household for ten generations now. This is my granddaughter Bijou." The girl curtsies again, lifting the sides of her strange robes as she does. I note her gloved hands and the patterned bonnet that conceals her hair and ears. Every inch of skin, apart from her face, is covered. The same goes for Chamberlain Kemi. "We will show you to your rooms so you can freshen up before you meet the other guardians," the chamberlain announces.

Maya clasps her hands together in delight. "They're here already?" she chirps.

"They arrived last night," Kemi confirms. "The other two from your quartet, as well as the guardians for Princess Chiwa, Prince Jahim, and Princess and Prince Adanna and Bem. You are the last to arrive." She tilts her head toward an arched wooden door behind her. "The fastest way to the princess's chambers is through the temple room."

I lean sideways, peering around her for a better look at the door, at the two moons stained into its dusty glass window. The door creaks as Kemi pushes it open. A small cloud of dust stirs at her feet. Bijou gently nudges Maya into the dim room and pushes aside an aged tapestry, revealing a dark wooden door that almost blends into the weathered stone wall. An old servants' path. Maya spares a single glance back at me before following Bijou into the darkness.

I start to follow, but I can't leave without first saying goodbye to Captain Aric. It feels important for some reason, even if he is a bit of a jerk. Maybe it's because he was the last person to see me with Ranee, the last person to glimpse who I was before coming here.

But when I turn back toward the carriage, I find both it and the captain already gone.

Kemi clears her throat. I push down my disappointment, turn around, and step into the temple. It is a plain room with a few benches and a small, round window high on the back wall. I tilt my head in confusion at the window's black panes.

"You cannot see it now," Kemi purrs in my ear, "but that window aligns perfectly with the old moon tower. In its prime, almost a thousand score ago, it was said to be quite a marvel." Something forlorn weighs on her voice as though she can remember such a long time ago.

"Doesn't anyone use this room anymore?" I ask, frowning at the two sets of footprints trailing across the dusty floor to the servants' path.

"Very few would even know how," she replies. "It has been many, many a score since the Order of the Two Moons. The knowledge of how to serve disappeared with the war. As it is said, what was written is lost, and what is lost cannot be written."

I suppose that explains why the storyguard and their oral storytelling traditions are so revered. They pass our history from mouth to ear so that, even if libraries burn, history is not forgotten. But what happened to this Order Kemi speaks of? That is something I've never heard of.

The chamberlain guides me into the servants' passage. I wince as the door swings shut, closing us in total darkness. But just a few notes later, speckles of purple light bloom across the stone walls, illuminating the path before us. Kemi already stands several feet ahead, smiling back at me and looking amused. I hurry to catch up with her.

The dimly lit tunnel unearths fresh memories of the thing lurking in the fog. Maybe Kemi knows something about it. "Have you ever noticed anything odd about this place?" I ask.

She chuckles. "Oh, there are a great many odd things in this palace," she replies. "I would beg you to be more specific."

But I have no concrete details to share with her. I settle for a sigh, deciding not to risk sounding crazy. "Protecting the princess is going to be even harder than I thought," I grumble.

That only earns another laugh.

"What's funny?" I demand.

"Oh, when you meet Princess Marleyn, then you will understand the joke," she says. "I would not want to spoil the punchline before then."

After a few twists and turns, we emerge into an ornate hallway, leading us to a round antechamber with five identical doors. Kemi guides me to the door just right of the one in the center. "Your room," she announces. She nods to the door left of the center one. "The guardian from Jara will stay there." Then the two doors on either side of the hallway's mouth. "The Guardians from Gedra and Zehir are there."

And finally, the door in the center. "And the princess's room."

Our rooms are determined by rank, I realize. As the supposed strongest, I'll reside at the princess's right. I push that alarming thought aside. "Is she in there?" I ask.

"At this measure? Unlikely," Kemi replies. "You'll find that girl to be a rather elusive Pulse, I'm afraid." She turns a key in the lock and pushes the door to my room open.

I suck in my breath at the splendor that awaits me—a room four times larger than the one I shared with Ranee, equipped with a private balcony and an attached bathing room. I stumble across the plush, sea-toned carpet to the canopied bed and run my hand down its smooth post. "This is *my* room?"

If only Katina could see it.

Kemi looks satisfied with the awe on my face. "You are here to fulfill the most vital duty in the empire," she remarks. "Surely you knew there would be rewards."

Her words sober me at once. I pull my hand from the wooden bedpost, letting it fall to my side. The room, just a beautiful perk for forfeiting my life, feels smaller all of a sudden.

"I'll draw your bath," the chamberlain announces, moving toward the bathing room. Her tone prompts me to raise my arm and sniff at myself. I'm certainly in need of one.

After bathing, I follow Kemi to the dining hall, dressed in my new uniform—a lightweight, long-sleeved tunic that reaches my mid-thigh. It's blue, like the sky, with darker blue accents and gold trim on the collar and cuffs. And apparently, it's the only thing I will wear here, because my wardrobe is full of exact copies.

At least it's as stylish as it is functional.

I hear chatter from the dining hall long before we reach it. I tug at the sash cinching my waist as we get closer, searching for something to do with my hands. Guardian Maya has been exceedingly kind to me ever since we met, but what if my other chorus sisters are less forgiving of my faults?

Large wooden doors swing open as we approach, revealing a long table lavishly spread with dishes from all four kingdoms. The chatter halts abruptly as five sets of guardians turn their gazes on me. I grab a fistful of cloth to steady my hand and, for lack of anything better to do, dip into an awkward curtsy.

It somehow works. A few of the guardians acknowledge me with a nod, and all return to their conversations.

There's no need for introductions. While helping me with my hair earlier, Kemi filled me in on everything I needed to know about the other guardians. I can identify everyone now just by their apparent ages and the dominant colors of their uniforms. Ages tell me which royal they serve. Colors tell me which kingdom they come from.

The eldest quartet, nearest the entrance, must serve Princess Chiwa. Technically, they're a trio since one of their chorus sisters perished in a childhood accident. Their blue-clad Maradi leader, with her rich brown skin and elegant braids that remind me so much of Katina, acknowledges me with a warm smile. There's such joy in her eyes but for the shadow left by her fourth sister's absence. She respectfully dips her chin before returning her attention to her remaining sisters.

Prince Jahim's quartet comes next. According to Kemi, they each hold twenty-five score, eleven score younger than Princess Chiwa and her trio. They hardly spare me a glance as I shuffle past them.

I pass by a spirited group of eight guardians, four young men and four young women, each nineteen and bound to one of Princess Marleyn's twin cousins, Princess Adanna and Prince Bem. They are the most jovial of the company, laughing boisterously, indulging heartily in food and drink, and enjoying themselves in a way I didn't know Guardians could.

But I suppose when we are together, our inhibitions are dropped. After all, guardians are permitted to love their chorus brothers and sisters, just not as much as they love their Pulses. I smile as I pass them. Maybe there will be time to befriend them later.

At last, I approach my own quartet, the youngest in the room. Clad in a deep red bandeau and flowing orange pants, Maya waves me over, her curls bouncing along with her enthusiasm. She sits with two others, a stunning Jaran girl and a neat-looking Gede.

"I was starting to think you weren't coming," Maya prattles, pulling me into the vacant seat beside her. "This is Guardian Rae."

The Jaran narrows her pretty emerald eyes, assessing me from head to toe. Judging by the downward curve of her lips, she finds something lacking. Her gaze snags on the pigtails, childish in comparison to her elegant high ponytail. I tug one of my pigtails self-consciously. Kemi had wanted to try a different hairstyle, but I couldn't bear it. Mercifully, the chamberlain let it go, not even questioning me for being sentimental.

"And this is Guardian Chyou," Maya introduces the Gede. Chyou, on the other hand, only offers me a fleeting glance before her focus drifts somewhere else—somewhere inward, if the distant look in her dull gray eyes is any indication. I note the quirky pair of furry brown muffs clamped over her ears and wonder how well she can even hear us.

"We were waiting for you to start eating," Maya says. On cue, Chyou wordlessly plucks a quail leg from her loaded plate and sinks her teeth into its flesh.

"Is tardiness a habit we can expect from our conductor?" Rae inquires, addressing me by my technical title.

I flinch. Rae looks like the punctual type of person who would ask a thing like that. She also looks like the type of person who wakes up at the crack of dawn to squeeze in a long run and a few hundred plank raises before breakfast, the kind of person I should be. "No," I stammer, even though tardiness is certainly a habit of mine, one Ranee tried and failed to eradicate. I change the subject. "What were the three of you discussing just now?"

Chyou rips a bite of meat from the bone. "King Felix's murder," she mumbles through a full mouth. Rae's grossed-out grimace doesn't seem to bother her.

"His body was discovered in the labyrinth at the west side of the palace," Maya pitches in. "Rae thinks we should investigate."

"Hm," I mumble, suddenly finding the bowl of bread rolls in front of me very inviting. I reach for one and bite into it.

Rae frowns, then looks pointedly at Maya. "Didn't you say that you both ate not that long ago?" she demands.

Maya bites her lip, glancing apologetically at me. "I guess we've sung through two measures since then," she says. "And anyway, we guardians do tend to burn our food off quickly."

Rae rolls her eyes. "So, it's agreed?" she demands. "We're going to the labyrinth?" She sends the question my way.

Right. Because I'm the conductor and all. I swallow a lump of bread and nod. "Mm-hmm." I don't trust myself to agree with actual words.

Rae narrows her eyes at my lips, and I'm suddenly aware of a few crumbs there. I wipe them away.

"We need to find out if he was felled by akbarrin or by something else," she muses. She lowers her voice. "Like his own kin, for example."

I glance at the other guardians down the table. With Princess Marleyn being too young to take the throne, their Pulses stand to benefit most from King Felix's death. If one of the other royals moves against Marleyn, we could find ourselves fighting *against* their guardians instead of alongside them.

That thought hadn't occurred to me until now.

As much as I hate to admit it, Rae is right. We need to investigate. "We'll go first thing tomorrow morning," I decide. "Before training."

Rae flicks her handkerchief open. "Good." She spreads the cloth on her lap, then picks up her silverware and neatly cuts into her food, throwing another disapproving glance toward Chyou.

Maya looks between the three of us, grinning. "It's so nice to be together at last." She sighs. She rests her forearms on the table and waits for the rest of us to finish eating.

We retire to our wing after dinner with instructions to report for training a half measure after sunrise. My chorus sisters and I stand before Princess Marleyn's door.

"We could knock," Maya suggests, wringing her hands, "or just wait until she comes out."

"She's the only royal who didn't present herself before dinner," Rae complains. "Why wouldn't she?"

"Yeah. That was kind of rude," Chyou agrees.

I frown. "She did just lose her father," I remind them. "A loss like that must be devastating." Am I the only one who understands grief? My chorus sisters turn and stare at me, none of them comprehending.

Apparently so.

"Let's wait until tomorrow," I propose. "I'm sure she's just as curious about us as we are about her."

Chyou yawns. "Maybe she's sleeping," she says, stretching her arms toward the ceiling. She shuffles off toward her own room.

"Or avoiding us," Rae mumbles, heading toward hers.

Maya and I linger behind. She keeps fidgeting with her

fingers but stops when she notices me watching. "Good night, Aryam," she says. "I hope you rest well after the journey you've had."

I start to point out that she's had the same journey, but then I realize that she's talking about what happened at the port back in Marad. I think, on some level, Maya gets it. At least a little more than the others.

Loss.

"Thank you, Maya." I think about hugging her but end up patting her shoulder instead. "Good night."

I crawl into my bed, sink into the cloudlike mattress, and revel in the sweet lullaby of the nightfalls chirping somewhere beyond my balcony. The curtains billow inward, stirred by a gentle breeze. Just before sleep claims me, I hear shuffling on the next balcony over, then a door shutting softly.

Princess Marleyn.

I half consider getting up and introducing myself to her, but that seems like it would be an imposition. Besides, my limbs are achingly tired.

I suppose we'll meet tomorrow.

CHAPTER SEVEN

Waking up the next morning feels like slogging through quicksand, every move threatening to sink me deeper into the realm of nightmares. Muffled voices linger at the surface, reeling me up through an onslaught of memories from the last few days. *Kyrel. Horses made of wind. A wooden-skinned deity and his serpentine wife. Soldiers turned into pigs. Ranee sinking below the surface.*

I gasp at the last of these terrors, as if I were the one being dragged down into oblivion at the hands of a vengeful demigoddess. I sit up too quickly, surprising the faces that stand over my bed. Everyone flinches except for Rae, who has a firm hand wrapped around my arm. She's been shaking me.

"What are you doing here?" The words spill out of my mouth as I fight to gain control of my breathing. How did they get in?

Maya moves first, perching herself on the edge of my bed, already dressed the same way as yesterday. Like me, she must have a lifetime supply of the same outfit. She rests a tentative hand on my knee. "Did you forget?" Her gentle voice is a murmur of waves brushing against a sandy shore. "We're going to investigate King Felix's murder."

How could anyone forget a foolish thing like that? I shake my head and wipe the sleep away from my eyes. "I remember."

"Then get dressed," Rae urges, "or we'll be late for morning drills afterward."

Sleep clinging to my bones, I rise and reach for my discarded uniform, draped carelessly over an armchair near the balcony. I see no point in putting on a new one when I only wore this one to dinner. Rae's gaze traces my movements. I can see her biting back a comment, but the criticism in her eyes only soothes a dull ache in my heart. I am already growing fond of her constant nagging. It is not much worse than Katina's teasing.

I dress quickly and meet my quartet in the antechamber.

"You didn't sleep well." There's no question about it in Maya's voice as the four of us pad softly through the dimly lit hallways, intricate coral sconces flickering at intermittent intervals.

"You say that as if it didn't take me summoning the strength of a land tremor to wake her," Rae retorts.

Even if her voice is dripping in sarcasm, her comment brings me relief. Sarcasm is easier to play off than concern. I brandish my disarming smile. "Yeah. I guess I really overdid it." I throw in a chuckle for good measure. Maya doesn't buy it immediately. I can see the doubt lingering in her eyes, but then she matches my smile.

"I guess you did," she agrees.

"I won't do it again," I promise.

"I somehow doubt that's true," Rae comments.

"Oh, c'mon. Do you all want to wake everyone up?" Chyou blurts out, even though it's her voice that's too loud. Still, we follow her cue and quietly file out onto an outer corridor that runs the east side of the palace.

The corridor is lined with arches that open onto the sea of rolling mist below. As we approach the rail, the labyrinth unfolds below us. A maze of hedges sprawl from palace to mist, black and shadowy in the dull moonlight. Heaviness anchors my feet to the ground as thoughts of that thing lurking in the fog race through my mind.

What if we encounter that phantom in corporeal form?

Just the thought of it chills my bones.

"Maybe we should come back after sunrise," I suggest, or preferably not at all. So that I don't sound like a complete coward, I add, "It would be easier to find our way in the light."

It's a sound reason. No one can fault me for wanting to make the best use of our time. The best use of *my* time would be to grab another measure of sleep, safe and warm in my bed.

But Chyou has already started toward the stairs that descend to the labyrinth's entrance. "I already know the way," she says.

Even Rae looks impressed at that. "You figured it out from just one glance?" I exclaim.

Chyou shrugs.

She leads the way through the maze, confident in every step, even though the path defies all logic. It is full of twists and turns that would leave me utterly lost if I were on my own.

Days.

A person could spend *days* lost in a place like this.

I stick close to the other members of my quartet, forcing myself to walk as tall and as unflinchingly as Rae, even though the writhing shadows and the gauzy veil of clouds make me want to jump out of my skin. I'm so focused on the shadows that I collide with Rae's back when she and the others come to an abrupt halt. "Watch it!" she hisses.

"Sorry," I murmur.

I sidestep around her and see that we've reached the labyrinth's inner garden.

"Exquisite," Maya marvels in one breath. She isn't wrong. This place is more than a garden. It's an oasis. Raised flowerbeds decorate the space, boasting exotic fragrances from the farthest reaches of the empire. Tucked between the beds are ornate bamboo benches with linen cushions, all facing the elegant fountain in the middle. A great stone egg sits at the fountain's center, cracked slightly, with water trickling into the serene pool at its base.

"An egg?" Chyou comments, her voice shrill with surprise. "That's weird." Her astonishment doesn't reach her face, still as impassive as stone. But her silver eyes are sharp as blades beneath her straight black bangs. They dart toward Rae the instant she speaks, even though the rest of her body remains still.

"I heard they found his body in front of the fountain," Ray announces. "It was drained of all blood."

I cover my mouth to suppress a gag. "You couldn't have told us that *before* we agreed to come here?" I complain.

Rae scowls. "Don't be a coward."

"There's a difference between being a coward and having good sense," I reason, not caring that she's right.

Maya fidgets. "Chorus sisters shouldn't—"

"Something's here, by the way." Chyou's observation silences us. I note the tension in her shoulders. Her entire body is on alert. I study the furry muffs on her ears and wonder if they actually extend her senses somehow, like a swift-footed hare on the Gede sands.

A song flows from the fountain's shadow, eerie and ancient.

When all was lost and all was vain,
you called to us; we burned your pain—

A glimmer of white flashes and a crescent of sharp little teeth appear. The figure that emerges behind the teeth is human-shaped and human-sized, but its movements are too still and too silent to be human. Chyou jerks and bares a fierce smile of her own. For once, she doesn't look bored.

Beside me, Rae tenses. "What are you?" she demands, trying to shake her arm free of my grip. It's only then that I realize I've grabbed on to her sleeve. I make myself let go.

A soft ray of moonlight slips through the veil of clouds and illuminates the creature's face, an ancient thing cascading with wrinkles, a face I recognize immediately. Maya's gasp behind me lets me know she remembers it, too. Just yesterday, this thing was an old woman who fed us soup.

I retch. Three bowls of it. I ate *three* bowls of something this wretched hag cooked.

"Hold it together," Rae hisses.

I force my chin up, even though every fiber in me screams to turn and flee. My gaze flits to each of the others—Rae, Chyou, Maya. Not one takes her eye off the creature in front of us. Not one looks afraid. Even Maya has recovered from her shock. And I am their leader. "Right." I push as much authority out as I can with the word. "What are you?" I repeat Rae's question.

A low chuckle emanates from the creature's cracked lips. She resumes her song.

—in vain, in vain, we burned your pain.
You called us and you left us stain.

Her voice is a crackle of fire and a hiss of steam. To my own credit, I don't flinch or run away screaming. A flash of green light, and then there's a glowing bow in Rae's hands, a rose nocked and aimed like an arrow. "We're not here for a lullaby," she warns.

The singing halts. "Pleasure to see you again, dearie," the old thing croaks, right before her sagging skin falls from her bones, pooling at her feet like a discarded bathrobe. She sheds her age along with her skin. The muscles and sinews twisting underneath radiate eternal youth.

And then she is engulfed in flames, a living, walking inferno.

Before any of us can respond, three blazing fires ignite in three corners of the garden. Their answering hackles cut through the air with chilling menace. A flash of brown light. Enormous gloves, like gorilla fists, encase Chyou's hands. The muffs covering her ears extend like the ears of a jackrabbit. The vicious smile on her face cracks wider as if she's been waiting for this moment, this thrill, her whole life.

A flash of orange, and Maya wields the flame sword. "They're called emberfiends," she says, a surprising harshness in her voice. "There are records of them in the archives at the Burning Temples of Zehir."

There should be one more flash—a flash of steel blue as I summon my own oju—but there isn't. The emberfiends rise into the sky and circle overhead. Rae traces their flight with the point of her arrow. "Anything about how to defeat them in those records?" she asks.

"I didn't have much time for reading while I was there," Maya answers.

"Moons," Rae mumbles. She glances at me. "What are you waiting for? Call your oju."

Before I can tell her that's not possible, one of the three creatures dives toward us with an ear-shattering screech. Rae unleashes her rose arrow upon it, and the monster banks left to avoid it. The rose arrow grazes against its embers, sparks flying from where a jagged thorn pierces the flames. The thing cries out angrily, before peeling off into the maze. With three new arrows knocked, Rae dashes into the hedges to hunt it down.

Another fiery creature swoops toward us. Chyou is prepared. She crouches, her fur-clad boots glowing just before she springs into the air. One leap propels her several feet skyward, and just when it looks like she'll start her descent, another burst propels her even higher. Her fists move faster than wind itself as they assail the emberfiend's flames, punching them out as fast as they can reignite.

Only one creature remains circling in the sky, and only one of my quartet standing at my side. The flames engulfing Maya's sword flare up, along with an intensity in her focused eyes. She doesn't take her eyes off the creature flying overhead. "Are you going to be okay?" she asks, her voice solemn.

"Just go." The resolution in my own voice surprises me. "We can't let them get to the princess." Wherever she is.

I don't expect her to hesitate, but she does. She looks at me, a fire burning in her eyes. "Just don't get hurt. You promise?"

Warmth at her concern flutters in my heart. I nod. "I promise, chorus sister."

The creature circling overhead peels off toward a distant corner of the labyrinth, as if to lure Maya away. Satisfied with my promise, Maya darts into the maze after her.

I am alone with the monsters' leader. Her flames flare and her skinless face stretches into a taunting sneer. "Very well, guardian," she jeers. "Let's see your oju."

As if I'm not reaching for it already, as if I haven't been reaching for it this whole time, pleading for akbarra to flood my blood and coagulate at my fingertips into my spirit weapon. But nothing happens. *Use wit if all else fails.* One of Ranee's old teachings floats to mind. My breath steadies. The fire creature in front of me wants a battle of words as well as one of strengths. I will give her one. "I don't need it to fight the likes of you," I say with feigned calm. *It is okay to be afraid.* Another of Ranee's lessons. *Your enemy will only see what you allow them to see.*

I can't allow them to see my fear.

"Oh?" The amusement in the creature's voice makes up for the lack of eyebrows she has to raise at my bold words. Her fire dances and crackles around her. A tendril of it snaps free and whips the night air with a smoky sizzle. My gaze shifts to the fountain bubbling behind her, to the water rippling in its basin.

It's a foolish idea, one that would never work.

"Then let's see what you've got." Her flame snaps forward, licking the air above my head as I duck and roll out of the way. I somersault onto my feet and dash for the fountain, evading balls of fire as the emberfiend flings them toward me. "Stop running, little sand scuttle," she hisses. Another ball of fire whizzes past my shoulder. I teeter on my right foot, twisting my body to avoid it.

I lunge for the fountain as soon as it's within one leap's distance and hurl myself into the water. Hovering above the ground, the emberfiend floats toward me, her head tilted in an exaggerated display of confusion. She's stopped hurling fire. "What are you playing at, scuttle?" she squawks.

The first splash of water fizzles into steam as it hits the flames engulfing her body. The second douses a patch of flame. The emberfiend screeches in pain. It's all the encouragement my arms need to scoop water out of the fountain faster, like a water wheel. Soon, dark spots appear on the emberfiend's body until her fire is completely extinguished. She screams and screams, dropping to her knees. "What have you done?" she rasps, clawing at her skin in horror.

I stand amazed. I can't believe that worked.

Except . . .

The emberfiend's cries turn to laughter. Her flames reignite, and she rises back to her feet. "Did you really think it would be so easy?" she taunts me. "Silly scuttle. We crossed the seas, too. Water cannot harm us." Her hoarse laughter rises.

Indignation flares in my chest. "Are you really teasing me?" I demand. An akbarrin, of all things.

And what does she mean by that? *We crossed the seas, too.*

The emberfiend carries on howling, wheezing with the effort it takes not to fall over. A noise like a thousand falling pebbles rushes through the air. The emberfiend halts, then turns her head slowly, slowly to look behind her at the bag of rice spilled at her feet. "No." The horror in her voice is authentic this time. "No," she cries again. And then she drops to her knees and desperately scrambles to collect the rice.

A girl stands over her, a beautiful girl with night for skin and golden braid rings glistening in her hair like stars. She holds an empty grain sack in her hand and beams triumphantly as the other three emberfiends drop from the sky, clambering to help their leader. The girl winks at me. "Marleyn at your service," she introduces herself, dropping the bag beside the frantic akbarrin.

Rae, Maya, and Chyou emerge from the maze, brows glistening with sweat. They approach, each taking in the emberfiends, and then Marleyn. *Princess* Marleyn. Rae speaks first. "Who are you?" she demands.

Chyou follows, looking like a petulant child not ready to end playtime. "And what did you do to our emberfiends?" she whines.

"She's the princess," I stammer, unable to believe it myself. I expected to feel something powerful when I first saw her. I thought I would be enchanted, maybe.

But I don't, and I'm not.

My quartet dip one knee to the ground, bowing their heads to show their respect for our princess. I drop a tick later, tucking my chin into my chest and wincing at my own clumsiness. Ranee would be so disappointed in me.

Rae clears her throat. "Don't you think we've bowed long enough?" she hisses, and I remember that I am their leader.

They won't rise until I do, even if I wasn't first to kneel. Even if I'm the one who wants to run a thousand miles in the wrong direction.

"You don't have to bow at all," Princess Marleyn intervenes. "I don't require it." She offers me her hand, and I take it, bracing for a jolt or a rush of power. Something that marks the significance of this moment. Still nothing.

"Thank you," I say. Is that what you're supposed to say to the person whose life you're bound to protect when she protects you instead? Why am I doing this all wrong?

The princess smirks, amusement radiating from her eyes. "I'm happy I could help," she says. Her eyes dance over the others, as if searching for something and coming up short. She frowns. "I'm surprised none of you knew how to handle this yourselves."

"We were handling it," Rae huffs.

"Drop a grain of rice on the ground and the emberfiend is compelled to retrieve it," the princess replies dismissively. "If the sun rises before she completes her task, before she puts on her skin again, she goes poof." Something bubbles in my gut at the haughtiness in her voice. An eye roll from Rae tells me it doesn't land well with her, either, but she holds her tongue. The princess glances at the emberfiends. "That should take them a half measure, at least, and sunrise is before then."

She turns to me, studying me. "Why didn't you summon your oju?"

Maya raises a hand to speak. "Aryam . . . doesn't have one," she confesses, casting me an apologetic glance.

Marleyn frowns. "Worse things than the emberfiends are coming," she declares. "You have no means of defending yourself against them. You will go to the palace library instead of training today. Maybe you will find something useful in the archives, something that can help you find what you need to unfetter your soul."

CHAPTER EIGHT

Unfetter my soul? So, the princess thinks I'm *fettered*? My head hangs low as Kemi shows me to the library after a breakfast where I watched Chyou scarf down more garlic potatoes and curried reef root than even I can eat. My chorus sister sopped up the spicy dish with the same fury she used to snuff out the emberfiend's flames with her oju fists. By the end of the meal, she had a mustache of tomato paste and a stomach the size of a watermelon, and her belch afterward sliced through the room full of chatter and made everyone stop what they were doing.

I can't even win at being a glutton.

And now Princess Marleyn thinks my spiritual connection to my oju is blocked, which means in a real battle against *worse things*, she thinks I'll be useless.

That's just great for my confidence.

I groan.

"Don't worry, Lady Sinanan. We're almost there." Oblivious to my misery, Kemi hums a lively, upbeat tune as she walks. For a woman with her score, she has a surprisingly buoyant gait. I wouldn't be surprised if she could do without the gnarled walking stick she uses to get around. Dropping my hands to my sides, I hurry to keep up with her.

The palace walls grow more ornate as we approach the library. Long, vibrant tapestries stretch from ceiling to floor, depicting fabled battles between the people of Beldemar and the akbarrin. Busts of ten generations of royals grace every corner. I stare at a full sculpture of Prince Donomar himself, clad in the shiny black armor crafted to resist a dragon's talons and to withstand its fire. Kemi's humming turns sharp and staccato as we pass that one.

The old woman's enthusiasm starts to rub off on me. Whether or not it contains any information on *unfettering* my soul, the library must be able to help me. Maybe I'll find something that will help me get home after I serve my purpose here, something to help me get free.

Although I may need some help knowing where to start.

"I've never been in a proper library," I muse aloud. Unless you count the cellar beneath Mr. Sama's washhouse, where Darien stocks a scant collection of weathered scrolls and tattered papers bound together by discarded scraps of linen.

"Then you're in for a treat," Kemi replies, and I sense another history lesson coming on. Kemi doesn't disappoint. "There were once five great libraries in the Beldemar Empire," she lectures, "one here, and one in each of the minor kingdoms. Only three survived the war: The oldest library at the Burning Temples on the northernmost tip of Zehir. The most sacred library in the Green Sands Desert on the southern coast of Gedra." She breathes in deeply, as if taking in the aroma of the knowledge enclosed in the library, and exhales with a flourish of her hand. "And the largest of the three, the library here at Capital Palace—the Library of Light."

The chamberlain stops before two elaborate wooden doors and taps her walking stick twice. The doors swing open, gusting me with the scent of old paper and wet ink. Two enormous wooden tables stretch out in front of us, crowded with white-clad scholars of all ages poring over ancient tomes. I tilt my head back and nearly collapse in awe. The library spirals upward, stories and stories of ancient books and dusty scrolls. A stained-glass dome shimmers overhead with vivid dragons dancing in colored light, casting gentle hues over the entire place.

Each story teems with silent scholars. Some are clad in Capital gray with red hems. They bustle about like the gray parrot darting between branches. Others wear a glossy white, with wide-brimmed hoods covering half their faces. I gaze on as they flit between shelves in an almost choreographed dance, stocking books here and plucking them from there. They work in silence, save for the gentle sounds of padding feet and flipping pages.

"Welcome to the Library of Light." Kemi beams.

"Who are all these people?" I ask.

"Traveling scholars," Kemi explains, her voice hovering just above a whisper. "They arrive at all times of the score, but the hooded ones have only arrived recently." She leans forward, the picture of conspiracy. "There is a rumor that they come from the Fallen Cities."

I gasp. "They're Amarishi?"

Ranee sang me histories of the dragon princess's favored acolytes when I was young. Silly nursery rhymes mainly. Myths. The Amarishi, mostly human, were said to dwell in Princess Nalini's floating cities high above the Jaran jungles. As it is sung, the cities fell when Prince Donomar placed the seal.

I don't realize I've shouted until every eye at the long wooden tables swivels toward me, and all those on the levels above us peer down. Kemi clears her throat.

I bow my head. "Sorry," I murmur.

The scholars resume their work, all except for two on the

second level. I look up to find them staring at me, a man with skin of onyx and a woman with skin like sand. White hoods cast shadows over the upper halves of their faces, but I make out enough to see that he has strong features, and she has a scar. Her lips curve into a playful smile as she whispers something to her companion. He clenches his jaw in response.

"This way," Kemi calls for my attention. She starts toward a narrow stairwell at one side of the room. I glance after her just long enough to ascertain her direction before I return my gaze to the second level, but the mysterious pair is gone.

It could be nothing. Curious scholars, maybe, surprised to find a guardian in their midst. I hurry after Kemi.

We climb one flight of stairs and swing left, walking past a small alcove that seems out of place in this grand library. Unlike the well-polished wood around it, its archway is mottled with pink paint, faded and chipping. A glimpse inside the alcove reveals once-bright floor cushions and colorful shelves that hold scrolls and bound books perfectly sized for smaller hands.

I tug on Kemi's sleeve as she hurries past, not even sparing the room a glance. "Kemi, what room is that?" I ask.

A sigh rattles the old woman's chest. "The late queen decorated that room long ago, while pregnant with the princess," she says, "but after she died in labor, the room was never used."

"That's so sad," I murmur, staring back at the alcove as Kemi leads me away from it. I can't imagine a childhood without stories. When I was little, Ranee sang them to me every night. It makes me sad to think that Princess Marleyn never had that with her mother—that she never knew her mother at all.

Of course, I'll never know mine, either. But it's different for people like me.

Kemi deposits me at a section on the fourth level, announcing that everything the empire knows about oju can be found on these shelves and wishing me luck. I wait a reasonable amount of time for an old woman with a walking stick to descend three flights of stairs and exit the library, then I steal back to the queen's abandoned alcove, dodging hurried acolytes and evading notice as best I can.

Curiosity has stolen my sense, but I'm sure there will be time for research later.

I liberate an armful of scrolls from a cluster of cobwebs and pull them into my lap as I plop down onto a dusty floor pillow. I spend the next measure losing myself in a web of fairy tales woven for small children. When I close my eyes and breathe deeply, I can see myself back in the room Ranee and I shared, small enough to sit in her lap and toy with her hair as she whispered the tales in my ear. She was a gifted storyteller, always whisking my mind away on some grand adventure. And these stories, written in swirling, elaborate strokes, do the same.

I find stories about trickster spiders and people who fly away from their troubles and trees that sing. I discover others about rabbits that outsmart their predators and girls who use akbarra to escape wicked families. Stories I know by heart, having heard my monitor spin them so many times.

My fingers trace the elegant penmanship, relishing each word, stopping at a title I've never seen before. *The One Who Wanted to Marry the Moon.* I study the illustration, as diligently drawn as the words are written. It shows a contemplative young man cloaked in shadow.

The fable follows a popular theme. A boy of humble origin falls in love with someone far above his station. At night, the boy dreams about a girl who weeps crystal tears beside the Moonsea. One day, he sets off on a quest to find her, falling more and more in love with her each time he dreams about her. On his journey, the boy encounters three animals in the middle of a quarrel. The animals—an ant, an eagle, and a wolf—have stolen a dragon egg and are arguing about who gets to eat it. Thinking to help solve the animals' dispute, the boy destroys the egg and divides it between the three of them.

I can't help grimacing when the boy strikes the egg. I don't pity the dragons their fate, but I know how they cherished their offspring.

The dragon egg transforms the three animals. The eagle becomes an enormous bird. The wolf becomes a shifter. The ant becomes king of the insects. So filled with gratitude, each one pledges loyalty to the boy and offers him their services should he ever need them.

The boy continues his journey, finally reaching the Moon Kingdom, and finds the girl of his dreams. But when he asks her for her hand in marriage, she rejects him, spurning his mortality. For she is the princess of the moon, and he is but a lowly human.

I reread the last line of the story and frown at the tragic and abrupt ending. That can't be it, can it? What kind of story is this, anyway? How is it fair that the boy traveled so far to find his true love, only for her to reject him in the end?

Ranee says that any tale worth telling holds a lesson, but I can't imagine what we're supposed to learn from a boy who gets his heart shattered. I scan the text again, searching for a hint. That's when I notice the hasty caption scrawled beneath the illustration:

Beware of the unrequited lover.

"Unrequited lover?" I repeat, tracing the warning with my finger. Could it truly mean the boy? I skim through the story a third time, running each detail through a sharp lens. Nothing jumps out at me to suggest that the broken-hearted boy is a villain, but now I'm even more certain that there's more to the story.

There has to be more.

I rummage through another armful of scrolls for a continuation of the story and come up empty-handed. There are no more stories of unrequited lovers here. I sink back onto the floor pillow, ready to give up, but a thought strikes me.

Maybe someone else took it.

Kemi says that no one's ever used the alcove, but that doesn't mean no one's ever borrowed from it. There could be someone in this palace who knows how the story ends, maybe even Princess Marleyn. If I were her, I couldn't imagine not exploring the beautiful reading nook my deceased mother built for me. Maybe the princess found the missing part of this story and took it.

I tuck the scroll inside my tunic and scramble to my feet, my mind made up to ask her about it.

A HAND SNAPS around my wrist just as I leave the secluded alcove, yanking me back into the shadow and out of sight of the open floor below. Another hand clasps over my mouth, muffling my grunt as I try to free myself. "Hush, or they'll know we're here," a hauntingly familiar voice murmurs near my ear, a voice like sand on a flame.

I catch a glimpse of the tan hand pressing against my lips, then the chestnut hair cascading over my shoulders. I gulp in her scent. She smells of amber and rain, like a fire crackling in the hearth of a cozy cottage. Like home, or some version of it.

"Ranee?" My lips flutter against the cool palm of her hand. I whirl around as soon as she releases me, hope flourishing inside my chest. It withers away just as quickly.

It's not her.

Of course it's not.

Am I so stupid, I forgot? Ranee's at the bottom of the sea now. Dead, or worse.

The woman standing in front of me has Ranee's sun-kissed complexion. She has her hair color. She has her beauty, even with the scar that cuts across the top of her left cheek. But unlike Ranee, she's tall and slender, like a reed. And her eyes lack the jovial, mischievous spark of my monitor's. Instead, they house a cool, raging storm.

She presses a single finger against her lips, commanding me to stay silent.

Then I notice how quiet the library is now, without even the sounds of shuffling feet and turning pages. The scholars who milled about when I first arrived are gone now. Had I been so lost in those stories that I didn't notice dozens of people leaving the room?

"We are *running* out of *time*." A woman's sharp voice slices through the silence. It's coming from the library's ground floor.

Steeling myself, I creep toward the balustrade and peer below. I can see two people, a man and a woman, each dressed in luxurious articles of purple-and-gold clothing. Royals. By their apparent ages alone, I can guess who they are. Princess Chiwa and Prince Jahim, sister and brother. But it's the thin crown resting atop the princess's head that confirms it.

While those outside the palace know nothing yet of the king's death, everyone inside its walls knows that Princess Chiwa is acting queen. At least until Princess Marleyn comes of age.

The prince perches on the edge of one of the long tables, filing his nails with an untroubled ease. Princess Chiwa's urgent proclamation fails to rattle him.

The princess stalks toward her brother and plants herself squarely before him. "The shadows will kiss any day now, and we still don't have it," she snaps. "He's going to be livid."

Jahim shrugs. "I warned you that the emberfiends would

fail, sister," he drawls. "Our little cousin is too much of a scroll spinner to not have known their weakness."

"Goody-goody little brat," Princess Chiwa snarls.

Princess Marleyn's own cousins sent the emberfiends after her? Did they also send them to kill King Felix? And who is the "he" that Princess Chiwa speaks of? I gasp, too loud.

"What was that?" Princess Chiwa demands.

The stranger behind me snatches me back by my shirt collar just as Princess Chiwa's and Prince Jahim's gazes snap in our direction. She pulls me back into the children's nook and prods at one of the shelves of scrolls. It slides aside, revealing a hidden passageway. I dig my heels into the ground. "It's too dark in there," I hiss, but the woman shoves me in and quickly shuts the shelf behind us.

The instant the darkness closes in on me, I feel it. That creature from the fog surrounding the palace. Its presence swirls around me, pressing in tighter and tighter, scraping its mental claws against the walls of my mind. A scream bubbles in my throat, but then an orb of blue light blooms in the woman's palm, bright enough to light our path.

"How are you doing that?" I demand.

The woman scowls and raises her finger to her lips. "They'll find us," she hisses. "This way." She starts down the dark passageway. I hesitate for two beats before following her. Facing Princess Chiwa and her handsome brother seems more daunting than following a mysterious stranger into a dark tunnel.

Several beats pass before the woman speaks. "I'm not from the Shadows, if that's what you're thinking," she says. "And I'm not here to hurt you or anyone else."

That's honestly reassuring. The last few days have been filled with creatures from the Shadows trying to hurt me and my friends. "Then where are you from, and why *are you* here?"

I ask. "And how can you do *that*?" I point to the ball of light still rolling in the palm of her hand. "Not that I'm not grateful for it," I add, ducking to avoid a cobweb.

"Who I am is not important," she snaps, her raspy voice filled with impatience. "And I'm here to take you home."

I stop walking. "Home?" I repeat. "Me?" That tiny smolder of hope fizzling out in my core sparks back to life, then recedes again. "But I can't," I say. Especially not now, not after what I've just read and heard. I need to speak to the princess and ask her about the boy in the story. I need to protect her from him if he's somehow a threat. "I must fulfill my oath."

She swivels on me with that storm blazing in her eyes. "You are not prepared to fill such an oath," she sneers.

I can't pretend that it doesn't sting. Even a stranger who's only known me for two beats can tell I'm useless, but I shake my head. "It doesn't matter," I say, hoping she doesn't hear the hurt in my voice nor the uncertainty.

Her brow hardens. "The princess will only get hurt if you stay here," she says. "Go back home and stay out of the way. *That* is how you can protect your princess."

"Do you really think that?" I curse myself for the words as soon as they tumble out of my mouth, but a small, cowardly part of me considers that she might be right. I think about all the things that happened today. The princess sent me to learn about my oju, and I wasted the day on stories. Instead of bringing her answers, I'm bringing her more questions—and none that will lead to me finding my spirit weapon.

And without my spirit weapon, does she even need me?

She seemed perfectly capable of handling herself this morning. She seemed not to need me at all. I'll just be in the way. Maybe that's what Kemi found so funny last night. Maybe getting back to Irez is easier than I thought.

I could go home. I could see my friends again.

"I know you're worried about the omission," she says, "but I can help you work around it. You can have anything you want —just away from here."

My heart leaps. Kyrel. I could see Kyrel.

And I could find Ranee. She would be so . . .

My growing excitement crumbles.

"No," I decline. Something inside me shutters as I say it. Ashamed. Ranee would be so ashamed if I turned my back on my duty. "I'm not going back. I want to, believe me, but I have a job to do here."

Her nostrils flare open. She opens her mouth as if to say something, but her anger fades, chased away by a wild, frantic look in her eyes. She glances over her shoulder as if she hears someone coming. "Blistering skies," she hisses. She looks back at me. "If you insist on staying, you won't find what you need here. Stay alert, and I will get you what you need."

I tilt my head. "How do you know what I need?" I ask.

But she takes a step away and deftly presses against a panel of the wall. It slides open, revealing a vacant hallway. The light in her hand blinks out, and before I know it, she's gone.

THE DINNER BELLS chime as I wander through unfamiliar hallways. Great. Now I'm lost *and* I'm missing dinner. I cradle my poor, grumbling stomach and stagger toward an ornate door coated with dust. Everything in this wing has a thin layer of it.

Stay focused, Aryam. Find Princess Marleyn. Warn her about her cousins. Ask her about the boy.

Part of me is glad to be missing dinner. I'm not exactly ready to face my chorus sisters and tell them that I *still* haven't found any information concerning my oju, nor am I looking forward to the judgmental look on Rae's face if she finds out

I've squandered the day reading children's stories. I don't think she'd even care if I told her they were really good children's stories.

Then there are the things I don't know how to tell them. What do I say about the scar-faced woman who can pool light in the palm of her hand? How do I explain that I let her walk away after she tried to get me to dissonate? Any decent guardian would have eliminated such a threat.

Suddenly, being lost doesn't seem so bad.

I reach toward the door at the end of the hallway, but just as my fingers graze it, it swings open, and I find myself bumping into a firm chest. The impact almost knocks me over, but a strong pair of hands reaches out and catches me. They hold on to me long after I'm steady, and I stare up into a pair of dark brown eyes. "Captain Aric?" I blurt out. "What are you doing here?"

The burly captain doesn't release me, not right away. He glances left and right and then behind me. Finally, after declaring us safe perhaps, he loosens his grip. "I could ask you the same thing," he says. "These are the king's quarters."

The door clanks shut behind him. I look around with a new awareness of where I've wandered. The halls here are quieter than in the rest of the palace, devoid of both residents and staff. Blackout curtains cover the tall windows, blocking out the evening light, and the few candles flickering in their sconces burn low, casting dancing shadows on the walls.

No one has been here in days. Weeks, maybe.

Captain Aric, Dex, and Joan retrieved me two days ago, but if I didn't know any better, I'd say the king has been dead for at least a month.

Maybe it's because that confuses me, or because I've been through numerous ordeals today, or because Captain Aric is my only connection to Ranee and the only person here who also stood with me in Irez, but I wrap my arms around him, pressing my face tight against his chest. His body tenses at first, then relaxes with a deep sigh. "Alright, kid," he murmurs. He lets me hold on for a tick longer before gently prying me loose.

Dark splotches mark his clothes where my tears fell.

"You shouldn't be here," he says. "Where's the rest of your quartet?"

I don't want to tell him how badly I've failed at everything since I've been here, including finding my oju and assuming leadership of my team. I don't want him to know that even the princess I've lost everything for thinks I'm useless. So, I just stare at him instead.

He sighs and walks away. He doesn't stop me when I follow.

CHAPTER NINE

"I didn't think I'd see you again." I jog a few steps to keep pace with Captain Aric as he strides across the sparring fields. This late in the evening, only the most dedicated soldiers are out honing their skills. Captain Aric swiftly maneuvers his way around them, dodging parries and ducking blows. I follow suit, albeit with much less grace.

Captain Aric glances at me like he's just remembered I'm following him and scoffs. "The palace is big, kid, but not that big. You're bound to see me around." He pivots out of the way of two sparring soldiers, who don't seem to notice him. I duck as a wooden stick swings over my head. Captain Aric reaches back for me and tugs me out of the way.

"It's getting late," he says. "You should be inside with your quartet."

"I'm looking for Princess Marleyn," I say, hoping he can sense the importance in my voice.

"And you think she's out here?" he asks incredulously.

"Maybe you can show me where to find her?" I ask.

"I have better things to do."

"Like what?" I ask, my voice coming out in a rush as he

hurries me across the rest of the sparring field, his grip tight on my arm. We crowd through a narrow gate that opens into a cobbled outdoor passage. Captain Aric merely grunts in response as we stop outside a splintered wooden door. He pounds on it, and two aggravated voices go silent on the other side.

The door swings open, and I'm surprised to see Dex and Joan again. Tall, strapping Dex holds the door open while Joan leans over a weathered map spread over a small square table. Dex looks flushed. "Did you find . . . " But he trails off as Aric pulls me into the light of the doorway. Dex flashes him a confused look, then just shrugs and returns to the table. Aric nudges me inside, checking over his shoulder before stepping in after me and closing the door behind us.

Would someone have followed us? Who? What was Captain Aric looking for in the king's quarters? I consider asking all my questions, but Captain Aric speaks first. He points toward a stool in the corner of the small room. "Sit."

I do, not because he ordered me to, but because I'm just now realizing how tired and hungry I am—and mostly because he ordered me to. Joan and Dex exchange glances before all three of their gazes fall on the map spread out on the table.

"What have you got?" the captain asks his second and third.

Joan pulls a pin from her coily hair and sticks it on the map, near what I can see is a bit of shore near a mountain range. "Here," she announces. "Right on Jara's northern coast."

He frowns. "By the Dragon's Back?" he presses. "You're sure?"

Joan's dark brown eyes flit toward me contemplatively. She bites her lower lip in thought.

"She's in Marleyn's court," Captain Aric reassures them, without even turning to look at me. "She can be trusted."

Joan's secrecy piques my interest. I lean forward, angling for a better look at the spiky mountain range known as the Dragon's Back, as Joan says, "I'm sure."

Captain Aric curses under his breath. "When?" he asks.

What are they talking about? I slide off the stool and tiptoe forward, prepared for any of them to send me back to my seat, but none of them do.

"The next whole moon is in a few days," Joan announces. "It has to be then. If we fail, we won't get another chance until— "

Captain Aric silences her with a raised hand. "I know." He frowns. "We'll handle it before then."

I'm standing over the map now. I can see that it depicts the four kingdoms and that there are red X's drawn all over them, all along their shores. "What do these X's mean?" I ask.

"You don't want to know, girl," Dex warns.

I have a feeling what he says is true, but I can't help myself. I wait for an answer. When Captain Aric nods his approval, Joan is the one to give it.

"Those akbarrin that attacked us on the way out of Marad weren't the first to slip out of the Shadows," she says, "nor were the emberfiends that killed King Felix and his court." She pauses to wipe her brow. "Creatures have been slipping out for near sixteen score now, attacking as soon as they're through, growing stronger as the seal between our realms continues to thin." She swallows, her eyes falling to the map. "One in particular has been attacking coastal villages," she says, "squashing villagers like insects in the dark of the night. It comes only on the nights when there's a whole moon." She gestures toward the hairpin near the Dragon's Back. "This is where we think it'll be next."

It squashes people like insects? "Wh-what kind of akbarrin is it?" I ask.

Captain Aric clears his throat. "They call it the Moongazer."

"It's the stuff of nightmares," Dex says. "You'll sleep better tonight if we don't tell you."

This time, I take his word for it. "What are you all going to do?" I ask.

Captain Aric runs a hand through his slick hair. "Well," he says, "I'm going to lead my men there and ambush the thing. That's what we're going to do."

It's not exactly a plan, but I'm just grateful that the soldiers will deal with this akbarrin instead of me.

"But we've got a problem," Joan says, more to the others than to me. She's about to say whatever Captain Aric didn't want her to finish before. The thing that first made him frown. "Shadowkiss."

"The shadows will kiss any day now," I murmur, repeating what Princess Chiwa said in the library.

Three heads swivel toward me. "What did you say?" Captain Aric demands. "Where did you hear that?"

The intensity in his voice makes me hesitate. "I . . . It was something I heard Princess Chiwa say," I explain. "What is Shadowkiss?"

A knock on the door sounds before any of them can respond. Dex goes to open the door while Joan gathers up the map, rolling it carefully and tucking it into a satchel at her waist. There's no one at the door. I watch as Dex squats and then stands again, carrying a tray of covered pots. There's a stack of three bowls. My starving stomach does flips at the aroma that steams out of them.

"Root chowder," Dex announces. The mere mention of the hearty northern Maradi novelty makes my mouth water. I lean forward, following the scent with my nose as Dex walks past me. He sets the tray on the now empty table, and Joan gets right to work setting out the three bowls. Three, not four. Right. I'm not supposed to be here. I fight back the sting of tears that threaten to fall at the thought that the others might not share. Captain Aric ladles heaping spoonsful of the soup into the bowls, and Joan drops a chunk of bread into each.

I know that by now the other guardians have finished eating in the dining hall. I won't have anything to eat until breakfast. If I can last that long.

Joan grins as she sets a bowl in front of Dex and another before herself, but the third she gives to me as Captain Aric proceeds to eat directly from the pot. I can't believe my good fortune. I dive in right away, savoring the delicious spices as soon as they hit my tongue. Joan and Dex laugh and even the dour captain smiles.

My hunger satiated, I wipe my mouth and ask again, "What is Shadowkiss?"

I might as well have thrown a bucket of ice-cold water on a fire, for my words put a damper on their joy. His face drained of color, Captain Aric chokes on a bite of bread, but he recovers and wipes his mouth with a handkerchief. "Joan, you tell it," he entreats.

I find myself approving of his request. Something about the woman, about the warm timbre of her voice, makes me think she'd be a great storyteller. Joan obliges us with a tilt of her head. "As it is said," she begins, in the formal way. Then she surprises me by gliding into song, her liquid voice both heavy and light.

Twin moons, Liora and Hama,
A tale of woe and hateful drama
Lady of moon's light, prince of shadow's night
Torn apart by a prideful heart

Only when the moon shadows kissed
did they make up for the time they missed

Ten hundred score and it was no more
Only gore for the love they bore

Joan's eyes twinkle with delight at the awe on my face. "My mother is a captain in the storyguard," she explains. "Trained my sister and I when we were young."

"But with a voice like that, why didn't *you* join the storyguard?" I ask.

Joan casts a fond look at Dex. "I am where I belong," she says. "As you can see in the tale of the lady of Liora and the prince of Hama, it is a privilege few can obtain."

"They were fated lovers," I reflect, "but they weren't allowed to be together." The tragedy behind the song hits even harder than that of the story I discovered in the library. "How sad."

"They found a way," Joan softly counters, "once every seven score when the moons' shadows overlapped."

"Shadowkiss," I realize. I tilt my head. "This story can't be true. We have only one moon."

"Hence the gore," Captain Aric cuts in.

"What do you mean by that?" I ask.

Joan's voice takes on a grave air. "There were two moons once," she explains, "according to many of the older songs. Somehow, we lost one."

Dex speaks up. "Haven't you ever wondered why your guardian symbol has two moons?"

"Or why there were two moons on that temple door?" Captain Aric follows up.

I shake my head. I'm too embarrassed to admit that I haven't spent very much time thinking about my guardian symbol at all. I've spent more time pretending it didn't exist.

Captain Aric sighs. "Things went badly for the lovestruck royals, and it resulted in the death of one of the moons."

"Went badly?" I repeat, trying to wrap my head around it. "Does that mean there was another war? Like the one between the humans and the dragons?"

Joan frowns. "No one can say. That song is lost," she confesses. "All we know is that there were two moons before, and now there's only one."

"If we only have one," I muse, a question starting to form, "how can there be a Shadowkiss? Don't we need the second moon for the shadows to overlap?"

Joan and Dex exchange glances, but it's Captain Aric who answers. "We know because they keep a calendar at the Burning Temples in Zehir." He pauses. "And we know because the seal on the Shadows is breaking. Before Prince Donomar, only the moons could open paths between realms."

Joan leans forward. "Our theory is that—"

"Welp." Before she can enlighten me, Captain Aric slaps his knee as if to summon the end of this conversation. He stands and heads for the door. "I think that's enough for now. It's getting late."

I stare at him, blinking slowly. "What? But what about—"

The captain opens the door. "Bad things tend to happen in the dark and it's almost here. You should return to your quartet and make sure the princess is safe," he says. "Go. Now."

I glance at Joan. She sits back, clearly unwilling to contradict the captain. "Leave us to worry about Shadowkiss and the Moongazer for now," she says.

Captain Aric clears his throat. I hurry to my feet and stumble past him, wondering what Joan had been on the brink of saying.

CHAPTER TEN

Instead of returning to my quartet, I strike out for a quiet place to quell my racing thoughts. I find the sparring fields calmer than earlier, Most of the soldiers have departed for their quarters, leaving only a few to idle and chat. I glance at the sky, pink with dusty purple clouds suspended overhead. That gives me at least a half-measure before nightfall. I skirt along the outer wall, trying to avoid attention.

In a few measures, I've learned two tales of unfulfilled love. The boy spurned by the princess of the moon. A lady of Liora forbidden to be with the man she loved—the prince of the dark moon. My mind swirls with questions. Who was the boy? How did he get to the Moon Kingdom in the first place? What happened to him? My mind shifts to the second story. Liora is our moon. What happened to the one Joan sang of—Hama? And what happened to its prince?

Some deep down, primal need to solve the mystery steers me to the Temple of Two Moons. Maybe I'll find something there about the Lady of Liora and Prince of Hama, something to help me understand why their love failed and how they dealt with the heartbreak afterward. Maybe I'll find something to help me deal with my own.

Because it's impossible not to see myself in these stories, impossible not to identify the similarities.

Each of us—the boy, the lady, and myself—have one thing in common.

Fate keeps us from the people we love.

I slip into the temple room, the door snapping shut with a resounding thud behind me. Dust eddies around my feet before settling. Muffled light streams in from the small circular window at the back of the room, stifled by the window's black tint. Still, there's enough light for me to make out what I missed during my first visit. Carvings line the walls on both sides of the room, each panel adorned with different phases of two distinct moons. The moons in the panels nearest the front of the temple are mere slivers, growing fuller with each step closer to the altar, achieving wholeness only as they overlap the black window.

I get it now. The black window represents the overlapping shadows from Joan's song—Shadowkiss. Its dark center blocks the light completely, letting it spill in only around the edges, like the halo of an eclipse.

I creep toward the altar, the floor creaking underfoot. A coolness at my chest bone beckons my hand to the crystal resting against my sternum. I fish it out from beneath my shirt and hold it in my palm, the chain still tangled between my fingers.

At first, nothing happens. The cool stone sits lifeless in my hand, with no trace of the glow I witnessed yesterday in the fog. Then, light shifts—just a flicker. I glance at the window and marvel as soft rays bend around its edges, pooling into a stream that flows directly into the crystal. The stone grows colder in my hand, colder until it bites into my skin. The coldness spreads, crawling up my arms and prickling through my veins. A strange, frigid wave surges through my body—not exactly painful, but sharp enough to steal my breath.

And then I'm flying. A force hurls me backward, flinging me across the temple and into the wall at the back of the room. The crystal flies from my grasp, clattering to the floor.

My shoulders hit first, and then my head smacks against the wood. Ears ringing, I scramble to my knees, panting, and stare at the fallen crystal now lying idly between the first two pews, its light drained.

I gaze at it, my heart thumping frantically.

What was that?

I struggle to catch my breath.

For a second, I consider leaving it where it lies—or picking it up and smashing it against the wall. I should destroy it if I can.

But then I remember Ranee's instructions.

Keep it hidden, she'd commanded.

Did she know that something like this could happen?

I snatch the crystal up, wincing at the pain in my hand. The icy chill is gone, as if nothing had happened. The stone is ordinary again. I glance around. Nothing has changed in the room, save for a crack in the wall where my body struck it. I quickly loop the chain back around my neck and shove the crystal beneath my shirt, hiding it from the window.

Ranee must have known.

What else did she hide from me?

"Where have you been?" Rae's voice smacks of irritation. She and the other two guardians block the way into my bedroom. Her harsh tone grates against the headache pounding in my skull.

"Please, Rae, don't yell at me," I murmur, swaying a little on my feet and grabbing the doorpost to steady myself.

Her eyes narrow as they wander over my body, assessing it. "What happened to you?" she demands, her tone only a shade softer. Still, the concern in her voice is almost enough to knock me off my feet entirely. I wasn't expecting it from her. "Did someone attack you? Was it"—she blanches a little—"another one of those things?"

A part of me is relieved that she cannot bring herself to say the word. *Emberfiend*. At least I'm not the only one who was shaken by them. Maya puts a hand on the small of my back as if afraid I'll topple over. Chyou's shoulders tense, rigid with anticipation. Her usually dull eyes sharpen like blades as she tilts an ear in my direction.

I shake my head. "No," I manage to say. "I just . . . " The words halt at the tip of my tongue. I realize I don't know how to tell them any of it.

Princess Chiwa may be evil.

A scar-faced woman tempted me to desert.

There's an akbarrin roaming Beldemar's coasts and squashing innocent people like insects.

There were two moons once.

My crystal attacked me. Or something like that.

I glance around at their expectant faces and see that I'm not the only one who's on edge. Maya fidgets, Chyou's deathly still, and Rae stares daggers at me, all three awaiting the worst. I can't weigh them down with what I know. Not now. Not while all the details are still so incomplete, and not before I've spoken to Princess Marleyn. How could I worry them like that?

I manage a practiced smile with just the right dose of nonchalance. "I was just a little careless and took a tumble," I blurt out.

Rae narrows her eyes suspiciously. I can't tell if it's

skepticism or disapproval, but then she sighs. "So, you're clumsy, too," she remarks, crossing her arms. Disapproval, then.

Chyou's shoulders relax, and the sharpness fades from her eyes, giving way to the usual boredom that typically resides there.

"We should get you to bed," Maya suggests, her hand pressing insistently into my back. I force myself not to wince at the tender pain. Rae opens the door, and the four of us file into my room.

"Bed sounds nice," I murmur my agreement, stumbling over the fuzzy carpet. I know I won't sleep well tonight, not after everything, but I make a show of being tired, of yawning and dropping onto my bed without even removing my uniform. Maya perches on the edge of the mattress, wringing her hands in her lap. The other two move around in my peripheral vision, Rae busying herself with the discarded pile of yesterday's clothing and Chyou taking up a post beside the balcony doorway.

"I can't believe you'd just throw your clothes on the ground," Rae criticizes.

"Ranee usually picks them up."

"*My* monitor would make me kneel on rice," Rae grumbles, earning a nod of agreement from Maya.

"I'm bored," Chyou complains.

"You know, you don't look so good," Maya frets, biting her lower lip as she scans my face.

I need to distract her. "Have any of you seen the princess?" I ask.

Maya hesitates as if aware of my attempt at distraction. "Not since the labyrinth this morning," she admits. She glances toward the door, then lowers her voice. "She doesn't seem that interested in getting to know us."

"She's rude," Chyou pitches in.

"She's our princess, not our friend," Rae reminds them, but I can hear the edge in her voice, the hurt she's holding back. We've all traveled great distances to get here and spent our lives training for this moment. And our princess seems to want little to do with us. "It's our job to protect her. That's it." She levels her sharp gaze at me. "So, at least tell us you've figured out your oju."

My answering silence, paired with a grimace, is clear enough even for Chyou. "Seriously?" my third shrieks.

Rae rubs her temples as if fighting off a headache. "Did you even get close?" she demands.

"Maybe we shouldn't be so hard on her," Maya intervenes. "We all know finding one's oju takes time. Besides, look at her. She's not feeling well."

I flinch at Maya's undeserved kindness. My quartet has every right to be upset with me. I didn't do the one thing I set out to do today. "It's not that bad," I reassure her, an outright fib. "No worse than the cramps you get during the monthly blood."

My chorus sisters freeze, shock apparent on all three faces. I sit up. "What?" I stammer. What did I say now?

"You bleed?" Rae inquires.

"Yes." There's an intonation at the end of the word that makes it sound more like a question. "I have since I held twelve score." How are they shocked by something so commonplace?

Maya cringes, pity and concern falling over her pale face. "Guardians don't bleed," she explains gently. "Not like that."

"And they don't have friends," Rae spews. "Or mourn their Monitors. They *can't* without being omitted."

Can't? I've always known that we shouldn't and that it could lead to omission eventually . . . but *can't*?

Rae's eyes burn with conviction, and I know that I've reached a new level of failure in her eyes. She's probably wondering how the oath hasn't omitted me, why it still allows me to walk this earth. I find myself wondering the same thing.

It's never occurred to me, but they must be right. Why should guardians bleed? We can't fall in love. We can't have children. I've never considered that the oath could *enforce* that, that it could take something like that away from us. My hands tremble at my sides. I clutch my bedsheets to steady them.

Something's wrong with me. Maybe failing to find my oju at a younger age irrevocably damaged me.

Maya's warm hand covers my own. A new determination burns in her eyes. "We won't tell anyone," she promises.

Rae's eyebrows arch. "We *won't*?" she demands. "I think Princess Marleyn should know if one of her guardians is compromised. Her life may depend on perceiving that"—she rakes me over with an unforgiving look—"dissonance."

The word cuts deep, striking a chord of my greatest fear.

"Aryam's one of us," Maya says, her voice surprisingly bold. She stares Rae down. "I know you both can feel it just as much as I do. She just needs help finding her way."

Rae scowls at her, rolling her eyes when Maya doesn't back down. "Fine." She turns and storms out of my room.

Chyou yawns, stretching her arms above her head. "Yeah, I guess I'll keep your secret," she mumbles. She follows Rae out.

Maya stays behind. "Would it be okay if I slept here tonight?" she asks. "I'm still a little freaked out by what happened this morning."

Somehow, I doubt that. I remember the way she held her oju, the daring smile she brandished when it was time to fight. She's a natural at this. They all are. But I'd be a fool to turn down her company. "Sure." I nod. A few beats later, I find her hand beneath the blanket and squeeze. "Thank you, Guardian Maya."

CHAPTER ELEVEN

Too soon. Morning comes too soon. I barely remember falling asleep.

"Wake up already." Rae's voice cuts through the haze.

"Maybe she could have just a few more beats?" Maya's gentle voice trails after.

"You really need to stop coddling her."

"She *does* look like she's been run over by a caravan," Chyou says.

I blink my eyes open and find the three of them standing over me, forming a triangle of annoyance, concern, and amusement.

"If she's going to *find her way*, then she needs to get up and train," Rae insists, narrowing her eyes at me.

"Yeah, but . . . look at her," Maya says in a tone that makes me wonder if I really do have hoof marks all over my face and body.

I close my eyes and assess every pain in my body. A dull ache pulses through my core. My muscles practically shriek as I rally to move my limbs. "Please tell me we aren't fighting more akbarrin this morning," I plead.

"I wouldn't call what you did fighting," Rae retorts. "Chyou says she saw you from the sky."

My eyes flash open. "Hey, that's unfair," I protest. "I made a valiant and respectable effort."

"You splashed water at it," Chyou remarks, looking unimpressed.

"I did the only thing I could."

"I thought it was a good idea," Maya pitches in, but the way she winces while saying it suggests that she didn't think it was a good idea at all.

"Thanks, Maya," I murmur, earning a relieved smile. My brain sloshes around in my skull as I sit up. I grimace against the protest of my muscles. "Rae's right," I grit out. "I need to train harder."

A crumpled-up scroll falls out of my shirt. I quickly tuck it back in, but not before Rae notices it. She narrows her eyes. "What was that?"

"Nothing." *Moons.*

My response only sharpens her suspicion. "Did you take that from the Library of Light?"

"It's just a children's story," I blurt out. "No one will miss it."

She folds her arms across her chest. "So, you weren't even researching your oju yesterday?" she says. "You wasted *a day* of training to read what? Fairy tales?" I shrink away from her, pressing a hand against my temple to stay my headache. Rae's eyes flood with surprise, chased by what I'm hesitant to call regret. She pulls back.

"Rae, breathe," Maya intervenes. "I'm sure Aryam didn't mean to waste so much time." Even though her voice lacks the bitterness of Rae's, the accusation of her words still stings.

I have to give them something, I realize. I owe them one truth, at least. I choose the one I think will rattle them the least.

"I didn't completely waste the day," I reassure them. "I overheard Princess Chiwa and Prince Jahim talking in the library yesterday. I think they had something to do with the emberfiend attack."

My chorus sisters blink, surprise registering on their faces, but I watch as they quickly come to terms with it. Royals attempting to eliminate threats to their power is not so surprising. "I'm sorry I didn't say anything last night," I apologize. "It was kind of a lot." I look up at them, the offer of peace in what I hope is an earnest gaze, but Rae shakes her head.

Her voice is softer now, some of the spark let out of it. "Sharing one truth doesn't absolve you of hiding another."

Guilt slams into me. "Rae, I didn't—"

"Don't," she cuts me off. "We know you did more than *fall* last night. We know you're holding something back." The tenderness melts away from her voice. "By whatever curse of fate, you're our leader. You can start acting like one by being someone we can trust." She shoots me a cutting glare. Her silence is an invitation to come clean.

"Rae," I stammer. "I . . . I didn't lie."

She frowns and, perhaps seeing that we'll get nowhere, sighs. "No, you didn't," she agrees. "You just didn't tell us the truth." She leaves.

"Training starts in twenty beats. Just try not to be late, okay?" Chyou says, before striding after her.

"They'll come around," Maya reassures me, nervously toying with the hem of her shirt. "It would be easier if you were a little more forthcoming." She hurries after the others.

I sigh and cover my face with my hands, pulling them away almost as soon as my fingers touch my cheeks. I don't have time to feel sorry for myself. If my chorus sisters want answers, I'll give them to them. But first, I need something concrete.

· · ·

"LOOK who's on time for once." Rae mutters the insult as the four of us stand at attention in the training square. "Barely."

My chest still burns from my brisk walk to the square. After forcing my sore body to get dressed, I nearly had to sprint across the palace to make it on time. But I *did* make it on time. I hold my chin up higher and try not to let Rae's words bother me.

"You haven't missed anything," Maya offers with a kind smile. "Mam Kadejah leaves us standing here for a few beats. Then she tells a story."

I arch an eyebrow. "A story?" I repeat. "Training doesn't seem so bad after all."

Rae rolls her eyes, but at least I earn a giggle from Maya.

"You're just obsessed with stories, aren't you?" Chyou observes.

I sigh dreamily. "Only ones about true love," I confess.

"Quiet, you four," Princess Chiwa's Maradi guardian hisses. "Mam Kadejah is coming."

It's impossible not to stare at her and wonder if she knows her Pulse is a traitor. I remember the smiles we exchanged when we first met. She seems like a nice person, Princess Chiwa's conductor, but would she act against the crown? Guardians can neither betray nor endanger their pulses, but can they disobey them if it comes down to something so serious?

A brown-skinned woman in a black uniform appears on the verandah, her gray hair neatly coiled. She walks upright, with the energy of a much younger woman and the authority of a panther. Part of me wonders if the cane is just for show, the way I suspect Kemi's might be, but then I notice it—a slight limp on her right foot.

"Mam Kadejah," Maya whispers at my side. "She is the highest-ranking official in the guard. She's trained dozens of the

Monitors who have lived here at the palace. Unofficially, she's retired."

I swallow as Mam Kadejah's eyes rove over the small cohort of guardians. "And officially?" I ask.

"Her job is to make our lives infernal," Princess Chiwa's conductor says over her shoulder.

"Silence." Mam Kadejah's surprisingly deep voice booms over us. Her eye lands on me, and one corner of her lips turns downward. "Guardian Aryam Sinanan," she says with a glare. "I see you've decided to grace us with your presence today."

I frown but hold my protest. Didn't anyone tell her I had direct orders from the princess to go to the Library of Light instead? Why can't just one small thing go my way?

"Your quartet will remain behind after training today to make up for yesterday's absence," Mam Kadejah declares.

"Yes," Chyou cheers at my side as I simultaneously groan. Rae and Maya carefully mask their reactions.

Mam Kadejah taps her cane twice. The thud echoes through the crisp morning air. "Recite the first tenet of the guardian's oath," she commands.

A chorus of voices responds, "The guardian will dedicate themself wholly to the protection of their Pulse against all akbarrin and partake in no distraction." As probably the most distractible person in this square, I wince at the last word.

Mam Kadejah seems pleased with our recital. She closes her eyes and inhales deeply as if savoring the scent of a fragrant candle. "Do you know *why* the guardian is forbidden to love another?" she asks.

I have a feeling she's going to tell us. I brace myself for words that will surely sting.

Mam Kadejah's eyes flash open, centering once again on me. "After defeating Dragon King Elrey, Prince Donomar enlisted the four minor kings and queens in a war against those akbarrin left who sought to annihilate mankind, among them being the Aziza Fae and the demigods and goddesses. With their help, and the help of Dragon Princess Nalini, the prince managed to banish those aggrieved creatures to the Shadows." She pauses, her stern gaze drifting over the ranks. "But Prince Donomar's victory came at great cost. He lost his wife, and soon after, the support of his friends. One by one, the four minor kings and queens turned against him, each led astray by agents of darkness who sympathized with the akbarrin and would see them restored."

My shoulders tense. I know this part of the story well, and I know exactly how it turned out for the four kings and queens. How it turned out for me.

"Prince Donomar retaliated by cursing their bloodlines," Mam Kadejah carries on. "One child from each royal bloodline of the four kingdoms would be bound to serve and protect each child from his, unable to turn against them, lest the oath in their blood rise up and destroy them." She pauses. "Yes, your duty was once a curse, but now, it is an honor"—she holds her head up proudly, resting both hands on the handle of her cane —"for such loyalty and diligence has preserved our empire for centuries. Do not be fooled into thinking that this is the *first* time the akbarrin have managed to slip from the Shadows.

"No. It has happened many times before, but each time, it has been quelled by capable and devout guardians." Her gaze stops wandering and lingers again on me. "Just one errant soul can unravel it all. That is why we must remain steadfast and honorable."

I swallow nervously. Mam Kadejah can't see through me that easily, can she?

She taps her cane twice more. "Very well, then," she says in a chipper voice starkly different than the foreboding tone she used during story time. "Let's begin."

. . .

We spend the next measure performing excruciating drills that leave my already sore limbs weeping. Mam Kadejah leads us through endless cycles of arm, core, and lower body exercises, followed by a measure of thrusts, parries, and lunges. I struggle to keep up with my chorus sisters. No matter how hard I try, I cannot match their strengths. Rae's uncanny focus and precision. Maya's effortless grace. Chyou's endless stamina. Mam Kadejah seems to notice, too. She administers sharp orders and corrections to the group, her stern gaze often settling on me when she does.

We pass the third measure sparring in pairs to practice offensive and defensive techniques. Mercifully, Mam Kadejah pairs me with Maya. I sigh with relief, thinking that she will take it easier on me than either Rae or Chyou would, since she is both the kindest in our quartet and the lowest ranked, but my relief quickly fades. Maya charges at me full force, her wooden practice staff poised for the strike. I barely manage to raise my own in time to block it. It falls out of my hands and rattles to the ground.

"Maya," I protest, gasping for breath.

She tightens her grip on her staff. "Focus on your grip," she advises. "It should be firm and flexible, like the branches of a tree. It'll prevent you from dropping your staff." And then she charges again. I roll out of the way, recovering my staff and raising it again in time to block another strike. Maya unleashes a flurry of attacks. I block again and again, always on the defensive, barely scraping by.

When it ends, I can hardly lift my arms. Instead, I shamelessly drop onto my back and stare up at the clouds drifting overhead.

"How are you so good at that?" I sputter between ragged

breaths as Maya appears in my line of sight.

She laughs and pulls me up. "The staff is my favorite weapon," she says, "next to my oju, of course."

I recall her oju, that bright flaming sword. I can only hope mine is something just as cool.

"Guardian Sinanan, your quartet may have a ten-beat recess before we begin our next session," Mam Kadejah announces. "The rest of you are dismissed."

I groan. "This is cruel and unusual punishment," I mutter.

"Don't be so dramatic," Rae chastises. "Besides, it's not like you couldn't use the extra practice."

"I thought she did well," Maya defends me as the two of them stroll off for water.

Chyou remains at my side. "Aren't you thirsty?" I ask her.

"No."

I decide not to drink anything, either. I can't help worrying that I won't be able to keep it down if we keep training this hard.

But Mam Kadejah changes tactics once the four of us reassemble. Instead of physical torture, she assails us with mental torment: meditation. We sit in an arc before her, legs crossed, hands resting on our knees with our palms open toward the sky. Mam Kadejah hums a throaty chant composed to lead the mind into a serene state of concentration. Judging by their absolute stillness beside me, Rae, Maya, and Chyou find it effortlessly.

I squeeze my eyes shut and try to quiet my mind, but I can't. Mam Kadejah's deep baritone only reminds me of how much I miss Ranee's sweet soprano. My monitor had an otherworldly voice that the whole forest seemed to stop and listen to. My thoughts are now wild birds in that forest, flitting from branch to branch, restless and yearning.

On the verge of quitting, I open one eye a sliver and peek

through it. My breath hitches as I lock eyes with the scar-faced woman. She stands on the verandah watching the four of us with keen interest. With a smirk, she salutes me before moving purposefully toward a potted plant at one end of the verandah. She scans the courtyard before pulling out a small scrap of paper from her pocket and tucking it into the pot. Then she turns a corner and vanishes.

I flinch forward as if to follow her, but then remember where I am and sit back with a sigh. Mam Kadejah's humming stops abruptly. Her eyes flash open before I can even shut mine again. "Guardian Aryam," she snaps. "Is there something more deserving of your attention than what you're supposed to be learning here?"

The others open their eyes and look at me expectantly. Heat rises to my cheeks as I note their disapproval and disappointment. "No, Mam Kadejah," I mutter, mustering as much contrition in my voice as I can. "I'm sorry."

"Sorry isn't good enough when the fate of Beldemar rests in *your* hands," the old woman quips. *"Focus."* She shuts her eyes again and resumes humming. I avoid looking at the others, even though I can feel their lingering gazes on me.

I manage to make it into the glen. The pristine valley manifests in my mind's eye, and I envision myself standing in a field, letting my fingertips brush against the tall grass. I feel my shoulder blades press together and my breath become tight.

Something's different.

The waterfall is closer than usual, and louder. Almost too loud.

A presence pushes against my mind—curious and prodding, like that nebulous shadow I encountered in the fog.

I snatch my mind back from the glen, careful to mask my breath and not to alert the others. Ranee would encourage me to engage the presence, to explore it, but I don't want to.

I can't.

Eons pass. Mam Kadejah hums her mantra, and my chorus sisters sit as still as statues. I wonder what it's like for them. Do they have their own glens, or do they go somewhere different? What do they do there now that they already have their oju? If I found mine, I don't think I'd ever meditate again.

It's so boring.

My mind drifts back to the scar-faced woman and the paper she placed in the pot. It's clearly a message meant for me. I bite back an impatient sigh as I wait for Mam Kadejah to wrap up the session. It takes an inordinate amount of self-control not to retrieve the message as soon as she does, and even more not to seem too eager for the others to leave.

"Aren't you hungry?" Maya asks, lingering on the verandah's steps.

"I'll be there after a few stretches," I say, pulling one arm across my chest to demonstrate. I throw in a chuckle. "I'm a little sore."

Maya hesitates. "That's probably a good idea," she says at last. "I'll save you a seat."

I wait a few more beats after they've all gone, then a few more to make sure the courtyard is well and truly empty. Finally, I rush to the pot and pull out the scrap of paper. In impeccable handwriting, the message reads:

If you insist on getting yourself killed, go to the Dragon's Back and seek there what you lack.

"Seek there what I lack?" I murmur, rereading the short, cryptic message again and again.

"And what do you have there?"

I jump, startled by the voice at my back. Slowly, I turn and face my quartet. Rae folds her arms across her chest. "I told you she was lying again," she says.

Moons.

CHAPTER TWELVE

It is one thing to withhold the truth from your friends. It is another thing entirely to outright lie to them. Not that I haven't done it before. I've lied to Darien and Kyrel every day I've known them. I lied about my identity and about what I was capable of. I lied to Katina until she pried the truth from me.

I remember how liberating it felt to finally give her a piece of the truth, and how dangerous. The scar-faced woman could be dangerous. What if telling my chorus sisters about her ends up hurting them? I weigh the paper in my hands, debating between coming clean and reaching for an alternative.

Go to the Dragon's Back.

I wanted to wait until I had something concrete to give them. Is this lead strong enough? I look my chorus sisters in the eyes and realize it has to be. I take a breath. "I'm sorry," I apologize. "I'm not used to being honest about these kinds of things."

"We understand that," Maya replies, and it dawns on me that, more than anyone, they really do, "but we can't help you if you don't tell us what's going on."

"Just hurry up and tell us everything," Chyou insists.

So, I take a breath, and I do. Almost.

They listen quietly as I tell them about the woman in the library, then about the meeting with Captain Aric and the others, then about what happened in the temple, and finally, about the message I now hold in my hands. I leave out the part about my crystal, still hesitant to disobey Ranee's instruction to keep it hidden.

For once, Rae's face isn't dripping with disdain. Instead, she looks contemplative. "We don't know if we can trust this scar-faced woman," she muses aloud, "but it's not like anything else we've done has gotten you an oju."

"What if what happened to Aryam in the temple was because of her oju?" Maya poses.

"That could be," Rae considers, "but it sounds strange. *My* oju didn't manifest that way."

"What *was* getting your oju like?" I ask them. It's a question that's been burning in my mind since I met them, but shame about my own situation kept me from asking.

"I felt fire in my arms, traveling from my elbows down," Maya shares, "and then the flame sword appeared."

Rae hesitates. She crosses her arms again, hugging them close to her torso. "I saw something I really wanted," she says. "The rose bow and arrows appeared, and I got it." I fight the urge to call her out for being vague, especially after giving me such a hard time for keeping secrets, but I can tell that whatever she's holding back is very painful. And just like I'm not used to being honest, I'm sure Rae's not used to sharing her troubles with others. She doesn't seem like the type to have friends, even if she could. So, I nod quietly, accepting this morsel of information. It's a start.

The three of us turn toward Chyou and wait for her to answer. She forms two fists and glances between them. In an effortless flash of light, her oju appear, two furry mits with retractable claws. "I don't remember how I got Boomi and Pao." She shrugs. "I only had three score."

We gawk at her. "You were *three*?" Rae exclaims. It's the first time I've seen her truly baffled.

"How could you even sit still long enough to meditate?" I ask.

Chyou's expression remains impassive. "I was a quiet kid," she shares. "I wasn't talking yet."

That somehow doesn't surprise me. I turn to the others. "How many score for you two?" I ask.

"Seven," Rae shares, a bit of pride creeping into her voice. Seven is early for most guardians.

"Twelve," Maya says, citing a more typical age.

And I have sixteen. I groan. "I really am a failure," I grumble.

"Stop feeling sorry for yourself," Rae commands, but there's none of the usual spite in her voice. "I think it's settled. We should go to the Dragon's Back and see if there's really something there that can help you."

"What about Princess Marleyn?" Maya inquires. She lowers her voice, even though the courtyard is empty. "We can't leave her alone with Princess Chiwa if she's trying to kill her."

What about the creature that's rumored to be smashing people to dust in that area? I want to ask, but I don't. I'm not willing to lose the ounce of ground I've gained with these girls. For the first time, I feel like they're starting to accept me. "We should convince her to go into hiding for a few days," I suggest. At least we can keep her safe.

"I think you mean *you* should convince her," Rae replies. "You're our conductor after all."

"Me?" I blurt out. "Don't you think it would be better if we approached her as a united front?"

Rae smirks. "Good luck," she says.

"Can we go eat already?" Chyou complains.

"I am kind of hungry," Maya agrees with a sympathetic glance in my direction. The three of them depart.

"You guys," I whine after them, but they don't turn around. And here I thought *I* was the coward.

Defeated, I trail after them, wondering how I'll gain an audience with the ever-elusive princess.

FINDING PRINCESS MARLEYN turns out to be easier than I anticipated. The next morning, a summons to her personal dining room awaits me at my door. Kemi leads the way, her jeweled bonnet glistening in the morning light. I trail behind her nervously, an uneasy feeling in my gut. At least the feverishness that's plagued my blood since the incident in the temple has dissipated. There's no trace of the power that flooded my veins and knocked me off my feet, and I haven't dare sought it out again.

I'm already sore enough from Mam Kadejah's torture session. My stomach turns at the thought of what she might have in store for us today.

But I grit my teeth, knowing I'll do whatever it takes to get stronger. If that means submitting myself to Mam Kadejah's torments, then so be it. I sigh.

"I take it you had a long day yesterday, Lady Sinanan," Kemi observes, glancing over her shoulder at the sound of my sigh.

"Try a long week," I grumble.

"Oh?" Kemi remarks. "Aren't you happy to be here in the capital? With your princess and surrounded by your chorus sisters? Most guardians do not receive such an honor in their lifetimes."

Moons. Now I sound ungrateful.

"Of course I'm happy, Kemi," I reassure her. "It's just . . . " I want to tell her that I wish Donomar had never cursed us, but Mam Kadejah's spin on the story is too recent in my head. He didn't *curse* the guardians. He *blessed* Beldemar. Only through our undying loyalty can Beldemar survive whatever darkness the akbarrin are stirring up. I sigh again. "It's nothing, Kemi," I murmur.

"It sounds like nothing," the old woman quips in a way that makes me think she knows it's something, but she doesn't pry. "And here we are," she announces with a regal flourish of the hand. We've stopped in front of a spiral staircase that ascends into an open-air garret, not far from my own room. I'm equally surprised and not surprised that Princess Marleyn would eat in such seclusion.

Kemi departs with an encouraging smile while I linger at the bottom of the staircase.

"Breakfast will get cold," a voice calls out from the room above.

Right. I fill my lungs and summon courage before ascending the stairs.

I don't expect to find her standing at the mouth of the stairwell, waiting for me with a table of untouched food steaming behind her, but there she is, looking almost as awkward as I feel. What can only be relief washes over her face. She releases her breath. "You don't *look* unwell," she comments.

Her words catch me off guard. "Why would you think I was?" I stammer.

"Mam Kadejah says you seemed rather sluggish at training yesterday," she replies.

I raise my eyebrows. "Mam Kadejah told you I was sluggish?" I repeat. "You and Mam Kadejah talked about me?"

The princess shrugs. "I told you," she says, "I can protect

myself, and part of protecting myself is keeping track of my guardians." She turns toward the table and indicates a chair. "Sit," she commands. "I'm eager to hear what you learned in the library yesterday."

I wince. "You say that now," I murmur.

She raises her eyebrows at me. "What was that?" she inquires. Her expression grows serious. "Did something happen?" She nods toward the chair. "Sit," she repeats.

Obediently, I slide into the chair and watch as she picks up a plate and piles it high with peppered fish, spiced potatoes, and tomato sundrop chutney. The plate lands in front of me with a resounding thud, and my mouth falls open. *She's* serving *me*?

Princess Marleyn slides into the seat across from me. "Tell me what happened," she demands.

I frown, trying to think of the best way to tell her that her own cousin might be trying to kill her. In the end, I decide the best way to share the information is to just come out with it. "I overheard Princess Chiwa and Prince Jahim discussing the emberfiends," I report. "It . . . sounds like they may have sent them after you."

Immediately, the tension melts away from her face, and she smiles, actually *smiles*. "And I thought you would say something I hadn't already put together myself," she says.

I gape at her. "You already knew?" I exclaim.

She picks up another plate and starts to serve herself. "I figured," she confirms. "Right before he died, King Felix had an argument with Chiwa. She's been acting oddly toward me since his assassination."

Sadness washes away my awe. "I'm sorry about your father," I say. "I know what it's like to lose someone close to you."

If she thinks that's a weird thing for a guardian to say, she doesn't comment, but her hand falters. She takes a breath.

"King Felix was a good man," she says. "I wish you could have met him."

If that were possible, if he was still alive, I mean, then I wouldn't be here at all. But I don't respond because my own grief gets stuck in my throat.

"Did you learn anything else?" the princess asks, casually slicing a square of butter onto her potatoes.

I nod. "I learned a story about a boy who may be trouble," I inform her. "I mean, if the story's true. It's . . . I found it among the nursery tales your mother arranged for you." I wince, waiting for her to scold me for wasting my time with fairy tales or lash out about me invading a personal space.

She does neither.

"Tell me about him," she instructs, calmly cutting into one of her potatoes. She raises an expectant brow when I hesitate.

"I don't know his name," I begin. "But he fell in love with a princess of the moon and traveled a great distance to find her, only for her to turn him away. There's a warning at the end of the tale. It says to beware of him, but I can't find any reason why. Have you ever heard a story like that? Do you know who the boy is or whatever became of him?"

Princess Marleyn chews thoughtfully, then swallows. "No," she admits. "I've never heard that story." She purses her brow. "Where did you say you found it?"

"Among the nursery tales," I repeat. "In the alcove the queen decorated for you." I pause, then dare ask, "Haven't you ever entered it?"

The princess looks surprised by my question. "The thought never crossed my mind," she replies. She rests her chin on the backs of her interlocked fingers. "Do you have anything else to tell me?"

I blink at her. Is that really all she has to say about it? She isn't the least bit curious about the alcove? Or her mother?

"Guardian?" Princess Marleyn looks at me, expectant.

"Right," I blurt out. "There is one more thing." I draw in a deep breath, steeling myself to ask her permission to travel to a place where a monster is murdering innocent people because a suspicious woman who tried to get me to defect told me to. I twist my fingers. "I may have found a lead on my oju," I confess.

The princess grins and leans forward eagerly. "Do tell."

"DID YOU FIND THE PRINCESS? How did it go?" Maya grunts out as the four of us hold plank positions on our toes and forearms. Mam Kadejah has left us in this position for nearly five beats now.

A bead of sweat coagulates at the tip of my nose and drops onto the cobblestone beneath my face. "I did, and it was . . . pleasant," I reply.

"*Pleasant?*" Rae bites.

I steel myself against a wave of pain that shudders through my shaking core. "Yes. She . . . isn't . . . that . . . bad?" How much longer until my strength gives out and I fall flat on my face? "I think . . . you guys . . . should . . . give her . . . another chance."

"We *would*," Rae grits out, "if she would stop avoiding us. The only time we've seen her was after we faced those emberfiends in the labyrinth."

My arms give out, and I drop onto my front, gasping through the pain.

"Guardian Aryam," Mam Kadejah reprimands. "I did not give you permission to rest. Everyone will start again." A chorus of groans rings out in the courtyard.

"Sorry," I whispered to my quartet. Maya manages to flash me a sympathetic smile.

"Did you ask her about the Dragon's Back?" Rae asks.

I nod, my core shaking too much for me to grunt out words. The others breathlessly await my response. Mam Kadejah finally releases us from our torment. I collapse onto my mat. "She . . . wants to go . . . with us," I inform them.

"What? No," Rae hisses, keeping her voice low so the other quartets don't hear. "It's too dangerous."

"It might not be such a bad idea," Maya interposes. "At least we could keep an eye on her."

"Maya, she could get killed," Rae argues.

A frown tugs at my lips. Then *we* would be killed, too. "But she could just as easily be endangered here," I point out, "especially if Princess Chiwa realizes she's unprotected." I glance at the elder princess's trio of guardians as they help themselves to the water bowl on the other side of the courtyard. Would they carry out an order against Princess Marleyn if their Pulse issued it?

"Don't be ridiculous," Rae murmurs. "If her life is truly threatened, the oju ajo will bring us all to her."

I purse my brows. "The *what*?" I ask.

Before Rae can answer, several spheres of light flash around us, emanating from the chests of two other quartets. The four of us scramble to our feet as lights bloom around Prince Bem's and Princess Adanna's guardians. I shield my eyes from the brightness of it. The lights vanish, the eight guardians with them.

Rae pants. "*That*," she says, "is the oju ajo."

"The royal twins are in danger," Maya exclaims.

"Guards!" Mam Kadejah calls simultaneously. "Guards! Quickly."

Soldiers storm the courtyard, then, at Mam Kadejah's behest, pour into the palace in search of the twins. Mam Kadejah looks at the rest of us. "See to your Pulses," she commands. "Hurry."

"How will we find her?" Maya panics.

"Stay calm," Rae commands. "We're lucky the oju ajo hasn't pulled us to her. That means she's safe."

But maybe not for long, I realize. "We should split up," I command. "We have better odds of finding her that way."

"No," Maya protests. "Pairs." There's something wild and frantic in her eyes as she looks at me. "We'd be better in pairs," she insists. "I'll go with Chyou. Rae will go with you."

I want to argue, but she looks so frazzled that I consider, for a moment, that maybe I'm not the only one who feels afraid at times. Besides, she's paired us well. From what I've observed, Rae is the strongest of us. Her skills will make up for my weaknesses. Chyou is the second strongest, with Maya close behind.

I nod. "Be careful," I say, and then we split.

Rae and I race through a maze of corridors, maneuvering around panicked servants and bustling soldiers. I lead the way, my heart beating against my ribs. Rae's reassurance echoes through my mind. The oju ajo hasn't summoned us. Princess Marleyn still lives. It hasn't summoned us.

I never knew such a thing could happen. Ranee *never* told me that the akbarra in our blood would whisk us away to our princess's side if she was ever in mortal peril. Why? She always took my preparation so seriously. Why would she omit this major detail?

I push my concerns to the back of my mind. I have to focus on finding the princess.

"Where did you last see her?" Rae huffs.

"Breakfast," I reply. "I saw her at breakfast." I lead her to the garret and clamber up the spiral staircase. But she isn't there.

The balcony is empty, and the table where we dined this morning barren. "She isn't here," I pant.

Sweet moons.

I have no idea where Marleyn runs off to during the day. She hasn't exactly told any of us.

Bright, shimmering, blessed moons.

It's just another way I'm failing. A competent chorus leader would be always aware of her pulse's location. I didn't want to infringe, to force her life to change any more than it already had. That courtesy may cost me all of our lives.

My chest heaves with sharp, shuddering breaths. I can't do this. I can't do any of it.

"Calm down," Rae commands, her sharp voice slicing through my panic like a sword through mist. It's enough to force me to slow down my breathing. Her eyes shimmer with a glint of determination. "We'll check the royal family's private chambers," she instructs.

I nod, some of the panic ebbing from my mind. This time, Rae leads the way. "How do you know where to go?" I ask as we wind our way through the halls into unfamiliar territory.

"While you were reading fairy tales all day, the rest of us decided to explore our new surroundings," she answers. There's only some of the usual spite in her voice. Most of it is crowded out by urgency. We clear a series of rooms: a small drawing room, a music room, a conservatory. All empty. One door stands ajar as we approach, a gentle rustling noise coming from within. There's a flash of green light, and then Rae's rose bow is in her hand, a quiver of rose arrows on her back.

I try not to get distracted by how effortlessly she called her oju.

She halts outside the door and rests her fingers against the glossy wood. It's a weird time for me to notice the green paint on her nails, but I do. Even now, she's just so . . . put together. Rae takes a breath, readying herself to go in.

"I'm here," Princess Marleyn's voice calls from inside. "Come in. It's okay."

Rae gives the door a gentle shove. I gag at the odor that blasts us in the face. It smells like sulfur and copper, a thick, tangy odor. Marleyn sits on the floor of what looks to be a solar room in complete disarray. Piles of steaming, blood-soaked clothes are scattered around her. A young man is dead on the ground in front of her, his head cradled in her lap, a trail of blood streaking from his lips. A few feet away, a young woman with almost identical features lies just as still, just as gone.

I count the piles of steaming clothes around us, realizing that's where the stench is coming from. There are eight. Eight piles of clothes. And eight missing guardians. My stomach turns.

"They died because they were too late," Princess Marleyn whispers, her voice hoarse. My eyes widen at the blood smeared on her bare arms. She slowly looks up and follows my gaze. A soft, reassuring smile graces her lips. "Don't worry," she says. "It's Bem's."

The door creaks behind us. I jump, spinning around. But it's only Maya and Chyou, having somehow found us. Maya blanches at the sight of destruction in the room, while Chyou just crinkles her nose.

I return my gaze to Princess Marleyn, sitting so still with her dead cousin's head in her lap. "How are you still alive?" I ask.

Her eyes glaze over. "I found them this way," she says. "Whatever did this was long gone." Carefully, she slides Bem's head from her lap, then stands. "I'm sure security will increase now," she says, with surprising steadiness. How is she not puking her guts out in fright? "If we're going to the Dragon's Back, we should leave as soon as possible."

I frown. "Maybe . . . maybe you should stay," I suggest. "Heightened security isn't a bad thing. It could help keep you safe."

It's Rae who opposes. "You were right," she explains. "She has to go with us. The oju ajo summoned Bem's and Adanna's guardians to them, but it didn't give them enough time. If that happens to us, Princess Marleyn's dead."

I swallow. And so are we. I nod in agreement. The Dragon's Back is in Jara, Rae's kingdom. "Are you . . . ready to go home?" I ask.

Her eyes harden. "Jara *isn't* my home," she replies before storming away.

CHAPTER THIRTEEN

We leave at nightfall. The moon hangs low over our heads, stretching our shadows long on the rocky path before us. The tide splashes against the cliff below, misting us with sea spray. "We must hurry," Princess Marleyn says over her shoulder. "The tide will soon cover this path."

I frown. That means there will be no turning back. I stumble over an exposed root. Right behind me, Maya catches me by the elbow and the small of my back. "Watch your step," she says. The kindness in her voice is almost enough to take the edge off my troubled mind.

We aren't going to the port. Princess Marleyn says Captain Aric's guards would never let us—let *her*—depart from there. She told us that King Felix kept a small fleet of ships stored in a cave system far beneath the palace. That's where we're headed.

"Does anyone even know how to sail?" Chyou asks before blowing a few strands of jet-black hair out of her face. Her furry brown muffs flash into place, covering her ears and pinning her bangs back.

I shake my head. Even though we lived near the coast, Ranee never took me out to sea.

"I can," Princess Marleyn speaks up. "King Felix taught me."

"Why do you call him King Felix?" Maya asks. "Were the two of you not close?"

Princess Marleyn stops walking, her shoulders tense. The rest of us pause behind her. "You must have been very close," I say, after a moment. "After all, he honored you across the entire kingdom for your sixteenth birthday." *Our* sixteenth birthday. I force myself to remember that the only one that matters, however, is hers. "That shows that he must have loved you very much."

My words do very little to ease the tension out of the princess's shoulders. She whirls around and stares Maya harshly in the eyes. "That is *none* of your concern," she declares.

Maya flinches, then takes a step back, dropping her head. "You're right," she murmurs quickly. "I'm sorry."

Princess Marleyn spins back around and marches on, leaving the rest of us to exchange confused glances. Maya blinks back tears, while Rae curls her fists to contain her simmering rage, and Chyou mouths, *Rude.*

We reach the mouth of the caves a few beats later. I halt before the gaping darkness and feel my knees lock up. Fear grips my chest, stopping my breath. Rae bumps into me. "Hey," she complains, shoving around me. "Don't go getting cold feet now."

She's right. Now isn't the time to panic, not when two royals have been slaughtered and their murderer could be after us right this tick. But . . . "I can't move," I grit out. It's as if a giant hand has wrapped around my body, holding me in place. Something probes my mind, a curious, menacing presence. The crystal hums against my chest, glowing gently. I gasp as coldness shudders through me.

And then it's gone.

The crystal's light fades, and the phantom releases its hold on me. I crumple inward. I'd fall if Rae and Maya weren't so quick to catch me. "What in the great moons was that?" Rae demands. She peers into the dark cave and then levels a suspicious glance toward the princess.

I push away from them, ignoring the weakness I now feel in my limbs. I must stand on my own feet if I'm going to convince them that I'm okay and that we have to go through with this. "We have to keep going," I insist. My eyes meet Princess Marleyn's and find them filled with horror. "I'm okay," I reassure her. The lie comes easily, even though I want to around and run away as fast as I can.

The fear ebbs out of her eyes, and she nods. She turns around. "This way," she commands.

Inside the cave, the water laps gently against the ridge we walk on. A vessel looms in the dim light, a simple, single-mast sloop. Princess Marleyn hurries us toward it, stopping at a wooden plank that serves as a bridge from ridge to boat. She quickly crosses it and begins readying the boat, throwing out instructions to Chyou and Rae. I hesitate at the edge, my stomach lurching at the sound of the water below. A vision of Ranee sinking below the surface flashes before my eyes. I close them, take a breath, and step onto the plank. Maya boards after me, and wordlessly, the two of us pull the plank aboard.

The boat coasts out of the cave, and soon, the capital of Beldemar is at our backs.

ONCE THEY'RE NO LONGER NEEDED, the other guardians settle in the front of the ship, as far from the princess as they can get. Chyou and Maya unfold their sleeping mats and lie down to rest, while Rae takes the first watch, keeping herself ready in case Princess Marleyn needs assistance with the boat.

I make my way to the helm, where Princess Marleyn stands, feigning indifference at being ignored. But I remember the kind girl who invited me to breakfast, and I think I know the truth.

"Did you have to be so rude to them earlier?" I ask.

"Was I rude?" she replies, not breaking her facade.

I cross my arms. Katina often acts—acted the same way when I used to call her out. She'd pretend she hadn't done anything offensive at all. But Katina only did so because making mistakes terrified her, and she didn't want anyone to look down on her.

I don't know why Princess Marleyn was rude, but I'll find out.

"Yes," I say. "You were. If you don't want to talk about him, that's all you need to say."

Her eyes widen, a brief crack in the facade. "I'm sorry," she apologizes.

I have to admit, I'm stunned to hear it—a princess apologizing to me. I recover my wits. "I'm not the one you should apologize to," I advise, before turning away from her and joining the others.

Rae doesn't say anything as I pull my mat from my pack and unfold it so that I can lie down beside the others. She doesn't even look at me.

I SLEEP UNTIL MORNING. The sun glaring down on my face wakes me. The others are already stirring, their mats neatly rolled up and stored to the side. Maya sits closest to me, carefully preparing a plate from our provisions. We have to be mindful with them. It will take longer to travel without the omiayo, and Jara is farther from Capital Island than Marad.

I quickly take stock of the others. Chyou flows through a

series of stretches while Rae fumbles with the sails. Princess Marleyn stands at the helm, one hand upon the spokes.

"Chyou, I could use a hand," Rae calls out, wrestling with the boom.

Maya smiles as I sit up. "Good morning," she greets me.

Behind us, Chyou doesn't break from her exercise. "I *always* do my stretches first," she replies steadily.

I gaze at Chyou in awe. It takes guts to say no to Rae. She really is a creature of habit. Maya slides a plate toward me. I note that she's put a little more on it than her own. She must not be that hungry. "You all let me sleep through the night," I observe. I feel a little guilty for being useless.

But Maya just shrugs. "We agreed you needed it most. This week has been . . . hard on you; and you're doing something very brave, going to the Dragon's Back to solve a mystery."

I shiver, finding the mist rolling off the sea chilling. "I'm not brave," I murmur.

Maya holds my gaze. "Would someone who isn't brave demand that a princess apologize to her servant?" she retorts.

My eyes widen. "Did she?" I ask. "Apologize to you?"

Maya laughs. "No," she says, "but Chyou heard you stick up for me. It turns out, those muffs she wears really extend her range. It takes courage to do what you did." She offers me a handkerchief. "Thank you, Aryam."

I just smile back at her and shake my head. "I'm not so sure you should be thanking me for speaking out of turn to our Pulse," I warn. Ranee would have advised against it, at least.

"Seriously, Chyou," Rae calls in the background, still fussing over the boom.

Maya stands and dusts off her pantlegs. "I should probably give Rae a hand." She lingers for a beat, a thoughtful look on her face. "Maybe you could try meditating," she suggests. "You might have some luck."

But the idea of entering the glen now and feeling that *thing* push against my mind feels too daunting. "Actually, I'm still a little sore," I say. "Maybe I'll join Chyou in stretching."

Maya's eyes dart between my limbs, assessing them. "That's a good idea," she agrees, after a beat. She extends her hand to me, clasping her fingers around my wrist, and pulls me up to my feet. Her grasp lasts a beat longer than necessary before she lets go and dashes off to assist Rae.

Chyou hardly seems to notice as I lumber toward her. She stands with her palms pressed together in front of her chest, her feet anchored steadily on the wood. As smooth as the breeze moving around us, she shifts her weight onto one foot, planting the sole of her other foot flat against her inner thigh and raising her hands above her head. I match her pose, and the instant my muscles begin straining to keep my balance, realize I've made a mistake.

Chyou's morning stretching routine is nowhere near as easy as she makes it look.

"You're breathing funny," she comments, without opening her eyes.

"Sorry." I reel in my breath and try to keep it quiet.

Chyou says nothing, but a faint glow shimmers through her muffs. I don't ask about it.

"I don't think stretching should be this strenuous," I mutter, clumsily following her into an awkward squatting position that makes us both look like grasshoppers. "*This* is how you start each day?"

"Yep."

"You never grow tired of it?"

"Nope."

I tilt my head, finding it hard to believe. "Ever?"

Chyou sighs, and I get the feeling that I'm interrupting her peace, but she humors me with a response. "I like my routine. I like training. I like fighting."

I nod, pursing my lips and urging myself to keep quiet. It must be a relief to be a person like Chyou. To wake up every day and know what you have to do and to like doing it. How many times did I drag my feet to the shore in the morning when Ranee insisted on meditating as soon as the sun rose? But I find it hard to believe that Chyou has zero interests outside of being a guardian.

"What else do you like?" I blurt out, unable to keep silent. "I mean, what else do you like doing that's not guardian related?"

Chyou groans. "I like it when it's quiet."

I frown. "Oh," I murmur. "Right." I take a step back from her. "I'll let you finish stretching."

"It's time for forms now," she comments, her face a mask of concentration.

"I'll let you do that, then," I amend. I hurry away, leaving her to practice on the main deck.

"She likes rocks," a voice rings out above my head.

I jump. Princess Marleyn stands at the edge of the quarter deck, her hands resting on the rail. It looks like Rae's taken over steering for a while. "How long have you been standing there?" I ask.

The princess shrugs. "A few beats. Your flexibility needs work."

I massage my shoulder and try to work out a knot. "What doesn't?" I sigh. I peer up at her. "How do you know Chyou likes rocks?"

Princess Marleyn leans against the rail. "Haven't you seen her room? It's like a shrine to mineralogy in there," she replies. "I have no idea where she got all those rocks."

"I got them from Gedra," Chyou calls out above the wind. I

glance back at her and recall what Maya said about the muffs. Range, indeed. Her oju must have also given her the strength to carry such a collection so far. I raise a hand to my chest, feeling the crystal hidden beneath my shirt. If Chyou really is into rocks, maybe she knows something about what kind of crystal this is.

Maybe I'll ask her later.

I glance up again to find the princess gone. It should surprise me more than it does that she knows what the interior of Chyou's room looks like, but at breakfast yesterday, she did say that she was keeping track of us. I guess that includes knowing our interests.

But if she notices personal details like that, why doesn't she use them to befriend the others? Does she really not care about her guardians?

A royal doesn't have to, I suppose.

TWO DAYS LATER, the lush forest of Jara swells against the shoreline as far as the eye can see, except for an expansive clearing where the port lies. No one should recognize us here, not even Princess Marleyn. Outside the capital, people only know the princess by name rather than by appearance. Rae stands stiffly at the ship's bow, her arms drawn tight across her torso as she stares solemnly at the approaching port. I sense that she hoped never to see this place again. Was it as bad for her here as Zehir was for Maya?

Neither Rae nor Chyou have told me anything about the Monitors who raised them.

She side-eyes me as I step forward and stand beside her, and I realize I won't be getting her to open up about it anytime soon. So, all I do is smile. She slides her icy gaze back to the shoreline. "Few roads lead to where we're going," she announces. "There are few cities near the Dragon's Back, and the coach company doesn't waste its resources by providing transport there. So, get ready to walk. A lot."

I nod. "Thanks for the warning."

"And try not to whine about it," she adds.

I hold my smile. Wow. Rae's meaner when she's nervous. "Okay, Rae."

I turn my gaze back to the island. From what I remember of Captain Aric's map, the Dragon's Back is on the other side, but we must dock on this side. The Sea of Scales is generally mild and easily traveled, but the seas on the other side of the island are treacherous. If we try to sail to the other side of Jara, we risk capsizing.

Princess Marleyn calls a meeting on the main deck. "Rae, as our emissary to Jara, you should serve as our guide," she says. To her credit, there is not an ounce of entitlement or arrogance in it. It's a request, not an order.

Rae can refuse if she wishes.

But instead, she clenches her fists and nods solemnly.

It's admirable, the way she accepts her role, putting aside her own discomfort. I don't think I've appreciated Rae enough for her dedication.

Rae glares at me. "*Why* are you looking at me like that?" she demands.

I lunge forward. My chin strikes her shoulders—I never realized how tall she is—and my arms wrap tightly around her body. She stiffens, and I can feel her heart pounding inside her chest. "*What* are you doing?"

I squeeze harder. "I'm hugging you." Hasn't she ever been hugged before?

She relaxes just slightly, and I hear her breathe an annoyed sigh. "You're so weird." She allows it for a few ticks longer before easing out of my grip and retreating to the other side of the main deck. Quietly, she kneels down and starts packing our things.

I sigh. Maybe one day, I'll be as selfless as her.

I turn to find the others staring at me as if they think I'm as weird as Rae says. Their confusion makes me laugh. "Don't any of you give hugs?"

At the mention of it, Chyou runs off, claiming the boom needs attention. Maya shrugs and walks away, and Princess Marleyn returns her attention to the helm.

We dock a measure later. The portmen who help us disembark are surprised to find five young girls aboard the incoming vessel, but otherwise they let us go easily. Princess Marleyn takes a draft of the damp, woodsy air. "It smells so earthy," she comments.

"It's Jara," Rae mutters.

A cloud falls over Princess Marleyn's face. Then she straightens. "I guess I deserve that tone," she admits, giving Rae an apologetic look. I think it's the closest Rae will get to an actual apology, and she seems to realize that, too.

The guardian and the princess exchange nods. A truce.

Princess Marleyn inhales. "Well, I suppose the first thing we should do is find a chaise to take us as far inland as possible," she suggests. "Then we can find shelter for the night. Somewhere discreet. We can start our hike."

Rae frowns. "I know a place where we can go."

The driver who agrees to take us inland charges an outrageous amount of coin and looks surprised when Princess Marleyn pays it, but he doesn't ask us any questions. Four roads emerge from the Jaran port. We travel down the narrowest and darkest of the four, the road growing narrower and darker the farther we go. Until suddenly, it ends, pinched off by a wild and impenetrable rainforest.

The driver peels off as soon as we disembark, without a care or concern for our safety. I think of the adults I knew back home in Irez and find it difficult to imagine any of them agreeing to drop five kids off in the middle of the forest with dusk approaching and no shelter in sight.

Princess Marleyn frowns at our surroundings. "Is there really an inn nearby?" she wonders aloud.

Rae steps past her, alerting my attention to a narrow trail. "Trust me," she says. "Where we're going is safer and more discreet than any inn. People in Jara aren't known for their hospitality."

Princess Marleyn considers Rae's response, then nods. "Alright," she agrees. "I trust you." She follows Rae into the dark. I hurry after them, leaving Maya and Chyou to take up the flank.

Not much time passes before the trail splinters off into two. Rae turns down a muddy, cramped path, just wide enough for us to walk single file. Princess Marleyn follows without complaint, not even batting an eye at the mud that besmirches her pristine shoes. Maya slips past me and follows her in, but I hesitate at the threshold, almost choking on the dank, swampy odor that creeps out of the darkness. I frown as a fuzzy, low-hanging moss brushes against my arm.

This is going to be gross, but I take a breath and step into the mud.

A whimper slips out behind me.

The line halts.

The four of us turn back to find Chyou frozen at the trailhead, her usually stoic face contorted with discomfort, eyes shut.

I step toward her. "Chyou?"

Her gray eyes flash open, riddled with anguish. I take stock of her shallow, rapid breaths. Something's wrong.

"Guardian Chyou," Princess Marleyn addresses her, frowning. "Why have you stopped?"

"We need to keep going," Rae agrees.

I raise a hand and find my voice. "Wait." Chyou clearly isn't well. I take another cautious step toward her. "Chyou, what is it?"

Chyou's eyes widen. She covers her hands with her ears and flinches when her elbow brushes against a mossy vine.

"Tell us what's wrong," I plead, earning another flinch from my chorus sister.

She takes a step back. "Just stop talking already," she lashes out, her voice one octave away from breaking. Her frantic eyes dart from my lips to my outstretched hand, then to the reeking, croaking darkness behind me.

Brown light flares from her muffs and then recedes, leaving them glowing. She closes her eyes and goes completely still, slowing her breaths. After a beat, she opens them again and meets my gaze. I can see that her mind is quieter, though not exactly calm. "There's too much happening," she explains after a few bewildering ticks have gone by.

"Too much happening?" I repeat.

She gestures at the forest. "It's too loud," she points out. "The animals. The twigs under our feet. And you're breathing so hard—you should really run more often, you know." She groans, her face looking a little greenish. "And it stinks." She gestures toward the hanging moss. "And I hate the way that feels. I hate this place." Her shoulders slump. "I miss the sands."

I've never considered how different Gedra is from the other islands, a desert in the middle of the sea. I soften my voice to accommodate Chyou's sensitive ears. "I bet it was really quiet there," I say.

Chyou nods.

It hits me. On the ship, Chyou wasn't being rude when she

said she liked the quiet. She was telling me about herself. I should have listened better.

I think about the way her muffs glow every time she complains about a noise. I point at them. "Do those help somehow?"

Another nod. "They let me hear only what I want to hear, but I have to keep adjusting them—and sometimes when I'm overwhelmed, I forget." She takes another deep breath. "But I just fixed it. Right now I can hear your voices."

That's good. I search my mind for a solution to her other discomforts, then remember the blanket folded in my pack. I pull it out. "Drape this over your head and shoulders," I instruct. "It's not the softest blanket, but at least you won't feel other things touching your skin." She accepts the blanket and wraps it around herself, the closest thing she can muster to a grateful smile on her lips. "I'm sorry I can't do anything about the smell," I apologize.

Chyou just plugs her nose with her fingers. "I've got it," she says, her voice chipper as if she wasn't just five seconds away from imploding. She brushes past me and the others, first into the awaiting darkness. I follow on my third's heels, emboldened by her bravery. The others fall in line, each giving me the same quizzical looks I received after hugging Rae.

THE TREES PEEL BACK from the path as we enter a misty bog, full of swamp grass and croaking frogs. Ahead, a stilted wooden shack sits atop the mist, its thatched roof sloping gently away from a grimy chimney that spits out black puffs of smoke. I scrunch my nose at the stink. Every instinct in my body screams to turn back, but my quartet, the princess—they all keep going. To my surprise, I do, too.

"What sort of place is this?" Maya's the first to ask. I stifle a scream as a slimy frog leaps across my path, its bulging eyes wild with warning. *Turn back*.

Rae's fists clench at her side, and she takes a breath before answering. "It's . . . the Bog House." If I didn't know any better, I'd say my unflappable chorus sister is rattled.

The feeling's contagious. "And who lives in this *Bog House*?" I ask.

Beside me, Maya's face is as pale and sticky as rice. She assesses our surroundings with flitting glances, and I wonder if her blood sings the warning, too. *Turn back*. Even Princess Marleyn seems a little perturbed.

But Rae doesn't answer my question. Instead, she ascends the rickety front steps and knocks politely on the door. I hear sharp footsteps on the other side of it, and then the door whips open so hard and fast that everyone except Chyou jumps.

An old crone opens the door, small and bony and curved. I know instantly that she's not human. I know it like I know every tenet of the guardian's oath. Sagging eyelids obscure her eyes, but she still gives the air of peering angrily through them. Her gaze lands on Rae. "What are you doing here?" she demands. Her voice sounds just like the frogs croaking all around us. "I told you never to come back."

Rae holds her ground. "We have nowhere else to go," she says carefully. "Please take us in, Mama Anura." Maya and I exchange glances, perhaps equally surprised at her deference.

The old woman grumbles. "Humph." She turns and walks away, leaving the door open to us. "I'll wager you have 'nothing to eat', either."

Maintaining that careful respect, Rae admits, "We would appreciate anything you could offer us."

Mama Anura has already hobbled her way over to a sooty stove, where a pot of soup bubbles. She lifts the lid and stirs, stifling an ugly cough with her thin lips. Rae turns sharply to the rest of us. "Eat *every* bite and be polite," she hisses. She glances at Chyou, a trace of apology in her eyes. "And unplug your nose." She turns back before the old crone faces us again.

"Sit."

Five bowls slamming down against the table punctuate Mama Anura's command. Five bowls all at once, out of thin air, like some horrid conjuring. I swallow a lump in my throat as beads of sweat sprout along my hairline. Not human. Not akbarrin. Maybe Mama Anura is some sort of enchantress. She heaves the large pot of soup to the center of the table, where a round coaster awaits it. My eyes almost bulge out of my head as I watch the ladle appear over the kettle and, on its own, lift the first scoop of soup.

Its base is a buttery yellow broth with a saccharine, almost rancid smell. Spare bits of chopped vegetables and slimy seaweed bob up and down inside it. The ladle deposits this first spoonful directly into my bowl with a splash. Then it fishes out a lump of white, rubbery meat and plops it in the middle of my soup. *Frog meat.* I appeal to Rae with pleading eyes, but she glares daggers at me across the table. *Eat it.*

With a shaking hand, I pick up my spoon and dip it into the broth. From one corner of the room, the old crone watches with expectant, piercing black eyes. I slurp up the first sip, hoping the sound will please her.

At my side, Chyou drums her fingertips against her thigh, murmuring a fervent, muffled meditation. At least she still wears her muffs so that she cannot hear my slurping, or the crone's rattled breathing, or the way the Bog House creaks every time someone moves. She's somehow found a way to cope with the smell, but if sounds and odors bother her, I wonder what the taste and texture of this atrocious dish will do. "Gross," she mumbles just once, when Mama Anura's back is turned.

But she eats. We *all* eat, and for once in my life, I'm grateful the old woman doesn't offer us seconds. Mama Anura inspects our bowls when we finish and seems pleased with finding them empty. Behind her, a door creaks open, and she says, "You can stay."

We spill through the door, eager to escape the old crone's prying eyes. As soon as I'm out of earshot, I gag, unable to help myself. The stew was as sweet and as bitter as it smelled, and the meat was too bland and rubbery to be pleasing.

The room we find ourselves in now is square and plain, with wooden planks for flooring and walls. Somehow, it has the perfect number of cots for five weary travelers.

Maya's face is pale white. "I thought Jaran frog meat was toxic," she whispers.

"She cures it," Rae replies. She doesn't look half as bothered by the meal as the rest of us. Even Princess Marleyn clenches a hand to her stomach and looks as though she'll hurl at any second.

"Why did you bring us here?" she asks.

Rae's nostrils flare with indignation. "Because we had nowhere else to go," she hisses. "I told you. Jarans are not exactly known for their hospitality." She wraps her arms around herself and lets out a breath. "And the inns here aren't safe for a princess," she mumbles. "Sure, Mama Anura can be terrifying, but the people out there? They're worse."

A heavy silence falls over us. I wonder what horrors Rae's encountered out there to make her choose a place like this, but I can see that she's near her limit for invasive questions.

Maya asks a safer one. "How did you know about this place?"

"You can always find her house inside a bog," Rae murmurs. "It doesn't matter where on the island. She'll be there. As it is said, she has many names. The woman of the bog, Mama Anura, Bogma. Regardless of what you call her, she will always take in lost children, feed them, and give them a room for a night, but the ones who are rude and ungrateful wind up on her stove as frogs."

I swallow. "Thanks for warning us earlier." I speak with sincerity . . . and sadness. "You've been here before. When you knocked on the door, Bogma knew you."

Rae nods stiffly. "She fed me often when I was young," she says tersely. "Unlike *your* monitor, mine was negligent and resentful and could hardly care to feed me. He was a miserable drunkard who hated that he'd been exiled here to train me."

I wait a beat for the anger in her voice to settle. "That thing you wanted when your oju manifested—you said you saw something you really wanted, and the rose bow just popped into your hand," I recall. "What was it?"

Rae's eyes flare, and for a beat, I think she won't tell us, but then something inside her caves. "It was a sundrop," she confesses, "one of Jara's rarest fruits. It was hanging high in the canopy, and I was too weak to climb to it. The rose bow appeared, and I shot it down."

I don't mean to gasp, but I do. "Rae . . . "

"Don't you *dare* pity me," she snaps, glowering. I have enough sense to school the compassion on my face. "And don't any of you worry about ever coming back here. If she sees me again, Mama Anura will probably cook me up next for taking advantage of her generosity." She glares at us before lying on her cot and turning her back toward us. "Go to sleep. Tomorrow, I'll lead you to the Dragon's Back."

CHAPTER FOURTEEN

I don't sleep. Not right away. The Jaran night air is too warm and humid, and the frogs croaking in the bog are too loud. Besides, I'm haunted by what Rae said earlier. Do those frogs really contain the souls of ungrateful children? That was only a local legend, wasn't it? She wouldn't feed children to other people, would she?

Oh, sweet moons. Am I a cannibal now?

I sit up.

No. I must believe that Bogma wouldn't really do that. It doesn't match up. How could a being kind enough to feed lost children be cruel enough to cook them? She may be strange and a terrible cook, but she took us in and kept us safe. That is who she has to be.

It's either that or I'm never going to eat *any* kind of soup again.

As my eyes adjust to the darkness, I peer around the dimly lit room at the sleeping lumps that are my chorus sisters. Maya lies peacefully on her back, arms positioned gracefully with one hand resting over the other on her abdomen. A look between the four of them and one would think that *she* was the princess.

Rae's position is similar, but there's tension in her body. She looks as though she's ready to jump up and fight in an instant. Chyou is curled into a ball and snoring. Princess Marleyn sleeps on her side, facing the opposite wall. Like Rae, her position is defensive. I frown, wondering what she's gone through these last few months to make her sleep that way.

Or maybe royals never relax. Maybe there's a reason why they need people like us.

A sliver of moonlight streams in through the circular window above my bed. I peer up at it, thinking of the way it looked that last night in Irez, when I almost kissed him. It was only days ago, but it feels like scores have gone by.

IN THE END, I don't sleep long. It's lighter outside, but the others are still sleeping. I roll over, feeling groggy, and check on them. Maya hasn't moved, still just as peaceful as when she first laid down. Rae looks stunning. And Marleyn now sleeps facing me. But Chyou . . .

I stare at the empty cot where she should be snoring.

Chyou's missing.

I sit up. The cot creaks beneath me, waking the others.

Marleyn's eyes flash open. "What's wrong?" she asks.

My chest heaves. Yesterday, at the dinner table, Chyou insulted Bogma's cooking when she thought the crone wasn't looking. Now she's missing. "Bogma cooked Chyou," I exclaim.

"What?" Maya's frizzy curls bounce as she whips her gaze toward me.

"Chyou's soup," I explain. I think of the steaming piles of guardians' uniforms in the solar, of Princess Chiwa's *trio* that should be a quartet. If our princess dies, we die. But if we lose a chorus sister, we have to live with that. Forever. I scramble to put my shoes on and race out of the room. "Chyou!" I cry. The others are on my heels.

The frogs' incessant croaking fills my ears as I burst out onto Bogma's porch. The creaky house shack groans on its stilts. "Chyou!" I start down the front stairs, rushing past the girl sitting statue-still to my left. Wait. I slow to a stop and turn my head slowly. Chyou sits on one wall of the porch, legs folded meditation style, eyes closed, seeming completely oblivious to my panic.

"Chyou!" I scream again, relief flooding my body.

One of her eyes slits open, then both. She looks at me with dull, mildly irritated eyes. She's wearing her muffs, but they must be allowing my voice through. She sighs. "You're very loud. You know that?" she complains.

"Chyou, you're alive!" I exclaim.

Maya crashes into my back and giggles at the sight of Chyou.

I look around. "But where's Bogma?" I wonder.

As if on cue, the crone emerges from the mist humming a cheerful tune. A long stick rests across her shoulders with a fresh supply of dead frogs hanging from it.

A sigh comes from the doorway. "Maybe next time, *check* before you cry murder," Rae scolds me. But there's no denying the relief in her voice.

Princess Marleyn stands behind her. "We should get going," she suggests as Bogma reaches the front steps.

The old woman pauses at the door. "Be careful out there," she says. "The little faceless ones warn me that he's coming soon."

"WHAT DO you think she meant by that?" Maya asks as we

walk away from Bogma's shack, a shack I hope we'll never, ever see again.

"Which part?" I shudder. "'Faceless ones'? Or 'he's coming'? Both sounded pretty ominous."

"We should just focus on one thing at a time," Rae suggests. "Like how we're going to get into Dragon's Back."

"What do you mean *get in*?" Princess Marleyn questions her. "I thought you said you knew the way."

"I *do* know the way," Rae retorts. "That isn't what I meant." She sighs, no doubt reining in her temper as she remembers that Princess Marleyn is the very Pulse that keeps us alive. "The path is guarded by this weird village. They don't allow anyone in."

"Maybe we can charm our way in," I suggest.

Rae shoots me an impatient glare. "You don't think I've tried that?" she demands.

I laugh nervously. Rae? Charm someone? I mean, I'm sure she *tried*.

"There's more of us now," Chyou says. "We could fight our way in." A wicked grin lights up her face.

Rae shakes her head. "No," she says. "That won't work."

"They'll let the princess of Beldemar in," Princess Marleyn says haughtily. "Otherwise, it's treason."

Rae scoffs at that. "I guess we'll see later today."

"Wait, what do you mean *later today*?" Maya asks. "We're only a few days' walk from the port, and the Dragon's Back is on the other side of the island. Shouldn't that take us a few more days, at least?"

Rae shakes her head and keeps walking. "The bog will let us out wherever we want," she says as she starts down the narrow path. "It's a part of whatever akbarra that allows Bogma's house to appear to lost children, no matter where they are. It should deposit us a half day's hike from the village."

Just as Rae said, we find a road awaiting us at the end of the path rather than the trail we took yesterday, deep in Jara's rainforest. Rae turns right. "It's a measure's walk this way," she says.

As the others fall behind, I race to keep up with her, in awe of how well she knows her island. Before Captain Aric came for me, I'd never even left Irez. But from what it sounds like, Rae's been traveling all around Jara since she was a little girl. "You're really brave, Rae. You know that?" I flash her a grin. Rae just sets her teeth and plows forward.

A while later, I strike up the nerve to show Chyou my sapphire stone. "Have you ever seen anything like this?" I ask, dangling the crystal in front of me.

Chyou glances at it briefly and returns her attention to the road. "I don't really like purple," she says with a shrug.

CHAPTER FIFTEEN

"Turn back from the Gate."

We approach Rae's *weird village* at dusk. The village is nestled at the tail of a mountain range that does resemble a massive sleeping dragon. By contrast, the village is small, with just a few stone houses, red-roofed and quiet. A bright red gate breaks the stone wall that circles the village, painted in white on its lintel: *The Gate at Eroden's Pass.* A man in ancient armor stands in front of the gate, fighting stick in hand. Two others stand behind him, similarly armed.

"I told you they were weird," Rae mutters, before stepping forward.

The man's knuckles tighten around the stick. "I said turn back."

"We seek shelter for the night," Rae intercedes, with so much ice in her voice it bites. I wonder if this is what she considers charm.

The man glowers. "You won't find it here."

"Let us stay," Rae insists. "We'll be on our way in the morning." She gestures toward the mountains that loom monstrously beyond the village.

He glares suspiciously at her. "Why do you seek to enter Eroden's Pass?" he demands.

Rae doesn't flinch, doesn't yield an inch. "We have our own reasons."

The man considers her, growing warier by the tick. Maya steps forward smoothly, unthreateningly. "Why won't you let us stay?" she asks, her voice gentler, kinder than Rae's. It has the effect of softening the man's posture and relaxing his shoulders, but his voice remains the same.

"Our children vanish at night," he said, "one by one. Anyone who dares to go search for them is found dead the next morning as if a boulder has fallen from the mountain and crushed them. Your timing is strange." He straightens his shoulders. "Besides, no one enters the pass."

"Crushed?" I repeat, feeling suddenly faint. So, this is one of the villages Captain Aric and the others mentioned, one of the villages where a terrible monster is scheduled to arrive by the next whole moon. *Tonight's* whole moon. But it sounds as though the akbarrin has arrived early.

I groan. Fate would have us beat Captain Aric's forces to the location. "Let us stay," I entreat, knowing what we have to do. "If there is any threat to your village tonight"—I try not to look squeamish—"we will handle it."

My chorus sisters whip their gazes toward me. I can see the shock and disapproval in their eyes. Princess Marleyn is with us. We should not engage in anything that would put her in harm's way, but I am their leader. "In return," I bargain, "you let us into the pass." Even if he said no, I would try to help. As awful as this akbarrin sounds, I can't let innocent children go undefended.

The guard narrows his eyes. "And how, exactly, do you plan to help?"

I cast a beseeching look at Rae. She sighs and summons her

oju in a flash of green. The bow appears in one hand, a rose arrow in the other. The man jumps in surprise. "Th-that's . . . "

"An oju," I confirm.

His eyes widen. "Then one of you is . . . "

"A princess," Princess Marleyn butts in, stepping to the front of our group. I see Rae's shoulders tense at this admission. "That would be me."

Immediately, the man drops to one knee. "Princess," he says.

Princess Marleyn frowns. "Rise," she commands. "I don't want anyone else to know."

He scrambles to his feet. "Princess," he says. "If . . . if you're here . . . If all of you are together . . . " His face pales.

"Beldemar is in danger," Princess Marleyn confirms. "Haven't you heard?"

He shakes his head. "Hardly anyone has traveled here in hundreds of score," he says. He looks perturbed. "Princess, I am *grateful* for your offer, but I cannot allow you to risk yourself. You can stay for the night. Take the pass. We won't interfere. But leave the kidnappers and murderers to us. We at the Gate are equipped."

"You do not decide what I risk," Princess Marleyn snaps. "We have business on the mountain, so we need to stay here for the night—that's true. But we will not ignore that the Protectors of the Gate need our help." She sees the shock in our eyes and shrugs, a smug look on her face. "Of course I researched the Dragon's Back before we left," she says. "The Gate is a warrior village, tasked with guarding Eroden's Pass. Every man and woman here is a warrior."

The man nods in concession. "Protector Jun at your service," he announces, looking around at all of us with sadness in his eyes. His gaze lingers on me a second longer than the others, perhaps weighing the worth of my words, before he returns it to Marleyn. "Your secret is safe with us," he says, glancing at Rae's bow just before it vanishes. "And we will accept your help, though I wish we did not have to let you face whatever darkness stalks this forest alone."

Princess Marleyn nods. "Show us to our quarters."

"Do you seriously mean to tell me that this entire village is full of warriors, and *they* couldn't stop this threat, but somehow *we're* supposed to?" I grumble to Princess Marleyn as Jun leads us into the village.

"Mm-hmm." Princess Marleyn nods.

"I bet you wish you knew that *before* you offered our services," Rae taunts.

"How's your splashing arm?" the princess teases.

I groan. "I never thought the two of you would team up against me," I mutter.

"You're really dramatic, you know?" Chyou—*Chyou*—chastises me.

"Yeah," Maya agrees, smiling. "No one's against you."

All around us, men and women hustle and bustle, carrying things to and fro, tending to livestock, and sharpening weapons. A handful practice sparring in a small enclosure with a wooden fence. They move with such speed and force that I'm glad we didn't have to go against them. I try to count them all. There are fewer than fifty, I think.

"For such a small village that hasn't seen visitors in over three hundred score, these people look less homogenous than I anticipated," I whisper to Maya.

Princess Marleyn overhears and snorts, the sound so unprincess-like that it makes us all turn our heads. "The Protectors of the Gate aren't *exactly* people anymore," she explains. "At least, that's what the scroll I read a few days ago said. They don't age."

"That's right," Jun proudly confirms, before I can consider where the princess encountered such a helpful scroll. "Princess Nalini herself gifted us with a life-sustaining akbarra to ensure that we would always protect Eroden's Pass. Makes us almost immortal—as long as no one kills us." He frowns. "But the downside is, we can't make more of us. If we lose an adult, the akbarra allows one of the children to age up instantly—but with the children disappearing . . . "

"Your numbers are in danger," I realize.

He nods. "And Eroden's Pass will be left undefended."

We stop outside one of the moss-covered, boulder-shaped homes that are scattered around the village.

I sweep my eyes once more over the village. There isn't a child in sight. "Who would want your children?" And who would want whatever lies at the end of Eroden's Pass? Could it be the "he" Bogma referred to? Or the one Princess Chiwa said is coming? The gears turn in my mind. Maybe it even has something to do with the jilted lover from the story. I glance up at Jun. "Can I ask you something?" If he really is hundreds of score old, maybe he knows the truth about the one who wanted to marry the moon.

Shrill laughter interrupts our conversation, followed by the sound of little feet pounding against a solid dirt floor. Jun chuckles. "Maybe later," he says, as a girl half my height bursts out of the house and flings herself into his arms. "Papi!" She giggles.

He lifts her up, swinging her in his arms, and squeezes her tight. Then he composes himself and sets her down, holding her sternly by the shoulders. "*Mija*, you're supposed to stay inside," he scolds. "You know it isn't safe."

The girl pouts. "You were taking too long to come in," she

says dismissively. She sizes up the rest of us. "Who are all these people?"

I offer her my hand. "I'm Aryam. What's your name?"

She seizes my hand and shakes it too firmly. "Valeria," she shares. She tugs my arm. "Come see my room." I laugh and go with her.

"She's so childlike," Maya comments at my back. "I wasn't expecting that from someone who's been alive for so many score."

"The children have no notion of it," Jun replies. "The akbarra preserves their innocence." He cups a hand around his mouth. "Don't keep her long, daughter," he calls after us, as Valeria pulls me deeper into the house. "Tonight, we'll have a feast."

"A feast?" I hazard a glance over my shoulder and catch the immortal man grinning. I don't think it's prudent to do something so festive when there's a Moongazer on the loose, or when children are vanishing, but I keep these comments to myself.

Jun's smile broadens, his eyes creasing at the corners. "A feast before the hunt," he says, "and to honor our esteemed guests who shall remain unannounced. You have my word."

My foot snags on my heel and I stumble forward, catching my balance just in time not to topple over Valeria. "Watch where you're going," Rae chides.

"Yes, please be careful," Maya agrees with much more grace than my other chorus sister.

"This way," Valeria says, tugging me into a small, cozy room. She waves her hand excitedly through the air. "This is where I sleep," she announces, gesturing toward a neatly made bed. She points at a dark blue ceiling painted with bright, yellow stars. "Mami painted that with special paint made from those glowing rocks in the caves, so it never gets dark in here." She tugs and pushes against the small of my back, driving me toward a small wicker basket filled with dolls and wooden toys —far more than a mortal child would own.

I guess whoever made them for her has had lots of time on their hands.

"These are mine," Valeria says. "Let's play." She plops in front of the basket and pulls out an armful of toys, pausing only when she notices I'm still standing.

"Oh." I join her on the floor and accept a wooden dragon. I examine the toy, frowning. "Isn't this toy a little scary?"

Valeria lets out a sharp laugh as if I've said something unbearably funny. I chuckle awkwardly. I suppose that in a village full of warriors, even the children laugh at danger. "Okay. Dragons it is," I concede.

The sweetest measure croons by as I play with the little girl, for once putting my worries aside. Near the end of it, a sweet scent glides into the room. Valeria perks up. "Honey cakes!" she exclaims, scrambling to her feet.

I follow her to the kitchen, where a small but powerful-looking woman is just removing a round, spongy cake from the oven. She smiles when she sees us. "Fortunately, I already had this one ready for the oven," she says, laughing at her dancing daughter. "I can't imagine a feast without honey cakes. Can you, sweet girl?"

"No, Mami," Valeria sings. "We must have honey cakes."

"Must," the woman agrees with an indulgent smile. "Careful of the oven." She straightens up, balancing the dessert on the wooden peel with expertise. She smiles at me, and I swallow the tender pain that such a sweet, simple gesture elicits. How my times has Ranee greeted me in our kitchen with a similar warmth shining in her eyes?

Valeria's mother carefully slides the cake onto a cooling rack before wiping her hands on her apron and turning to me. "I'm

Nanda," she says. I tilt forward at the waist, prepared to greet her respectfully, but she envelops me in a hug. "I'm so happy you're here," she says, squeezing a grunt out of me.

Right. The promise I made at the village gate resurfaces in my mind. "We'll get to the bottom of whatever's happening here," I vow.

Nanda releases me and winks. "I believe it."

The clang of metal draws my attention to my left. My mouth falls open at the sight of Rae standing in front of a stone basin, vigorously scrubbing a pot. "What?" she demands. "While you were having playtime, the rest of us decided to make ourselves useful."

Nanda ruffles Valeria's hair. "Keeping this one out of my hair while I cooked was plenty useful," she reassures me. She hands me a pan of goat meat cut into tender, juicy strips. "Will you carry this out?" She gives Valeria a basket of soft, unleavened bread. "And you, Miss, can carry these."

A collection of tables that weren't there when we arrived now runs the length of four houses, loaded with an assortment of random foods. As we get closer with our contribution, I doubt Jun's claim about this feast being for the hunt. It all seems rather improvised. I glance around at the other protectors, whispering among themselves as they bustle about with final preparations.

I bump into Maya setting silverware out at one of the tables. "I wonder how well Protector Jun kept the secret about the princess being here," I whisper.

Maya giggles. "Very well, I'm sure."

I sigh. "At least they all seem friendly," I murmur, setting the pan on a vacant spot on the table.

A quarter measure later, I sit with Princess Marleyn and my chorus sisters at the table, a mountain of food before us. "We should go easy on it," Rae commands, her imperious gaze traveling slowly between Chyou and I. "We don't know what the night will bring."

"For once, I agree with you," I murmur. I don't want to stuff my face only to chuck everything up again if we wind up facing some terror. I scan the wall of forest that half-encircles the village. "At least things seem pretty quiet now."

"Not to say they can't change quickly," Maya weighs in. "So maybe it would be best to restrain ourselves."

Chyou lets out a little whine at that but gives in with a sigh. "Fine."

A high note whines through the nighttime air, warm and inviting. Our attention snaps to a patch of road beaten brown by excessive foot traffic—the dancing floor. There, a man plays a stringed instrument so ancient that I don't know the name for it. Another man joins in, striking a drum, and a woman begins to sing.

Princess Marleyn grins. "Let's dance," she says, hopping to her feet.

"Seriously?" Rae questions her, frowning.

"What?" The princess crosses her arms, looking smug. "Don't you know how?"

Rae narrows her eyes. "Of course, I know how, but I didn't come here to dance."

"I'll pass," Chyou yawns, reaching for a bread roll.

Princess Marleyn glances at Maya, who shrugs timidly. "I should keep an eye on the forest," she says.

"I know a dance," I blurt out before the princess can get to looking too dejected. Princess Marleyn rewards me with a genuine smile before running off to the dance floor, where a few protectors are already in motion. I lean toward my chorus sisters. "The next time she tries to be nice to you, just go along with it," I suggest.

That only earns me three puzzled stares.

Princess Marleyn returns to snatch my hand and drag me off to the dance floor. She launches into a dance of elbows and legs and awkward twists. I blink at her. Princess Marleyn is a *terrible* dancer.

She laughs wildly. "I'll admit," she says. "I never paid much attention to my dance lessons, much to King Felix's chagrin." She takes my hands and squeezes them. "Show me your dance, Guardian Aryam."

I gently pull my hands away and nod, closing my eyes as I summon Ranee's teaching. I concentrate on the drums and chase after the rhythm with my heart. My body begins to sway, catching the notes like a current, and carve through the air with my hands, turning slow circles to the beat. The music spirits me away, almost to beach where my monitor first taught me this flight.

It isn't until the song ends and my feet stumble to a halt that I realize everyone around me has stopped dancing. For a beat, silence reigns.

And then, applause—sporadic and stunned—breaks the silence.

"That was a beautiful dance," Nanda comments, later, as we file into the house. "Where did you learn it?"

"My monitor taught it to me," I reply. It feels strange to be complimented for doing something well after doing so many things wrong.

Nanda raises her brow. "Your monitor?"

I release a nervous laugh. "If only I paid as much attention to her combat lessons as I did to her dance lessons," I mumble, followed by a wince. Maybe that isn't the best thing to say to someone who's counting on me to keep her daughter safe from akbarrin.

Mercifully, Nanda doesn't comment.

After the feast, Jun returns to guard the red gate while

Nanda frets over finding us all a place to sleep. In the end, Princess Marleyn and the others unfold their mats in the sitting room, and Valeria insists that I share a bed with her.

"Appropriate," Rae remarks. "Aryam is a child, after all."

I only stick my tongue out at her as Nanda ushers Valeria and I into the nursery. Valeria's bed is just big enough for the two of us. We squeeze in together, and Nanda tucks us in. "Story, please, Mami," Valeria yawns.

Nanda runs a hand over her daughter's forehead. A knot clenches in my stomach at the familiarity of it. How many times did this exact scene transpire between Ranee and I? "*Mija*, it's too late for a story; besides, you've heard all the ones I know."

"Then tell me one I've heard before," Valeria pleads.

I'm too embarrassed to pitch in and say that I want a story too, specifically one about a dissatisfied peasant boy who aspires to marry a moon princess, but now doesn't feel like the right time to ask.

"Not tonight, *mija*," Nanda maintains. She leans forward and presses a kiss on her daughter's forehead. "Go to sleep." My breath stops when she surprises me with a kiss to my own forehead. She pulls away, smiling kindly, though there's a weary sadness in her eyes. "You too, Lady Aryam."

Beneath the blanket, Valeria fishes for my hand, squeezing it tightly in her own once she finds it. She clutches it to her chest as she drifts away. "Good night, Lady Sinanan."

NANDA'S EAR-PIERCING scream wakes me. By the time I sit up, she's already sunk to the ground in a heap of pitiful tears. "I should have just told her a story," she whimpers.

Realization slams into me, obliterating the fogginess of sleep. I note the absence of warmth at my side, where a small body should be curled up and sleeping. Valeria's spot is empty.

. . .

"We'll find her."

I swear this vow at the red gate. Princess Marleyn and my chorus sisters stand at my back. Before me, Jun embraces his inconsolable wife. "I'll bring her back to you," I promise.

The wind tows Nanda's gut-wrenching sobs behind me. I tighten my grip on the fighting stick Princess Marleyn insisted that I borrow from the warriors. She walks beside me, carrying a stick of her own, along with the two daggers she brought from home.

Valeria went missing on my watch. She and I were in the same bed. I owe it to these people to bring her home safely.

I lead the way.

The nighttime forest is preternaturally quiet. I know for a fact that there are at least frogs here, but none of them croak. No owls hoot. The air is eerily absent of chirps, squeals, grunts and growls. Nothing. It's as if even the animals are too afraid to breathe. We take our cue from them and proceed with cautious, quiet steps, our backs ramrod straight. My shoulders, back, and quads ache from hiking through the forest and carrying my pack yesterday, but I won't let any of it stop me.

Not when Valeria needs my help.

Shortly after setting out, we emerge onto the narrow bank of a brackish river glittering in the whole moon's light. I gaze down the shoreline, toward a channel that likely lets out into the ocean. No sign of Valeria or any of the other missing children. A firm, insistent tug on my shirttail yanks my attention in the other direction, and what I see is enough to make me yelp.

Luckily, Rae is close enough to shove a hand over my mouth and stifle the noise. She glares at me with a stern warning in her eyes. Beyond her, the other three stand ready, their eyes fixed on the horrifying creature before us.

It's several times taller than a human man. Its alabaster white skin stretches taught over long, slender muscles. That's all it is—bone and muscle and glaring white skin. The creature stands with its back to us, its face tilted toward the moon. Its massive white hands, the fingers more like claws, hang idly at its side, while its feet straddle an offshoot of the river. Everything about it is unnaturally still, as if the moon has bespelled it. It is the Moongazer.

Rae slowly lowers her hand from my mouth and shoots me another warning with her eyes. She doesn't have to tell me twice. The last thing I want is to attract that monster's attention.

Sand shifting softly underfoot, we creep onto the riverbank, fanning away from each other to become five targets instead of one. I grip my staff, steeling my nerves against the overwhelming impulse to *run*.

It is one of Mam Kadejah's quiet mantras that helps me to quiet my thoughts. *Steady breath. Focused mind. Quiet, seek. Quiet, find.* I repeat it again and again until . . .

Snap!

A branch cracks beneath my foot. I stare at it with a mixture of awe and horror. How can a twig betray me like this?

The Moongazer doesn't appear to move, yet when I drag my eyes up toward its face, I find it directed toward me, its depthless eyes peering pointedly at the staff in my hand. And then the rest of its body adjusts, its neck rotating slowly, then its shoulders, torso, and legs.

"Roaring seas," Rae swears.

But I don't draw my eyes away from the Moongazer's face. It's both horrifying and lovely, if you can forgive the fact that its eyes are just two black chasms. It might have been a very beautiful man once. The confusion on its face morphs into silent outrage. The ground rumbles as the Moongazer thunders toward us, sprinting with the precise form of an elite runner.

The others disperse, spreading out farther, ojus glowing. "Aryam, *move*," Rae shouts. She nocks a rose arrow, aims, and lets it loose. It strikes the Moongazer's thigh. The flower blooms and turns the veins in the creature's legs green. The Moongazer stumbles to a halt. Its face contorts with pain as it opens its mouth skyward and unleashes a silent, furious roar. Then it focuses on Rae and lumbers toward her.

My legs remember to work.

I veer to the left just as the Moongazer pivots right, toward Rae, one arm arching back as it prepares to strike her. She runs parallel to the forest, fumbling with nocking another arrow. The others have already cleared out of the Moongazer's range, but Rae won't make it. The few ticks she spared to buy me time have cost her too much.

Something cold and desperate lances through my chest—something like the power that overtook me in the temple room. But this time, I can tell that the power is not coming from the crystal. The power comes from me.

Weightlessness spreads in my core as a familiar light blooms in my chest and pools in my hand. The light expands wider and wider until it is a sphere around my body, lifting my feet off the ground.

Mam Kadejah's mantra loops through my mind, fueling the energy somehow. Is this it? Have I found my oju at last?

Whatever it is, I need it. I need it to save Rae.

I tug at the power and, finding that I have little control over it, funnel it into my voice. "Moongazer!" I yell.

The riverbank goes still. The Moongazer freezes. And then those dark eyes are on me. It turns slowly, one section of its body at a time. Then it runs toward me. The power in my chest flares, and the sphere of light waxes and wanes. I sag toward the ground and bob up again, pulling on the power inside me to *do something. Save my friends.*

But the power peters out completely, and I crash to the ground.

"Aryam!" The cry comes from Princess Marleyn, and that's sheer terror in her voice. The Moongazer plows toward me, but in another instant, it surges forward, its legs entangled by a fluorescent green vine. Chyou holds the rose arrow end of it while Rae and Princess Marleyn tug the other end. Then, faster than any human should be able to move, Chyou laps around the Moongazer's legs, binding them.

The Moongazer pitches forward, its bony, spindly fingers crash down just inches from my feet. Maya, with her oju sword blazing, hops onto the creature's hand and sprints the length of its arm, leaping onto its shoulder. She swings her blade down against the back of its neck and severs its head.

THEY SPRINT FOR ME. My heart pounds inside my chest, and blood sings in my ears. The world dances as Princess Marleyn and my chorus sisters pull me to my feet. My eyes lock on the viscous black blood seeping from the Moongazer's neck. A whole river of it.

"What *was* that?" Rae demands. But it's not anger or contempt in her voice. It's fear. "Aryam, you . . . you were glowing."

My head throbs. "Maybe it was my oju?" I suggest.

Rae shakes her head. "No. Oju don't do that. I've never seen anything like that."

I wrap a hand around my crystal. Did it do something to me that evening in the temple room? Pass something to me, perhaps?

Princess Marleyn steps forward. It's her voice I hear screeching through my mind in terror. *Aryam!* That terror still lingers in her eyes as she speaks. "We should keep—"

A whistling sound cuts her off. An arrow lands at my feet. Princess Marleyn cries out, blood seeping from her upper arm. The arrow must have grazed it.

My chorus sisters launch into action. Rae fires a rose arrow toward the tree line. It lands, emitting a cloud of thick green gas that obscures us from view. Maya's and Chyou's ojus flash back into their hands.

"I'm okay," Princess Marleyn huffs, tearing a strip from her shirt. She quickly wraps it around her arm. Her eyes dart between me and the tree line, and if I didn't know any better, I'd say she's more worried about me.

That's fair. My body feels strange after what happened, and I need my staff for balance almost as much as I need it for fighting. I start to reassure her, to lie and say I'll be fine, but armed men and women emerge from the gas cloud. Soldiers. And the insignia on their chest . . .

Princess Marleyn and I lock eyes. Those are Princess Chiwa's soldiers.

They must have tracked us here. But how and why?

Princess Marleyn seizes my arm and drags me out of their line of sight, hiding me behind the Moongazer's body. Rae launches five rose arrows at once, a vine net between them. She manages to ensnare a handful of soldiers. Chyou and Maya charge into the fray. The princess assesses the battle, then me. "Stay here," she pleads.

I sway on my feet. "But . . . "

She smiles disarmingly. "I know," she says. "It's your duty to protect me, but you can't really do that in your condition." She firmly presses me back. "I'll be fine," she promises. And then she races toward the fighting.

CHAPTER SIXTEEN

I really, really don't want to, but I fall back against the Moongazer's body. It's cold and still and as solid as a wall. All around me, battle sounds clang through the midnight air. I heave myself forward and stagger into the Moongazer's muscular arm.

Princess Marleyn strikes and parries with power and finesse, gracefully carving her way through the throng of soldiers. It's no wonder that she neglected her dance lessons as a child. Evidently, the battlefield is her dance floor. She and Rae fight in concert, Rae slicing through enemies with the blades that have manifested on the ends of her bow. Either of them alone would make a formidable opponent, but together—they're a tempest, sweeping through the battlefield with devastating precision.

Chyou and Maya unleash a storm of their own, with Chyou zipping through the field at twice the speed of her opponents. With a single, powerful strike, she sends soldiers soaring. Maya wields her flame sword with steady, practiced ease. She's not as fast as the others, but her sword's flames buy her the space she needs, keeping the soldiers around her at bay.

There is something mesmerizing and poetic about the four of them fighting together.

There will be songs written about their greatness.

I sigh as I drop to my feet. And parodies sung about my uselessness.

I must join the fight.

The aftereffects of that power surge linger in my blood, but I find that I can stand without clinging to the Moongazer's corpse. I adjust my grip on my staff and take one step toward the fight.

"Aryam!"

My name on the wind halts my feet. The hairs rise on my arms.

"Aryam!"

That voice.

I glance toward the princess and my sisters. It isn't coming from them.

"Aryam!"

Ranee.

I whip my head toward the trees. It's coming from there.

"Aryam! Aryam! Aryam!"

I find the strength to run, pumping my arms as hard as I can. I run toward her voice, leaving the battlefield behind, leaving the princess and my chorus sisters behind. "Ranee!" My chest and throat burn as I force her name through my lips. I stand at the jungle's edge, searching frantically.

She isn't here.

"Aryam!"

It's her. Ranee is alive. "Ranee!" I glance back at the fighting. The faint lights of my quartet's oju glimmer in the distance. I'll come back. Ranee and I will help them.

She calls to me again, but her voice is far away, and growing farther still. I follow it deep into the forest, and then I lose it entirely. And when I stop to look around, I realize I'm terribly, terribly, terribly lost.

I WALK FOR MEASURES, calling every name I can think of. "Princess Marleyn! Rae! Maya! Chyou! Ranee! Jun! Nanda!" No one responds. The forest swallows my voice whole. I go until I can't go any farther, and then I collapse on an exposed tree root and fall into a deep, vulnerable sleep.

Thirst and hunger torment me when I wake. I walk again, sleep again, wake again.

This time, there's laughter.

Children's laughter.

I sit. "Valeria?"

Something rustles in the bushes. I crawl on my hands and knees toward it. The laughter rings out again. It definitely belongs to a child. I push aside leaves and branches, and I find feet, small, dirty, and bare. These ones are a darker shade than Valeria's. Another one of the missing children, then?

The feet point away from me. I sit back on my heels and draw my gaze up a tiny pair of legs, a grass skirt, a round belly.

I pause. That isn't right.

My eyes dart back down to the child's heels. The toes point away. I saw that right the first time. I drag my eyes up again. The knees point away. But the stomach faces me, as do the bare chest, the chin, and the mischievous grin full of sharp little teeth.

And that's it. Where there should be a nose and eyes, there are none, only a large, broad-brimmed hat casting half the akbarrin's face in shadow.

I scramble backward, scraping my arms and legs against thorns.

The akbarrin child's smile widens. Its lips part. "Aryam!" it cries with Ranee's voice.

"Aryam! Aryam! Aryam!" the forest echoes as more faceless children emerge from the thickets around me.

I scream. I scream and plead and scream some more. "Leave me alone!"

But I feel their hands on me, tugging, shoving, turning. I curl into a ball, shielding my face from them as they keep it up. It takes one of them tugging on my pigtails for me to sit up and bat their hands away. *"Stop!"*

They do. The akbarrin children go completely still, and if they had eyes, I'd imagine they'd be blinking right now or watering, properly chastised. My chest heaves as I stand, and the children scamper back as I tower over them. I think of the way they used Ranee's voice to lure me here. "You tricked me," I accuse.

The biggest one, still hardly reaching the middle of my thigh, says, "He made us."

He.

The little faceless ones warn me that he's coming, Bogma had declared.

I ask the question I'd rather not. "Who's he?"

The faceless children gasp. Some of them scatter, returning to their hiding places.

Only the biggest of them remains. It doesn't speak.

I swivel around, scanning the forest for threats. "Is he here now?" I ask. The child shakes its head. "Good. Then take me back to the village." I try to muster as much authority in my voice as I can.

But the child just vanishes with a poof of black smoke, and the others after it. I hear their laughter again, just beyond the thicket. I push through it and emerge onto another riverbank. The faceless children are there, prowling the water and overturning stones with sticks. One sits on a smooth rock and bites into a crab, shell and all. It wiggles in his mouth. It's a sight I wish I could unsee at once but one I know I'll never be able to.

I drop to my knees and watch as they trawl for more crabs. When I can stomach it, I ask the bigger one, "Why did you bring me here?"

It considers me with a tilt of its head, carefully clutching its prey as if I might try to take it. "You hurt Papa," it says before biting into the shell with its sharp little teeth.

Something swims toward us, parting the water with a long, flat nose, as gray as the mountain. Two eyes poke above the water's surface. The faceless children squeal and scatter, vanishing into the forest with squirming crustaceans in their grips. Only the biggest one remains.

I jump to my feet. "What is that?" Only now do I realize I left my staff where I slept. *Careless, Aryam.*

The child stands. "He only said we had to take you and the others," it says. "He didn't say we had to hurt you. Goodbye, Aryam." He disappears.

A beat ticks by before I realize "the others" means the children of the Gate.

I spin around, searching desperately. "Wait," I yell. "Where are the others? Give them to me."

A bush rustles. A child steps out of it, this one taller and fully clothed. A girl. A normal girl with eyes and a nose. More rustling. More children emerge from the bush. Ten in total. The last one runs into my arms. "Aryam!" she cries.

I stoop to catch her and squeeze her tight. "Valeria," I sigh. "You're okay."

Water ripples behind me. I turn, pressing Valeria behind my back, as a great beast emerges from the water. It is a gray, corpulent thing, with a barrel-shaped body and stubby legs. Its face is long and flat, with eyes at the top of its head, and two long floppy ears behind them.

Valeria snakes her arms around my waist and squeezes tight, hiding her face in the small of my back. The ground shakes as the thing moves toward us.

"I won't let it hurt you," I promise, scanning the beach for anything that can be used as a weapon.

The beast shakes its head and laughs dismissively. "You fell for the faceless ones' nasty little trick," it says in a woman's voice. "Don't you know they call a child's name at night, using its mother's voice to lure it away?"

My heart pounds. I disregard her taunting. "What are you?"

The animal shakes the water from its skin, jiggling rolls and rolls of fat. "I am Nasha," it says. "This is *my* river. I've come to take you to a friend."

I hold tight to Valeria. "I won't leave them," I say.

Nasha moves her head around, eyeing the whimpering children. "Sleep," she commands, and they collapse onto the sand.

I catch Valeria as she falls and lay her gently on the ground. "What did you do to them?"

"They will be safe until we get back," Nasha replies, "as long as we're back before dark. Climb onto my back. I will carry you across the river." She chuffs when I don't move. "You waste precious time. How long do you think my children can hide your whereabouts from *him*?"

I narrow my eye at her skeptically. "Those faceless ones are *your* children?"

She smiles, if such a creature can do such a thing. "Sometimes mine, sometimes no." She turns, stamping her feet and flashing me her hindquarters. I'm surprised to see that she wears a skirt of vines and palm leaves. I can't help but stifle a laugh. It looks ridiculous.

Nasha chuffs and steps toward the river. "I'm going to lower myself in the water now. Climb on."

"How do I know I can trust you?" I ask, straightening up again. Every ounce of sense I have warns me not to.

"Precious time, girl." She stomps her hooves impatiently. "Climb on. That is, if you'd like to get your little friends here to safety by nightfall."

I don't like it. I don't like it all, but as she lowers into the water, I wade in after her and slide onto her back. She's wearing something else around the front half of her body, tied in the back with a cord. A bra, maybe, which is another silly, ridiculous article of clothing for a creature like this. I grab on to it as she begins to drift toward the middle of the river. "How do I know you won't just eat me?" I ask. Ranee told me a story once of a crocodile that carried a monkey on its back with every intention of stealing its liver for a soup recipe. The monkey was clever and evaded the snare, but I'm too tired and hungry and weak to pull off a similar feat.

Nasha chortles and I have to grip the cord harder to keep from slipping into the water from the way her body shakes with laughter. "If I wanted to eat you, girl, I could have already."

CHAPTER SEVENTEEN

The river splits around a small island. I slide off Nasha's back as she clambers ashore, relieved to have my liver intact rather than carved up for soup. "This way," she says, shuffling toward two slender trees with pale, peeling trunks. She strides between them and vanishes, leaving a clear view of the boulder that sits behind them.

I weigh my options. Follow the talking hippo creature into a mysterious portal or risk the arduous swim back to shore in my weakened state. But if I don't go, perhaps Nasha will leave Valeria and the others in their slumber. I groan and follow her in.

It is not the hippo creature that I find awaiting me on the other side, but a woman. She is short and squat and half-naked, apart from the grass skirt and brown bandeau wrapped around her chest. I know she is Nasha at once. I eye her warily. "How?"

She waves a hand, gesturing to the land around her. It is like the jungle we left behind, tree for tree, but dimmer, and the river has run dry. "Welcome to the Shadows," she says. "Here, I can easily shift between forms."

I nearly jump out of my skin. "You brought me to the

Shadows?" I hiss. "How is that better than being hunted by this mystery man in my own realm? Won't it be easier for him to find me here?"

"Which is why you'd be wise not to mention it until we get inside," she warns icily. "Even the winds report to him."

I slap two hands over my mouth to stifle a gasp. She's brought me to a hell.

Nasha turns for a round, stone cottage where the boulder from my realm ought to be. She waddles inside, and this time I follow without hesitation, if only to escape prying winds.

The space is much more commodious and inviting than I expected. Incandescent stones glow bright, lighting up the space, and colorful tapestries adorn the walls. A large stone table, hollow and filled with water and petals, takes up the center of the room. Leaning over it is a breathtaking boy with brown skin and red hair. He turns as we enter, flashing a charming smile when he sees me. "Hi, pigtails."

"KYREL!" His name bubbles out of me amid a rush of tears. I lunge for him, falling against his flat chest and wrapping my arms desperately around his firm waist, not caring what Ranee or Rae or anyone else would say. He's here—in my arms.

Kyrel's eyes widen with surprise, then crinkle with delight. He carefully frees himself from my grasp. "Still a crybaby, I see."

"How did you get here?" I sputter. He looks the same as I left him—tall and strong, but also a little happier. There's a joyful glimmer in his red-brown eyes that wasn't there before. A tick later, I realize I've asked a serious question. My smile fades, and I step back from him. How *did* he get here?

Kyrel's smile vanishes, too. That glimmer in his eyes gutters out. Hesitation contorts his handsome face. "I . . . " He hooks the palm of his hand on the back of his neck, then drops his hand to his side, and dread builds up inside of me as I realize I've never seen him hesitate before.

Kyrel sighs. He gestures vaguely with an open hand. "The Shadows are my home," he confesses. "This is where . . . this is where I hatched."

The word may as well be a sledgehammer and me a sheet of ice. "Hatched?" I repeat. I take another step back.

Kyrel raises both hands, palms facing out, as if pleading with me not to do anything crazy. "I'm a dragon."

I think my heart will punch its way through my rib cage. "You. Are. A dragon?" Each word tastes bitter with the tang of fear.

His silence confirms it.

"At Dragon's Fall," I murmur, "you didn't like the play."

"Elrey's fall signaled the imprisonment of my people."

I gaze up at him. "Your eyes. Your hair."

"The only trace of my kind," he explains. "Unlike Nasha, I can't transform. Whatever Nalini did to contain her father, it bound my powers, too."

I shake my head, hardly able to hear his words over the roaring of my blood. "Are there others?" I demand. "Others like you in the human realm?"

He shakes his head. "I don't think so. I might be the only one, or at least the last one."

So many things make sense now. His strange features. The way he's so handsome and charming and confident, bordering on arrogant. He looks and acts like a dragon. I was just too infatuated with him to see it. How could I be so blind?

"Ary," he says carefully, as if he can read the panic in my eyes. "I'm *good*. You *know* I'm good."

He's not. He's a dragon. Dragons are bad.

I turn and find Nasha blocking the door with her plump body. "Take me back."

I can't believe I almost kissed him. I *wanted* to kiss him. It would have been even more of a betrayal than I thought. Before, I only thought I'd be breaking a blood oath that would never be called in, not betraying all of humanity.

"Don't be ridiculous," Nasha says. "You've both come all this way. You can at least hear the boy out."

Wood scrapes against wood. I turn to see Kyrel pulling back a chair from the table. He smiles. It's as charming as ever, if only a little nervous. "Please," he says. It's a word I realize I've never heard him say. "Sit."

I do, but not because he asks. Because I'm tired. *So tired.* I could sleep for days. "A dragon in Irez for almost a score," I murmur numbly. My gaze flutters to his. "You lied to me."

"I didn't," he retorts. "I just . . . didn't tell you."

I huff. "You know I don't like secrets."

He pulls back another chair and sits down. "You kept a few of your own."

But we're not here to talk about me. We're here to talk about him. I narrow my eyes. "Why did you come to Irez in the first place?" I demand. I won't let him charm me into being a hopelessly romantic, fawning fool. Not again.

He puts on an air of contrition. "I was looking for Yara's teardrop," he confesses. "The crystal Ranee gave you. Do you still have it?"

My hand flies to my sternum and grasps at bare skin. "It's gone," I exclaim, jumping to my feet.

But then I remember the way the little faceless ones grasped at me in the jungle before I found the courage to bat them all away. I turn to Nasha. "Your children."

Nasha rolls her eyes. "I will retrieve it." She vanishes through the door, and I almost think to follow her. But she's right. The least I can do is hear Kyrel out.

I glare at him. "Did you manipulate me?" I demand.

He frowns. “I don’t know what you mean.”

“I am a guardian. I am not supposed to have . . . feelings like the ones I have—had—for you.” My cheeks flush at the admission. “Did you somehow change me?” Because it shouldn’t be possible for me to feel the way I do—did. The more time I spend around the other guardians, the more I realize that.

He bristles at that. “I told you. I don’t have any powers, especially not that sort.” His expression softens. “You . . . really don’t know. Do you?”

“Know what?”

He shakes his head and mutters something to himself. “The faceless ones say you glowed.”

“The faceless ones don’t have eyes,” I point out.

“That doesn’t mean they can’t see.”

Whatever he’s getting at, I don’t want to be a part of it. “I only glowed because of the crystal,” I say, “or the teardrop, or whatever you call it. What’s the deal with that thing, anyway? I think it did something strange to me.”

Kyrel leans forward. “That teardrop was a gift from the Moon Princess to the Dragon Princess’s daughter. It brought something out of you, maybe.”

“It brought what out of me?” I ask, not sure I want to know.

“Your true power,” he says.

I shake my head. “I don’t have power.” Not inherently, at least. “Humans don’t have power.” Only akbarrin do. Even guardians only borrow their power, yielding it back to the earth when they die.

Kyrel pauses and then says, “Yara’s tear would only react that way to a direct descendant of the dragon she gave it to.”

He’s lying.

"You're lying," I blurt out. What kind of sordid game is this?

He shakes his head again. "When you met me, did your heart sing? Did you feel it rejoice? That's what dragon's blood does when—"

I find the strength to stand. "I do *not* have dragon's blood."

"Not a lot of it," he concedes. "Not enough to ever transform, even if the barrier between our worlds was completely removed."

"I don't have *any* dragon's blood," I argue. "Guardians are fully human. They must be to wield an oju."

"Yet, you don't have an oju."

"Because I never bothered to learn," I reason. "Because I was lazy, and childish, and always pining after . . . " I stop myself from saying it—*you*.

He stares me down before trying another approach. "The name Ranee means queen. Did you know that?"

I'm shaking now, backing toward the doorway. "Ranee was *not* a queen," I explode, and I think of what he's implying by insisting that she was. "And she was not my . . . "

Nasha's words from earlier slam into my mind. What she said about the faceless ones. They call a child's name at night and use its mother's voice to lure it away.

Mother.

Nasha had deliberately used that word. Those creepy little akbarrin can only fool a child by using its *mother's* voice.

I think I might faint, but I force myself to remain standing. He's telling the truth. I know it now in my soul, no matter how much I wish it weren't so. Kyrel is telling the truth. Ranee is my mother, and *I* am not a guardian. My heart stutters. "Then Princess Marleyn . . . "

"Is likely *your* guardian," Nasha's voice confirms from behind. She's returned with Yara's tear dangling in her hand.

"The little ones tell me how she cried out for you on the riverbank. My guess is that she's known it all along."

My heart. It's pounding so fast. I press my nails into the palms of my hands to keep from keeling over. Then I reach out and snatch the teardrop from Nasha's hand. Kyrel eyes it as I loop it back around my neck. He could take it, I realize, if this is really what he's been looking for, but he doesn't make a move on it. "Take me back to them," I demand. I don't bother to stop Kyrel when he insists on coming along.

THE CHILDREN STIR awake as we approach the shore. Valeria splashes into the water. "Aryam!" she cries. I slide off Nasha's back and wade toward the girl, wrapping her in a hug when I reach her.

"I'm taking you home now," I promise.

"The faceless ones cannot take you home without risking their necks," Nasha says. "He is bound to be furious with them for returning the teardrop to you." She tilts her head down the river. "Go that way, and you'll find a bog."

"How will a bog help us find her friends?" Kyrel asks.

But I think I know, and the thought is enough to make me want to vomit. I groan and turn to the children. "Whatever you do," I warn them, as Rae warned me just a few days ago, "eat every bite and be polite."

CHAPTER EIGHTEEN

Bogma shelters us for the night. The children manage to scarf down Mama Anura's cooking with hardly a grimace between them, a sign that they're surely starving. I suppress the wave of nausea that threatens to overtake me and lift a shaky spoonful of frog soup to my lips. Valeria giggles at me before draining her own bowl with a hearty slurp.

I wince and then smile. She reminds me of Darien's little sisters and brothers. How I miss them all.

For once, guilt doesn't hound me at the thought of home—only confusion. I am not a guardian. I am allowed to feel. It's an unsettling concept.

A glance at Kyrel's bowl finds it as empty as Valeria's. He winks at me when our eyes meet, and out of instinct, I try to subdue the flutter in my heart.

I am allowed to feel.

The next morning, I lead the children away from Bogma's house. I have no idea how the trails work, but Rae said that the Bog House will let us out wherever we want to go. *Take us back to the Gate,* I plead.

Relief washes over me as a familiar road comes into view, the one that led us to the Gate yesterday. "It's only a few measures' walk away from here," I announce to the children, eliciting delighted giggles. They race ahead, leaving me and Kyrel behind.

Warmth flushes my cheeks as we walk awkwardly beside each other. *Say something, Aryam. Sweet moons, anything.* But I come up short.

Kyrel watches me. "Do you want to talk about Ranee?"

"No." The rejection is quicker and sharper than I intended. My gaze cuts to the ground. I stare at my feet for a few ticks, feeling the heat of his gaze on me, and sigh. "It's just . . . she lied to me about everything." She told me that I was a guardian and that she was my monitor. She told me I couldn't have friends or love. She pushed me to search for an oju she knew I would never find. Even in the end, even when they came for me, she didn't tell me the truth."

"I understand," he says. Even though he says it so earnestly, I want to tell him there's no way he could understand, but . . . "Sometimes, I wish I could speak to my parents, too."

My resolve sputters.

"They died almost a thousand score ago," he shares. "My egg was hidden and enchanted with protection, meant to hatch in a time safe for dragons, but I hatched sooner."

"I'm sorry," I apologize. That he lost his parents. That I could be so inconsiderate. That both of us must be so alone. But then I realize it. Maybe we don't have to be. "I'm not a guardian," I blurt out.

He stares at me. "I'm not sure I follow," he says. "We've established that."

I nod. "I'm not a guardian," I repeat. "Maybe I can look past your not being entirely human, and we can . . . " For a tick, his stern gaze makes me pause. I find myself rethinking every interaction we've had, that attraction I thought I felt between us. What if I only imagined it? What if he was just playing me the whole time?

But then I remember the way he stared into my eyes that night at Dragon's Fall, the kiss we almost had, the smile he reserves only for me. No. I didn't make it up, not any of it.

"I'm not saying we should be together," I say—even if I can get past his ancestry. "I just think we don't have to be alone."

We've stopped walking now. The children's peals of laughter have grown distant.

Kyrel regards me with a pained expression. I can see him weighing his words as he sorts through the turmoil in his mind. "You don't get it. Dragons do not fall in love with humans." The hope that had begun to blossom in my chest flickers out as he walks away.

THE GATE IS a smoldering mess by the time we reach it. Kyrel and I find the children whimpering at its entrance, clinging to one another in sorrow. There are three adults among them, a woman and two men. I quickly count their heads and realize we're missing just as many children. "Where is Valeria?" I cry. Panic grips my heart. I promised her mother I'd bring her home.

The young woman steps forward. "I'm here," she says, cupping my chin and turning my eyes to meet hers. I know it instantly. These are Valeria's eyes, the same she shares with her mother. But Valeria is just a little girl. At least, she *was* just a little girl only beats ago. Now she towers over me the way her father does.

"How?" I stammer.

Pain lines her gaze. "If I'm big, it means one of my parents . . . " Her eyes widen in horror as silent tears spill down her cheeks. She releases my face and sprints through the gate. Doing so must trigger some akbarral alarm because all throughout the ruined village, guardians stumble out of their homes. Jun is among them, one leg bandaged and an arm bound to his chest. He hobbles toward his daughter and manages not to topple over when she crashes into him, sobbing for her mother.

A fist grips my heart. She sounds so much like Nanda the night I departed.

I look around at all the damage. "What happened here?"

A flash of green yanks my attention to the front of Jun's house. I focus my eyes and find Rae standing there, rose bow in hand. The instant our eyes lock, her oju vanishes and she charges toward me. I freeze, steeling myself for a verbal lashing, but it never comes. Instead, she slams into me, wraps her arms too tight around my neck, and squeezes.

"What are you doing?" I choke.

Her soft face presses against mine, smelling like flowers and soap, even as the village around us still reeks of carnage. "I'm hugging you."

Despite everything, that makes me laugh. I don't have the heart to tell her that this isn't hugging; it's choking. When she pulls away, she's smiling, too—Rae, *smiling*. But she discards that smile as soon as she notices Kyrel at my side. The rose bow blinks into her hand once more. "Who is *he*?" she demands.

Kyrel extends a hand. "Kyrel Durago," he introduces himself, wearing an arrogant smile that has the same effect on Rae that it had on the villagers back in Irez. I watch as her suspicion morphs into outright disdain. Her gaze slides to me, harboring the question of whether she should put an arrow between his eyes.

I slide between them and say, "We can trust him." I hope.

Her eyes narrow into slits, but after a second, the rose bow vanishes.

I glance over the village, my eyes resting on Jun and his

grown daughter sobbing in each other's arms. "What happened here?" I ask again.

Rae casts another mistrustful glance in Kyrel's direction before replying. "Those soldiers attacked the village before they tracked us down." She glances toward Jun and Valeria. "Nanda and a few others didn't make it."

Sorrow washes over me at the thought that Valeria will never see her mother again. I push it back, trying not to think of my own 'mother.' "Where are the soldiers now?" I ask.

"Dead," Rae replies. "Jun and his people regrouped and reinforced us on the beach. It was . . . brutal."

A vision of an arrow grazing Marleyn's arm flashes before my eyes. I gasp. "Where's Princess Marleyn?" Calling her *princess*, at least out loud, is a force of habit now, and one I'll happily cling to. I'm not sure I'm ready to give up the ruse or to face the truth about myself.

"This way," Rae murmurs. The glare she levels at Kyrel makes it clear that he's not welcome to follow. I flash him an apologetic wince. One thing at a time.

Marleyn sits on the bed in Valeria's nursery, a room I guess will no longer be needed. She's shirtless, wearing only the bandages wrapped tight around her torso. Relief eases my worries as I realize that her wound is only of the flesh. Maya sits beside her, her brow bent low in thought. It seems as though the two of them are in the middle of an intense conversation, but they look up as we enter.

At the sight of me, Marleyn leans forward, as if to get up, but winces and falls back. It looks like she's been hurt elsewhere. I rush to her side and assume the stool that Maya vacates. I press her back down. "You're okay" is all she says, her voice heavy with relief.

I nod and confirm it. "Yes, princess. I am."

She tenses. It's enough to confirm what Nasha said after

Kyrel told me who I really am: Marleyn's known all along. That's why she's been so distant to the other guardians, and maybe why she wishes I could have met King Felix. Why she calls him King instead of Father. He wasn't *her* father; he was mine.

A tender pain aches in my chest. That evening in Irez. I'd chastised Ranee for thinking that the king would send gifts to our village to honor two humble servants. I scorned the idea that he cared for us at all. I thought he'd only done it to honor his daughter. It turns out, I had no idea how right I was. But Ranee. She knew.

Why didn't she tell me then?

I fight back the tears that threaten to fall. I should tell Marleyn that I know the truth, but I *can't*. "What happened to you?" I ask instead. The only wound I saw before I left was the one to her arm, but now there's the bandage around her torso as well. She'd been fighting so well. How could she have let her guard down?

She frowns. "I got distracted," she murmurs.

The realization sinks in. She got distracted because of me. She must have when she realized I'd run off. I swallow. "Well, I'm glad you're okay," I murmur. I look around. "Where's Chyou?"

Maya stirs behind me. She's been posted at the door during our conversation. "I'll find her," she offers, slipping out of the room and leaving me and Marleyn alone.

"I won't be able to move for a few days," Marleyn murmurs. "We won't make it out of Eroden's Pass and back to the capital in time to stop Chiwa from making a move on the throne."

"Then you stay here," I suggest, squeezing her hands, "and I'll take Eroden's Pass myself."

She shakes her head, eyes widening. "Aryam, *no*," she protests, and I finally understand her fear. It's a guardian's fear.

It's been her fear since the morning since she saved me in the labyrinth.

I don't let up on the pressure on her hands. "I have a duty," I remind her, though now I know it's bigger than finding an oju. Marleyn must have known that, too, must have known that whatever lies at the end of Eroden's Pass is just for me. "I'm going to fulfill it."

She smiles or winces. It's hard to tell. Then she sighs. "You're very brave, Aryam," she whispers, closing her eyes. "You don't know it, but you are."

A shuffle of footsteps sounds behind us. I turn to see Maya and Chyou, the latter covered in sweat from head to toe, her long, dark bangs plastered to her forehead. Surprise and awe register on her usually stoic face. "You're really here," she says as Rae squeezes in behind her.

I offer her an earnest smile but don't move to hug her. Something tells me she wouldn't appreciate a hug. "Hi, Chyou," I say instead.

Chyou grins. It's the second time I've seen her smile so brightly away from the battlefield. I gaze between my chorus sisters, seeing them all in a new light. They are bound to me, and now I know that I am bound to them. I choose them.

One day, I will free them from this bond so that they can choose me, too.

MARLEYN INSISTS that I wait one full day before venturing into the mountains, and I don't argue. The next morning, I wake up to the tantalizing aroma of peppers, onions, and salted fish. I follow my nose to the kitchen, where Valeria labors over the stove, humming a sweet melody as she cooks. I stretch, alleviating the soreness in my back. "When did you learn to cook?" I ask, stifling a yawn.

She turns, setting her stirring spoon on the counter, and smiles her mother's smile when she sees me. In another tick, she's crossed the room and swept me into a warm, tight hug, clutching my head to her chest. She kisses the top of my head and holds on a tick longer. "Good morning, Aryam," she says, before releasing me and returning to her work. I follow her to the stove and peer into the skillet. "I've helped my mother in this kitchen for hundreds of score," she explains after a long pause spent watching the vegetables sizzle in oil. "The children at the Gate lose their memories over time. It preserves their innocence and protects them from the boredoms of immortality, but shortly after I transformed, it all came back to me. I now know everything I need to know to defend this village and keep Eroden's Pass safe."

I nod. I suppose it makes sense, in a strange way. "Do you also know a story about a boy who married the moon?" I ask. Her stirring hand halts, and then she quietly nods.

"I remember that, too," she admits. "Why don't you help me with breakfast, and I'll tell you the story?"

"I NEED you to stay and look after the princess." Outside Jun's hut, three members of my court stand before me, looking none too pleased with my request. No, it's not a request. It's a command. They may see me as their leader, but I am also their princess.

They're covered in sweat and grime from cleaning the village and tending to the wounded before breakfast, even Rae. "You can't go alone," she counters. "It's too dangerous."

"I won't be alone," I point out, nodding toward Kyrel, who helps one of the villagers right a livestock fence on the other side of the pasture.

Rae narrows her eyes. "I know you think that boy is your friend, but I don't trust him."

"Me either," Maya agrees honestly.

"Yeah, he's weird," Chyou pitches in.

"He's always been good to me," I reassure them. I clasp my hands around the crystal and remember that he let me walk out of Nasha's home with it, and he saw me safely back to my friends. I set my chin. "I'll be safe." I need them to stay with Marleyn. We'll need her at full strength.

Rae continues to smolder. "If you aren't back in three days, I'm going in," she says.

"Noted," I agree. "Then, I guess we'd better go now."

I say goodbye to them. Valeria rushes out to supply me with a pack stuffed with a sleeping mat, food, and supplies. "Look after yourself, little one," she says, heaving the pack onto my back. My shoulders protest the weight with a whining ache.

But I laugh. "Yesterday, *you* were a little kid," I remind her.

She tilts her head. "An immortal little kid," she reminds me, "much older than you." She tugs fondly at one of my pigtails. "You saved my life and my friends' lives, and you brought me back to my father. I am indebted to you." Her shoulders grow tense as Kyrel approaches, and I realize with dismay that she trusts him about as much as my guardians do. She hands him his pack with less care.

I suppose Kyrel has *always* had this effect on strangers. I was the bridge to help him connect in Irez. I can do the same for him here.

"Look after her," Valeria commands. She turns to me and smiles. "And if you aren't back in three days, *I'm* coming in, too."

So, she'd heard that. I nod, mustering bravery.

"You know you don't have an oju," Kyrel says, after we have passed through the iron gate at the head of Eroden's Pass, after the others are well out of earshot. "So, why are you still doing this?"

I gaze down the path ahead, a dirt road wedged between rock walls. "Marleyn knew I had no oju, too," I reply, "and yet she still deemed this mission necessary. I am meant to find whatever awaits us at the end of Eroden's Pass."

CHAPTER NINETEEN

"I'm surprised, pigtails," Kyrel comments a few measures later, after the two of us have ascended the sharp incline at the trailhead. We now walk the narrow path along the mountain range's spine, the part of the trail that gives this region its name. Dragon's Back. On both sides, rocky slopes slide into a lush forest below. I shudder at the thought of what creatures, besides the faceless ones and Bogma, lurk there now that there's an opening between our world and theirs.

"Why?" I ask. I walk carefully in front of him. Since we left, the only noise between us has been the sound of gravel crunching underfoot.

"We've been hiking since early morning, and you haven't whined once."

"Hmph," I remark, feigning indignation. But the familiar ease of his voice as he makes his jest brings a warm smile to my face. He's laying it on thick, all the teasing, but maybe he's making up for lost time. I suppose I can't really blame him for trying to force things to seem normal.

"It's getting dark," he says, after a few more measures trickle by.

"We should stop." We've reached a spot wide and round enough to unroll our sleeping sacks. I can't be sure that if we keep walking, we'll find another spot like it; and it wouldn't be wise to keep hiking in the dark, not when the path is treacherously thin at times.

I nod and lower my pack from my aching shoulders. He's right. I haven't been complaining, even though my back and shoulders and the arches of my feet scream with soreness. But I can't complain, and I can't turn back.

Kyrel drops his pack, then stoops to one knee to rifle through it. "I'll start a fire," he offers.

"Can't you just spit one out?" I blurt the words out before I can consider how insensitive they might be. His freezes, his shoulders pinched tight. *Smooth, Aryam.*

His shoulders relax, and he lets out a breath. "Again, I can't access my powers."

"Is that what you want?" I ask. "To break the seal on your powers?" Bring back the akbarrin and the certain end of humanity?

He bristles at my questions. He's always done that, I realize, bristled when anyone questioned or challenged him. Dragon pride. Many in Irez called it arrogance. I soften my voice. "I need to know," I plead. Even if he says he can never fall in love with me, there must be some small part of him that cares. Why else did he go to Irez? Why did he stay there all those months and befriend me?

It couldn't just have been for the teardrop. If it was, what's to stop him from taking it from me now?

His pupils flare, then shrink with focus. They expand again as he studies me, staring at my face as though he's seeing me differently than he ever has before.

"You've seen the Shadows," he says slowly. "You know the bleak world I hatched into, the place your ancestor condemned all akbarrin to live in for eternity. My people have lived and died in that darkness."

Hatched. My breath catches at that word as if I need to continually remind myself that he's not human, even as his words border on treasonous. Treason against *me*, against the nation of people I am destined to serve. "Donomar gave everyone the chance to live here," I remind him.

His nostrils flare. "Only if they denied themselves and renounced their gifts," he snarls. I flinch away from him. I've never heard him make such a sound, never heard him raise his voice at me.

"The Shadows have cracked open and akbarrin are wreaking havoc," I reason. I rattle off a list of the terrifying creatures I've encountered over the past week. "The Moongazer, the faceless ones, the emberfiends! Look at what they did to my father . . . to my parents." My voice cracks. Why can't he see that allowing the akbarrin back into Beldemar would pose danger to us all?

"Akbarrin have existed quietly in this realm for sixteen score, and no one besides the people they have helped have noticed," he argues. "Nasha protects the forest. Father Wood and the little faceless ones mind the animals. Bogma feeds the orphans."

The third example hits its mark. I imagine a little Rae, defenseless and neglected by her monitor, surviving off of frog soup, so desperate for survival that her oju manifested just so she could shoot down a piece of fruit. "Maybe you're right. Maybe *some* of the akbarrin are good."

He exploits my admission. "Those people don't deserve to rot in the Shadows," he says.

I frown. "But what about the ones who do?" I ask. "Breaking the seal doesn't just let the good akbarrin in. It lets *all* of them in, including the ones who hate mankind and want to destroy us."

"The risks that akbarrin pose to humans have been

egregiously exaggerated," he says, "and there are far more *good* akbarrin who would aid man against those who do intend harm."

"It's a lot to think about," I admit, wishing suddenly that I could consult either of my parents. I collapse on the ground. "How am I going to do this?" I whisper. "How can I be responsible for decisions like this?" Alone.

"You're young and inexperienced," he says, as if he isn't also, "but that isn't a weakness. Your strength is that you can do things differently and not make the same mistakes as your ancestors."

I shudder. Who, exactly, *are* my ancestors?

IN THE MORNING, we eat a breakfast of dried salt fish and raw peppers before setting out again. I devour mine too quickly and am left wanting. Days of trekking through the forest really build up an appetite. Hunger must be written clear across my face because Kyrel breaks his fish in two pieces, offering me the larger of the two. "Take it," he insists when I hesitate. "I've never required much in this form."

In this form. I would be lying if I said hearing him say such a thing didn't freak me out just a little. I nod and take the fish, demolishing it in three bites.

Kyrel laughs.

I've forgotten how much I love his laugh. It's such a rare thing. But something about it seems off. Forced. I shake it off and smile back at him. A peace offering.

Maybe I can't bring myself to agree with everything he said last night, and maybe I'll never fully trust the akbarrin, but I know that I can trust this one.

Kyrel reaches toward my face and wipes a crumb away from the corner of my mouth with the tip of his thumb. I see it in slow motion. His thumb. My lips. Our smiles. "Still a glutton, I see," he teases, knocking the smile right off my face. He's up and on his feet before I can defend myself, strapping his pack to his broad, muscular shoulders.

Moons. How can he do that? Pretend everything's normal, as if he didn't trample my heart the other day with his cool declaration.

Dragons do not fall in love with humans.

I crumple up the cloth my food was wrapped in and throw it at him. "Don't be so rude."

He catches the cloth in one hand before it strikes, thanks to his stupid dragon reflexes, I suppose, and laughs again. Twice in one morning. "Forgive me," he entreats, shoving the cloth in his pocket. A dragon asking for forgiveness? *There's* something you never read in the scrolls. It's too bad it's just a joke.

We set off as soon as the first rays of sunshine light our path. If we're lucky, we'll reach the fifth peak before noon. A piercing glimmer in the distance marks our destination, as bright as a star. "What do you think is there?" I ask, carefully evading a treacherous patch of loose gravel.

"I don't know," he admits.

Things aren't awkward between us like they were yesterday. We talk. We talk as we always have. I ask after the place and people I once considered home. Disappointment sinks in when Kyrel tells me he hasn't spoken to Katina or Darien since I left. I'm not sure I expected Katina to stick around, but Darien . . . he promised. When Kyrel showed up to our village the way he did last summer, everyone wanted to run him out of town, but Darien promised me he'd try to be his friend no matter what. He promised to do that for me.

I couldn't do it for myself.

At least I thought I couldn't.

It turns out I was capable of making friends all along.

In fact, I've always had everything I ever wanted. Friends. Family. Desires of my own that had nothing to do with protecting Marleyn. I should have seen it. I hesitated to bow when I first met Marleyn. I resented her because I thought my life was chained to hers.

But it was the other way around.

The guardians are chained to me.

My vision blurs.

Kyrel stops walking and sniffs. "I can smell your tears," he says. He turns and studies me. "What's wrong?"

I wipe my eyes with the back of my hands and shudder. "I don't want to be a princess," I confess. "I want that even less than I wanted to be a guardian."

He goes unnaturally still for a beat before asking, "What *do* you want, Aryam Sinanan?"

His words startle me into drawing a sharp breath. No one has ever asked me this question before. But I know the answer almost instantly.

Marleyn, Rae, Chyou, Maya. They each deserve lives of their own. No one should be chained in service to another unless they choose it, and even then, they deserve the chance to change their mind. To walk away. I release my breath and say, "I want my people to be free, too."

CHAPTER TWENTY

As we crest the fourth peak, the fifth looms into view and the shining light atop it morphs into a golden palace as a chilling gust of wind slams against us. I stumble into Kyrel, and he catches me, setting me back on my own feet as the wind dies down. "A palace," I exclaim, taking in the towering, claw-sharp spires and thick, thorny vines that snake around the edifice, shrouding the translucent windows that shimmer like gems.

"The Golden Palace," Kyrel murmurs. His eyes, for once, are as wide and surprised as mine. "They've really let this place go."

"It's magnificent." It takes a beat for his words to catch up with me. "Wait," I say. "You've been here before?" I recall Jun telling me that no one had entered the pass in almost a thousand score.

Kyrel's eyes narrow. His pupils slide in my direction. "I've heard tales of this place," he says, with a shrug. "It's just not what I was expecting."

You can trust him, Aryam, I remember, chastising myself for my momentary lapse of faith. I try to shrug it off. "Well, I think it's more exquisite than anything I've ever seen." If not a little creepy at the same time.

He nods. "Dragons love their riches," he comments.

We descend the ridge to find a rope bridge awaiting us. My stomach lurches at the sight of the ancient thing swaying over a perilous drop. A white-capped river roars hundreds of feet below. "That doesn't look safe," I comment. Nor do the derelict stairs on the other side of it, jutting toward the palace and narrowly hugging the cliff wall.

A pebble falls at my feet, having tumbled down from overhead. Kyrel and I whip our gazes upward just in time to see a flash of black. He snarls, the sound so guttural that I have to force myself not to flinch. "We're not alone," he says. Then he darts onto the bridge, each wooden plank groaning beneath his feet.

A wave of nausea overwhelms my gut, threatening to liberate its contents, but I think of everyone depending on me and fight it back down. I have to find whatever's in that palace, and I can't die while doing it. Because if I die . . . The nausea surges again . . . Rae. Marleyn. Chyou. Maya. They die, too. Instantly.

So, I study the planks, noting every darkened mossy spot that suggests rot and weakness. My eyes travel along the ropes, eyeing the areas where they've begun to fray. I count the missing planks. Then I gather my breath, drop my pack onto the ground, and step onto the first plank, balancing my weight as best I can. It holds. I sigh in relief.

"Hurry, Aryam!" Kyrel yells back to me. Moons. He's already on the other side. The bridge sways gently in his wake. My stomach roils.

"Don't think I haven't noticed that you left me here to face this on my own," I mutter, steeling myself for the next step. If I fall, the oju ajo blinks my guardians right to me. In mid-air. None of us would stand a chance.

Decide your path and commit to it. Do not falter. Ranee's voice fills my mind, almost as though she's here with me. I take one more decisive breath, and then I move. My leaps are quick and light. If I hesitate even briefly, I risk a misstep or putting too much weight on a plank. The bridge creaks and sways as I go, a treacherous dance partner, but I keep moving. *Don't look down, Ary. Keep moving.* Ranee's voice again, clear as a bell inside my head.

Maybe fear and adrenaline are making me hear things. But she sounds so . . . close. I do the opposite of what her voice says. I stop. The wind howls around me, and the bridge lurches. I look down at the river that churns in the abyss beneath our feet. Maybe I imagine it, but I see a splash and a frantic blur of silver. *Go, Aryam. Keep going.*

"What are you doing?" Kyrel yells from the other side. "Keep moving."

"Right." I nod, determined not to let anyone down. A shadow blocks out the sun, but by the time I look up, whatever cast it is already gone. The bridge lurches again, swayed by an overpowering current of wind. I cling to the ropes, my heart thrumming in my ears.

"Run!" Kyrel shouts.

And I do.

The sound of splintering wood explodes behind me as my feet reach solid ground. The black shadow zips by again in my peripheral vision. I barrel into Kyrel, and he steadies me, his hand gripping my arm firmly. The surprise in his eyes as he gazes toward the bridge is enough to make me whirl around, dread cooling my blood.

The bridge is gone.

I try not to faint as I watch its shattered pieces plummet

into the river far below. "What was that?" I gasp. I turn and search his face. "What did you see?"

His eyes harden. He releases my arm. "Let's move," he instructs, sounding more like an army general than my friend. He hurries up the first set of stairs, leaving me open-mouthed near the cliff's edge. I wonder, suddenly, if I've done anything to offend him since this morning.

But I chase after him. Fire courses through my lungs as we ascend a few flights of switchbacks. I try not to think about the fact that the only way back to the Gate is in pieces at the bottom of a river.

The doors open right into a throne room. It's a beautiful palace, but not a very large one. A resplendent carpet stretches ahead of us, lined with jewels and treasures on both sides, right up to a golden dais, upon which stands a brown-skinned woman in a flowing black dress. Her massive mane of woolly black hair is cleverly bound down her back with golden netting and rhinestones. She stands proudly at the edge of the dais, her gorgeous face marked with contempt.

Kyrel spots her as soon as I do. His shoulders tighten.

"State your purpose here," the woman commands. Her voice, despite the intended harshness, is soft and airy. Something inside my blood eddies at the sound of it, something surprisingly warm and pleasant.

Her eyes widen, then sharpen, centering on me, as if she feels it, too. She doesn't take them off me as she descends the steps of the dais and strides toward us. With one swift swipe of the hand, she brushes Kyrel aside and towers over me. She peers into my eyes, searching them, and then her own soften with awe and brim with tears. "You have her eyes," she whispers.

Then the great, breathtaking woman dips her head and bows before me. "I am in your service," she vows. "Princess."

I choke. "Um. Why?" I have to say, this is the last thing I

thought I'd find here. I offer her my hand and she takes it, clasping it in her own as she rises to her feet.

She searches my eyes again. I see such joy in hers, but it's incomplete and paired with longing. "You don't recognize me," she says, with an amused smile. "Lazy girl. You should have figured it out by now. You haven't changed, after all these score."

I scratch the back of my head. "Um, miss, I think you're mistaking me for someone else."

She winks before straightening up entirely. The amusement falls from her face as she turns from me to Kyrel, who stands rigidly to the side. "You, on the other hand, know very well who I am."

Kyrel looks shocked, but then he laughs. "Eroden Truthsayer," he sneers. "So, you're alive? I'm not surprised you see through this disguise."

"Disguise?" I repeat.

Eroden, apparently, angles herself between us, keeping me at her back. "Show your true self, skin thief," she commands.

Skin thief? My heart races. What is happening?

Kyrel is gone in a flash. In his place stands a man I've seen only once before—the dashing, dark-skinned man from the mezzanine in the Library of Light, the one who stood with the scar-faced woman who sent me here.

Eroden growls. "Why have you come here, Adisa?"

CHAPTER TWENTY-ONE

Adisa?

Every interaction we've had over the last two days flashes before my eyes as horror creeps in. "I . . . " Everything I said to him, everything I *confessed*. And it wasn't even him. "This whole time?" I exclaim.

The man apparently called Adisa tips a pretend hat toward me. "Nice to properly meet you, Princess."

Princess. Hearing the word used to address *me* makes me shudder, and he knows that because *I* confided in him. Devastation and hope burn in my chest like twin flames, one because I've shared a deep secret with a stranger and the other because there's a chance that what he said while pretending to be my friend isn't true.

Maybe there's hope for Kyrel and I after all.

I step around the woman called Eroden, emboldened by this hope. "Where is he?" I demand. "Where is the real Kyrel?""

A sharp sound breaks out of the woman beside me. She covers her mouth."Ky-Kyrel?"

A glint shines in Adisa's eyes. "Son of Zorel," he confirms. "You didn't think the egg could stay hidden forever, did you?"

Eroden snarls. It's a feral sound, too animal to comc from a human throat. The black shadow that swept away the bridge flashes across my mind as a terrible understanding overwhelms me. That shadow belonged to her. What *is* she?

Something tells me that I don't want to stick around to find out. It's already bad enough that Adisa is not what he appeared to be. Maybe I've gotten in over my head. Maybe I should have taken Rae up on her offer to accompany me. Please, Moons, don't let it be too late now.

As Eroden and Adisa spat, I start inching away from them.

"It was obvious," Adisa goes on, "what Nalini offered you. Sequester yourself here. In return, she would protect your egg even as Donomar destroyed all the others."

Donomar destroyed dragon eggs? That doesn't make sense. He was a hero. But my train of thought snags on something else Eroden said.

Her egg?

That means that Eroden is Kyrel's mother, making her a dragon. I see that shadow from the bridge in my mind again. Does this mean she can transform? It shouldn't be possible. Donomar made it impossible.

"He hatched human, you know," Adisa says. "Shameful for a male of his breeding. She may have hidden him for you, but she couldn't spare him from the wretched curse that binds the rest of your kind." He passes an evaluative gaze over her. "It does beg the question of how *you* seem to have evaded that nasty little affliction."

Eroden growls, and the sound sets my feet moving again. "I swear on both moons, Adisa, if you've hurt my son . . . "

"Hurt him?" Adisa presses his hands against his chest as if pleading innocence. "Jesminder and I raised him while his own mother abandoned him." His eyes slip toward me. "It seems to be a trend."

A sick, wet feeling creeps into my throat. Ranee didn't abandon me. She lied to me, sure, but she didn't leave me. Not on purpose. I glare at Adisa, stopping my retreat just shy of the open door. He has the decency to at least look remorseful, as if he's sorry for all of it. For insulting me. For fooling me. For whatever horror he plans on inflicting next.

He scans the sparkling treasures piled on the floor and gazes up at the golden arches above us, tracing them, searching for only the moons know what. "What did the Dragon Princess ask you to guard here?" He looks pointedly at Kyrel's mother. "Was it worth giving up your son?"

Eroden bares her teeth at him. They're sharp. Too sharp. "Jesminder put you up to this," she assumes. "How dare you remove an egg from its nest?"

"It would have been worse if you-know-who got his hands on the egg," Adisa says. That remorse glimmers in his eyes again. When Eroden's eyes shoot wide, I know she sees it, too. Still, her nostrils flare as Adisa declares, "Mindy and I made the best choice we could. We've never hurt him."

Mindy. He says it with such fondness; it's as though the name should mean something to her, too. That same warm, pleasant feeling that stirred in me when I first saw Eroden flurries up again in my chest, but there's a twinge of something else. Something sad.

A face forms in my memory, Ranee's but not. A scar across her cheek and a cold flame raging in her eyes. And somehow, I know exactly who this Jesminder is. In fact, the first time I saw her, she was with Adisa. Did she orchestrate all of this? Did she send me here just so that he could come, too?

I feel like a fool, a kora with its strings plucked.

Taking advantage of Eroden's silence, I ask, "Is Jesminder . . . "

"She's your aunt."

Her proclamation may as well be a scythe that cuts the breath right out of me. "My . . . my . . . " I stagger back a few steps, stumbling over some loose treasures. Adisa's eyes light up with amusement.

"Ranee seriously told you none of this?" Eroden demands.

"How do you know Ranee?" I ask, feeling numb all over. Ranee's only thirty-five score, yet Eroden speaks as though she knows her intimately. That isn't possible. Eroden is at least a thousand score, older, by the sound of it.

The look Eroden gives me is a mixture of pity and exasperation. "Ranee and Jesminder are Nalini's daughters. The Dragon Princess was their mother, your grandmother."

I reward her explanation with a blank stare, and she frowns, turning to Adisa. The skin thief tilts his head as if he shares her disappointment. "What else would you expect? Ranee left the Fallen Cities to marry that human. She sealed herself in a mortal frame and betrayed us just like her mother did."

I shake my head, squeezing back the tears that threaten to fall. "Ranee's no traitor," I say. No matter what I learn about her, I won't believe that. "She's the one who trained me. She taught me everything I know about honor and duty."

Adisa sighs, as if his patience is being tested by a headstrong child whom he pities. "She didn't even tell you who or *what* you were," he says. "Human though you may be, in part, you are also the granddaughter to Nalini Heir Tivinia, favored daughter of Dragon King Elrey, only son to Dragon Queen Tivinia. You are heiress to not *one* but *two* thrones."

"You're lying," I accuse him.

Eroden's voice is soft, all the fire and snarl gone. "He tells the truth," she says. "The Golden Castle would not have permitted you entrance if not for Nalini's blood coursing through your veins." She takes a breath and swivels her head back toward Adisa. "Thank you for keeping my son safe." Her voice hardens, and a terrible energy descends upon the room, stirring my blood. "But even so, you are not welcome here, for *your* kind deal in favors and debts, skin thief."

Then, in true nightmare fashion, Eroden's beautiful black skin ripples and splits in a thousand places as it morphs into obsidian scales.

AN UNEARTHLY SCENE flashes before my eyes. In one instant, Eroden appears human. Terrifying, but human. In the next, she's five times bigger, with wings and scales and gnashing teeth. A dragon as black as coal. Adisa changes, too. He doesn't grow like Eroden did, but his skin turns leather. His fingers sharpen into claws, and his pupils morph into vertical slits. Eroden chuffs at him, full of disdain. Adisa bristles.

"I'm not what I once was," he acknowledges, and I wonder if she said something mind-to-mind—the way only dragons can. "Nalini made sure of that."

Something in my chest aches. I desperately need to make this stop. "Don't fight," I plead. The words come from somewhere deep within me, somewhere that doesn't feel entirely like me.

Eroden snaps her teeth at me. Not viciously. It's more like she's warning me to get back. To stay out of harm's way. For the sake of my guardians, I do. My head swirling with the revelations of the past measure, I take shelter behind a pillar and watch as the two beasts lunge for each other, claws and teeth gnashing.

Adisa is a blur of blackness, of raging talons and fanged snarls. With just one swipe, he could shred through flesh and bone and almost does as he dives beneath Eroden and tears at her underbelly, showering himself in a spray of her blood. She roars in pain as he springs onto his feet, then slams her tail into his side, sending him flying into a pile of treasures.

The fire that erupts from Eroden's maw burns black as she unleashes it upon him. I cringe and squeeze my eyes shut. I don't want to see a man burned to death. Or hear it. Or smell it. Or *taste* it. Because some smells are so bad, they have a taste. But no such assault batters my senses. When the roar of Eroden's flame subsides, there is nothing left where Adisa fell. No body, no scorch mark, not even the pile of treasures he plummeted into, just a coat of black dust.

There's a whooshing sound as Eroden shifts back into her human form. Blood soaks her shirt and seeps through the fingers she presses against her abdomen. Horror fills me. Horror at her injuries. And at Adisa's . . . "Did . . . did you . . . " I can hardly bring myself to say it. "Is he dead?"

Eroden limps toward me, grimacing at the pain. "No," she says sharply. "We don't have time." She towers over me, searching me with frantic eyes. "Where is it?"

"Where's what?" I ask, distracted. If Adisa isn't dead, what did her black flame do to him? He is a liar and a creep, but he raised Kyrel, and he didn't hurt him. Or me. He could have.

Eroden's hand falls heavily on my shoulder, snapping me back to attention. "Where is the tear?" she demands. "I've heard on the wind that it was near. You must have it."

My breath hitches. I press one hand against my chest, feeling the crystal that lies beneath my shirt.

Eroden's eyes narrow on the thin chain around my neck. She brushes my hand aside and yanks the crystal from under my shirt. I reach for it. "Hey! That's mine."

But Eroden crushes the pewter casing around the crystal and drops the chain.

"Eroden!" Adisa's indignant voice tears through the air. He sounds like he's far away and in the same room with us all at once. A black orb flickers where I last saw him, then vanishes again.

Eroden presses the crystal into the palm of my hand. "Eat it," she instructs me.

I glance at the rock in my hand. "What?"

The black orb flashes into sight again. This time, Adisa sounds closer. "That was a nasty trick, Eroden."

Eroden pushes my hand toward my mouth. "For Moons' sake, eat it, girl."

I look at her like she's crazy. Maybe being sequestered in this palace for near a thousand score has made her so. I try to keep the judgement out of my voice. "I think you're confused."

Metal clangs as treasures pour out of the rippling black orb. Adisa's hand pokes through, clawing for purchase.

"Eat it!" Eroden shouts.

Her urgency makes me plop the crystal into my mouth. I bite down, expecting to break all my teeth and prove to the batty dragon that the crystal is inedible. Instead, the crystal shatters in my mouth, and a burst of flavor rushes over my tongue, salty and sweet. Unfathomable cold explodes through my body, stealing my breath.

Adisa's other hand breaks free. He grasps the outside of the orb and starts to pull himself through as more golden trinkets and jewels tumble onto the floor.

Ice thickens my blood. "Eroden," I stammer. "What did I just do? What's happening to me?"

Her bloody hand clamps around my wrist as she stumbles toward an alcove at one side of the room, toward the base of the stairwell that resides within it. "Hurry."

We barrel up the stairs. A wooden door clangs shut behind us, its latch falling into place as if sealed by invisible hands. My body feels sluggish and numb and impossibly cold, but somehow, I manage to climb the stairs without tripping over them. Eroden's grip digs into my skin.

Adisa's angry voice rings out behind us. The door rattles from the other side. We keep running.

The stairs spiral up to a tower. I gasp at the two moons on the tower's door. They're just like the ones in the temple room.

Eroden pushes the door open without a second thought, revealing a room with a stone table supporting a single scroll. "You are like us now, Aryam," she says hurriedly. "You can read the songs of the dragons, but you are also something more than us. You can *use* them." As she speaks, she reaches for the scroll.

A spot of black darts between my feet, then skirts around Eroden's ankles. A beetle of some sort. I jump back, startled and disgusted. Eroden turns toward me, her face questioning, and then there's a burst of air behind her. Adisa stands behind the table, the scroll clutched in his hand. "I don't believe it," he says, a grin stretching across his face. He unrolls the scroll. "'The Song of Binding and Unbinding.' It was here. All this time."

Dread and fury sharpen the dragon's voice. "Adisa," she cautions. "Don't be a fool."

His eyes light up with triumph. "My queen will be pleased with this."

Eroden scoffs. "Queen?" she spits out. "Is Jesminder already calling herself that? Adisa, *think*, you amorphous idiot. If she uses that scroll—"

"Dragons will fly these skies once more."

"*One* in particular," she warns, "and if I recall, he wasn't very happy with Jesminder when he went under. She will be sealing her own death."

Adisa wags a finger. "Elrey will understand now that Jesminder tried to warn him about her mother," he says. "He will see the error of his ways and restore her to glory."

"The Dragon King?" Eroden tries to reason. "Confess to an error?" She lays the skepticism on thick, perhaps trying to get him to see how foolish he sounds.

"The Dragon King?" I interrupt. "Elrey the Dragon King? But he's . . . " Dead. He's *supposed* to be dead. But even as I think it, I know it isn't true. "No," I whimper. Something was *off* about Capital Island, and now I know what. That presence in the fog, that consciousness brushing against my own.

Adisa's grin widens as he watches the realization dawn on my face. "Yes," he says. "The Dragon King, your grandfather, lives. He rests beneath the mountain."

I shake my head, breaths punching out of me like fists. "No, no, no," I repeat. This is worse than anything I could have ever imagined. Oh, I should have stayed a coward. I should have stayed home in my bed instead of going to that *stupid* Dragon's Fall. Why did Ranee let me go? Why did she put that crystal around my neck?

I have to stop things from getting worse.

I push down the panic that threatens to paralyze me and look Adisa in the eyes. "I *sensed* him," I say. "You can't let him out." It would be the end of the people of Beldemar. Maybe even the end of the akbarrin. The being that I sensed was so, so angry. "He will destroy us all. You understand that. Don't you? Dragons *do not* forgive."

Adisa sighs. "You have known of your dragon heritage for five beats, and suddenly you are an expert on them," he says, shaking his head. The scroll rolls shut in his hand. "I am sorry, girl. I truly am. But these things are well beyond your understanding. It would be foolish to entrust this key to a child."

I hold out my hand. "Adisa, give the scroll to me. I have to bind the Shadows again, but this time, I'll make sure the akbarrin are better cared for."

Adisa frowns. "And which realm will *you* reside in?" he asks. "Don't you see? You are one of us."

In a flash, the older man is gone, and Kyrel stands in his place. "Fight for your true people, and you can have everything your heart desires."

"Be wary, child," Eroden snarls in my ear. "His kind take the skin of those you desire and make bargains that leave you broken."

Something inside me cracks. "I won't turn on the people of Beldemar, not even for him."

Adisa furrows his brow. A shadow falls over his face. "Then the people of Beldemar will turn on you."

Another flash illuminates the room, this one so bright it blinds us. When it recedes, Adisa is already gone. A bird has taken his place, clutching the scroll in its talons. He darts out the window, narrowly evading Eroden's outstretched hands as she lunges after him. "No," she cries, just before she tumbles out of the window and plummets to the rocky surface below.

A tremor rattles the Golden Palace. I run to the window and peer down. The black dragon writhes at the tower's base, a mangled wing crushed beneath her, the other outstretched and twitching. Adisa screeches as he shrinks farther and farther in the distance.

CHAPTER TWENTY-TWO

I sprint down the spiral stairwell and dash through Nalini's hoard. By the time I reach Eroden, she has shifted back into her human form. Instead of a broken wing, she has a shattered arm. Blood streams out of her torso in rivulets of red. I drop to my knees beside her and push my freezing hands against her side. The cold makes her flinch and cry out in pain. "I'm sorry," I apologize, but I don't take my hands away. "What can I do?" I ask. "How do I fix this?"

I know little about the healing arts—always fell into a daydream when Ranee droned on about them. But now my attention is sharp and desperate. I'll do anything she tells me to. I'll do something right. For once.

Eroden's bloody fingers close around mine. She squeezes. Her grasp is weak. Too weak. "There's another," she says, blood spluttering from her lips. She draws in a painful gasp before continuing. "Another who has the song you need. He will be much harder to find than this place"—another sharp gasp—"and reluctant, perhaps, but you must find him, Aryam." A dimness settles over her eyes. Her breath grows shallow. "Find him before Adisa and Jesminder find a way to use the song. Go now."

I fret over her body and over the blood that doesn't seem to slow down no matter how much pressure I apply. "Find who?" I ask. There's no way I'm leaving her like this, but I'll say anything to keep her talking. Kyrel's mother.

Her eyes meet mine. They're sharper than they should be with death drawing so close, but they hold no trace of fear. "Aryam," she says, "find Chori. Find the griot they call the Songkeeper."

"Chori?" I repeat. The Songkeeper is the highest rank in the storyguard, but I know from all Darien's obsessive rambling that the current one is not called Chori.

It doesn't matter. Eroden needs to focus on staying alive.

"Eroden," I say. "Kyrel's going to be so happy when he finally meets you. He thought he was alone. He thought he had no one."

Her eyes soften. "I am happy that he lives," she says. "And if he never changes, if he is *human* . . . " Her eyes meet mine again, searching. Knowing. "He has you now." Her lips tick up slightly as she murmurs his name. "Kyrel. Son of Zorel."

She dies with a smile on her face.

NIGHT DESCENDS UPON THE MOUNTAIN. I sit cradling Eroden's body in my lap, my teeth chattering against the cold that plagues my body. Colder and colder as time seems to stagnate around me. She died before I could even ask her about the tear I ate, about what it did to me, about what she meant when she said I *should have figured it out by now*.

A slurry of questions eddies around in my sluggish brain.

Who is Chori?

How will I find him?

Why does it have to be *me*?

Worst of all, how will I tell Kyrel that his mother died in my arms? That I couldn't do anything to help her?

Something stirs in my chest. A faint warmth. A gentle tug urging me to get to my feet. I ignore it, not ready to leave Eroden's body behind. Besides, there's nowhere for me to go, anyway. The bridge is gone. Even if I could cross the chasm, the journey back to the Gate is too perilous to attempt in the dark. And since Adisa is airborne with the scroll, there's no way I can beat him back to Capital Island, no way to stop him from unleashing the Moons'-given *Dragon King* upon the world.

It is only when Eroden's body evaporates out of my hands, disintegrating into a fine black mist and floating toward the heavens, that I scramble away and race back into the palace. With no place else to go, I return to the tower and curl up beneath the window.

I WAKE up to the sound of metal striking stone and the clamor of human voices. "Again!" a man shouts. *Clink.* "Again! Fire the hook!"

Rubbing sleep from my eyes, I stumble over to the arched window. My eyes shoot open at the small troop of soldiers gathered on the path, firing grapples across the chasm. They are led by a tall, blond-haired man. Captain Aric. And at his side, those are Joan and Dex and few others I don't know. One of the grapples finds purchase, and Captain Aric tugs the line taught.

Joy and disbelief well up inside me. "Captain Aric!" I shout.

It takes him a few ticks to locate me. Dex is the one to point me out. The lanky man raises an arm in solute, while Joan fires another hook across the gap. I plow down the stairs, back through the treasure room, and out into the crisp morning air. Before heading for the stairs, I glance at the place where

Eroden's body had lain and sigh when I see that it's no longer there.

That hadn't been a dream, then.

Captain Aric's feet strike the ground just as I turn around a switchback. I let him unhook himself from the line and clear the edge of the cliff before I barrel into him, wrapping my arms around him.

He stiffens, then wraps an arm around me and squeezes me back. "Alright, kid. Settle down."

"How did you find me?" I ask. "What are you even doing here?"

Captain Aric glances around, awe filling his eyes as he takes in the palace. "We came to defeat the Moongazer," he says, recovering from his shock, "but it appears we were beaten to it." His eyes drop to his hand, which grips my arm. "You're freezing," he observes. "What happened here?"

I just stare at him. "I'm not sure you'd believe me if I told you," I reply.

Captain Aric sighs. "The things I've seen in the past few weeks?" he mutters. "You'd be surprised what I'm willing to believe. Humor me."

I nod, choosing my words carefully for once. "You remember that crystal I wore around my neck?" I ask. "The one Father Wood tried to take?"

"I do," he confirms.

A gush of cold blood eddies in my core as I say, "I ate it."

Captain Aric's eyes widen, but he doesn't seem as surprised as I expected. "What else happened?"

I wait until he swings me across the chasm into the awaiting arms of Joan and Dex, who reel us in, before I tell him the rest. As we trek back toward the Gate, I tell them what I can about the events that transpired at the Golden Palace. "You saw a real dragon?" Dex exclaims in disbelief.

"And a skin thief," Captain Aric muses, "who's on his way back to the capital to free the Dragon King from a prison beneath the palace."

That last revelation zaps the excitement out of his soldiers' faces. Somberness falls over our party. I frown. "You're the captain of the guard," I say softly. "Did you know that he was there?"

Captain Aric pauses. "Yes."

A beat. "Does Princess Marleyn know?" I ask.

"King Felix did not tell her," Captain Aric says slowly, "but I did."

Joan makes a sound of disapproval. "Captain," she chides. "Why would you tell that sweet girl something so terrible?"

Captain Aric's brown eyes meet mine. "Because I'm her monitor," he announces, "and it is my job to prepare her for any threat against the princess."

Shock tears through me. "You *knew*," I accuse him. "From that first night in Irez, you *knew* who I was this whole time?"

He nods. "Yes," he confirms. "I knew who you were."

I can't believe this. "And Ranee?" I demand.

"She was my queen," he admits. "Before he died, King Felix sent me personally to retrieve the two of you."

No wonder I got a personal escort when the other guardians had to make their own way. "What about the crystal? Did you know what it was, too?"

"I know that it belonged to your mother," he confesses, "and that her friend the Moon Princess gave it to her to consume if she ever wanted to return to the way she was before. I know that she gave it to you instead. To protect you in case you needed it."

A tender pain lances through my anger. I stop walking. "Why didn't she tell me what it was?" But I know the answer to my own question.

I've given you what childhood I could, Ary.

She'd been against letting me go to Dragon's Fall, but she allowed it because she wanted me to have fun. To make memories. She'd added the teardrop to my costume not as decoration, but as protection, because I was her daughter and a princess. I glance at Joan and Dex, both of whom have been uncomfortably silent for the past few beats. "Did either of you know about any of this?"

Joan throws her hands up in deflection. "This is news to me."

"They didn't know," Captain Aric confirms.

My chest heaves. "I couldn't find my oju. I thought I was broken." Tears blur my vision as I look up at him. "Why would she let me believe I was a guardian?" And a dissonant one, at that.

"The king and queen needed to keep you safe and secluded," Captain Aric explains. "If she told you that you were a princess and that there were people hunting you, you would have grown up in fear. By telling you that you were a guardian and training you like one, she gave you courage, among other things. The crossings from the Shadows started happening the score you were born. Your parents were afraid that even if you learned your identity in secret, the wind or trees could report your location before you were old enough to defend yourself."

His words strike a chord of fear. I often felt that something was watching me in the Immortal Soul Forest. Now I know that I was probably right. "And why not tell me once I reached the palace? Why make me continue the charade of looking for an oju?"

"For the same reason," he says. "It's safer."

"How so?"

Captain Aric runs a hand through his hair, pausing mid-motion. "You should speak to your chorus leader about that.

The two of you can decide how you want to proceed from here."

Marleyn, I realize. Stunned, I nod.

A slow, relieved grin creeps across Captain Aric's face as he leads the way. "Right this way, Your Highness."

Your Highness.

The title rings in my ears all the way back to the Gate. Captain Aric knew. Has always known. He and Ranee have known each other since before she carried me to Irez. He had served her. His queen. From the moment they climbed into that carriage together, they knew or suspected how everything would turn out.

And I was the fool.

It's enough to provoke bitter tears to my eyes throughout our silent journey. When we reach the Gate, I find the village already reconstructed and its Protectors, new and old, already going about their normal business. Nanda and the other fallen seem sweetly forgotten, as if their deaths had occurred near a thousand score ago and were no more than a distant ache.

Another of Nalini's mercies toward them, I guess.

Captain Aric doesn't delay taking me to Marleyn. A disgruntled Rae directs us toward a clearing in the forest. "She doesn't want any of us near her," she gripes. "Which is fine by me."

But she's hurt.

She's spent her whole life preparing to protect a princess who seems to snub her at every opportunity. It makes my heart ache. Maybe I should tell her the truth now—tell her the real reason why Marleyn avoids her. But the words get stuck in my throat. I turn and follow Captain Aric into the forest.

Sweaty and out of breath, Marleyn turns to face us as we

emerge from a thicket, a wooden practice staff resting idly in her good arm. Her other arm is still in a sling, bound tightly to her chest. Despite everything that she's lied to me about, concern for her swells in my heart. "You should be resting," I say.

Her silver-brown eyes shimmer as they land upon my face. "I have," she says, bluntly. Her emotions are guarded, but I can still tell what she's feeling. Relief. Her gaze slides to Captain Aric, and he nods and takes his leave. Marleyn studies me closely. Finally, she asks, "Are you going to say what you wanted to say to me the other day?" she asks. "That morning in the nursery?"

I'd called her princess, and she'd flinched. Sadness had crept into her eyes.

Moons. She's always wanted to tell me. She wanted to tell me then. I can see that now.

"Why didn't you tell me?" I ask, hurt leaking out through my voice.

She tilts her head, ever so slightly. "Tell you what?" she asks.

Fine. So, she needs me to say it first. "You aren't the princess," I say as steadily as I can manage. "I am."

Relief floods her face, and she grins. "Guardian Marleyn," she announces with a bow, wincing at a pain the movement inflicts on her. "At your service."

Before I can respond, Marleyn's arm wraps around my neck, and she squeezes me into a surprisingly strong hug for someone with one good arm. "You can ask me anything," she breathes into my ear, the weight of scores of secrecy rolling off her shoulders.

I wait until she releases me and draw in a breath. "Have you always known?" I ask.

Marleyn shakes her head. Then she tells me her story.

She was six when she realized she was different than her cousins, Adanna and Bem. She was not careless the way they were, and she couldn't make friends. She was seven when the man she thought to be her father told her that he was, in fact, not. She was seven and a half when King Felix's captain, Aric, and Mam Kadejah started giving her private combat lessons in a chamber hidden beneath the palace.

That was where she spent much of her time, and why we always had so much trouble finding her.

"He said that the ruse was an important part of protecting you," she concludes, "and that the right time to tell you the truth would be when you were ready to hear it."

"Who said that?" I ask, my mind numb and heavy with the sadness and isolation of her tale. Sadness she can't even detect, because in her mind, all that time, she was doing it for me. She would do anything to keep me safe.

Marleyn's eyes glimmer with tears, not for herself but on my behalf. "King Felix," she answers. "Your father."

So, she kept that secret. Even though it's obvious she's been dying to tell me these past few days. Even until this last beat, when she allowed *me* to be the one to say it. She did what she thought was best for me. Not herself. My eyes drift to her arm in the sling, to where the arrow grazed her skin. "You could have been killed," I murmur.

Marleyn holds my gaze. "I wasn't."

"But you *could* have been," I insist, helpless tears welling up in my eyes. "You can't take risks like that. Not for me."

"I will take *many* more risks for you," she insists, her voice hard with determination. "I can tell that you hate the guardians' oath. It was forced on you, and you never wanted it. It was only made worse by the fact that you never really *had* it. Try to understand that you don't really know what it's really like. It doesn't hurt us, having such a pure and singular purpose."

"But it does hurt you," I protest. "Don't you see how sad

the others look when you're cold toward them? When you don't let them serve you?"

Marleyn frowns. "That's because, deep down, they know something's wrong," she says. "They know it isn't me. Think about it. Maya was drawn to you at the border port between Marad and Zehir. She could have departed from *any* port to get to the capital, yet she happened to be just where you needed her to be at just the right time. Rae, even though she'd never admit it, feels fiercely protective of you. When we lost you on the beach, she made Chyou and Maya carry me back to the village while she searched for you in the forest. Alone."

I hadn't known that. Marleyn smirks at the surprise on my face.

"And Chyou," she says, contemplatively. "Chyou was terrified to take the path to the Bog House, but she overcame herself for you, for your mission. There's not one of us who wouldn't do anything for you. If the others feel sad, it's because serving me feels wrong, but they're too afraid of the Omission to admit it."

A heaviness weighs on me. "They know," I realize, "but they don't know that they know, so . . . *I'm* the one who's hurting them." I sigh. "Maybe I should tell them."

"When you're ready," Marleyn agrees. "If they don't figure it out for themselves." She straightens up. "In the meantime, I think we should keep up the ruse when we return to the palace. I'm not comfortable with all the attempts on my life recently."

I raise my eyebrows. "*What* attempts?" I demand.

But Marleyn just smiles daringly. "That one on the beach, for starters," she says. "And a few more since the king died. But don't you worry. I can handle it."

I shake my head. Of course she can. A tightened string eases inside my chest. "We need to get back to the capital."

CHAPTER TWENTY-THREE

Captain Aric summons his omiayo to take us back to the port. It's a relief that we won't have to go on foot or make another stop at Bogma's froggy nightmare. At the red gate, Valeria pulls me into a tight hug, lifting my feet off the ground, and whispers into my ear, "Stay safe, princess." She laughs at the shock on my face when she sets me down. "If your face hadn't given you away from the start," she says, "that dance you performed would have."

"My face?" I repeat. But then I recall the way Jun stared at me when he first met me, and the way the protectors whispered among themselves as I helped Nanda carry the goat meat from the house.

So, Jun kept his promise after all. He didn't tell anyone that the princess was among them. They saw for themselves.

"Do I really look that much like The Dragon Princess?" I ask.

"There's a resemblance," Valeria confirms. "But you also *feel* like her."

I tilt my head. "How do you mean?"

Valeria shrugs. "I can't really explain it, but maybe it's

because she made us into what we are," she tries to explain. "Maybe there's a part of us that will always sense her."

"Maybe," I agree. "But I *do* wish one of you would have said something."

Valeria laughs at that. "We are your humble servants," she says. "If you introduce yourself as a guardian, who are we to say differently?"

I raise my brow. "I didn't say anything when I came back from the pass," I point out. How does Valeria know that I know the truth now? "Shouldn't you still be addressing me as a guardian?"

That earns another shrug. "You didn't say anything," she acknowledges. "But you came back changed. That's all the confirmation I need."

Changed? I start to ask her what she means by that, but Rae calls me from the coach.

"Come back and visit me," Valeria pleads as Rae starts to tug me toward the coach.

"I will," I promise, squeezing Valeria's hand for as long as I can before Rae drags me away.

Captain Aric's boat carries us swiftly across the Sea of Scales. It's another relief that we won't be at sea for too long. Less time on the water means less time thinking about Ranee and the possibility that Mama River will emerge from its depths and drag me down, too.

I expect the worst when we arrive at Capital Island. Shuttered buildings. Panicked citizens. Fleeing boats. Smoke rising from the skies. But there's no sign that Adisa has returned here and managed to free the Dragon King. Instead, the city continues in its revelry. Its streets remain adorned with posters, ribbons, and floating lanterns of purples, gold, and silver. Music and singing fill the air as, all over the city, story grunts sing about the end of the war. I pull the carriage curtain back just enough to peer out and wonder if, somewhere in this city, the griot Eroden mentioned is among them.

"Tomorrow, there will be a final parade," Marleyn announces. "Following that, there will be a feast. We should enjoy ourselves."

I close my curtain. "But what about the griot?" I ask. Over our journey, I told her everything that happened to me in Jara. Then, together, we told the others as much as we could without revealing who I really am. They know that the Dragon King inhabits the mountain. They know that there is a griot out there somewhere who can help us keep him there. They know that an akbarrin dragon queen deceived me into getting her the key she needs to free her father.

Maybe it's wrong not to tell them everything, but after feeling like I wasn't good enough for so long and finally earning their respect, I'm scared of losing it all over again. What would they think if they found out I might be the very thing they're supposed to destroy?

Marleyn responds with unflappable calm. Sometimes, listening to her speak, I can't believe that I didn't notice it all along. She is the true conductor of this quartet, a born leader. "Captain Aric has a network of spies that can lay their webs for us," she announces. "In the meantime, I think it's important to rest, and . . . I'd like for us to honor the king, even if we can't tell anyone he's dead." Her eyes hold mine. "He was a devoted father who spent every waking moment remembering his wife and loving his daughter."

I swallow back a lump in my throat to keep it from bubbling into a sob. I think again of the gift he sent to Irez. For me. I nod.

Marleyn smiles. "Anyway," she says. "You have training to do."

My eyes widen. *What? Still?* I want to shout, but I don't.

She's right. I need to understand what consuming Yara's tear has done to me. I shiver against the ice swirling in my blood.

As if she knows exactly what I'm thinking, Marleyn smiles again smugly.

Unaware of the friction between us, Chyou blurts out, "I'm good at finding stuff, too, you know."

Marleyn nods. "Okay, then it's settled," she says. "Captain Aric's spies will search for news of this griot. Chyou, you'll help, and Maya, *you'll* assist her." She slides her imperious gaze to Rae. "And you will help Mam Kadejah get Aryam battle-ready." Rae's stoic face doesn't flinch, even though I suspect it must annoy her to be ordered around so callously. Marleyn raps her fingertips against her kneecap. "I'll do some research of my own in the meantime."

The carriage rattles to a stop at the palace gatehouse. "But," Marleyn says softly, "we've all had a difficult journey. We can afford to rest until after the parade. That's an order."

MARLEYN'S ORDER is one that I'm more than happy to follow, even if, technically, I'm not bound to Marleyn's orders. It's evening when we arrive. Kemi has dinner set out for us in our rooms: lime soup, curried meats, rice, and pastries. I don't know who informed her of our prompt arrival, but I bless the soul who did. After stuffing my face, I indulge in a lavender bath, then fall into a freshly made bed soft as a cloud.

A tart knock at my door wakes me up too early in the morning.

"Lady Aryam, you have a visitor." Kemi's sweet voice filters through my morning haze as she lets herself into the room. She draws open the balcony curtains, letting sunlight stream in. I shield my eyes and roll over, groaning.

"That's impossible," I grumble.

For once, the idea of being a princess seems enticing. At least, once everyone knows, I can make a law that states it forbidden to disturb a person who has just returned from a long and harrowing journey.

Kemi's already rifling through my wardrobe, all for show, I think. There's nothing there but a sea of blue. Law number two. No more traditional colors. Anyone from any nation can wear any color whenever they want. Though that does make me wonder. What *would* I wear as a princess? Marleyn seems to stick to black with gold or silver trim.

Kemi snorts. "Tell that to the young lady sitting in the princess's personal dining chamber. She says she's traveled a long way to see you—all the way from Irez. Princess Marleyn offered up her personal dining tower for you to use. Such a sweet girl that one."

I sit up, blinking in disbelief. "Irez?" I exclaim.

A young lady?

It can only be one person.

I tumble out of bed and snatch my uniform as Kemi pulls it from the wardrobe. I put it on quickly, tripping over my own feet as I rush into the bathing room to freshen up. Kemi tries to get me to sit so she can tackle my hair, but I never took the bubble braids out from last night and they sort of held, so I brush her off.

The old woman frowns. "You should really tidy it," she insists, but I'm already halfway out the door.

Katina sits primly at the breakfast table, back as straight as a rod and legs crossed at the ankles as if *she's* the princess, as if this dining room is hers. She tries to school her face when she sees me, but her eyes light up with mirth and I know she's beyond excited to be here. She keeps up the facade for a tick longer and then breaks it with a squeal, leaping out of her seat and running in short, choppy steps to throw her arms around my neck. "Ary," she cries. "I can't believe this. Look at where we are."

She releases me from the hug but takes both my hands in hers, interlacing our fingers. She assesses me. "You look . . . good," she says.

I laugh because I know I look terrible. "I have so much to tell you," I reply. "But first, *what* are you doing here?"

"So, listen," she says, lowering her voice conspiratorially. "I *live* here now."

My jaw drops. "What?"

She shakes her head up and down, biting her lip to suppress another squeal. "My mom sent for me a few days after they took you away. When I got here, she told me that the king is dead and that I'm going to live here now—at least until things calm down."

"Are things bad in Irez?" I ask, imagining the village in a frenzy.

"Not bad, just strange," she replies. "People don't know about King Felix yet, but most people know there's something weird going on. My driver refused to travel at night. That's what took me so long to get here."

She resumes her seat at the table and bids me to sit down with a flick of her well-manicured hand.

I slide into the seat next to her and decide not to tell her that her driver may have saved her life. No need to scare her. "I can't believe I haven't thought to seek your mom out yet," I say instead. "What does she do here?"

It's the wrong question. I can see it in the way she tenses her shoulders. Even back in Irez, Katina got tight-lipped whenever any of us asked about what her mother did in the capital. I've always thought it was something important, but Darien thought her mom was a maid.

"Never mind," I stammer. I watch as relief floods her eyes. Maybe Darien was right. "I have so much to tell you," I say.

Katina leans forward, ever the lover of gossip. "Tell me everything."

So, I do, ignoring the slight pang of guilt for not doing as Marleyn and I agreed and keeping my identity a secret. Katina and I are best friends. We've had each other's backs since we were little, and she's always kept my secret. Why should now be any different?

"Remember the game we used to play in the washhouse?" I ask, at the conclusion of my tale. Katina and I would play princess, guardian, and servant. Katina used to think it was so funny to make me play guardian when Darien had no idea it was true. She would always play the princess, of course, and make our friend fetch her whatever she wanted to eat and drink. I look for the light in her eyes when she realizes the irony of my being the true princess all along.

But her eyes are dull and emotionless, her face vacant. "You're the princess?" she murmurs.

Her lack of enthusiasm sounds a warning bell inside my head. "Yeah," I murmur. "But you can't tell anyone, okay? It's a secret."

Her shoulders tense. She sits up a little straighter. "Obviously."

I frown. "Kati, did I say something wrong?" I ask. She's only just gotten here. I never thought I'd see her again. I don't want us to fight already.

She releases a long sigh. "Whatever. I'm just tired, I guess. I had a long journey."

She's just heard the harrowing details of my journey and knows it was much longer, but I don't say anything to worsen the argument I sense brewing between us. I wonder what could have set her off this time.

"I need to go," she says. "I just wanted to say hello and let you know I was here."

I glance at all the untouched food on the table. "Don't you want anything to eat?" I ask.

"Bye, Aryam."

I remain behind at the table, blinking in confusion. What just happened?

I gaze over the spread of delicious foods and fail to find my appetite, the one thing I always thought I'd be able to rely on in life, next to Ranee. I sigh and push away from the table. There's a parade today. At least I'll have something to distract me from whatever just happened between Katina and I.

CHAPTER TWENTY-FOUR

The Dragon's Fall celebrations die down two days after the parade, and I'm glad for it. Foods and parties that would have delighted me weeks ago only set my heart racing. The morning after, Rae bursts through my door and drags me to Mam Kadejah's training square a measure earlier than the guardians are scheduled to arrive.

"Do not think that I will go easier on you now that you know the truth," Mam Kadejah warns me while Rae flows through her morning stretches. "Indeed, I will only train you harder now that you know what's at stake."

The elder keeps her promise. By the end of the day, I am so sore, I can hardly lift a spoon to my lips without wincing. Her relentless ministrations make Ranee's morning exercises seem like splashing in tide pools at the children's beach. But at the end of one month, her methods start to pay off. I can at least hold my own a few beats longer in a sparring session with Maya.

We neither see nor hear of Jesminder and Adisa, and no other akbarrin attack the palace. After training, Chyou and Maya take daily excursions to find the griot Eroden told me of, while Rae and I stay back to guard the princess. But one day, Marleyn sends Rae on a private mission. Rae's verdant eyes narrow as Marleyn whispers her instructions. Then she departs after a curt nod, her mouth set in a grim line.

"Shouldn't she partner up with someone?" I ask as Marleyn and I set out through the palace. She's asked me to accompany her somewhere, which soothes my hurt feelings over the fact that Katina seems to be avoiding me.

"Rae can handle herself," Marleyn reassures me. "She is my second, after all."

A fair point. "Where did you send her?" I ask. "She didn't seem all that happy to go."

"Really? I thought she looked eager," Marleyn beams, but she doesn't answer my question. "You should probably be more concerned about where *we're* going."

She whisks me to King Felix's quarters. The fixtures in the hallway leading to his rooms have acquired a few more dust layers since I unwittingly wound up here some weeks ago. I drag a finger along the bald head of a sculpture and rub the dust between my fingers, pursing my lips with distaste. The king's wing seems to have been shut off entirely since his death. Even the staff are not permitted inside to clean it.

What must they all think of all this?

My thoughts drift to Chiwa, still playing queen regent. We thought that she would do something to solidify her claim to the throne in our absence, but she hasn't made another move since dispatching that troop to assassinate Marleyn.

"What are we doing here?" I ask.

She shushes me, glancing behind us before grabbing my wrist and pulling me into a study. I shiver as she bolts the door shut behind us. It's cooler in here than it has any right to be. A metal clang rings through the chilly air as Marleyn slides the last of four deadbolts into place.

"That's a lot of security for a study," I comment.

Marleyn flashes me her signature smirk before striding to the large oak desk at the center of the back wall. Like everything else in these quarters, its surface is coated with dust. A thin scrap of tree bark lies slightly curled in the center, beside an empty bottle of ink and a feather pen. Marleyn glances at these items before opening a drawer and rifling through it.

I turn away from her and examine the rest of the study. Its design is more modern than the library's. There are mostly books on the shelves instead of scrolls. A round, three-quarter couch upholstered in a luxurious blue fabric sits in one corner. The square shelf on the ground level has a circular center. Up on the mezzanine, there are more shelves and a sliding ladder for reaching the books at the top.

I turn to Marleyn, who has moved on to rifling through another drawer. It dawns on me that this study must be where she learned about the Protectors at the Gate, and where she gets information that none of the other guardians seem to know. "Why don't we help the others search for the griot?" I ask.

She closes the drawer and stoops down to the one below. "Actually," she says, pulling it open and rifling through its contents, "we'll be doing a different sort of searching today." She moves to the drawer on the other side. "If I can just find where Captain Aric left the key."

"The key?"

"He's always moving it," she says. Her hand stops searching and she plucks a brass key from the drawer. "Aha!" she cries triumphantly. "Retrieving the song from the griot won't matter much if you don't have the power to put behind the words. So, today, we need to find out what Yara's tear did to you."

"And that key is going to help?" I don't bother to clamp down on the skepticism in my voice.

Marleyn laughs, something she does a lot more now that the

truth is out between us. She turns to face the bookshelf at her back, removes a book from the center, and inserts the key into a lock hidden behind it. A clanking noise rings out from what sounds like a hollow chamber behind the bookshelf.

I lean forward in anticipation.

The round part of the bookshelf swings inward, revealing a spiral staircase that descends into darkness. A burst of frigid air greets us, and I suddenly understand why this study is so cold.

I gape at the hidden passage, my eyes wide and unblinking. "Where does it lead?"

Marleyn steps in first. Darkness envelops her like a shawl. "To your grandfather."

As if on cue, the darkness turns its eye on me. The hairs on my skin stand alert as its gaze rakes over me. A shard of coldness pierces my heart, its tendrils spreading like icy veins. My foot falters at the threshold. Marleyn halts at the first landing, watching me with blade-sharp eyes. "You sense him. Don't you?" she asks.

I nod.

"Don't worry. He's trapped inside the stone. He can't get out."

"Why are we going down there?"

Marleyn just grins. "We're already late," she says, before skipping off into the island's bowels. "Close the door behind you!" she calls up, her voice echoing off the obsidian walls.

I leave it open a crack, allowing a sliver of light to illuminate the stairs, but from farther below, Marleyn calls, "All the way."

I wince and pull the door shut, expecting terrible, complete darkness. Instead, I am met by the gentle blue, green, and pink glow of minerals embedded in the rock wall. I exhale my relief and proceed down the spiral stairs, which seem to reach far below the palace.

The stairs deposit us in a large, bean-shaped chamber with one other entrance on the opposite side. It appears to be a tunnel, and Captain Aric stands at its mouth with a lopsided grin on his face. Or should I call him monitor Aric now?

He chuckles at my shock and greets us. "Marleyn." He bows his head to me. "Princess."

My heart races. "Please. Don't call me that."

The monitor and guardian exchange looks. Then Captain Aric nods. "Why are we here?" I ask, my eyes darting over the black walls glinting with minerals. I look anywhere but at the two people in front of me, all the while thanking the moons that I don't find a dragon peering back at me.

Mercifully, Marleyn explains. "We're here because this place amplifies akbarra."

I blink rapidly. "It does *what*?"

Marleyn continues with imperturbable poise. "My oju is strongest when I unleash it here," she says. A spark of silver ignites in her eyes as she summons it. The light of her oju glows so brightly that I must shield my eyes. When the light dims, I see that she holds a serpent's fang, a silver chain with a curved blade dangling at one end of it and a circular disc at the other. The oju vanishes. "Captain Aric and I would like to know what this place can do for you."

"For me?" I protest. "But I don't have an oju. Royals don't have any abilities."

"Royals *didn't* have abilities," Captain Aric confirms, "before you. Nalini left Donomar before they could conceive a child together. His descendants hail from his second wife, but when your mother fell in love with your father . . . Well, you may as well say Nalini came home. You are her descendant as well as Donomar's."

"And you've eaten Yara's tear," Marleyn points out. "It was

already affecting you when it was outside of your body. Let's find out what it did to you after you consumed it."

I WAVER between skepticism and denial, but there is no point in arguing with the two of them. Besides, they're right. I can't afford to ignore what's happening to me any longer.

I follow Marleyn deeper into the chamber. It is bare, except for a large, square mat covering the floor's center. Marleyn deposits her shoes at the edge of the mat before treading to the center of it. Captain Aric and I follow suit. "So," I say, "how do we figure it out? Please don't say we meditate."

Marleyn rolls her eyes, smiling. "You don't like meditating because you've always been sent on a rainbow chase," she says. "It will be different this time. The thing you are seeking actually exists inside you." She nods toward Captain Aric. "Let Captain Aric be your guide."

I sigh and drop onto my knees, then slide them out from under me as I settle into position. Captain Aric and Marleyn sit, too, the three of us forming a triangle.

I close my eyes, sitting with my legs crossed, my hands lying palm up on my knees. I breathe in, hold my breath, release, hold, and repeat. Captain Aric guides me, his voice surprisingly soothing and calm, but it's hard for me to surrender to it—the calmness. Even though soft light fills the chamber, I can still feel the darkness from before. Its eyes are watching me. Curious. Probing. I can feel it shifting around me, like a great beast sniffing potential prey.

"You have to relax," Marleyn intercedes, her voice soft and encouraging.

Easy for her to say. She doesn't have this darkness purring against her mind.

"Relax," Marleyn says again, a little more firmly this time.

It takes conscious effort, but I let my shoulders drop. I inhale. The darkness stays; I acknowledge it and release it, directing my attention to Captain Aric's words. "Steady breath. Focused mind. Quiet, seek. Quiet, find."

He repeats the mantra again and again. I drop into the glen and, this time, stay still as the force probes my mind. I breathe in. I've spent too long being afraid of it. I have to face it head on.

"*What are you?*" I ask it. "*What do you want from me?*"

A single word resonates through the glen. "*In.*"

I inhale sharply. Captain Aric's voice deepens as he anchors me again with the mantra. *In.* Ranee always told me that if something strange ever happened in the glen, I should just go along with it. I'm not sure if this is what she meant by strange, but I have to try.

"*In,*" I concede.

The glen dissolves into darkness as the mysterious entity melds with my mind. Silence fills my head, then roaring water, so much louder than before.

I open my eyes.

I see water. It falls in force. I am in a cave, nestled high above a forest. The glittering sunlight blinks through a curtain of water. It's a waterfall. I gasp. It's the *waterfall. The one from the glen. I'm on the other side of it.*

"Steady breath." Captain Aric's voice breaks through.

Far below, the water crashes to the ground, its steady roar a soothing white noise. I inhale and curl my talons . . .

Talons?

I have talons, as black as lava rock and as sharp as shark teeth. I curl them around the edge of the cave and stretch my back long, all the way through my tail. I fan my wings out at my side.

Tail. Wings.

Talons.

This can't be real.

"Focused mind," Captain Aric chants.

I acknowledge and release.

On the other side of the waterfall, an eagle cries out, the same one who greets me each morning. Joy fills my heart. I leap through the cool, refreshing waterfall to greet my friend. The two of us soar over valleys, wind caressing my periwinkle scales as they sparkle in the sun.

I bank toward an iridescent pond, nestled in the heart of the forest, and land on its shore. The earth is soft against the balls of my feet, allowing me to carry my statuesque figure with grace and ease. I approach the pond and lower my neck to drink, only to find a woman staring back at me. She is brown-skinned, dark-haired, and breathtaking. She is my human form, and men will fall at her feet.

Nalini.

The shock steals the air right out of my chest.

"Steady breath."

The woman in the pond looks afraid. Her eyes scream with warning.

"Steady breath."

She recoils, retreating from the surface of the pool. Her features grow murky as the water ripples red.

A stabbing pain seizes my chest. I try to back away from the water, but I'm frozen in place.

"Aryam?" Marleyn's voice is sharp, worried.

"Control your breaths," Captain Aric snaps.

I cannot respond.

The red in the water takes the shape of a dragon's face—wider, sterner, older than my own. A red dragon with white hair and blazing eyes. A dragon king.

"Aryam!"

The darkness crashes in on me, wraps its tendrils around my

throat, and squeezes. I claw at it. I'm twice trapped—at the pond's edge and in the chamber's darkness. I claw and claw and claw. *The dragon king's face glares back at me from the pond, eyes bright orange, anger palpable.*

With my heart beating fast, I blow out a white mist. It rolls over the pond, obscuring it. When it dissipates, the pond is frozen, and the dragon king has vanished.

"Aryam!"

"*Release me,*" the Dragon King speaks into my mind. The darkness releases its hold around my neck, and I fall onto my side, gasping for air. My hands lie before my face, tiny flakes of ice coating my fingertips. A tiny cloud of frost puffs out from my lips. Marleyn doesn't hesitate to gather me up in her arms, squeezing me tight, as if willing her warmth into my skin.

"Aric, what did you do?" she chastises.

My teeth chatter against each other. "It wasn't him," I say. The darkness—that curious, awful, darkness—the one from the physical world, hovers nearby. But it doesn't reach for me again. "I know what the tear did to me." What Eroden thought I should have figured out—what she must have sensed in me the moment I went near her.

Lazy girl, she'd said. *You should have figured it out by now.*

All those score, I should have been more curious about the waterfall. I should have gone to investigate it. Is that what Ranee was waiting for?

"The teardrop awakened Nalini's spirit inside of me." It let her *in*, into my mind. "The ice in my blood. It's hers. Now that she's awakened, I . . . maybe, I can use it."

And as if all this time she has been waiting for me to acknowledge it, my grandmother's spirit tugs gently at my heart, as if to say hello.

. . .

BACK IN KING Felix's study, Marleyn drapes a blanket over my shoulders while Aric serves me a hot cup of tea, both still reeling from the revelation I sprang on them down below. Coldness nips at my bones, completely at odds with the fire that plagues my fears. King Elrey's fire burning Beldemar to a crisp.

He wants to kill us all.

I tug the blanket tighter around my shoulders, but it does little to thaw the ice in my veins.

"We need to find the griot," Marleyn asserts.

"I'll send out more scouts and upgrade the priority," Captain Aric announces. The study door clicks shut behind him after he leaves.

My teeth chatter against the cold. "Marleyn," I stammer, "if Jesminder manages to free the Dragon King . . . " Hundreds of thousands of people will die.

Her eyes glisten with steel. "We *won't* let that happen."

I want to be comforted by her words, but the truth is that Jesminder has outsmarted us from the beginning. She manipulated us into getting the key to the king's prison. She is over a thousand score older and smarter. We need all the help we can get to outwit her. "We need to bring the others up to speed," I assert. "About everything." They have a right to know what we're all involved in.

Marleyn nods. "It's time," she agrees.

We walk silently through King Felix's hallways, the mystery of the griot stifling any hope of conversation. My mind drifts forward, to the moment we'll tell Rae that *I'm* the princess. The only satisfaction in it is that she won't be able to criticize me as much as she does now. My mouth twitches into a half smile and I start to share my revelation with Marleyn, but the shock in her eyes halts me.

That's all the warning I have before a flurry of blue and brown and green befalls us, leaving Marleyn pressed against the wall by two members of Chiwa's trio and myself arrested by the third. The Maradi conductor pins my arms behind my back. My blood thins at the sight of the Jaran's and Gede's hands clasped around Marleyn's wrists, at the way they prevent her from uniting her hands to summon her oju.

They know.

Marleyn struggles to free herself, but the women, who have at least fifteen score of training on us, are too strong. "How . . . dare . . . you?" she grunts out between breaths.

"How dare they *what*?" a voice calls from the darkness of the hallway before us. Princess Chiwa steps into the light, a cruel smile on her face. She reaches Marleyn in five crisp steps, the sounds of her heels echoing down the hall. She peers into my conductor's face. "You have his complexion," she says softly, "his hair texture even. It's easy to see how we were all fooled by you, *Guardian Marleyn*, especially without that freakish wife of his around to compare you to." She turns away curtly, and lowers her severe eye on me. "But *you*," she says. If I didn't know any better, I would say it's amusement that colors her voice. But I do know better. It's hatred. "I should have recognized *you* the moment I saw you snooping in the library, sitting up there in *her* little nook, spying on me and Jahim."

"How did you find out?" I ask.

A feline grin stretches Princess's Chiwa's lips. "Do come out now, dear," she instructs.

My heart clenches as Katina emerges from the darkness, taking up Chiwa's side. There is a hint of concern on her face when she sees me. Then her eyes dart away from mine.

"She's so much more useful than her mother," Chiwa sneers. Her hand falls on Katina's shoulder. "Well done, girl. It would be such a waste to have you scrubbing floors like your mother. I'm glad she begged me to bring you to the capital, where you will be protected when the world falls to pieces."

Tears sting my eyes, the betrayal cutting deeper than anything I've ever felt before. "Kati, how could you?" I stammer. "You are my friend."

"*Friend?*" Chiwa spits. "How can she be *friends* with you? You are an abomination and a traitor to mankind."

"That—that isn't true," I protest.

Chiwa's voice hardens. "You *colluded* with dragonkin and gave them the one thing they needed to destroy us all."

"I didn't know what they were," I defend myself.

"So, you admit it?" she says. "Admit that you sympathized with the dragons? That you sympathize with them yet?"

"I don't," I deny. She's twisting this all up, making it sound so much worse than it is.

"Is she not friends with Kyrel Durago?" Chiwa demands, her calculating gaze sliding to Katina. "Isn't that what you told me?"

Katina raises her eyes to meet mine, hardening them as she says, "Yes."

"He's your friend, too," I blurt out, struggling to get free against the Maradi. At my movement, Marleyn renews her efforts to free herself as well. Neither of us succeed.

Princess Chiwa sighs, as if our demonstrations bore her. Only when we settle does she say, "Katina had the good sense to renounce the akbarrin the moment she knew what he was. If you had done the same, then perhaps I would not have to do what I must do now." She looks up into the eyes of the person restraining me. "Princess Aryam is a traitor and a threat to all humanity," she declares. "Dispose of her."

The Maradi's grip tightens on my arms.

"Oh, but kill her guardian first," Chiwa says, "and don't forget the captain you left tied up just down the hall there."

Too fast, the Jaran summons two green thorns, no larger than needles, and flings them into our thighs. Numbness spreads rapidly through my body, and I sink into the Maradi's arms. Paralyzed.

The Gede steps away and returns, dragging a bound Captain Aric by his ropes. The three guardians drag us swiftly and silently out of the palace.

CHAPTER TWENTY-FIVE

The paralysis lasts long enough for the trio to bind our arms behind our backs and drag us out of the palace and into the forest at its backside, into the ring of fog that swirls around the mountaintop. Capital Island's forest is nothing like Jara's or Marad's. The trees here are slender and far apart, their crowns thin, as much as I can tell through the mist. The forest seems younger than the others.

"Moons, this place is terrifying," says the Gede, a short, stocky woman with stern features. "Let's just do it here and get it over with."

"We keep going." The Maradi tightens her grip on my binds and presses her blade against my side. Marleyn's eyes flare with panic as the metal kisses my skin. I flash her a look of reassurance to let her know I'm alright. For now.

We walk deeper into the forest, the fog thickening around us. "Here?" the Gede pleads four beats later, when the mist has turned the trees into shadows. "I feel like something's watching us."

She isn't wrong. King Elrey's gaze is upon us. I can feel his presence in the chilling wind and hear his breath in the rustling leaves. "*Release me,*" he purrs.

"So that you can kill us all?" I have no idea how speaking mind to mind works or if he will even hear my response. *"No thanks."*

"Keep moving, Tess," the Maradi snaps at the Gede.

King Elrey groans. The sound is a millstone in my head. He's in pain. "*The shadows will kiss,*" he declares, "*and he will have your hand. Release me.*"

"Here." The Maradi shoves me forward. I stumble over a rock and fall to the ground, my knees sinking into mud. To my left, an inlet glistens in the fading daylight. "We can dump their bodies in the sea when we finish." Captain Aric and Marleyn fall to their knees beside me, neither daring to retaliate as the Maradi's oju flashes into her hands—a scythe with a blade of blue steel and a wooden snath. She raises it, poised to strike.

"Wait!" the golden-skinned Jaran cries. The Maradi halts, her scythe suspended in midair. "We're really going through with this? Just because Chiwa tells us to?" I can't help thinking she seemed ready to go through with it when she stabbed us with those poisonous spikes.

"If we don't, Chiwa dies for her crimes, and then we do," the Gede insists. "She killed her own cousins and attacked the princess. They will execute her for treason if they find out. Is that what you want, Mora?"

Mora's hazel eyes look haunted. "It's murder and treason."

The Maradi's hands tremble as she grips the snath of her scythe tighter. "We don't have a choice."

Mora stands her ground. "There's always a choice, Andra."

The Maradi lowers her weapon. "Kill or be killed is *not* a choice." Her voice softens, filled with tenderness only for her chorus sisters. "We've already lost our sister before we'd even met her. I won't lose another of you, not after we've all been alone for so long."

A heavy silence hangs between them. Most Monitors leave their guardians after eighteen score. That means Chiwa's guardians have lived alone for at least that long.

I glance at Marleyn, then down at her hands, slowly picking away at the threads that bind her. So, we have the same thing in mind. I rub my thumbs and fingertips together, feeling the cold that gathers there.

"There can be no dissonance amongst chorus sisters," Tess, the Gede, speaks up. "What will it be, Mora?"

The Jaran sighs. "We only need to kill the princess. The other will die with her, and the man will have the sense not to return to the capital if we set him free."

The Gede hesitates, then nods. "One murder, not three," she agrees. She approaches the Maradi and me and rests a hand on her chorus sister's shoulder. "Let me bear this burden, sister." Andra steps aside. Tess frowns down at me. "This brings me no joy."

I hold her gaze. "I don't blame you," I admit, feeling the icy chill in my hands, "but I will stop you." Crusted with ice, the ropes tied around my wrists shatter into pieces. I roll out of the way just as the Gede's oju, two giant claws, smash down where I sat. Chiwa's guardian swings for me again, but silver light flickers through the air, and the weighted end of Marleyn's serpent's fang meets her attack. The weight strikes Tess's claws with a resounding clang and deflects the blow.

My guardian springs to her feet, slashing Captain Aric free with the blade end of her fang before twirling it overhead and swinging it in a wide arc for Tess's legs. Tess leaps, narrowly evading the strike, and crashes back down. Andra and Mora rush to her side as Marleyn and Captain Aric take up mine.

Where the captain managed to pull a dagger from, I can't even fathom, but he's armed.

"You should retreat," I warn Chiwa's guardians, hoping they don't see through my bluff. We may be three on three, but they have the upper hand. It's three guardians against one. "You no longer have the advantage."

Tess sneers. "You're no match for us, girl." She scrambles toward us, her giant claws snapping, ignoring the warning cry of her conductor.

"Tess!"

But it's too late. The serpent's fang wraps around the Gede's right wrist and, with a forceful tug, severs her hand from her arm. Bright, red blood sprays in the air as the Gede screams. Her oju vanishes, and she collapses to her knees.

I turn to my guardian and behold her with a mixture of awe and horror. Not an ounce of regret registers in her eyes.

"What did you do to her?" the Jaran screams. She rushes for her chorus sister, catching her just as Tess starts to fall backward. Andra charges with her scythe, ignoring me and going right for Marleyn. As Marleyn runs and lures her farther along the bank, I realize that this is exactly what my guardian planned. She's incapacitated one opponent, lured the strongest away, and left the third with unfavorable odds. Two against one.

I glance at Captain Aric and note that he sees it, too.

Mora carefully lays Tess aside and rises to her feet. "You will pay for this."

I raise my hands. They're still so cold. "Mora, you don't want to do this."

Green light flares, and her oju appears—a green gauntlet of thorns. She looks so devastatingly gorgeous, like a deadly flower. She steps toward me. "You're wrong. I *didn't* want to do this."

Captain Aric positions his dagger. "When I say go," he whispers.

But I see the way he limps and sways on his feet. They were rougher with him back at the palace than they were with Marleyn and me. "I'm not leaving you." Not again.

"Princess." His voice drops into a low growl, but there's desperation in it. Fear that can't be quelled.

I clench my fists, reaching for that strange power. "I'm not leaving."

The captain snarls softly, "Fine. Stay behind me, princess."

I do as he says, sliding behind him, still quietly reaching for the ice. Mora's hands shimmer as she conjures two long, razor-sharp spikes, wielding them like daggers. She charges with a feral cry, closing the distance between us in an instant.

Captain Aric meets her advance, raising his own dagger. Mora strikes first, thrusting one spike at his chest. Aric parries the blow with his dagger, the blade cutting into the spike's woody fiber as he deflects the attack to the side. Mora follows with a swift slash from another spike, aiming for his throat.

He swiftly ducks under the strike and counters with a quick jab at her midsection. Mora twists away, just out of reach. She spins back, slashing two fresh spikes in a brutal crosscut. The captain blocks one, but the second catches his arm, leaving a shallow cut. He grits his teeth but keeps his eyes locked on the fuming guardian.

Mora sneers at him. "Not bad for a monitor," she spits.

The captain pants, reestablishing his position in front of me. "I knew yours," he retorts. "Came back eighteen score ago happy to be rid of you."

Mora's face hardens, and I wonder if she's just another of many guardians with a terrible monitor.

Captain Aric labors to get his breath under control.

"He trained you well," the captain goes on, "but he was always lousy on the left. It looks like you inherited the flaw."

Mora snarls at that and charges the captain with two

enormous spikes protruding from her arms like sharp-edged lances. "How's this for lousy?"

"Duck!" the captain commands.

We drop in unison as Mora's lances close over our heads in a clear move to separate them from our necks. Captain Aric rolls one way, and I roll the other, flanking the guardian between us.

"Seas," the captain swears as he marks our distance from each other. He grunts, putting a hand to his side. The hand comes away bloody.

That's when I notice the dripping spike protruding from Mora's knee. She distracted us with the lances overhead only to catch Captain Aric in the side with her true attack.

"Captain!" I cry.

He falls onto his knees, then face-first into the mud, spasming in pain. Then, still. He goes so still.

Mora turns toward me, her eyes burning green and wild. "Now," she mumbles. "I'll make you wish you'd listened to him when he told you to run."

Impossibly fast, Mora leads with her elbow, a spike as long as a dagger protruding from its tip. I grasp for Nalini's power, but it doesn't come. That little trick with the rope seems to be all I could manage. I could run, but I'll take that spike in the back if I try. I have only enough time to shield my face with my arms.

The blow I expect to take my life never lands. Instead, I'm blinded by light. Then Rae stands between Mora and me. She raises her bow just in time to deflect Mora's attack. Chyou appears at Mora's side. She strikes Mora with a powerful blow, sending her flying, flying toward Maya, who with one swipe of her flaming sword, cuts the guardian in half.

I barely register Andra's scream, devastated and feral, before I crumple into Rae's arms and lose myself to darkness.

. . .

I WAS GOING TO DIE. The oju ajo brought the rest of my guardians to me, and they saved my life. But they took someone else's. Someone who didn't deserve it. Guardian Mora is dead. Tess may be, too. After I fainted, Marleyn permitted Andra to drag her away. They've gone back to Chiwa. I have no idea what happens next for them.

Rae paces the muddy bank. "We should go after them," she says. Her oju still glows in her right hand. She hasn't released it.

"We have bigger problems." Marleyn hoists Captain Aric's unconscious body upright, sitting it against a small boulder at the water's edge.

The shadows will kiss, and he will have your hand.

"He's coming for me!" I blurt out. Until now, I've been resting against Maya, lamenting everything that has happened, but now I make myself sit up.

My guardians whip their heads toward me. Rae narrows her eyes. "*Who* is coming?"

"The jilted lover," I explain. I suspect I know what it means now. The boy in the story still wants a bride. The details Valeria filled in for me back in Jara come to mind. After the moon princess rejected him, he killed her father and conquered the moons. Still, he was left without a princess as his bride.

I bring the others up to speed.

"That doesn't explain why he's after you," Rae muses.

My words tangle in my throat. I haven't told them. "I . . . um . . . " I decide the best thing to do is just come out with it. "I'm sort of the princess of Beldemar."

Maya giggles. The sound is so surprising that I twist around to look at her.

"Yeeeaah, we kind of all knew that already." Chyou punctuates this revelation with an exaggerated yawn, as if to say it's old news.

I jump to my feet. "You *knew*?" I suspected that they knew on some subconscious, heart level, but consciously? "When? How?" I glance at Marleyn and can tell by the surprised look on her face that she hadn't known, either.

"I suspected it that night on the beach in Jara," Rae confesses. "After you . . . glowed." Rae had gone out looking for me that night on her own. She'd left Marleyn behind, even though she was injured. I hadn't stopped to think about that.

"I knew from the moment I met you," Maya admits, "when I slew Father Wood. I felt drawn to protect you."

"And I know because we just oju ajo'd to you." Chyou shrugs.

"I didn't understand why you introduced yourself to me as a guardian," Maya says, "but I went along with it, and eventually, I realized that you needed to believe it, so I didn't say anything. To anyone."

I'd suggested that we split up to find Marleyn after Adanna and Bem had been murdered. Maya had fervently protested. She'd *known*. In the labyrinth, she'd needed to be sure that I would be okay before she went off to fight the emberfiends. Even then. She'd known.

Tears dot my eyelashes. "I'm sorry I didn't admit the truth sooner." I could have spared them all a great deal of pain.

"We're happy it's out now," Maya replies, a genuine smile on her face. "It means we get to protect you."

"And to do that, we need to know why the boy in the story wants to marry you," Rae doubles back. "It's not just because you're a princess."

I purse my brows. "I don't know," I admit. I turn to Marleyn. "Do you think the griot would know?"

Marleyn blows out some air. "We'll have to locate him to find out."

"Oh, we found him," Chyou says, a sly grin on her face. But then it fades.

"What?" Marleyn asks. "What's that look?"

Maya nervously wrings her fingers. "He's just not what you would expect, and there's a problem."

Chyou airs a dramatic sigh. "The griot lost his kora."

"Pity." A hard but enchanting voice rises from the sea behind us. We flinch, turning to see Mama River emerging from the water, her serpent's body dragging behind her. "You've all come so close to figuring it all out, but you're too late."

A sharp pain sears through my ankle. Numbness spreads rapidly up my leg. My guardians cry out, and the world spins as the five of us drop into the mud. Mama River's snakes slithering into her embrace are the last thing I see before darkness takes me again.

CHAPTER TWENTY-SIX

Sunlight dances on my eyelids as consciousness slowly seeps in. Muffled voices hum at my side. I blink my eyes open to a haze of color and shapes. A few ticks later, the muffled voices and blurred shapes grow clearer. I am sprawled out on a luxurious sofa, in some sort of elegant parlor with ornate furniture and golden accents. A calming, floral fragrance greets me and almost lulls me back to sleep.

But then my memories come crashing back. I sit up with a gasp. Two firm sets of hands arrest me. "You're okay." My heart beating rapidly, I turn and stare into Marleyn's steadying gaze.

"Where are we?"

"Amaro Bay," Rae announces at my other side. "Mama River's queendom under the sea."

I tug my arms away from them and grip my head as a splitting pain strikes behind my eyes. "Oh, we're under the sea?" I shoot a petulant look at Marleyn. "I thought you said I was okay." Last I knew, being trapped leagues under the sea at the mercy of a vengeful demigoddess does not mean *okay*. The pain digs deeper, and I grimace as my vision flickers.

"She means you're not dead," Chyou proclaims from the

other side of the room. I blink up at her. She's blurry. They all are.

I blink again and then they're gone. *The room is different. Small and wooden, bare except for some fish netting and a plain wooden chair. A woman stands before me, but she is not one of my friends. Jesminder's worlds'-deep eyes meet mine.*

I gasp, flinching away from her. Hands grip my arms again, steadying me. "What's wrong?" Marleyn, Rae, Chyou, the fancy parlor. It all comes rushing back. Jesminder vanishes.

I struggle for my breath. "I . . . I . . . " I look around, taking stock of the room, of the gossamer curtains fluttering gently in the wind, of the seagulls squawking in the distance. How any of this exists at the bottom of the ocean, I don't know. But it seems real. What I saw just now—that was . . .

What was that?

I scan the room again. My spine straightens. "Where are Captain Aric and Maya?" Neither are here.

Marleyn squeezes my arm before letting it go. "Mama River will only speak to you."

I scramble to my feet. After what happened to Ranee on the beach, I never would have thought to run after the aggrieved demigoddess, but I will do it if my friends are in danger. I sense that they are. "Take me to her."

We emerge from a townhouse at the edge of an ancient and sprawling city. Overhead, sunlight shimmers against a dome of pure akbarra, swirling in mesmerizing patterns with the current of the sea above. An enormous shadow passes along the barrier, and I snap my gaze away. I don't want to think about the crushing weight of all that water.

Marleyn smiles knowingly. "If it makes you feel any better, it freaked Chyou out, too."

"Did not!" Chyou objects.

But I smile, a weight in my heart lessening at the freedom Marleyn has to be herself now that she's not pretending to be me. We're all going to be great friends if we get through this.

"Mama River is this way," Rae announces, striding toward a grassy knoll just outside the city.

As we approach the small hill, I hear singing. A woman's voice, sweet and alluring, rides the wind. We crest the hill, and there sits Mama River on the shore of a creek, singing and staring into the palm of her upraised hand, as if she holds a mirror there. Her singing stops when she notices our presence, and she turns sharply, her eyes narrowing and cutting directly to me. In an instant, she coils her serpentine body and springs for us, for me.

Marleyn and Rae close in front of me, but neither calls her oju. Can't, I realize. The same way I can't feel Nalini's powers cooling my blood. I wedge between my guardians, nudging them aside. If Mama River wanted to kill me, she would have done it back on the surface world.

Mama River circles around us, ensnaring us with her scaly body. She stops before me, peering down into my eyes. She sniffs, her lips curling with distaste, and I realize I must smell awful after being dragged through the forest and mud. I bow my head. "Forgive me, Mama," I plead.

My deference seems to please her. She huffs and backs off, just a little. I decide to press my luck. "I come to you with a humble heart and seek your forgiveness."

"For what crime, daughter?" she demands.

I clench my fists to keep them from trembling. "For my mother's," I say, "and my friend's." Ranee attacked her, and Maya killed her husband. "They did not know what they were doing. They were only trying to protect me."

Mama River darts away a few steps, turning her back on me.

"Their crimes are unforgivable. I thought you came here to worry about yourself. You do not have much time after all."

Pain nips at the space between my eyes again. My vision blurs. I fight it off and force myself to speak through it. "Please, Mama. What can I do to free them?" I ask. "There must be something."

Mama River turns back toward me and eyes me up and down, as if considering, but I can see by the gleam in her eye that she has already decided on her price. Hope flares inside me. Ranee. She must be here. I'm going to see her again.

"I will let the girl go," Mama River offers. "However, she has taken a husband from me. You will give me another."

I furrow my brows, trying to grasp at her meaning. I can't even secure my own love life, and now I am to play matchmaker to a demigoddess? "I'm sorry, Mama," I say. "I don't know anyone."

"She means Aric," Marleyn murmurs at my side. There should be horror in her voice. There should be pleading and shock and disbelief. But her voice is steady. "You should agree."

I whirl to face her. "I should *what*?"

Marleyn's solemn gaze doesn't falter.

"He's your monitor."

"He's prepared me well," she responds. "If he were here right now, he would tell you the same thing. Do it."

I shake my head, struggling to believe the words coming out of her mouth. "It isn't right," I reason. She must see that it isn't right.

But she can't.

She can only see me.

I glance at Rae and Chyou. They can all *only* see me.

I turn back to Mama River. She watches me quietly, a small, pretty smile on her face. I shake my head. "Please, Mama. There must be another way."

She turns back toward the water. "I will return the three of you to the surface, daughter," she says, her tone dismissive, "and you will be grateful for your lives."

She starts to hum again, and I remember the way we found her, staring into her hand. "Where is your mirror?" I ask.

Mama River swivels around, glaring at me. "What do you know of my mirror?" she demands.

I smile. Good. "What if I retrieve it for you?" I bargain. "Will you release Captain Aric then?"

Mama River roars with laughter. "Foolish girl," she barks. "You do not know what you promise. To retrieve my mirror, you must approach the very one you should be running far, far away from."

My skin crawls. "You mean Anton?" I stammer. That's the name of the boy in the story, another helpful detail from Valeria.

Mama River scowls. "He has taken something from all of us," she snarls. "It is why we do his bidding." She paces on the riverbank, darting to and fro with the speed of a mamba. She halts. "Fetch my mirror," she agrees, "and I will return the man to you."

"Aryam," Rae hisses. "Don't do it."

"Deal," I agree. "And Maya?"

Mama River flicks her hand, and a crop of curly blond hair emerges from the creek behind her, followed by Maya's face, torso, and . . . tail! The scales of her tail, golden-orange and iridescent, flicker and flex as they fade back into human legs. She collapses onto the shore, coughing up water. Rae and Chyou rush to help her to her feet.

My heart pounds in my chest. "And Ranee?" I sputter. "C-can I see her?"

Mama River sneers. "You already have."

My mind flashes back to Eroden's Pass, to that blur of silver

I saw flicker in the raging river far below the bridge, to that voice in my head urging me to keep moving. It was her. *Ranee* had helped me. I reach for Mama River. “Please,” I plead. “Just let me talk to her.”

But Mama River’s snakes sink their fangs into my ankle once more and the world fades away.

CHAPTER TWENTY-SEVEN

When I wake this time, dawn streams between the trees, shining pockets of light into the dark forest. It was night when Mama River took us. I groan, rolling over in the mud, only to bump into something hard and hollow. I open my eyes to see a round calabash covered in hide. A long, wooden neck protrudes from it, with strings running from the gourd to the tip of the neck.

A kora.

As my guardians awaken around me, I sit on my knees a pluck and folded scrap of paper from the instrument. In swirling, elegant handwriting, it reads:

Tell the drunken fool I have no need for this.

We soak ourselves in seawater, rinsing mud from our skin and wringing the water out of our uniforms as best we can. Rae and Marleyn exchange soft-spoken words. Then Rae shoots me a withering look before darting off into the forest. "Where's she going?" I ask Marleyn. Part of me is relieved I won't have to endure her rage over the deal I struck with Mama River. The other part of me worries for her safety.

"I sent Rae to hunt something down for you," Marleyn

replies. "She was just closing in on it when the oju ajo whisked her away." She turns to Chyou. "Take us to the griot."

Chyou leads the way, wearing the griot's kora on her back. Maya wraps her arms around herself and shivers at the cool water still clinging to her skin and clothes. "How do you think she got Chori's kora?" she asks me, her teeth chattering.

I bite back the urge to ask her for the fifth time if she's okay. Moons know I wouldn't be if I'd been turned into a mermaid, but she'll only tell me that she's fine. "People used to give gifts to Mama River all the time, whenever they wanted something. Maybe he gave it to her." I glance up at a patch of sky peeking through the sparse canopy above us, at a strange flicker of light beyond the clouds. "Do you see that?"

"See what?"

A searing pain ignites between my ears. I stumble, reaching for the nearest tree to steady myself.

I am looking at the sky but through someone else's eyes. I see a faint trace of metallic black glimmering beyond the atmosphere. I turn, and there is Jesminder again, staring at me as if I'm her world. She looks scared.

The vision vanishes.

"What was that?" My guardians stand rigid and alert, like sentries on the lookout for an invisible foe. Marleyn fixes me with an assessing look. "What's happening to you?"

"I don't know." My breath cuts out of me like ragged shards of glass. It's the truth. I don't know what's happening to me, but I look up at the sky, at the faint flicker of black beyond the world. "But I *do* know what that is." In my vision, I was in someone else's head, and it became clear. "That's the dark moon."

Marleyn traces my gaze. "Hama," she murmurs.

I nod. "Shadowkiss is happening today."

She pivots. "We need to hurry," she says, before striding swiftly uphill.

"THE GRIOT LIVES HERE?" I ask, gazing at a makeshift village that sprawls across a verdant slope. It's a haphazard collection of shacks fashioned from discarded materials.

Chyou shakes her head and points higher, toward a jagged cliff that oversees the village. "No. He lives up there."

Above us, a small cave is barely visible against the exposed rock face. It's more of a hole than a cave, patched up with rusty planks, except for a triangular slit between them, serving as the entrance. Sallow-faced elders, lean and ancient, poke their heads out of shanties made of rusted metal sheets and peer at us as we walk by. Some sit outside, fine-tuning weathered instruments and cooking meager provisions over smoky fires. A toothless old man grins at me, his clothes little more than tattered rags. I force out a polite smile and wave hello.

I ignore the barking in my aching legs as we begin the ascent up to the griot's hovel. When we finally reach the entrance, Chyou shifts the kora on her back and bangs on one of the metal sheets. "Hello! We're back!" she yells into the darkness. "Come out already."

Twirling a lock of her hair around one finger, Maya smiles at the confusion on my and Marleyn's faces. "Chyou has a way with him," she explains.

A round, brimless cap emerges first from the darkness, followed by an old man hobbling out of the hole. Once out, he straightens up as much as his timeworn body will let him and grins a toothless, *tongueless* grin when he sees the instrument strapped to my guardian's back.

I fail to stifle my gasp.

Marleyn politely covers her mouth.

The old man reaches into the pocket of the burgundy pants sagging from his wasted frame and pulls out two smooth stones, which he proceeds to tap together in a display of enthusiasm. I watch as Chyou's eyes shift to the stones, deep in concentration.

Maya leans into my ear. "He's communicating in Gidi," she whispers. "It's an ancient language once used in Gedra's mountains between human acolytes and the rock dragons they served."

I glance at Chyou. "And she knows this ancient rock language?"

Marleyn shrugs. "It suits her. Don't you think?"

"I guess it does," I agree.

"I'm *trying* to concentrate, you know?" Chyou complains, and the three of us fall silent as the griot taps out the rest of his message. Chyou's jaw tightens. "Do we really have time for that?" she groans.

"What did he say?" Marleyn asks.

Chyou faces us. "Songkeeper Chori thanks us for returning his treasured kora and invites us to tea."

I glance up at the sky, at the shadow looming beyond the clouds. Soon, there will be two moons in the sky. I face the Songkeeper. "Thank you," I say, "but Guardian Chyou is right. We're in a hurry."

Chori's wrinkled hands bring the stones together once more, and he clacks out an insistent message to Chyou. I guess the gist of it before Chyou even translates. "Songkeeper Chori insists. He says it's poor conduct not to properly bestow his thanks, and besides, he needs some time to refresh his memory."

I glance again at the sky. "Fine, but we can't stay long."

The Songkeeper beams and ducks into his cave. Chyou removes the kora from her back and sets it against the rock wall as Chori reemerges with a wooden crate. He drags the crate to the center of our circle, then returns for a cloth and a surprisingly nice tea set. Not long after, the five of us crowd around the crate and sip on an herbal tea imbued with jasmine and mint. Chori attends to our cups with utmost hospitality, refilling them almost as soon as we take a sip.

"What happened to your tongue?" I ask, as he pours more tea into my cup. His hand falters. Then he sets the tea kettle aside, picks up his rocks, and taps out another message. Chyou translates.

"It was cut out after the war, after I helped the Dragon Princess create the seal."

I frown. "That must have been horrible," I say. "I'm sorry that happened to you." I don't know which thought is more unsettling—that the man before me holds at least a thousand score or that he's spent most of those score completely silent. It must be a terrible fate for a man of griot caste.

The griot clacks the stones together again. "You seek to reinforce the seal. To trap akbarrin again."

I nod.

His lips turn downward. "It was a mistake. Nalini regretted it, in the end."

I press my hands against the warm china of my teacup, willing the coolness out of my fingers. "If I don't do it, the Dragon King will unleash his wrath on my people." I think of the faceless children and their horrid pranks and the Moongazer and countless other creatures that will inhabit Beldemar. "Horrible things will keep happening."

Chori pulls a small flask from the folds of his clothes and tilts it into his cup. A foul-smelling liquid splashes into his tea. He brings the flask to his lips and drains it before picking up his tea. My guardians and I exchange glances, and I recall what Mama River called the old griot. A drunken fool. He slams his empty cup down on the crate and belches before clumsily grabbing the stones and slapping them together.

"I will help you."

Tension melts out of my shoulders. I offer Chori a grateful smile. His answering smile is cooler than mine, but I hardly have time to ponder it as a piercing whistling sound slices through the air. A burst of green darts above the forest's canopy below us and explodes into a cloud of green smoke. Marleyn hops to her feet. "She did it," she exclaims. She turns to the griot. "You said you need time to remember the song. How long will that take?"

He clacks his stones together. One tumbles out of his hand and rolls to the ground as he releases another belch. A drunken smile spreads across his face.

"A measure," Chyou translates, wrinkling her nose at the Songkeeper's odor. "Give or take a quarter."

Marleyn nods. "Stay here and make sure it gets done," she commands Chyou and Maya. Her hand slides around my wrist, and she tugs. "Come with me."

CHAPTER TWENTY-EIGHT

It's midmorning when Marleyn and I find Rae in the forest. She stands proudly beside her quarry, two boys wrapped back-to-back in glowing green vines. "I caught a dragon," she announces. "And a fool."

My feet stumble to a stop. "Kyrel?"

His eyes rise to meet mine and widen at the sight of me. "Pigtails?"

The boy on the other side of him pauses his squirming at the sound of my name and then renews it with increased vigor. "Aryam?"

A gleeful laugh escapes my lips. "Darien!" I lap around them, then stand face-to-face with my oldest friend. Less than a quarter score has passed since we last saw each other, but I think he's grown even taller. I spot the few squiggles of hair on his top lip. "You're starting to grow a mustache to match your sideburns," I squeal. That elicits laughter from both of us. His is pitchy and deeper than I remember.

I dash back around to face Kyrel, and my laughter tapers off as I meet his sobering gaze. "How did you get here?" I ask. I take a step back. "How . . . how do I know it's really you?"

A hand reaches past my face and tugs on Kyrel's ear. "Because," Marleyn says as she steps between us, "you can make a skin thief drop their skin by pulling their ear like so." She reaches around and yanks Darien's ear, eliciting a yowl. My guardian grins, not even folding under Kyrel's incensed glare. She shrugs. "The ear trick works, but if you pay enough attention, you'll also see that a skin thief is a terrible actor. They usually overcompensate."

I think about how Adisa behaved on Eroden's pass, laying the teasing on thick—being *too much* Kyrel.

Kyrel stares daggers at Marleyn.

"Sorry," I apologize, drawing his eyes back to me. I resist the urge to touch his face, to run my fingers along his skin. "I . . . " I start to tell him about Adisa and how he deceived me, but he cuts me off.

"I know," he says. "When a skin thief wears your skin, he's connected to you."

My blood chills. "Connected? Connected how?"

His eyes darken and grow distant. "You see glimpses," he explains. "Glimpses of what they see." Focus returns to his eyes and he trains it on me. "I saw you when you almost fell from that bridge." Something like horror takes over his gaze, but the mask falls quickly back into place. He doesn't say what else he saw.

My heart quickens. I press a hand against it. "Untie them," I plead.

Rae glances at Marleyn for approval before making the vines vanish, but her bow appears in her hand, and I know she'll use it without hesitation if she even suspects that either of them poses a threat to me. I shift my body, angling myself between her and Kyrel. "How does a skin thief get your skin?" I ask.

He frowns. "They just have to touch it."

I find it hard to breathe. "He touched me twice," I whisper, remembering the crumb he wiped away from my lips and when he caught me after I made it across the bridge. How could I have been so stupid?

When I look into Kyrel's eyes, I can tell that he already knows. He saw that, too. My shoulders slump as shame settles in. Kyrel grips my chin, his hands strong and gentle, and raises my gaze to meet his. "That wasn't your fault," he says, a hard edge to his voice as if he can command me to believe it.

Tears roll down my cheeks and onto his fingers. "I thought you were acting differently," I say. Adisa had been distant at first. He'd sounded older and wearier of this world than anyone our age should sound. "I should have known it wasn't you."

Kyrel's lips press against mine and everything stops. My worries. My heart. The world. The kiss is soft and firm and everything I ever wanted it to be. My knees buckle as a fierce, prickling wave sweeps through me, leaving me breathless and giddy. He pulls away, a faint gleam in his eyes. My breath hitches.

"Ahem." Behind Kyrel, Darien clears his throat, looking as stunned as I feel. He coughs out an awkward laugh, but I see a flicker of something else in his expression. Hurt?

Kyrel looks pleased, and I wonder if he's been thinking about kissing me for some time now.

I straighten myself out, fighting through the elation that weighs down my limbs. I shake it off. "What are you both doing here?"

"We left when I saw you in the Shadows," Kyrel explains. "Through Adisa's visions. We went to Jara first. The Protectors at the Gate were rightfully mistrustful of us, especially Valeria."

"They locked us up," Darien jumps in.

I don't know why, but the thought of Valeria getting the better of my friends makes me want to laugh. I turn to Darien. "You came to save me?"

He glancecs between Kyrel and me, and I can swear he stares at our lips. "Kyrel told me the truth about the two of you," he says, after a moment. He opens a satchel at his side, revealing rolled-up scraps of parchment. "I thought if I could collect your story, I'd finally get a chance at joining the storyguard."

I smile. "Of course." But something tells me he would have come for me even without that chance.

Marleyn steps forward. "Captain Aric's spies caught wind of these two sneaking around," she said. "I had Rae hunt them down."

I look at her. "Why?"

She levels her eyes on Kyrel, and there's not an ounce of the kindness there that she reserves for me and the others. "Because I did some research of my own," she shares. "I thought about what you told me of Liora and Hama, and I wondered why they needed Shadowkiss to meet—not just why they needed it, but *how* they used it."

"They needed love." Kyrel's voice carries the weight of a world on his shoulders.

"Love?" I repeat, feeling the same heaviness come crashing down on me. If I've learned anything from all the stories I've heard, love ends poorly for people like us. The princess of the white moon loved the prince of the dark moon. Nalini loved Donomar. My mother loved my father. I look at Kyrel and feel my heart withering. Before, I would have given anything for him, for the kiss that still lingers on my lips.

But we can't be in love. Adisa was right.

He takes my hand in his, and I tremble at the touch that, before, would have stolen my breath. He squeezes. "Our hearts sing to each other," he says. "It is why we'll always find each other. I know you feel it."

I blink back tears. "I don't want to feel it." His pupils flare, but the rest of him is frozen. I ease my hand out of his. "Maybe this is another reason why Ranee hid the truth," I say, the words spilling out of my mouth. "Maybe she did it to protect us from the fact that love leads to tragedy for people like us."

His pupils constrict again as determination sets in. "I won't let anything happen to us, Pigtails."

I shake my head. "You don't understand. If I . . . " My voice breaks. "*When* I close the seal again, you will go back to the Shadows, and I will stay here." And I will do it. I will send him away because I am no guardian bound to a princess. I am a princess bound to an empire. It is my duty to keep it safe.

We must put duty before self, Ranee's words echo through my mind, *now, more than ever.*

He grabs my hand again and presses it flat against his chest. My insides melt at the firm muscle beneath his shirt, but then I feel what he wants me to feel. His heart beating forcefully inside his chest. "It sings for you," he repeats. "That won't change whether I'm here or in the Shadows."

Rae rolls her eyes. "We can deal with that part later," she interrupts. "We need to know what that skin thief wants with Aryam's skin."

"I agree," Marleyn speaks up, but amusement flickers in her eyes as she glances at my hand, still pressed against Kyrel's pectorals. I pull it away and hide it in the folds of my skirt, averting my eyes to Darien, whose face is about as flushed as mine feels.

Kyrel stares steadily at me, ignoring the others. "Close your eyes," he instructs.

I do.

"Seek the thread that connects your mind to his. It will feel like a tickle behind the eyes."

"I feel it." It's there, just as he described.

"Pull it."

I pull.

My eyes flash open, but I am no longer in the forest with my friends. I'm limping into the gatehouse, bleeding down my arm. "Is that the princess?" Joan lowers her voice as she says my title. She and Dex scramble to their feet. She reaches me first. "What happened to you? Where are your guardians? Where's the captain?"

"I . . . I don't know." It's my voice but not me saying it. "Chiwa's guardians attacked us."

How does he know that?

Joan and Dex exchange looks. Dex's hand goes to the hilt of his sword as he scans our surroundings for danger. "Come with us," Joan says, taking my arm. She leans into my ear. "Our theory was right. The dark moon was never destroyed—it was in the Shadows all this time!"

And now it's coming back.

So, that's what she wanted to tell me before.

The vision snaps. I stumble backward into Marleyn's arms. "What happened?" she asks.

"He shut her out," Kyrel assumes. "You can only hold the thread for so long."

I nod because that's what I felt, like Adisa cut the thread that links our minds.

"It will grow back," Kyrel reassures me. "It's like spider's silk blowing in the wind."

I turn to my guardians. "He's with Joan and Dex." I look at Kyrel. "Are my friends in danger?" I ask.

He furrows his brows. "Adisa is like an uncle to me. I've never known him to be violent," he says, and it's hard for me not to get caught up on that word. *Uncle.* "But I do know that he's desperate."

I straighten up. "We need to hurry."

I turn for the griots' village, and the others follow suit, but Rae steps in front of Kyrel. It's only now that I realize she still holds her oju. She's almost his height, almost tall enough to look him straight in the eye. It doesn't matter that she's not. "So, what side are you on, dragon boy?" she demands.

I want to protest. I want to scold her for being mean to him, but she's right to ask. We need to know if Kyrel will help us with the seal, even if it means he ends up on the other side of it.

He raises his hands, showing that he's not a threat, and nods toward me. "I'm on her side."

Rae holds his gaze a few ticks longer before sliding her own toward Darien. My friend flushes. "I'm on her side, too," he sputters.

Rae's oju disappears.

Music, bright and clear, weaves toward us. It starts softly, an otherworldly melody that lures the heart one plucked string at a time. Marleyn exhales. "It sounds like the griot is ready."

CHAPTER TWENTY-NINE

The music has stopped by the time we return to the village, but we can see Songkeeper Chori, Chyou, and Maya awaiting us on the ledge. At my side, Darien can barely keep a lid on his excitement. "I can't believe this is happening," he squeals, his voice cracking a little.

Marleyn glances at him. She leans into my side. "What's wrong with your friend?"

"He's never met a real griot," I explain.

"Only the story grunts that get sent to villages like ours," Darien says.

Marleyn smirks. "Then you're in for a treat," she says. "This one's unlike any griot I've ever met." I remember the wine and rot of Songkeeper Chori's breath and think she's telling the truth.

I turn my face toward my friend and offer him an encouraging smile. "Just keep an open mind," I suggest. "Oof." My face smacks into Kyrel's back. "Hey," I protest, but he doesn't budge. I follow his gaze to the sky, to the pale yellow orb just barely visible in the morning light. *Liora.* Kyrel makes a low growling sound, his eyes darting between the two moons. Not knowing what else to do, I slide my hand into his and squeeze, the touch sending shivers up my arm. I sense his body relax. "Let's keep going," I whisper.

He doesn't move at first, nor does he let go of my hand. "I can hear them," he says. "They're singing."

It takes me a few ticks to get past how unsettling his words are, and then I hear it, too—two distinct notes humming at a low frequency. Marleyn takes my free hand and gently tugs me toward Chori's ledge. I follow, pulling Kyrel behind me.

Chori sits on a stump beside his crate, holding his kora by its neck. A blank sheet of parchment lies on the crate before him. If he's surprised to see us returning with friends, it doesn't show. The old griot just starts to play.

The music sweeps over us like a tidal wave as he plucks the first strings. Kyrel squeezes my hand as we brace ourselves against the wind. In the village below, the other griots stumble out of their shacks, blinking their ancient eyes in surprise. Then a flautist raises his flute to his lips and joins in, followed by a woman with a voice of timber humming a wailing tune. Someone plays a hand drum. Another plays the lute. Soon, an intricate song fills the forest.

And words inked in gold appear on the parchment, one by one. I stumble toward the crate and read them. Tears stream down my face by the end of it.

At my side, Marleyn asks, "What does it say?"

And I realize she can't read it because it is written for dragons. *You are like us now, Aryam,* Eroden had said. *You can read the songs of the dragons.* I look up at my guardian through blurry eyes. "It is a story," I explain. A story and a warning.

The song is about Nalini. Nalini, who was wise and foolish. Nalini, who saved and cursed us all. The song obliterates everything that I thought was true about the romance between the Dragon Princess and the Human Prince. In fact, it wasn't a romance at all.

Donomar *used* her.

He tricked and betrayed her, and by the time she came to realize it, it was too late. She was left with only terrible choices to make, choices that hurt the people she loved.

After explaining to my friends, I turn to Chori. "The Dragon King *was* a threat to humans," I confirm, "but humans deserved it. Anton destroyed his egg." I think of the fountain that sits at the center of the palace's labyrinth, a fountain shaped like a cracked egg. The water dripping out of it is the akbarra that Anton stole. "Then Donomar seduced his daughter and turned her against him."

An ache throbs in my heart, and I know it is Nalini's spirit weeping with regret.

Chori nods.

"Even when Nalini realized it," I carry on, "she imprisoned her father."

Chori's frail fingers reach for his stones. Chyou translates for him. "The Dragon King was furious. He wanted to purge humans from these lands because humans are treacherous beings, but his daughter still loved them."

"So she drained the dark moon of its power," I conclude, "and used it to bury him in the island."

Chori nods again.

"And in doing so, she trapped Anton."

Another nod. Chori clacks his stones together. "It was Anton who corrupted Donomar. The great dragons were dying out, and he needed another youngling. He wanted Nalini to bear an heir."

"But she'd already had my mother and aunt," I point out. It still makes me squeamish to think of how long they've both been alive.

Chori shakes his head. "Too old. To get the power he seeks, Anton needed a youngling."

"But Nalini and Donomar never had children," Marleyn speaks up. "There never was a dragon heir." Her eyes widen. She looks at me. "Until you. That's why he wants you."

Kyrel growls. "I am a dragon," he says. "Why doesn't he come for me instead?"

Chori eyes him before clacking the stones. "You come from good stock. Zorel and Eroden were powerful dragons, but they were not greater dragons. Only Elrey, son of Tivinia, is a great dragon. He is the last great dragon. His offspring are still more powerful than any other."

I shudder, thinking of what Anton did to Elrey's egg, how he let the ant, the wolf, and the eagle devour it. How it gave them all great powers. "So what?" I say. "Does he want to eat me?"

Chori barks out a laugh. It is a creepy, raspy sound. He taps the stones together. "If you were an egg, he would most certainly eat you, but you are alive. There is another way he can claim your power. He aims to marry you."

Kyrel snarls, and for a second, I think he'll rip the old man to pieces. The sound sobers the old man. "If you want to stop him," he taps, "you must sing the song. Let your hearts' melody intertwine with that of the moons when the shadows kiss, and you will seal him away for good."

I put a hand on Kyrel's shoulder, and it seems to calm him. Chori raises his eyes to the sky. "Go to the moon tower," he instructs. "That is where you must be when the time comes." Then he plucks a few notes on his kora and he, his griots, and their entire village shimmer out of sight.

. . .

"Did that really just happen?" Darien stands flabbergasted on the ledge, several beats after Chori vanished.

"You kind of get used to crazy things like that," Chyou mutters. She squints her eyes at him. "Who are you, anyway?"

My head still spinning from Chori's revelations, I hurry through the introductions. "Chyou, Maya, my friend Darien. Darien, my guardians, Chyou and Maya."

Only Maya has the presence of mind to smile politely and hold out her hand. "Nice to meet you," she says. He shakes it, and if I didn't know any better, I'd say he was blushing.

We don't linger long. Rae quickly enlists Maya and Chyou to help her scavenge for freshwater mussels in the nearby stream. With practiced hands, she wraps them in banana leaves, seasoning them with wild onions and garlic left behind by the griots, then roasts them over a flame kindled by Maya's sword. Chyou takes a bite and gags at the texture. "Bleh. Tastes like survival," she complains, scrunching her nose.

My heart aches at the reality of her words. Rae once had to fend for herself like this. For her, this was survival. She shoots Chyou a withering look.

"I like it," Maya says, though the wince in her smile gives her away.

Darien slurps the tender meat out of a shell and agrees. "Honestly, it's the best mussel I've ever had."

I flash him a knowing smile. It's the *only* mussel he's ever had. These creatures aren't native to Marad.

Rae rolls her eyes, but she doesn't tell anyone to shut up, so I think she appreciates the gesture.

After we eat, Marleyn holds her hands against the sky. She squints, peering through the triangle formed by her fingers as if she can calculate the distance between the two moons. "I think we have two or three measures before they meet," she estimates. She winks at me. "Let's get you to that tower."

"There are just two problems," I remind her. "Chiwa's trying to kill me, and Captain Aric's guard thinks they already have me."

Marleyn shrugs. "Chiwa's down a few guardians, and we'll deal with the rest if it becomes a problem. Are you ready?"

I nod, clutching Chori's song to my chest. The forest resonates with the moons' steady tunes, low, pulsing notes that only Kyrel and I can hear. He stands tall beside me, staring in the palace's direction. I can practically see the weight of his resolution as he fortifies it in his mind. He's on my side, no matter what, even if being so means that we end up in completely different realms. Forever.

Something shudders inside me. Today ends with a broken heart.

That kiss may just be the death of me after all.

As if he can read my thoughts, Kyrel takes my hand in his. "Together," he says. "We'll face this together."

Because both of us have spent our lives so very alone. I blink back my tears and force myself to nod. I wonder if, when all this is over, I will still hear his heart singing from the Shadows. I wonder if he will hear mine. Because knowing all that I know now, my heart will never stop singing for his.

Darien steps forward, fumbling awkwardly with his satchel full of parchment. I swallow the lump in my throat and push out a laugh. "Did you really need to bring so many?" I ask.

"Did he need to bring *any*?" Rae mutters as she brushes past us toward the path that will lead us to the service road.

"I thought griots were supposed to remember everything," Chyou comments.

Amusement glistens in Marleyn's eyes. "Yeah. What will you do if those notes catch fire or get wet?" she teases. She tugs the satchel's strap, laughing when it snaps back into place.

Darien clutches the bag to his chest. "Hey," he protests. "I'm not a griot yet. I'm still in training."

Marleyn shrugs and joins Rae at the front of our group while Chyou and Maya fall behind. I offer Darien a sympathetic smile. "I'm sure if you keep working at it, you'll get the hang of it," I promise. "Especially now that you don't have to spend all those measures working in your father's washhouse."

His face brightens up. "Thanks, Ary."

Rae yells back for us to start walking. We oblige. Kyrel releases my hand and goes before me. Darien walks just behind me. "Do you think you'll ever go back there?" I ask. His relationship with his father has always been strained, so I can't imagine that his leaving went over well.

Darien rubs the back of his neck. "Let's just say I'm sort of disinherited."

"The old man told him if he wants to chase after an illusion to never come back," Kyrel translates.

I wince. "I'm sorry. That had to hurt."

Darien shrugs. "He blubbered like a baby when I told him Kyrel was going with me." There's an ounce of sourness in his tone, of jealousy, I think. It's no secret that after Darien's father got over his xenophobia, he treated Kyrel like the eldest son he wished he had. Sometimes, it makes me feel guilty, knowing I'm the one who convinced him to hire Kyrel in the first place.

I put some steel in my voice. "You'll become the greatest griot in the empire," I proclaim, "and your father will see how foolish he's been all along." I glance over my shoulder to find him smiling, the dream shining in his eyes, and I turn away before he can see the concern in mine. He just has to stay alive first.

We reach the service road a quarter measure later. Marleyn halts us at the forest's edge and bids us to be quiet. "Something's not right."

I peer up and down the vacant road. "I don't see anything."

"That's the problem," Rae catches on. In a flash, her bow appears. "This is a service road. Goods should be getting transported at all measures of the day." Three flashes later, Marleyn, Chyou, and Maya are armed.

I grasp Darien's forearm. "Stay close to me," I urge. Because, if it comes down to it, I am the only one the others will protect. Darien looks like he doesn't need to be told twice.

The underbrush rustles on the other side of the road, and then she emerges. My aunt. Jesminder. And in her wake, four hooded female figures step out from the trees.

CHAPTER THIRTY

"Hello, niece." Jesminder's airy voice is laced with menace. She scans our group, a dangerous glint in her eye, and snags on Kyrel. "So. This is the thanks Adisa and I get for raising you. You side with the humans."

Kyrel doesn't rise to her bait. "Where is Adisa?" he asks. "I'd like to have a word with him."

She answers with a smug smile. "I bet you would." She spots the paper in my hand. "What do you have there?"

I hide it behind my back as my guardians fan out in front of me, the brightness of their ojus flaring with their tempers. Without moving, the hooded figures standing behind my aunt clock my guardians' movements. I note their unearthly stillness and the strange sheen of their half-covered faces.

Jesminder smiles. "Oh, don't worry about my handmaidens," she says, knowing full well that's all I'll do. As if she senses my fear, one of the handmaidens curls her mouth into a smile, showing a glimmer of perfectly white teeth. Perfectly *sharp* white teeth.

I swallow hard and try to appeal to my aunt. "I thought you wanted to help me," I say. Isn't that why she tried to convince me to leave the palace when we first met? Even if she did end up using me to get the scroll, she'd tried to spare me first.

Her face hardens. "You are my sister's youngling," she snaps. "Of course I wanted to help you. I tried to get you away from here, but you're just like her. Too stubborn. Too weak. Now it is too late. He knows who and what you are, and he's coming for you."

"You tried to take me home," I recall.

"To the Fallen Cities," she confirms, "to your mother's childhood home, where I could have kept you safe."

Marleyn's serpent's fang flares. "She's safe with us."

The handmaiden to Jesminder's right snarls, baring bright, fanged teeth. I flinch. Darien claps a hand over his mouth, muffling a yelp of surprise. "What are those things?" he squeaks.

"They've had many names, boy," Jesminder obliges. "Names that come from before the time of our islands. Our songs call them Aziza." As she speaks, the female creatures remove their hoods, revealing impossibly divine brown faces and long, pointed ears.

"The Aziza abandoned these islands before the war's end," Marleyn challenges.

Even though I see them standing before me, I nod my head in agreement, remembering what I've been taught. The Aziza once mediated between humans and dragons. They were a benevolent race of peacekeepers. Then, one day, they went to sea and vanished.

"And yet," Jesminder says, airing a bored sigh, "here are four right in front of you."

My knees tremble. Four Aziza. My guardians have their oju, but those hold only a fraction of the power the Aziza were said to wield. I can't let any of my friends get hurt. "What do you want with me?" I ask. I glance up at the sky and note the moons' position. They're closer. Kyrel sees it, too. He purrs a soft growl as his hand closes around mine.

"I want you to break the seal," she says. "It turns out the song is useless to Adisa and me. One, it requires my mother's spirit." As if in answer, Nalini's life force swirls in my blood, cold seeping through my very bones. "And two, it requires the singer to be madly in love."

I bristle at that, my ears burning hot. "I'm not *madly* in love," I protest.

"Seriously?" Rae hisses.

"I'm not," I insist, under my breath. Infatuated, maybe. But love? Love is dangerous. I offer Kyrel an apologetic glance, but his eyes are set on Jesminder.

"I am," he says. Those two simple words shatter right through me. "And I'm going to help her reinforce the seal."

Jesminder looks unimpressed. "That *is* madness," she sneers. "Have either of you stopped to consider what happens to the two of *you* if the seal reinforced?"

I lift my chin. "We know," I reply. "That won't stop us from doing what's right."

Jesminder's lips curl upward. "And what happens to my dear sister Ranee?" she asks. "Last I heard, she's no longer a mortal. Does *she* get trapped in the Shadows with the rest of the akbarrin?"

My breath catches in my chest. I break into a cold sweat. I haven't considered what would happen to Ranee now that she's a mermaid. If I fix the seal, she will be banished from Beldemar. I will never see her again.

The moons hum louder in my ears, a sickening tone that reverberates through my core. I sway on unsteady feet. Kyrel anchors me.

Duty before self.

What kind of selfish princess would I be if I let millions of my people die at the hands of vengeful akbarrin just so I could see my mother again? I push through the nausea rolling in my stomach. "I will do what I must to keep the people of Beldemar safe."

My aunt's beautiful face hardens with displeasure. "Like I said," she scorns, "stubborn and weak."

Two of her handmaidens charge forward, releasing their robes to flutter off into the bush. "Chyou. Maya," Marleyn calls, and the two guardians rush to meet them. A wave of terror hits me as Chyou throws a punch, only for her opponent to blink out of the way and slam an elbow into Chyou's spine. Chyou's body arches forward as she takes the hit. She cries out.

"No," I stumble forward as if to help her, but Marleyn and Rae move shoulder-to-shoulder, sealing me behind them.

Maya learns from Chyou's overzealous attack and feints toward her opponent, then swings her flaming sword in a wide arc and catches the Aziza's arm when she blinks behind her, leaving a shallow gash rimmed with charred flesh. The Aziza shrieks in pain and rage as the smell of singed flesh fills the air. Chyou's opponent lunges for Maya, then blinks as Maya swings for her, aiming to get her from behind. But Chyou covers her, catching the Aziza in the gut with a punch that sends her flying.

Relief floods my heart. "The Aziza aren't at their full strength." Kyrel confirms what I am seeing. "They won't be unless the seal is broken."

On the other side of the road, a third handmaiden starts to circle around the fight as Jesminder and the fourth slip back into the forest. Rae trails her with a rose arrow until she is obscured by the fighting. "Moons," Rae mutters. Her oju vanishes, and she unsheathes two daggers instead. She starts toward the fighting.

"No." Marleyn catches her by the wrist. "Get Aryam to the

tower." The serpent's fang sways idly in her hand as she watches her mark. "We'll catch up."

"We're not leaving you," I protest. "I can fight." Not as well as they can, not nearly as well, but I've spent scores of my life training, and Mam Kadejah's lessons have made me stronger. I can help.

Marleyn smiles. "I know you can," she says, "but you don't have time."

"She's right," Kyrel urges. "We have to go." I let him pull me away.

CHAPTER THIRTY-ONE

We race uphill, Rae ahead of us with her rose bow nocked and ready. Darien pants and wheezes at my back, struggling to keep up. "Please tell me it isn't much farther," he huffs.

The others don't even glance back at him. "No one's trying to kill *you*, you know," Kyrel points out. There's no malice in his voice. "You could just splinter off. Someone will find you when this is over."

"I'm not leaving Aryam," Darien protests. And even though he's foolish for staying, it warms my heart to hear him say that.

"I'm not against another body getting between Aryam and those Aziza if they catch up to us," Rae says.

"Rae, that's so mean," I object.

She shrugs. "Try to keep up, story boy."

But it isn't Darien who slows us down. Yards before we hit the wall of fog, I stumble to a halt, my vision blacking out as Adisa's thread snaps into place. Kyrel catches me.

I am in the tower where Marleyn and I once breakfasted together. Chamberlain Kemi and her granddaughter Bijou are here. Bijou stands guard at the door, while Kemi peers out at the rolling clouds on the sea. No, not clouds. Sails. Ships' sails.

Kemi turns, moving with a grace and youthfulness uncommon to women of her age. She carries her walking stick flat in her hands.

I knew it! She doesn't need it to walk.

She twists the handle and pulls, unsheathing a long, slim blade. "Don't worry, princess," she says. "You are safe with us."

Princess? Chamberlain Kemi knows!

The chamberlain and her granddaughter remove their bonnets, revealing pointed ears poking out of their wooly hair. Aziza! The chamberlain and Bijou are Aziza!

"Aryam!" Rae's desperate voice snaps me out of the vision.

I swoon. I would fall, if it weren't for Kyrel holding me steady. Rae's face hovers inches from mine. Relief floods her eyes. Kyrel sets me on my own feet. "What is it?" he asks. "What did you see?"

My chest heaves as I try to make sense of it all. I remember the armada on the sea. "Something's coming," I inform them. "Something bad."

THE MISTS ARE EERILY QUIET. No sign of Jesminder or the Dragon King anywhere. Barely able to see our own feet, we walk for fear of falling or colliding with one another. The glowing vine Rae summoned to tether us all together by the waist produces the only light.

When we emerge, it is to a hazy orange sky. Like dusk, but not. Kyrel frowns up at the sky. "It's starting."

I turn my head for a glimpse of the sun, only for Rae to slap her hand over my eyes and turn my head. "Don't *look* at it," she exclaims. "Are you crazy? You'll ruin your eyes."

I shake my head. "You're right. That was not smart."

We've emerged from the fog east of the main road. The service road continues across the field of gnarly trees to the staff entrance. "There will be guards," Rae muses. "We don't know if they'll be friendly."

Or if they're loyal to Chiwa.

We can't afford a fight.

I gaze at the palace, tracing its walls to King Felix's quarters, to his study. When Marleyn took me to the chamber beneath, Captain Aric had already been waiting for us. He'd used another way to get in. A tunnel. "I think I know another way in," I announce.

Concealing ourselves in the fog, we skirt along the mist toward the palace's rear. I keep my eyes on the windows of King Felix's quarters. Soon, we're directly behind what must be his study. A slick, stone wall looms behind the palace, pushing us against the swirling fog. "It should be close to here," I murmur, scanning the wall for an entrance.

"What about there?" Darien asks, pointing toward a lone wooden post, just barely visible in the fog. "It could be a marker."

Rae darts toward it, summoning her oju. She fires an arrow of green flames into the fog. The blaze cuts through the mist and strikes the ground, illuminating a few feet. Another post appears. "There," she says. She runs to it and fires another arrow. Another post peaks out of the fog. "There."

We follow the posts down and down and down. All around us, the forest is remains silent. Even the animals have gone quiet.

But then a sound whistles through the air. A howl, followed by others.

We freeze, all of us. "What was that?" I ask.

"You don't want to know," Kyrel answers.

We move faster. Down, down, down, until we reach a

massive boulder with an iron door set into it. Rae kneels, using the stem of a rose arrow to pick the lock.

The lock clicks open.

The tunnel that swallows us whole is cool and damp and dark. Our feet squelch in mud as Rae leads the way, using one of her arrows as a torch. It isn't long before we reach Marleyn's training chamber. I brace myself for the Dragon King's assault on my mind, but nothing happens. He doesn't say a word.

"What are you waiting for?" Rae asks, watching me carefully.

I shake my head clear. "Nothing. This way." We head for the stairs that spiral up and up to the king's study. I'm grateful for the glowing minerals that light our way. As expected, the door is locked at the top, and unsurprisingly, Rae picks it.

Darien's eyes widen at the size of the king's personal library. "Unbelievable," he murmurs.

Suddenly, I know how to keep him safe. "You should stay here," I suggest. Before he can protest, I add, "See if you can find something useful. Something that will help us." I don't expect him to find anything, but leaving him here will keep him out of harm's way.

He looks like he might still argue, but then he nods. "Maybe I can find a way for you to save Ranee," he says, and after a pause, "and Kyrel, too. Maybe you don't have to banish them to the Shadows."

A lump lodges in my throat. I nod, unable to trust myself not to cry. I grab his hands and squeeze. "Thank you."

Darien locks himself in behind us.

"I can't believe Kemi and Bijou are Aziza," I whisper as Rae leads us stealthily through staff passages, which we find as empty as the road that led us here. I wonder if Chiwa sent them all away. Maybe she did to spare them.

"I honestly thought they were strange," Rae comments.

"Jesminder has handmaidens," Kyrel points out. "Maybe Kemi and Bijou were something similar for Ranee."

"Then that would mean they've known who I was since I got here," I say. "And they kept that secret. Maybe that means we can trust them."

Rae glances at me, then looks pointedly at Kyrel. "I don't trust anyone," she replies. "Not when it comes to you."

Another barrage of howls cuts through air, stopping us in our tracks. They're closer this time, impossibly closer. Whatever creature made those horrid sounds must be moving at remarkable speed.

We run toward a window at the end of the hall and peer out at the forest behind the palace. I clap my hands over my mouth and stifle a scream. On the sea below, the first ships of the armada have drawn to shore. Trees shake violently as unseen creatures barrel through the underbrush, yipping and howling. Rae whips her gaze to Kyrel. "What *are* those things?" she demands. Only the slight panic in her eyes belies her harsh tone.

He furrows his brow. "They're *his*," he answers. He looks at me. "He's sent them for you."

But it isn't terror for myself that shudders through me. "Marleyn, Chyou, and Maya are still out there," I exclaim.

"They can handle themselves," Rae insists, but there's fear in her eyes, too. She must protect me first, but she's allowed to also care for her chorus sisters. She exhales. "We have to trust them." She pivots away from the window. "Come on."

CHAPTER THIRTY-TWO

I hear howling. "Wolves," I say.

Chamberlain Kemi peers over the balcony. Her face pales at the sight below. I rush to her side and see them clambering over the palace walls, wolves four times too big. "He's here."

Kemi pulls me away from the window. "Get back, child," she exclaims. There is fear in her voice. She is right to be afraid. I wrestle away from her and run back to the edge. I look down, straight into the eyes of one of the beasts.

"What is he doing?" The words tear out of me as I come back into myself. I lean against a wall of the cellarway outside the palace kitchen. Beyond the kitchen garden and field looms the Moon Tower, black against the darkening sky.

"What happened?" Rae asks.

But Kyrel doesn't give me a chance to explain what I saw. Instead, he steps out into the garden.

"Wait!" Rae commands. "We don't know if any of those things are lurking around."

"They're not," he replies, strolling coolly into the garden. "They're going for Adisa, instead."

I straighten slowly. "How do you know that?" I ask. An uneasy feeling settles in my gut as Kyrel turns to face us.

"Because he is doing exactly what we planned." Jesminder's voice projects out of thin air, and then she materializes beside Kyrel.

He looks at me, true apology shining in his eyes. "Sorry, Pigtails."

I spin around. "Rae . . . " But before I can warn her, help her, the fourth of Jesminder's handmaidens appears at her side and slams an elbow into her head. Rae's body crumples to the ground. I scream.

"No time for dramatics, niece," Jesminder scolds, with a roll of her eyes. "She'll live." She glances at Kyrel. "It was one of *his* stipulations. We do not hurt your guardians—as long as you comply."

I throw a harsh look at Kyrel. "If you think that means I'll forgive you for betraying me—"

"I don't," he cuts me off. "And I don't expect you to understand. Not now."

Tears stream down my cheeks. "I understand," I reassure him. "I understand that you've played me from the beginning. You were never in love with me. You never even wanted to be my friend."

He shakes his head. "I *do* love you," he says. "You won't understand how much."

Cold hands seize me by the shoulders. I struggle against Jesminder's handmaiden, but she is too strong. Jesminder approaches and wrests the parchment with Chori's lyrics from my grip. "He's telling the truth," she says, her eyes gleaming as she unrolls the paper. "This song won't work without two enamored hearts."

I glare at her. "It doesn't matter," I say. "Those lyrics are to seal the barrier, not *un*seal it."

Jesminder chuckles. "Poor fool," she says. "We weren't the only ones playing you." She gives a pitying look at the confusion on my face. "Do you think really think Nasha and Mama Anura were fooled by Adisa's disguise? Mama Anura only shelters defenseless children for the night. She does not permit adults to enter her home, nor children if they are in the presence of an adult capable of caring for them, but the night *you* visited her, she made an exception. Do you really think Mama River believes that you, a *child*, could retrieve her mirror from the King of the Dark Moon? Why would she give you the griot's kora, otherwise? And why would he be so eager to help you? They all want the same thing."

She watches as I struggle to grasp her meaning. It all starts to make sense. Adisa stole the lyrics from the Golden Palace so that I would need to find the griot to rewrite them, but instead of writing me a song to reseal the barrier, Chori wrote me one to open it. I swallow. "They want to free King Elrey?" I ask.

She scoffs. "Those imbeciles only want their petty trinkets back," she says.

The memory of Mama River's words slams into me.

He has taken something from all of us. It is why we do his bidding.

My heart thunders in my chest. I fight against the rising tide of panic. "They want to free *Anton*?" I exclaim.

"Then they each get what was taken from them," Jesminder confirms. "The river demigoddess gets her mirror. The griot gets his tongue." She flicks her own as if to emphasize the word. "Even Chiwa gets something. Don't you think it strange how empty the palace is? How no sirens cry out at the armada on Capital Island's shores? She was *expecting* his forces to arrive today."

Fury washes over me.

And she called *me* a traitor to mankind.

I try to quiet my racing thoughts and focus my mind. I stare at Chori's song. "So, if we sing that," I say, "your grandfather gets freed—"

"Our grandfather," she interrupts.

"But so does Anton?" I shake my head. "It's dangerous. He's a power-hungry madman. He'll *destroy* Beldemar. Don't you see?"

She shrugs. "Only if he gets his hands on you," she says. "Which won't happen." Something like regret flickers in her eyes, and I remember the vision where she stared into Adisa's face as if he were her entire world.

"You love him," I say.

"Apparently not more than I love myself," she mutters. "If our love were pure, perhaps we could have unsealed the barrier ourselves."

I jerk my body, trying once more to free myself from her handmaiden. "I won't sing that song," I say. "I won't help you let out two monsters."

She doesn't look bothered. "You will," she says, her voice crisp. "If you want your guardians to live." Kyrel's eyes widen at that, but rather than protest, he sets his mouth in a firm line. Jesminder turns on her heels and strides toward the tower. "Bring her."

JESMINDER KICKS in the ancient wooden door at the base of the tower. There's such unexpected strength in her lithe figure. The sky is a deeper orange as the moons loom overhead. Kyrel enters the dark stairwell first, followed by Jesminder. The handmaiden nudges me in after them.

"Guard the door," Jesminder instructs, and the handmaiden releases me to follow her orders. I hesitate on the third step. Since we set out this morning, I have put Beldemar first at every turn. When I thought I would lose Kyrel. When I thought I'd lose Ranee. But now . . . could I really refuse to sing and doom my guardians?

They would fight for me until their dying breaths.

Jesminder halts a few steps ahead but says nothing. Through the darkness, I can almost see her smile as I resume climbing.

No. I won't let them die. The five us are linked. I won't face this world without them.

We reach the top of the tower and enter a circular chamber. The walls curve inward, and everything here is dark, except for the soft glow streaming in through a moon-shaped window. A crescent light cast shadows on the walls, illuminating hieroglyphs. Kyrel steps onto a dais at the center.

The humming of the moons is so loud here that I cover my ears.

Kyrel turns and reaches back for me. I glare at him and ignore his hand, raising my foot to lift myself onto the dais, when suddenly, Adisa's consciousness slams into mine.

"Grandmother!" Bijou cries over Kemi's lifeless body. Wolves demolish the room. One swipes at Bijou and knocks her aside. Her eyes flare wide as blood spurts from her lips.

I back against a wall as one of the beasts approaches me and sniffs. It growls and snaps its teeth at me. "Where is she, skin thief?" it snarls.

I smile. "How about a bargain?"

I'm surprised to find Jesminder holding me up when I return. "Is that it, then?" she asks. "Is he dead?"

I reel from the sudden shift. "I don't know," I stammer. "I didn't see." But Kemi is dead, and Bijou may not be far from it. I pull myself away from Jesminder. "Let's get this over with."

After a pause, she nods. "When it is finished," she says, "I'll be able to transform. I will fly you to safety. Somewhere where Anton can't get to you."

"I'm not going anywhere with you," I snap.

She holds my gaze. "And I'm not letting him get his hands on you."

"I'll take her," Kyrel says softly. "I'll be able to transform, too. Right?"

Jesminder hesitates, then nods.

I shake my head. "I'm not going anywhere with *you*, either."

"The moons are aligning," Jesminder announces. "There will be darkness. Then silver. Then you sing."

I don't look at either of them. "I haven't heard from the Dragon King since yesterday," I say, "and he seemed pretty weak. What if he's dead?"

Jesminder's voice is cold. "Then we are all doomed."

THE CRESCENT LIGHTS shrink into darkness. Through the moon-shaped window, the moons have become one—a silver orb surrounded by a ring of fire. Their distinct notes blend into one intoxicating chord as their power surges into our bodies. I feel it hit Kyrel at the same time it hits me. Our bodies go taut. Our chests arch forward. Despite ourselves, we link hands and clasp them tightly as everything around us morphs into liquid silver.

We sing, our voices one, male and female. I don't think I could resist, even if I tried. The silver moons' chord is the most enchanting sound I've ever heard and devastatingly compelling, as is the union of our singing hearts. I cling to him as if being ripped away from him would be the same as having my heart torn from my chest.

I can no longer deny it. I've loved him since the day we met.

I *am* in love with him. I *will* love him even when this is over, even when I should hate him for what he's done.

Our song ends, and Kyrel draws in a sharp breath, his hand crushing mine. I mirror his reaction as a cold draft of pure akbarra floods my body. We close our eyes against a blinding flare of light, and then the moons spirit us away.

THE AIR CRACKLED with infinite akbarra. I stood at the edge of my balcony, eyes fixed on the dark moon rising on our moon's horizon. A lifetime had passed since I last saw him. We'd been born and dead many times before. But that day, our moons would become one. A bridge would form when their shadows touched, and we would walk between worlds.

"Yara." My mother's voice was soft at my back. Yes, my mother. The songs the humans sing do not mention her, but she was there. She was complicit. I turned to face the resplendent queen of the moon. She was clothed in sparkling silver that day, as all on Liora were, to celebrate the coming of Shadowkiss. It was the one day in a hundred score that we deigned to fraternize with the citizens of the dark moon, and the war between our worlds halted.

The Moon Queen moved toward me, her silver garbs flowing about her, her crown of white locks coiled atop her head. Her stunning brown face was the perfect picture of concern. "It has been almost ten lifetimes now," she said. "When will you put this affair between you and that lowly prince to rest? He is beneath you."

I was long tired of my parents' objections. I yanked my hands away when my mother tried to grab them. "Says who?" I demanded. "I love him. That alone makes him my equal in every way."

My mother scoffed. "Stupid girl. You know nothing about love."

I glowered at her. "Would you rather I marry that human boy?" I demanded. He had arrived in our world only that morning upon the back of a great bird. My father had been amused and immediately taken with him. "I've seen him whispering into Father's ear. I've seen the way he looks at me. I know what he wants."

Power. Perhaps to rise against the dragons and Aziza who ruled his world. Perhaps for an ugly, nefarious reason.

My mother bristled at that. "Theron would never promise you to a mortal." Her hatred contorted her face. "He is only entertaining the boy because the boy has promised a way to rid us of our little Hama problem. That prince will not cross the bridge today when the shadows kiss."

I turned toward the dark moon with a gasp. "Hadi!" I cried, gravely concerned for Hama's prince. "What have you done to him?"

"We have done what is best!" my mother called, but I was already running down the stairs of my balcony. I ran to the Moonsea, toward the dark moon glistening in the sky. I fell in a heap, my cumbersome gown puffing up around me, and cried.

My tears hardened into crystals, as they often did whenever they were born of such devastating emotion. I held three of them in my hand. That is when he found me.

The human boy called himself Anton. He told me that he had dreamed of me and that his dreams were no match for the reality of my beauty. He had the gall to ask me to marry him.

I rose in anger and shouted at him. "Marry you?" I cried. I spat such malice at him, filled myself with my parents' scorn for all things lesser. I am not proud of the things I said, but in short, I told him that I would never marry him.

Anton's face turned to stone. He threw himself upon me, tearing my dress, and wrested one of the crystals from my hands. He ate it, and the rest is recorded in your human songs—the ones your people seem to have lost. My father came, Anton slew him, and I fled.

I fled to the floating cities in the human world. I learned of Hadi's fate, that he was cursed to be a silent, wandering creature, destined to gaze at the white moon for all eternity or until someone relieved him of that burden. I have you and your guardians to thank for that, Aryam.

I gave my tears to my dear friend Ranee. She ate one to make herself mortal when she fell in love with a human king by the name of Felix. I told her to keep the second in case she ever decided to return to her immortal form, but I always suspected she would give it to you. She was a better mother than mine ever was.

The crystal grants wishes, Aryam. Yours is that you will never be alone. Your wish is granted.

CHAPTER THIRTY-THREE

Yara's voice fades from my mind with a final petition. *Love is a gift and a right. Never let anyone take it from you.*

My eyes flutter open, and I gasp as the weight of my body settles back in. The hum of the moons tapers into silence, and unobstructed sunlight streams in through the window. I shield my eyes. Kyrel does the same. He stumbles off the dais, pulling me along behind him. I trip, falling into him, and he catches me. For a moment, I am stunned stupid. I rest against him and gaze up into his earnest eyes, Princess Yara and Prince Hadi's tragic love story looming fresh in my mind.

And then I remember that in *our* story, Kyrel *isn't* Hadi. He's Anton. I push away from him.

Something inside of him caves. I can see it on his face. He reaches a hand for me. "Ary . . . " I can see his heart breaking in his eyes. I stumble away from him, my head spinning. Whatever desperation I felt for him beats ago was only a spur of passion, a result of the intoxicating music thrumming through my blood. Wasn't it?

A thundering crack shatters the silence. Capital Island groans.

"It worked!" Jesminder's voice is ecstatic. "You've broken the seal, girl. It worked." She holds her hands in front of her face, turning them over in awe. They ripple with purple light as a wave of scales travels up and down her forearm.

Kyrel looks like he's going to be sick. His legs buckle. He drops down to one knee, clutching his stomach with one hand and steadying himself against the ground with the other. "Ary." There's fear in his voice. He doesn't know what's happening. It chips away at the ice wall I've slammed between us.

I whirl toward my aunt. "Did you even prepare him for what happens now?" Whatever that is.

Jesminder stops admiring her own hand. The scales ripple away, leaving behind human flesh. A sinister smile spreads on her lips. "He needs to hunt," she says, teeth gleaming as if already drenched in blood.

Kyrel and I lock eyes. The horror I find in his mirrors my own. I shake my head. This can't be happening. Kyrel tries and fails to rise, collapsing back onto all fours as a horrible shift takes over his body. Bones crack. Skin ripples. A vicious, animal sound tears through his throat.

I back away.

A howl echoes through the stone stairwell below, followed by a scream. The handmaiden. Jesminder turns toward the entrance. "We have to go," she says.

Footsteps thunder up the stairs. Sharp claws scrape against stone.

I meant what I said before. I'm not going anywhere with her. I stumble away when she reaches for me. "*The window,*" a faint voice cries in my head. *"Get to the window."* I lumber toward it.

A flickering blue light tears from my chest and hardens

around me as I crash into the wall beneath the window. A crack splinters from the window to the floor, and the wall crumbles outward. I plummet toward the earth, toward a horde of massive wolves clawing to get into the tower. Above me, the top of the tower explodes, raining down a shower of stone.

The light around me hardens again, and the stones bounce, pelting the wolves below. "*Brace yourself,*" warns that voice in my head, and I curl into a ball, wrapping my arms around my head.

My cocoon of light slams into the ground, carving a scar into the earth as it skids away from the tower. I cry out at the sharp pain that bites into my side. The light flickers away.

A roar tears through the air. I blink up at the sky as an enormous dragon soars overhead, its purple scales scattering the sunlight. Jesminder. A second dragon tumbles out of the tower, smaller and weaker than the first. Its wings twitch awkwardly as it plunges for the ground.

My heart seizes. I sit up, fighting against the pain. "Fly!" I scream. But Kyrel doesn't know how. "Fly!" I shout again. I push to my feet. My body barks at the movement. I limp toward the tower. "Fly." My voice is a hoarse, desperate whisper. He straightens a wing. His talons dig into the tower wall, slowing his descent, and then he shoves off it. The second wing stretches wide. A gust of wind catches under his wings, lifting him shakily into the air. With a few unsteady flaps, he gains some height.

I stop walking and crane my neck to gaze up at him as he flies overhead, just barely clearing the palace before he disappears from sight.

The wolves go silent. I lower my gaze to find them looking at me. Those who were clawing to get into the tower drop onto their paws and turn toward me. I take a step back, feeling the world sway beneath my feet. That is all the invitation they need. The beasts charge toward me with gnashing teeth.

When it is only a few steps away, the first leaps into the air, claws outstretched. That faraway voice in my head cries out. *"Ice. Summon my ice."*

Coldness pools into my fingertips, but the most I can manage are thin flakes of ice on my skin. The beast crashes into me, slamming me back. His massive paw pins my chest to the ground as he snaps at my face, his sharp teeth clamping shut an inch from my nose. The wolf howls as others close in around me.

I squeeze my eyes shut as drool drips onto my face.

A whistle sings through the air, and the wolf yelps in pain. Another gush of hot liquid spurts onto my cheek, reeking of copper. I open my eyes to see a green arrow right through the wolf's head. It collapses on me, pinning me beneath it.

The others yelp and scatter as a barrage of arrows rains down on their furry bodies. Then the one pinning me down lifts suddenly. Chyou stands over me, holding the wolf's body over her head. I gape at her. I knew her oju makes her stronger than the average human, but not this strong. She tosses the body to one side as if it were a stone instead of a giant wolf.

I cry at the sight of her. "Chyou!" She reaches down and pulls me to my feet, grinning wickedly. I gaze in awe as the rest of my guardians dispose of the wolves. From one side of the field, Rae fires arrow after arrow, striking her prey with supernatural precision. Marleyn wields the serpent's fang in a tornado of fury. And Maya's sword blazes hotter than ever.

"Is it just me?" I ask, "Or are you all stronger and faster than before?"

Chyou's grin widens. "Yeah. I think we got a power boost."

I think of the light that wrapped itself around me as I fell from the tower. The reason I'm still alive. "Yeah. Me too," I mumble.

Beats later, the field reeks of slain wolves. The air is full of whimpering from the few who survive. My guardians pick their way toward me. Marleyn crashes into me. My bones cry out at the strength of her hug. "I'm so happy you're okay," she murmurs into my ear.

"Did I really just see you jump out of a window?" Rae snaps.

Despite every ounce of pain I'm in, I laugh. "I didn't really have a choice," I reason.

"What was that light that surrounded you?" Maya wonders.

"It looked like a dragon," Chyou remarks.

"A dragon?" I repeat.

"*That's right,*" says the voice in my head. *"Hello, granddaughter."*

THE DRAGON PRINCESS lives inside my soul. "*I was always here,*" Nalini explains. *"The crystal made it so that you could feel me. Yara made it so that you could* hear *me."*

So that I will never be alone, I realize.

"That's right."

"What's happening?" Marleyn asks. My guardians watch my face. "Is it Adisa?"

I shake my head. "No," I reassure her. "That's over. He's . . . I think he's dead." I stare back at them, unsure of how to tell them that I now share a soul with my grandmother. Maybe they will think I've hit my head too hard. "I'm fine," I say. "I'll explain it later."

The ground rumbles before our feet as Capital Island groans again. "*My father,*" Nalini warns. *"His prison is crumbling."*

My eyes widen. The island is his prison.

"*Everyone here is in danger,*" Nalini confirms.

"We have to speak to Chiwa," I blurt out. "And we'd better do it fast." Because Anton had an entire armada at our shores, and the troop of wolves we've defeated is only just the start.

My guardians don't question me. Instead, they fall in rank around me as we move into the palace. We find my cousin sequestered in the throne room with Jahim and a host of nobles and staff. Andra, her Maradi guardian, stands at her right, and Tess, with one hand missing, at her left. I'm happy to see she survived, even as her eyes narrow on me with hatred.

Chiwa springs to her feet. Her guardians' oju flash into place. Jahim's guardians follow suit, causing my guardians to summon theirs. "I'm not here to fight," I announce, hoping to calm everyone down. "You need to evacuate the island. Everyone here is in danger."

"Everyone here is *safe* under my rule," Chiwa counters. "I've taken precautions to ensure their safety."

"You've made a deal with a madman," I retort. "What did he promise you? Do you even know what happened to the last royal he made a bargain with?" But she doesn't. Yara only disclosed King Theron's fate to me.

"You shouldn't be here, girl," Chiwa sneers. "If there is any danger to be had, it is because *you* endanger us with your presence. You are what he wants, after all."

"Is that why you tried to kill me?" I ask. I raise my voice over the gasps my revelation elicits. "So that he couldn't have me? What will he do when he finds out you betrayed him?"

A malevolent smile curves her lips. "I suppose I haven't betrayed him after all," she answers. "I had hoped to prevent his escape by getting that crystal from you or killing you. It is an ugly deed, but it would have saved us all. Now he's out, and I will have to honor the bargain I made with him. You're here, and I will deliver you to him."

And lay easy claim to the throne without Adanna and Bem around. Unlike Jahim, they must have challenged her.

The serpent's fang flashes so bright that a chorus of startled cries rings out from the listening crowd. Several shield their eyes. Even Andra and Tess's faces tense with surprise. "I wouldn't try it, if I were you," Marleyn threatens. "You know what happened the last time you came for our princess."

I lament the hurt her words inflict on Chiwa's guardians, the pain evident in their faces.

"Guardians are born to live and die for their pulses," Chiwa says dismissively. "Even if I lose all of mine, I have an entire army at my disposal."

Gratitude swells in my heart for Ranee. For once, I am grateful that she raised me as she did. At least I didn't turn into a monster like Chiwa. At least I can feel sympathy for my guardians. "Then you'd better put that army to work," I suggest. I'm not here to argue semantics, to point out that *her* army is actually *my* army. "The Dragon King is coming, and he is very unhappy."

My warning hits its mark. Chiwa's bottom lip trembles. "Traitor!" she shouts. "What have you done?" She turns to the crowd before her. "Do you see?" she cries. "I told you that she sympathizes with the akbarrin. She has killed us all."

I scan their faces and see that they believe her. My breath hitches as I lock eyes with Katina, standing beside a timid, pretty woman who must be her mother. Katina shrinks away from me and hides behind the woman.

"You can't believe her," I plead with the crowd. "I didn't want any of this to happen."

"Liar," Chiwa exclaims. "You are a traitor and a liar. Now the Dragon King will burn us all."

The room erupts into a frenzy. Men and women scream. Some faint.

"Aryam," Marleyn whispers at my side. "You've warned them. We need to go."

But then I remember. "Darien."

My guardians exchange glances. I can see it in their eyes. They will do whatever they must to get me away. Now. A detour to the king's quarters is not a part of their plan. I turn and find Katina in the crowd. I find her staring at me. "Darien is here!" I shout. "He's in the king's study. You have to get him out." She blinks slowly at me. My voice breaks. "Kati, please."

Katina glances at the door, then looks back at me and nods.

Marleyn and Maya take me by my arms and guide me out of the room. Rae walks ahead of us. Chyou flanks behind. I struggle to keep up with them, the pain from my fall catching up with me at last. Marleyn drapes my arm around her neck, and Maya does the same. I cast a silent plea to the moons for my friends. For Katina. For Darien. For Bijou. For Joan and Dex, wherever they are. Let them all be safe.

CHAPTER THIRTY-FOUR

Black smoke steams from every crevice of the island behind us as the Dragon King's prison breaks. Molten lava seeps through the island's pores. It looks like a volcano on the brink of eruption. *How long?* I wonder. *How long before he's out?*

"*It will take time,*" Nalini reassures me. "*Lots of time.*"

Either way, the island is no longer habitable. I feel a surge of relief as large ships flee the island in our wake. Chiwa may be a monster, but at least she is getting my people out. I can only hope that the friends I've left behind have made it aboard.

Marleyn stands beside me at the ship's stern, gripping the rails as we watch the chaos unfold. Rae works the helm while Maya and Chyou handle the sails. "I'm sure your friends will be okay," Marleyn tries to console me.

"It's not just them I'm worried about," I admit. "Chiwa is right. I betrayed my people."

"You made a choice," Marleyn asserts. "In my opinion, you made the right one. Jesminder's handmaidens were toying with us, keeping us away from you. They would have killed us if she'd commanded it, and you would have no one to protect you. Anton would have found another way to get to you, and Beldemar would be in just as much danger as it is in now." I feel her staring at me, even as I am unable to draw my eyes away from the smoking mountain. "You will make this right, Princess," she says. "I know that you will."

I shake my head, tears glistening on my eyelashes. It is too much to do alone.

"You are not alone, Moonsong," my grandmother counters. *"I am with you, and I will teach you to use my ice."*

"Moonsong?" I murmur. Ranee calls me that.

"It is because the moons sang when you were born," she explains. *"How else do you think the Shadows cracked?"*

The revelation startles me. I am the reason the akbarrin returned to the human world?

"My girl. You must realize by now that you are as much of an akbarrin as I am."

"Adisa said something similar," I reply, *"but he failed to recognize that I am human, too. The humans and the akbarrin are all my true people."*

"And you will be the one to unite them and usher them into a new millennium," Nalini foretells.

"A new millennium," I repeat, letting the words sink in. Humans and akbarrin together. In peace.

"What was that?" Marleyn asks, watching me with a confused look on her face.

I flush. Of course. I look like I'm talking to myself. "It was nothing," I say, forcing out a giggle.

Marleyn mirrors my smile, but hers fades as quickly as it comes. Her eyes widen with shock, and I trace her gaze back to the ships escaping the island. Two are in flames now; a third is under attack by a young black dragon.

Harpoons fire at him, and he dodges them on shaky wings. "No!" I cry out.

"He can't control it," Nalini explains. *"He is young, and it is in his nature to hunt on first flight."*

The dragon flees the ships' hostile fire, flying straight toward us.

Marleyn seizes my wrist and yanks me back. "Get down into the hold," she cries. She shouts for Rae. In an instant, Rae is at the stern, oju nocked with three roses and aimed. She traces Kyrel's flight with her arrows' tips.

"Don't hurt him," I plead.

"He betrayed you," Rae snaps.

But I know now that he didn't. He lied to me, but he never betrayed me. He's known since the beginning what I was, what would happen to me if I'd succeeded in strengthening the seal. "He *saved* me," I reason.

But Rae unleashes the arrows, and they strike true. Two catch his wing. One strikes above his foreleg, tearing into his flesh. He screeches and peels off into the distance, fading from sight.

I turn on Rae. "*Why* would you do that?" I shout.

Rae looks surprised, but not regretful. She gestures toward the burning ships at our backs. "That's reason one," she declares. "He was coming in hot—reason two. I am your guardian—reason three." Her voice rises with each reason until she is shouting back at me.

"Rae." Marleyn steps between us, speaking softly. "Go back to the helm."

Rae swivels on her heels. "I didn't even aim to kill," she mutters.

And despite my rage at her, part of me is present enough to realize that she's right. She could have brought him down. Instead, she scared him off. But I'm too mad at her to admit I understand. Marleyn wraps her arms around me as I fold into her and sob.

. . .

Two moons glow in the nighttime sky when, days later, we finally reach Jara's shores. It was Nalini's idea to return to the Gate, since she herself granted them the powers that made them immortal.

"*They are the only people we trust,*" she'd said. "*For now.*"

Maya disembarks beside me, glancing between each moon. "That's going to take some getting used to," she murmurs, "having two moons in the sky."

"So weird," Chyou agrees as she strolls by with a suspiciously noisy bag in her hand.

"Chyou, are you seriously going to carry those rocks all the way from the shore to the Gate?" Rae calls after her.

"What? I have to rebuild my collection." Chyou shrugs.

Marleyn catches up to us. "I have a feeling those two are going to bicker the whole way," she says, a laugh bubbling out.

"I think so, too." Maya frowns, wringing her hands together.

Marleyn throws an arm across my shoulders. "Well," she says. "It's what sisters do, isn't it?"

I catch the true meaning of what she's implying. I'm not ready to forgive Rae for what she did to Kyrel, but that doesn't mean that I never will. I sigh and change the subject. "Can we please *not* go to Bogma's this time?" I ask. "I'd rather starve."

Marleyn laughs. "Coming from you, that's grand," she says.

I pinch her side. "Hey," I protest. "That's so rude."

Marleyn laughs and runs ahead to catch up with the others.

Maya beams at me.

"What?" I demand.

She shrugs. "Nothing," she chirps. "It's just that we're all together, for a breath, and no one's actively trying to kill you. It's nice."

We fall silent as we enter the jungle together. The thought that there could be creatures watching us from the darkness doesn't creep me out the way it used to. They are my people, too, and I am bound to protect them. I reach for Nalini's cool power and toy with the frost that coats my fingers. My sisters and I will train at the Gate, and we will grow stronger. We will set Beldemar free.

I slide my hand into Maya's. She flinches at the iciness of my fingers and giggles. "It is nice," I admit.

And when we defeat true love's greatest adversary, I will fight again and free my sisters.

KING OF THE MOON WASTES

A boy named Anton dreamed of a girl named Yara. He dreamed that she wore swathes of moonlight and cried tears of crystal. When he woke up, he could not stop thinking of her.

Anton shared his dream with his mother, who said, "You dream of the Moon King's daughter. She lives with him in his tower overlooking the Moonsea."

Anton decided he would go to the Moon Kingdom. The next day, he set out. He encountered three creatures on his way: an eagle, an ant, and a wolf. The three were quarreling over a dragon egg stolen from the nest of the dragon king's consort. Anton destroyed the egg and divided it evenly between the three of them.

Each of the three received a gift in turn for consuming the dragon egg. The eagle became the griffin, the ant became the king of insects, and the wolf became the great wolf.

"I swear allegiance to you," cried the griffin. "Wherever you find trouble, summon me with this song: *O griffin with wings unfurled, lift me high above the world*. Then I will carry you great distances."

"I swear allegiance to you," cried the king of insects.

"Wherever you find trouble, summon me with this song: *O king of insects, king of dreams, weave for me my moonlit beams.* Then I will build you a great kingdom."

"I swear allegiance to you," cried the great wolf. "Wherever you find trouble, summon me with this song: *O great wolf with fangs so bright, bring the fury of the night.* Then I will tear your enemies limb from limb and devour them."

Anton went on and on until he reached the end of the world. There was nothing he could do, so he sang,

"O griffin with wings unfurled, lift me high above the world."

Then, the great griffin came down and carried Anton on its back. They flew and flew until they reached the edge of the Moonsea, where the Moon King's daughter wept. Anton said to the girl, "Marry me."

"I cannot," replied the Moon King's daughter. "You are mortal."

Anton saw three crystal tears glistening in Yara's hands. "Then give me your tears," he commanded. "I will eat them and become immortal."

But Yara refused to hand over her tears, so Anton seized one and ate it.

From his tower, the Moon King saw what was happening and rushed down to defend his daughter. Despite having more power, Anton saw that he was still outmatched. He sang,

"O great wolf with fangs so bright, bring the fury of the night."

Then the great wolf came and tore the Moon King limb from limb and devoured him, destroying the Moon Kingdom as well.

Anton saw the damage and frowned. He sang,

"O king of insects, king of dreams, weave for me my moonlit beams."

Then the king of insects came and built Anton a new kingdom.

Anton prepared to marry Yara, but when he looked for her, he learned she had fled during the fight, taking the last two tears with her.

Then the Moonsea dried up, and Anton became king of the Moon Wastes.

COMING IN 2025

Aryam and the guardians will return in Book 2: *A Chorale of Beating Hearts.* Be sure to subscribe to the author's newsletter for updates and sneak peaks.

ACKNOWLEDGMENTS

Writing and publishing this book would not have been possible without the support of so many people. I'd like to thank my grandmother, Bonita Shepherd, and my parents, Shanada and David Washington; my grandparents, Starlon and Diane Washington; my sisters, Jaalyn and Sade Washington, and my brothers, David Washington Jr. and Caleb Washington; my beta readers, Anthony McDonald and Stephanie Reynolds; my editors, Christopher Morgan and Misha Kydd; and a beacon in my community, Nyshell Lawrence. I'd also like to thank my friends, Christina Bhattacharya, Patricia Buttrey, Candace Potts, Ruth Cogan, Skye Fernandez, Callie Smith, David Tran, Precious Noble and Maggie Cosand for their encouragement and support. I especially want to thank the following people for their generosity and kind words: Joanna Chen, Ashley Neblett, Marissa Dierlam, Michele Robinson, Tangela Curtis, and Christine Heaps. Last but certainly not least, thank you to my fellow indie authors Andrea Rose Washington and Nico Vincenty for your support and guidance! Thank you all for believing in and supporting me and for being the first champions of my work. I am beyond blessed to have such wonderful people in my life.

Forever grateful,

Ty

ABOUT THE AUTHOR

A proud graduate of the University of Michigan, Tylisha Washington is an author and teacher based in Lansing, Michigan. With a passion for storytelling, she began writing books at the age of ten. Tylisha is passionate about education and inspiring young writers. When she is not writing, she teaches English as a Second Language and tutors bright young writers. For fun, she enjoys reading, exercising, watching anime, and playing The Sims.

You can connect with Tylisha by following her Instagram account, @tywritenow or visiting www.tylishawashington.com.

ALSO BY TYLISHA WASHINGTON

Songs of Aryam

Made in the USA
Las Vegas, NV
10 November 2024